THE
DEATH
OF A
MAFIA
DON

THE DEATH OF A MAFIA DON

MICHELE GIUTTARI

Translated by Howard Curtis

ABACUS

First published in Italy in 2007 by Biblioteca Universale Rizzoli
First published in Great Britain in 2009 by Abacus
Reprinted 2009 (twice)

A CIP catalogue record for this book is available from the British Library.

ISBN 978-0-349-12162-8

Typeset in Horley by M Rules
Printed and bound in Great Britain by Clays Ltd, St Ives plc

Papers used by Abacus are natural, renewable and recyclable
products sourced from well-managed forests and certified
in accordance with the rules of the Forest Stewardship Council.

Mixed Sources
Product group from well-managed
forests and other controlled sources
www.fsc.org Cert no. SGS-COC-004081
© 1996 Forest Stewardship Council

FSC

Abacus
An imprint of
Little, Brown Book Group
100 Victoria Embankment
London EC4Y 0DY

An Hachette UK Company
www.hachette.co.uk

www.littlebrown.co.uk

For my parents, Tindara and Giovanni.
And for Zanego, where I finished this book
looking at the sea

PART ONE

THE ATTACK

According to Pliny the Elder, the basilisk is a
small snake, less than eight inches long,
but by far the deadliest of creatures,
highly poisonous and able to kill
with a glance.

1

When Officer Franchi saw the unmistakable figure of Chief
Superintendent Ferrara – the light raincoat, the impeccable
blue suit, the inevitable half-smoked Toscano cigar in his
mouth – leaning on the left-hand parapet of the Ponte di
Santa Trinità, waiting for him, he cursed under his breath and
checked the time, first by the Swatch he wore on his wrist,
then on the dashboard clock in the brand new Alfa Romeo
156 from the Headquarters pool. Both showed 7:40, which
meant he wasn't late but Ferrara was early.

As usual.

He drew up at the kerb.

'Good morning, Sebastiano,' Ferrara said, getting in the car
and shifting the pile of newspapers Franchi had left for him
on the back seat.

'Good morning, chief,' Franchi replied, turning immediately on to the Lungarno Corsini, from where he would
take the next bridge, the Ponte alla Carraia. 'Well, maybe
not so good,' he added, seeing the banks of dark clouds
advancing threateningly from the direction of the Parco
delle Cascine.

'I think you're right,' the head of the *Squadra Mobile*

replied, his glance falling on the front-page headline in the *Corriere della Sera* of that Monday October 1, 2001:

COUNTDOWN TO ATTACK ON AFGHANISTAN
British sources: Only a few hours to go
Threatening silence from USA
Blair: Conclusive evidence against Osama.
FROM OUR WASHINGTON CORRESPONDENT:
The attack on Afghanistan will begin in the next 48 hours, according to British sources quoted in the London *Observer*. The targets will be Osama Bin Laden's training camps and hideouts and the Taliban air force and missile positions. The offensive will begin with a massive—

'Seems to me it'll start before we get in.'

'What will?' Ferrara asked, not sure what he meant.

'The rain,' the driver replied, and to confirm this there came a muffled roll of thunder from the distance.

Ferrara smiled. If only the one problem facing him that day was rain!

But the day had already been ruined for him by the prospect of the mass of work waiting for him at Headquarters. The end of an investigation always leaves a long trail of reports to be completed, charges to be formalised, evidence to be sifted through, statements to be taken, all the myriad formalities and documents which reminded Ferrara of the old proverb about guests and fish stinking after three days.

Many more days than that had passed since August's massive operation – an operation that had put an end to the drugs ring masterminded by the Mafioso Salvatore Laprua, otherwise known as Zi Turi, had seen the same Laprua arrested for the murder of the journalist Claudia Pizzi, and had swept like a cyclone through the top echelons of the Prosecutor's Department of Florence, leaving his friend Anna Giulietti in temporary charge as Acting Prosecutor.

'Have you seen the papers, chief?' Franchi asked, as he turned on to the Lungarno Soderini.

'Yes. More stormy weather there.'

'Poor bastards. If I'd joined the Carabinieri, as I'd planned, they might have sent me over there. It gives me the shivers just thinking of it. My mother would be sick with worry.' He chuckled. 'She crosses herself every time she sees me in my police uniform. She's convinced our job is the most dangerous in the world!'

'How right you are, Sebastiano. You should tell my wife, she's just the same. She sees dangers everywhere, and the longer I stay in the job, the worse she gets. She keeps telling me it's time I put on carpet slippers and did the crossword – or wrote my memoirs!'

'For heaven's sake, chief! I'll tell her the head of the *Squadra Mobile* is living the life. The trouble is, women watch too many thrillers where the police solve everything at gunpoint. If only my mother knew the biggest danger I face is having to change a tyre!'

They had just passed the Red Cross building when Ferrara's mobile phone rang. He glanced at the display, and saw a name he had only recently added to his address book: Laprua's lawyer, Silverio Liuzza, who had been bombarding him with ambiguous messages lately. Ferrara was surprised. It was only 7:46, an unusual time for a phone call from a lawyer – he surely couldn't be in his office at this hour. Better to stop the car, he thought: that way, they could talk at ease and not run the risk of losing the signal. Perhaps this time the lawyer would put his cards on the table.

'Park as soon as you can.'

Noticing an Audi A3 that had put on its indicator and was preparing to leave a parking space on the left-hand side of the street, just before the Piazza del Cestello, Franchi braked somewhat abruptly, forcing the mail van behind him to do the same.

'Good morning, Signor Liuzza,' Ferrara was saying into the phone.

'Good morning to you, my dear Chief Superintendent Ferrara,' Liuzza began. He was a long-winded Neapolitan, who loved the sound of his own voice, and Ferrara prepared himself for the litany of high-flown civilities with which he invariably prefaced his phone calls.

But he was not destined to hear them.

It was only a matter of seconds – fractions of seconds.

The Audi had only just moved out of the space and Franchi had begun edging his way in when a huge explosion shook the buildings within a radius of several hundred yards. The thick walls of the old churches from San Frediano to Santo Spirito shook, and the windows of the shops along the Ponte Vecchio, and the window panes in the Palazzo Pitti. The shockwave caused by the explosion could even be felt on the north side of the Arno, although some of the shock was absorbed by the river, the waters of which seemed to hang back for a moment at the edge of the Santa Rosa weir, as if anxious to beat a retreat.

The Alfa Romeo 156, newly assigned to Ferrara by Police Headquarters, was pushed back by the rush of air – Franchi had just hit the clutch and the car was in neutral – and slammed into the mail van which was coming up from behind, ready to overtake. Fragments of steel, branches torn from the oaks on the square, and the heavy chain marking the boundary of the parking area all hit the windows of the car, shattering them. Ferrara watched, stunned, as a ball of fire rose into the air and the front seat came dangerously close to him. The phone he still clutched in his hand pressed painfully into his ear.

The last thing he saw was the blood on the dazed face of his driver, who had turned to him as if to apologise for not protecting him.

2

Tucked in between the Borgo San Frediano and the Arno, the Piazza del Cestello takes its name from the imposing church of San Frediano in Cestello with its rough stone façade, which is situated on the side of the square facing towards the river, along with a little theatre and a hotel. At right angles to the church on one side is the Archbishop's Seminary, and on the other side the administration building of the Army's Logistical Command. The fourth side of the square, the one closest to the river, shaded by age-old trees, marks the limit of the car park which fills the square, a car park which is always packed.

The first people to emerge after the explosion were a small group of soldiers led by the lieutenant on duty, who came stepping over the carpet of shattered glass in the doorway of their building.

The square was filled with a dense cloud of black, acrid-smelling smoke.

Their eyes watering, the soldiers squinted through the layers of smoke and came to a halt, stunned by what they saw.

'But . . . but . . . oh my God, Lieuten—!' the youngest of the soldiers, a tall, thin, fair-haired young man, exclaimed, staring incredulously at the crater and the burning hulks of cars beside it, and he stood there with his mouth open on the last syllable, lacking even the strength to close it. The lieutenant was gazing in horror at what looked like human remains adhering to the twisted sheets of metal and even to the wall of the Seminary.

Immediately afterwards, an inspector and five officers from the nearby Oltrarno police station emerged from the Via del Piaggione adjacent to the Army building. The inspector was speaking excitedly on his mobile phone to Police Headquarters in the Via Zara. On the other side of the square, three soldiers came running from the barracks of the Customs and Excise Corps on the Lungarno Soderini.

The unreal silence following the explosion was broken by the echo of the first siren, still some distance away, and then by a feeble moan. As if they were signals, the two sounds immediately set off the acoustic inferno that accompanies every atrocity of this kind: screams, cries for help, weeping and, over everything, the sinister cacophony of other sirens coming ever nearer – ambulances, fire engines, police cars – each with its own distinctive and agonising sound.

In the premises of the Operations Room on the top floor of Police Headquarters, Commissioner Riccardo Lepri was personally making sure that the emergency plan set up by the Public Safety Committee of the Prefecture was being correctly carried out. Beside him was Francesco Rizzo, deputy head of the *Squadra Mobile*. In the centre of the room, the operator, with a microphone in his hand, was trying frantically to reach the patrol cars scattered throughout the city. Given that they were all tied up with other things, the responses were slow in coming.

'Operations Room to Central Patrol,' he said, making a second attempt to reach that particular car.

'Go ahead,' a voice finally replied.

'Proceed with all haste to the Piazza del Cestello – there's been a big explosion.'

'We'll be right on it.'

'Good, bring yourselves up to date when you're on the scene.'

'OK.'

'Operations Room to Novoli Patrol.'

'Receiving you.'

'State your position.'

'Viale Redi.'

'Proceed to the Careggi Hospital – the wounded should be arriving. Identify yourselves and report back.'

'Roger, we're on our way now.'

'Use your siren. You have authorisation.'

'OK.'

'Operations Room to Poli 476.'

'Go ahead, we're just taking off.'

The noise of the helicopter's propellers could be heard.

Commissioner Lepri intervened at this point. 'Fly over the area between the square and the outskirts. Notify us immediately of any suspicious movements.'

'Anything particular to look out for? A specific vehicle?'

'No idea. We're completely in the dark about this. We leave it up to you, but if you do see anything suspicious, inform us immediately and wait for instructions.'

'OK. We're in the air now.'

The noise grew louder.

After the umpteenth fruitless attempt to get his chief, Michele Ferrara, on the phone, Superintendent Rizzo found the tension impossible to bear any longer.

It was Rizzo who had received the news of the explosion

and who had guided the men in the chaos which had followed – sending some to the armoury to pick up M12
submachine guns and put on bullet-proof vests, others to the
courtyard to start the cars and wait for their colleagues. He
had stayed in Headquarters because he wanted to find
Ferrara, who should be in charge and who was usually in his
office by this time of the morning, but all he had been able to
do was follow events passively alongside the commissioner.
He felt superfluous.

'Still nothing?' Lepri asked, although he already knew the
answer from the disappointed look on Rizzo's face.

'No reply. Not even on his home phone. Nothing but
recorded messages! I'm going to the scene, Commissioner.'

'All right, but keep in touch. Whichever of us tracks him
down first informs the other, understood? Or rather, if you
find him first tell him to phone me straightaway.'

'Of course,' Rizzo replied, almost shouting because he
already had one foot out of the door.

He rushed downstairs and got in the first car he found,
which already had a light flashing on its roof.

'Let's go, quickly!' he ordered, simultaneously dialling
Inspector Riccardo Venturi's number.

'Are you at the scene?' he asked Venturi as soon as he got
an answer.

'Just arrived.'

'How's it looking?'

'Like Beirut.'

3

When the bomb went off, Ferrara's wife Petra was just going inside the little greenhouse. She had been standing on the terrace of their top floor apartment, watching her husband's car moving away until she had seen it cross the Ponte alla Carraia. She had also seen the storm clouds gathering, and it had occurred to her that it might be an idea to clean the plant boxes before she did the breakfast dishes, for fear she'd be unable to do so later on because of the rain.

But the thunder which made the floor and the window panes shake slightly did not indicate rain, but something far worse: the kind of thing she always dreaded, embodied in the dense cloud of black smoke rising from the Piazza del Cestello.

'*Mein Gott!*' she cried out, staggering back. Then she rushed inside the apartment, picked up the receiver and dialled Michele's mobile number.

'*The number you are calling is unobtainable.*' The hateful automatic message echoed in her ears with the force of a sinister premonition.

She could have called the driver, or Ferrara's ultra-efficient secretary Fanti, or his deputy Rizzo, or even the commissioner.

Someone must know where the head of the *Squadra Mobile* was at that moment.

She could have done that.

But women don't waste time on things they know will get them nowhere. When something needs to be done, they do it.

She threw on a raincoat, closed the door behind her, not even bothering to double-lock it, and ran down the stairs without waiting for the lift – if she had stopped for a single moment, her legs would probably have given way.

'It's like an anthill down there,' the helicopter pilot said a few minutes later to his co-pilot as he flew low over the square, which was hidden beneath a curtain of smoke. It was a centre of both attraction and repulsion, with people either dazedly stumbling away in fear or running towards it to offer help, report back or be there out of simple, reckless curiosity.

Her vision fogged by tears she couldn't hold back, Petra was unable to get through the crowd of onlookers being held back from the site of the explosion by the police, who were starting to cordon off the square and the Lungarno Soderini. She felt lost. But just as she was thinking she would have to give up, she heard a familiar voice.

'Signora Ferrara, Signora Ferrara!'

It was Rizzo, who was coming towards her. Held up by the crush of ambulances, fire engines and cars, he had left his own car in the Piazza Goldoni, on the other side of the river, and had reached the scene panting for breath.

'Rizzo, where's my husband?' Petra somehow found the strength to ask.

He had been hoping she could tell him that. 'We haven't seen him, but don't worry. What are you doing here?'

'This is the way Michele came this morning to get to

Headquarters. The explosion happened just after he left home. You don't think—'

'No, I'm sure there's no connection. This is a terrorist thing, the whole of the West is under attack. Look, I'm going to see what's happening, but first I'll have one of my men take you home and as soon as I see the chief superintendent I'll tell him to call you.'

'I want to come, too.'

'I'm sorry, Signora Ferrara, that's not possible.'

'Rizzo,' was all she said, and there was such a mixture of authority and entreaty in her voice and eyes that Rizzo knew there was no point in insisting.

'The chief will never forgive me,' he said, walking ahead of her and showing his police badge to get through the crowd.

Ahmed Farah, the Egyptian journalist from *La Nazione*, who had helped Ferrara in the past, recognized Rizzo and fell into step behind him.

'This is a terrorist attack, isn't it?'

'We don't know that yet. It's too early to say.'

'Do you need another September 11 before you wake up?'

'You have your theories, we have to investigate.'

'If they don't blow you up first. These guys mean business, Superintendent.'

'I know, but for now let me do my work.' Rizzo let Petra through the cordon, but stopped Farah when he tried to follow them. 'Not you, you stay here.'

'So you don't want to make a statement to the press?'

'No, Chief Superintendent Ferrara will do that when the time is right.'

'By the way, where is he? I haven't seen him.'

'He'll be here.'

'Tell him to call me. I may be able to help him in this

business. I'm a Muslim, I know these people. I know this whole scene much better than you do.'

'All right, I'll tell him, but—' Rizzo broke off in consternation: he had lost sight of Petra.

Ferrara's wife had walked away, heading unsteadily but without hesitation for the mail van, behind which she had glimpsed the Alfa Romeo 156.

Rizzo found her again, ran to her side and was just in time to catch her as she fainted in his arms.

She had walked past the van and had found herself facing the shattered car windows.

The crushed, twisted and bloodstained car was empty.

4

Petra had been lifted up by two officers who had come running at a signal from Rizzo and was taken in a semi-conscious state to the superintendent's car. Now the car was speeding to the Careggi Hospital, its siren blaring. The piercing sound shattered Petra's eardrums, increasing the nausea she was already feeling as the driver wove in and out of traffic.

The first drops of rain smudged the windows.

Rizzo was talking excitedly on the phone. His voice was muffled by the siren and the windscreen wipers, and their hypnotic rhythm felt like hammer blows as Petra struggled to make sense of the muttered words.

'How long ago? . . . Serious? . . . We're on our way . . . Ten, fifteen minutes at the outside . . . Yes, Commissioner.'

When he had finished with the call, Petra tried to speak, but the effort simply made her retch.

'They're both injured, but alive,' she heard Rizzo say to the driver. 'The commissioner's already there, so hurry.'

'Yes, chief, but how seriously injured?'

That was the question Petra was also dying to ask.

'He doesn't know, he's only just got there.'

They were silent for the rest of the journey, Petra's muffled sobs swallowed by the wail of the siren.

The square in front of the emergency department was filled with police cars. Among them, Rizzo recognised Riccardo Lepri's car. An officer led them to the room where the commissioner was sitting impatiently, his right leg moving back and forth in a nervous manner.

Rizzo would have preferred to entrust Petra, who was still unsteady on her feet, to the care of a nurse, but she had been so firm in her objection – predictably – that he had given up the idea.

When they entered the room, the commissioner stood up, went to Petra and took her hands in his, solicitously.

'Don't worry, he's going to be all right.'

'Where is he? I want to see him.'

'They took him to X-ray.'

'How is he?' Rizzo asked.

'We just have to wait. They only brought him in a little while ago, still unconscious. Doctors never say anything until they're sure. But I'm very confident,' he added, presumably for the benefit of Petra, who could feel her nausea coming back.

Noticing this, Rizzo walked her to one of the cold, grey metal chairs lined up along the walls of the room.

A man in a white coat came in through a frosted glass door and signalled to the commissioner. Leaning on Rizzo's arm, Petra made to stand up, but the doctor shook his head. With a reassuring gesture, Lepri asked her to wait.

'But I'm his wife,' she protested weakly, collapsing back on the chair as the door closed on Lepri and the doctor.

When at last it opened again, the commissioner was accompanied by another doctor, an older man with an authoritative air. His round pink face, with its crown of snowy white hair, was grave but serene. Lepri, on the other hand, looked really grim, and it was his face that drew Petra's anxiety like a magnet.

But it was not Lepri who went to her. Instead, he called Rizzo over, while the doctor shifted one of the chairs and sat down facing her, smiling good-naturedly.

'Good morning, Signora Ferrara. And it is a good morning, I can tell you. Your husband is a very lucky man. I'm Professor Giombi, the consultant. I can assure you you have nothing to fear. We have to operate on his jaw and remove a few small foreign bodies, but it's really not serious, believe me. There are a few cuts from flying glass, a few minor burns. But we haven't found lesions in any vital organs. With all these various things, though, he will have to stay here for a while. He needs complete rest, and I mean complete. Do you understand? No visits from colleagues, no work until further orders. Consider it a holiday.' It was a feeble attempt at a joke.

'Can I see him?'

'Not now, we're getting him ready for his first operation.'

'All right, I'll wait here,' she said wearily, closing her eyes and leaning back in the chair. With her left hand she gripped the back of the chair next to her to stop herself falling to the side.

She wasn't feeling at all well. And she didn't believe him.

While the doctor had been reassuring her, she had several times taken her eyes off his face and glanced over at Commissioner Lepri and Superintendent Rizzo, who were whispering together, their expressions a clear denial of everything the consultant was telling her.

At the same time, he had noticed that her condition gave cause for concern.

'Please, don't move,' she heard the doctor say, as he pushed back the chair with a metallic squeak.

Petra wouldn't have been able to move, even if she had wanted to. She felt dizzy, and very close to fainting again.

5

'He's a lucky man.'

Again.

This time the voice was Rizzo's.

He had taken the consultant's place without her even noticing.

She had not fainted, but had slipped into a kind of emotionless limbo. Shaking herself out of it, she realised that the commissioner and the consultant had gone, leaving only Rizzo and her in the room. She also saw that Rizzo was not smiling.

'The truth, Rizzo. I'm prepared to hear it, whatever it is. I don't want soothing platitudes, I want to know, do you understand?'

Rizzo gave her a bewildered look. 'The chief isn't seriously hurt. Didn't Professor Giombi explain?'

'What was he supposed to say? He could see the state I'm in. But I wasn't born yesterday. I saw you – you and Lepri. You looked as if you were at a funeral. So don't tell me everything's fine. I want the truth, Rizzo, the truth!'

Rizzo swallowed and bowed his head.

Perhaps he didn't want her to see his watery eyes.

'Your husband is going to pull through very quickly, Signora Ferrara, thank God. He isn't seriously hurt. Unfortunately,

Officer Franchi wasn't so lucky. He probably won't make it.'

Petra burst into tears. It was not just a release of the tension that had been accumulating, it was also remorse: all this time, she had been thinking only of her husband, not of the innocent driver who had shared his fate. A woman as solid and down-to-earth as her German origins, Petra Ferrara, having chosen to spend her life in the shadow of her Michele, had always had a kind of respectful fellow-feeling for the men in her husband's team. Now she realised how weak she'd been and, worse still, how selfish.

Rizzo waited for her tears to subside, then said gently, 'I'll take you home, there's no point in your staying here. Don't worry, they'll let us know when you can see him. Let's go.'

At that moment, the door opened and the consultant came in, accompanied by a nurse.

'No, no, you go, Superintendent, the commissioner is waiting for you. But I'd like to keep Signora Ferrara under observation. She needs medical care. I've given instructions to the staff and we've got a room ready. It's a double room, the best we have. The other bed is reserved for Chief Superintendent Ferrara.'

Although he was impatient to return to the scene of the attack, Rizzo could not refuse when the commissioner insisted on buying him a coffee in the hospital cafeteria. Given the circumstances, this wasn't going to be a break, but a 'working coffee'. That was the way of the world, even in Italy, even in Florence. The old habits were dying, no one had time for anything, everyone was always in a hurry.

'This is a bad business,' the commissioner began.

'Terrible,' Rizzo agreed.

'Were you expecting it?'

Rizzo did not understand. 'I'm sorry, how do you mean? Oh, because of September eleventh? Well, obviously, we've all been on our guard since that circular from the Ministry, and Florence is a potential target, but to tell the truth . . .'

'Of course, of course. But that wasn't what I meant. I was referring to the fact that Ferrara was there. What was he doing?'

'He was on his way to work.'

'But to get to the Via Zara from the Lungarno degli Acciaiuoli where he lives, why cross the river?'

'It's one of the possible routes. For security reasons, the driver never goes the same way twice in a row.'

'That's as maybe, but doesn't it strike you as odd that a bomb should go off just as the head of the *Squadra Mobile* is passing? We all know how Ferrara is, how he thinks of himself as a maverick. If I find out that he was following some private lead . . .'

'No, Commissioner. I really don't think so. I would know. It was just a coincidence.'

'If you say so, but it is very strange. But then we're living in strange times! Any clues so far, any leads?'

'It's too soon to say. Right now, I think I should get to the scene.'

The commissioner regarded him with what Rizzo interpreted as a doubtful expression. 'Yes, you're right,' he sighed. 'Strange times!'

'I'll be going, then. Thanks for the coffee.'

'Yes, go, and keep me up to date. And please, Superintendent Rizzo, I want maximum cooperation with all the investigative bodies, don't be like your chief. Everyone's going to want to put their nose into this thing. Military Intelligence are saying they want to send someone from Rome, they don't want to rely on their Florence bureau!'

'Don't worry, Commissioner,' Rizzo said to cut him short, glancing irritably at his watch.

It was 10:05.

6

'Like a lion in a cage,' Mafia boss Salvatore Laprua had said disdainfully to his wife only two days earlier, and he had thought of the other Lion, who was free and safe and crouching in his lair, depriving him of the support on which he had stupidly counted.

He wasn't used to being behind bars. He had defied the boss of bosses, Antonio Caputo, who was still in charge in Sicily even though he was on the run. He had left Sicily for the Versilia coast and set up the biggest drug trafficking organisation there had ever been. He had robbed, embezzled, blackmailed, killed and ordered killings, and had reached the age of seventy-seven without ever having been convicted of a crime. There was no way he was going to resign himself to rotting in jail now.

That was why he had yielded in the end to his lawyer's entreaties. Not that he trusted him: like all lawyers, he was all talk and no action. But it was possible this lawyer had found the only way out. Ferrara, the head of the Florence *Squadra Mobile*. It was Ferrara who had pursued him in August, Ferrara who had put him in the frame for the murder of the journalist Claudia Pizzi, Ferrara who had confiscated two hundred and fifty kilos of heroin hidden in blocks of marble in the port of Carrara, ready to be shipped to America. But Ferrara was a Sicilian, and a man of respect, unlike this timid attorney Liuzza, who was now sitting opposite him in the interview room, looking pale and agitated, a bird of ill omen.

'Did you talk to him?' he asked, without any preamble.

'I nearly did, Don Laprua. I've been after him for a while, as you know. It isn't easy . . . this is a delicate matter . . . it takes tact, you need to find the right moment.'

'You didn't talk to him! You're taking all this time to tell me you didn't talk to him!'

'That's not true. I phoned him this morning as we agreed. Really early, in fact, so we'd have a chance to talk in peace. He answered the phone, and we said hello, exchanged the usual greetings, but then . . .'

'Then what, Liuzza?'

'Then the bomb went off.'

'The bomb? What bomb? What the fuck are you talking about?'

'I was just opening my mouth when I heard this terrible explosion and we were cut off. It was like an atomic bomb! They're saying on the radio there was an attack in the Piazza del Cestello, near where Ferrara lives.'

'Is he dead?'

'No one knows, they took him to hospital. We don't know anything for certain yet.'

For a moment there was a gleam in Laprua's eyes, but it immediately vanished. He bowed his head, passed a bony hand through his white hair, let out a long sigh and muttered something in Sicilian dialect. To the lawyer, it sounded as if he was saying, 'The fools!'

'Fools?' he echoed. 'Who do you mean?'

Salvatore Laprua looked at him with the contempt he reserved for the incompetent. 'You're the only fool here.'

Silverio Liuzzi's dense, confused expression almost amused him.

He lowered his voice abruptly. 'In my village, Bellomonte di Mezzo, we grew up on bread and proverbs. One in particular. "The man who talks too much is a cuckold." Do you know what that means?'

'Of course,' the lawyer replied promptly, and a touch smugly. 'It means you shouldn't tell tales.'

'Wrong. That's what I said to my father when I was thirteen. I was cocky, sure of myself. It was like a leaving examination, only in the school of life. All I got in return was a slap. "The man who tells tales is dead," he said. "But the man who talks too much doesn't do much. He wastes time, and the others get off with his wife!" I learned three things that day. That actions speak louder than words, that men with white hair are to be respected, and that before you say anything you should think, not twice, but three times. I was thirteen. How old are you?'

Liuzza ignored the provocation. 'All right, I understand,' he said, anxious to redeem himself. 'But there are other avenues we can try. There's the prosecutor who co-ordinated the investigation, her name's Anna Giulietti. I can get to her.'

'You don't understand a thing. You didn't do what you were supposed to do. Now it's over.' His voice had dropped almost to a whisper. 'Over.'

'What do you mean? Is this a joke? I assure you I still have several strings to my bow – I have my ways, my contacts—'

'Contacts!' Laprua cried, his body suddenly shaking with anger. 'What use are fucking contacts when you couldn't even make the phone call you were supposed to? I don't want you to do anything more for me, have you got that? Anything. You're no use to me now. That's it, this conversation's over. Everything's over. Guard!' he yelled. 'I want to go back to my cell!'

7

It was raining hard by the time Rizzo got back to the Piazza del Cestello.

He felt doubly depressed. By what had happened to Sebastiano Franchi and by that hint from commissioner Lepri, which rather stuck in his craw.

Given the current climate in Italy, and the seriousness of what had happened, it was natural that Military Intelligence should be involved, along with Internal Security and Counter-Terrorism. But it was as if the commissioner had been determined to underline it, introducing a note of mistrust which hurt his pride. It was the police who had paid the highest price so far, which meant that they had the strongest motivation to solve the case. Whether this was a terrorist attack or not, they should take priority in the investigation.

Inspector Venturi led him to the scene. The epicentre of the conflagration was a deep egg-shaped crater near the chain that marked the boundary of the parking area. All around, over a radius of a hundred yards, amid the carcasses of burnt cars, lay broken glass, tree branches, debris, even pieces of door and window frames and cornices.

The grisliest part of the work had already been done. The

remains of the victims had been taken to the Institute of Forensic Science for identification and post mortems.

The forensics team in their white overalls were picking their way through the debris in the rain, under the orders of their chief, Gianni Fuschi. Some of them were photographing every detail with an almost maniacal precision, others were collecting objects and placing them in numbered plastic envelopes, while a different group was exclusively concerned with finding traces of explosive.

There was no blood to be seen now on the asphalt: it had been washed away by the rain and the water from the firemen's hoses.

Rizzo walked up to Deputy Prosecutor Luigi Vinci, who was standing talking to Superintendent Gianni Ascalchi, nicknamed The Roman.

'Good morning, Signor Vinci,' he said, closing his umbrella and sheltering under theirs.

'Good morning, Superintendent.'

'Have you all heard?'

'Unfortunately, yes,' Vinci said.

'It's a slaughterhouse,' Rizzo observed, looking around and seeing the fragments of human flesh still stuck to the walls.

'A real massacre.'

Rizzo nodded. 'So what happened exactly?'

'The bomb must have been in a parked car – we'll have to find out which one. It hit the cars next to it, including an Audi A3 directly in front of Ferrara's car, which as far as we can see had stopped.'

'Stopped?'

'According to the driver of the mail van that was following it.'

'The one that crashed into the chief's car?' Rizzo asked, looking towards the two tangled vehicles.

'Yes, only it seems to have been the other way round. In other words, Ferrara's car reversed into the van.'

'Does that seem right to you?' he asked Ascalchi.

'Not really. Sebastiano is a first-class driver. Even I wouldn't do something as stupid as that.'

'Where's the van driver?'

'The Carabinieri are questioning him.'

'When he's finished, get him over to Headquarters, I want to talk to him.'

'All right, chief.'

The word sounded strange, coming from Ascalchi, but it was true: in Ferrara's absence, he was in charge of the investigation.

'Are there any other eye witnesses?'

'We're doing a house-to-house. Someone must have seen something.'

'Right. Do we know anything about the device?'

'Fuschi isn't saying anything yet, except that it was probably in one of the cars that were seriously damaged.'

'In other words, we don't know anything definite?'

'Unfortunately not. They'll photograph and video the scattered pieces in the positions they were found in, then collect them and take them away. Hopefully we'll have some useful information as soon as possible.'

'It wouldn't surprise me if one of them turned out to be stolen,' the Deputy Prosecutor said.

'More than likely,' Rizzo replied. 'All right,' he said to Ascalchi, 'as soon as you know anything definite, let me know.'

'Don't worry, Francesco.'

'We need to identify the owners of all the damaged cars as soon as possible and question them. We need to know when they parked here – one of them may have noticed something or someone suspicious.'

'If only! It's going to take quite a time, though. For some of the cars, the only way we're going to be able to trace the driver is by matching the engine and the chassis.'

'Right.'

Unfortunately, time, as usual, was what they did not have. *It's best if I make a move*, Rizzo told himself, *I'm not really needed here any longer.*

He said goodbye to the two men and left.

His mind was in a greater turmoil than ever. He couldn't stop thinking about Franchi, and he couldn't yet see any chink of light, anything that could help him to orient the investigation in a particular direction.

It was only when he realised that he had not reopened his umbrella and was soaked through that he grasped the full truth of the matter: he was badly shaken. He had seen plenty of violent deaths in the past, but never carnage on this scale.

8

Superintendent Rizzo was chilled to the bone by the time he got to Police Headquarters. He went straight to the secretary's office.

'Fanti!' he cried.

'Yes, Superintendent,' the secretary replied in a thin voice.

Sergeant Fanti, Ferrara's indispensable assistant, was naturally thin, but that day he seemed really drained, his cheeks even more hollow than usual, if that was possible. His laptop was connected to the radio in the Operations Room; he was desperate to find out how his chief was. He had tried several times to reach the officer on permanent duty at the hospital, but there had been no reply.

'Get me Acting Prosecutor Giulietti on the phone,' Rizzo ordered before entering his office, ignoring the silent question in Fanti's eyes.

Anna Giulietti, an attractive woman from an aristocratic Florentine family, who had devoted her life to her work, had coordinated Ferrara's operation against Laprua.

Rizzo had only just collapsed into the armchair behind the desk and closed his eyes when the telephone rang. He automatically reached out his left arm and grabbed the receiver.

'Hello! Acting Prosecutor Giulietti?'

'Yes, this is she.'

'Good morning.'

'Good morning to you, Superintendent Rizzo. You beat me to it. I was just about to call you.'

'Go ahead.'

'Could you come to my office?'

'Of course. Straightaway?'

'If possible.'

'I'll be right there.'

He stood up. Before going out again, he went back into the secretary's office, where Fanti sat with a hangdog look, with his ears still glued to the radio.

'He'll pull through, don't worry.' Rizzo assured him. 'He isn't seriously injured. In the meantime, I want you to send the usual telegram to the Ministry, I'm off to the Prosecutor's Department.' He preferred not to mention Franchi: Fanti would find out about him in due course.

'Who shall I send copies to?'

'The usual. The office of the Head of the State Police, the Criminal Investigations Section and the Central Operational Service. And add Counter-Terrorism, though they probably know it all already.'

It was five minutes to midday by the time he reached the Prosecutor's Department.

He climbed the stairs to the first floor and knocked on Anna Giulietti's door.

'Please sit down, Superintendent Rizzo,' she said in greeting. She was wearing a pair of grey slacks and a black silk velvet jacket over a white blouse with the collar raised to frame her face. The only adornment was a pair of discreet but luminous pearl earrings. Neatly presented as she was, she did not look her best. Her beautiful, still youthful face looked hard, her eyes weary.

'Good morning, Acting Prosecutor,' Rizzo said as he sat down in front of the walnut desk.

'The first thing I need to tell you,' she began without further ado, 'is that my colleague Deputy Prosecutor Vinci and I will be co-ordinating the investigation into the attack.'

Since August, when Ferrara's investigations had led to Prosecutor Gallo being implicated, the Prosecutor's Department had been without a head, and executive duties had been carried out by Anna Giulietti as the longest-serving of all the deputy prosecutors.

In reply, Rizzo nodded.

'I've already drawn up a file against persons unknown for mass murder and criminal damage, as well, of course, as illegal possession and transportation of explosive material.' She paused. 'But that's not why I asked you here.' Then she paused again.

Rizzo wondered why she was keeping him on tenterhooks.

'I know Chief Superintendent Ferrara isn't seriously hurt' – and here she seemed to brighten up for a moment – 'but he's going to be away for a while, so I want you to be in charge of the investigation.'

Again, Rizzo nodded.

'I'm sure you realise there's not a minute to lose. The fact that Ferrara is absent mustn't be allowed to slow down the *Mobile*'s activities.'

'He'd never forgive me!' Rizzo interrupted her.

'I'm sure he wouldn't. So, what have you got so far?'

'What can I tell you, Signora Giulietti? We've only just started.'

'Don't you have any theories? Is there any reason you can think know of, other than chance, why the chief superintendent might have gone by way of the Lungarno Soderini this morning?'

Rizzo recalled some of the odder aspects of the incident, especially that curious halt his chief had made. Why had they stopped? Had they seen something? And why had they suddenly reversed? This could be crucial, he felt, perhaps even the deciding factor, and he couldn't wait to talk to Ferrara about it. Not knowing what answer to give for the moment, he preferred not to venture any theories.

'No, Signora Giulietti. As far as I know, it's simply the route he was taking to come to the office.'

'Pure chance, then? I find that hard to believe. Ferrara's not just any police officer. But it's true, we're living in strange times. The attacks in New York have changed everything, and that's the only thing people can think about. And Florence is certainly an attractive target, is that what you're thinking, too?'

'Well, it's a theory. In fact, Military Intelligence are sending us someone from Rome.'

'How do you know that?'

'Commissioner Lepri told me.'

Anna Giulietti did not seem pleased to hear this. For a while, she was lost in thought. Then she dismissed whatever she was thinking with a gesture of her hand, as if swatting flies. 'That's neither here nor there. What matters is what you think.'

She gave him a questioning look, which made him feel uncomfortable.

'It's too soon to say. Until we get the results of the tests—'

'If that's your attitude,' she burst out, 'the Secret Services will get the results first and you last! We can't afford to wait, don't you see that?'

Yes, he did see that, but what could he do? The Secret Services, being secret, were justified in following their own methods, and they had precedence where threats to national security were concerned.

Anna Giulietti waited, knowing he had no answer, and in those few moments she calmed down. 'There are two reasons I asked you here, Superintendent Rizzo,' she resumed. 'I want this investigation to be quick, and I want it to be conducted with an open mind, do you understand? If Military Intelligence and Counter-Terrorism want to pursue their own leads, let them. Whatever they find out they'll pass on to the police and the Carabinieri. But as far as the terrorist theory goes, it's only one of several, and they're all equally valid. Is that clear?'

Rizzo could not have agreed more, and said so.

'Good. I shall, of course, ask for the full cooperation of the Carabinieri.'

Rizzo said nothing.

'Don't think I don't trust the police. But the more of you there are, the better. There's no point in making the investigation too personal. Have I made myself clear?'

'Perfectly.'

'Good. Then you can make it clear to the commissioner. As soon as possible, I'll be writing with instructions to both you and the Carabinieri.'

'Of course, Signora Giulietti. You will have the fullest support of the State Police, and the *Squadra Mobile* in particular.'

'I never doubted that for a moment, Superintendent. Let me tell you now that, once the crime scene investigations are complete, I'll be calling an operations meeting today at Police Headquarters. The head of the Regional Forensics Department will be attending, and so will Major Alibrandi and other senior officers of the Carabinieri.'

'Fine.'

'I'll see you later, then, and . . .'

'Yes, Signora Giulietti?'

'I think we should increase security around Ferrara, don't you?'

'Do you think he could have been the target of the attack, and they could try again?' Rizzo asked incredulously. He realised that until that moment he had not even entertained the possibility. The implications were enormous.

'You read my mind. If we're keeping our options open, we can't rule out that theory, can we?'

'No, of course not . . .'

'Then please get it done as soon as possible.'

On his way out, shaken by this new perspective, the super-intendent suddenly wondered if Ferrara's safety had been the real reason for his being summoned. He had been aware for some time that there was an unusual understanding between Ferrara and Anna Giulietti, an understanding which perhaps went beyond the respect they felt for each other as profes-sionals.

9

Rizzo got back to Headquarters to find Fanti waiting for him.

'Signor Spano is in your office, Superintendent.'

'Who's he?'

'I thought you sent for him. Superintendent Ascalchi brought him, he told me—'

If it was the driver of the mail van, so much the better. Rizzo's hands were itching – he needed to be active.

'It's all right, Fanti. I'll take care of it.'

He entered the office and saw a well-built man of about forty, with black hair, sitting with his back to the door.

'Hello, I'm Superintendent Rizzo.'

'Hello,' the man replied, getting up to shake his hand. 'Spano, Francesco Spano, you sent for me.'

'You were driving the van, is that right?' Rizzo asked, sitting down at his desk.

'Yes, that's right, Superintendent.'

'And can you tell me exactly what happened?'

'I just told the Carabinieri.'

'Do you mind repeating it for me?'

'No, of course not.'

'Go ahead.'

'I was driving along the Lungarno Soderini, and just before the Piazza del Cestello the car in front of me, a blue Alfa Romeo 156, suddenly stopped. So I slowed down and put on the indicator to overtake, but then I braked because I saw that another car, an Audi, which had been parked on the left-hand side of the street, was starting to move out. Practically just in front of the Alfa Romeo. I waited for it to come out into the road and move off before overtaking, but just as I was about to start the van again, the bomb went off, and then I didn't know what was going on. I heard the explosion, and I've never seen anything like it – I saw the Audi leap into the air in a ball of fire, and things flying everywhere and the Alfa Romeo reversing right into me.'

'Are you sure?'

'About what?'

'That it was reversing?'

Francesco Spano frowned. 'Well, I didn't see its lights, I just saw it coming towards me, and I didn't have time to avoid it.'

The man was very specific, and so was his reconstruction. The only thing that was not clear was why Sebastiano Franchi had suddenly stopped. Police drivers are given very specific instructions, and Franchi's were to get the chief superintendent to Headquarters as quickly and safely as possible.

'Did you have the impression that the Alfa Romeo had to brake suddenly because the other car was blocking the street?'

'No, Superintendent, though it did wait to let the other car come out and I had to stop, even though I wasn't all that close to it.'

The reason they had stopped like that, apparently deliberately, had to be that they had seen something suspicious. Could they have actually seen the bombers? If that were the case, their testimony would be vital to the investigation. One

34

more reason to tighten security at the hospital. And he really had to talk to Ferrara.

'But the Alfa Romeo . . .' Francesco Spano said. 'Well, in the end, it got off lightly.'

'Not really,' Rizzo said, thinking of the two men in hospital.

'But if it hadn't stopped, it would have been the Alfa Romeo that went up in a ball of fire and not the Audi, don't you think?'

'So what you're saying is that the Audi shielded them?'

'I think that's obvious, Superintendent, at least from what I could see.'

'Thank you,' Rizzo said. 'You've been a great help.'

Once Spano had gone, the superintendent called Fanti and ordered him to make sure that there was constant twenty-four-hour surveillance, both around the hospital and outside Michele Ferrara's room.

Rizzo spent the hours that followed alternating calls to Careggi – Ferrara was undergoing his first operation, and Franchi's condition was still giving cause for concern – with calls to the Operations Room and the patrol cars.

The number of victims had been established: four dead and sixteen injured, two of them seriously. Commuters on their way to work, most of them. Among them were some non-EU immigrants, a number without work permits, who would be deported as soon as they had recovered. They had been lucky, though, compared with the victim closest to the car at the time of the explosion, whose scattered remains might remain forever unidentified, unless someone – a friend, a relative – notified the authorities of his disappearance. The one thing that was certain at the moment was that he or she had been of Middle Eastern origin, and if they had also been an illegal, that was likely to be all anyone ever knew.

Thanks to the discovery of a driving licence, though, they had been able to identify the driver of the Audi A3, a university student named Achille Bruno. His father had recognised him from a few particulars: a ring and the scars left by a back operation he had had two years earlier after an accident in the snow.

Early in the afternoon, Inspector Venturi knocked at the door.

'Come in!'

'Hello, chief,' he said as he entered. 'Why don't you open the window?'

'I'm sorry, you're right. Do you mind doing it for me?'

Rizzo had been chain-smoking, and the room was thick with smoke, the air unbreathable.

The inspector threw the window wide open, and the smoke started to disappear as if sucked out by a vacuum cleaner.

'Thanks, sit down.'

The inspector took a seat on one of the visitors' chairs.

'I have the first results,' he said, placing a file on the desk.

'Good.'

'We've identified the car that was carrying the device.'

'Go on.'

'It was a Fiat Uno. There's not much left of it, but we managed to match the chassis with the engine. Can you imagine? The engine had ended up in the river, surrounded by fishing rods! Then, when we searched through the debris, we found the registration document under a parked Renault about thirty feet from the crater.'

'Intact?' Rizzo asked, incredulously.

'Perfectly intact, chief. I could hardly believe it, but Dr Fuschi says it's quite normal. Paper is able to bend with the shock waves, so it doesn't break easily.'

'It's a good thing it didn't catch fire.'

'Absolutely. The chassis of the car was found on the other side of the square near the river.'

'Good God! And who did this Fiat belong to?'

'It's registered to Arturo Poli, of 44 Vie Giosué Carducci, in Prato.'

'Any criminal record?'

'No. It looks like the car was stolen.'

'Did he report it?'

'There was nothing on the database, but I called our colleagues in Prato and they told me he reported it this morning but they hadn't yet had time to send it in.'

'What time this morning?'

'Eight-thirty. I asked them to fax me a copy, it's there in the file.'

Rizzo opened it. It was a standard form, and in the section reserved for the statement of the party reporting the theft, Arturo Poli, a clerk at Prato Town Hall, declared that he had parked the car in the usual place in a street outside his home at about nine the previous evening. At eight the following morning, when he had gone to pick it up, it had disappeared. In answer to a question from the officer taking the statement, he had said that he did not suspect anyone.

'That's good, Ricardo. Send for him. We need to find out if he noticed anything suspicious over the last few days. And send a couple of officers to Prato to go over the Via Carducci and the surrounding area. You never know, someone may have seen something.'

'I'll get right on to it, chief.'

'Let me know what you find out.'

The inspector left the room, and Rizzo, alone again with the voices coming over the police radio, picked up the phone to bring Acting Prosecutor Giulietti up to date.

10

The meeting began at exactly 8 p.m.

The crime scene investigation had been completed less than an hour earlier and the forensics team had returned to Headquarters.

The room where the meeting was being held was on the second floor, in a quiet wing of the building. All the chairs round the solid walnut table were occupied. Acting Prosecutor Giulietti sat in the middle with Deputy Prosecutor Vinci. Sitting beside Anna Giulietti were Rizzo and Fuschi, and beside Vinci, Major Angelo Alibrandi, commander of the special investigations unit of the Florence Carabinieri. Also present were a number of police superintendents and inspectors and an equal number of marshals from the Carabinieri.

The walls were bare apart from a framed photograph of the President of the Republic; a document, also framed, listing the names and dates of all the commissioners who had served over the years; and a photograph of a police officer who had been killed by a terrorist during an attempted prison break from Murate prison in the late 1970s. On the table were some bottles of mineral water and paper cups.

Acting Prosecutor Giulietti spoke first.

'Today has been a tragic day for Florence and for all of us,' she began. In a calm but firm voice, looking from one man to another as she spoke, she went on to emphasise how important it was, given the size and complexity of the investigation, that everyone cooperate fully. 'Anybody might have been the target of whoever planted that bomb, but the fact is that by involving two representatives of the police it has struck at the heart of the State which we represent. I ask you, therefore, to act together in perfect harmony. In fact, that's not a request, it's an order.'

The infighting and bureaucratic wrangles between the various bodies, and sometimes within the same body, were an endemic ill which nobody had ever managed to eradicate, but they could be kept under control if the prosecutor in charge of the case had a strong enough personality to impose his or her will on everyone. Anna Giulietti had personality to spare, and that made all the difference.

'There won't be any problem about that,' Rizzo reassured her, and his assertion was immediately echoed by Major Alibrandi. Everyone else nodded.

'Having got that over with, I'd like Superintendent Rizzo to tell us what we know so far about the bomb.'

'Thank you, Acting Prosecutor.'

He went over what he had already told Anna Giulietti and then informed them of the latest developments.

'We've questioned the owner of the car, but didn't discover anything that wasn't already in the report. As far as we can tell at the moment, it does appear to be a theft by persons unknown. Unfortunately, none of the neighbours noticed anything or anyone suspicious in the last few days.'

'But they must have had a safe place to prepare the car,' Anna Giulietti said. 'Isn't that so, Dr Fuschi?'

The head of Forensics looked particularly tired and drawn.

Like everyone else, he could not get Sebastiano Franchi's condition out of his head, nor the absence of Chief Superintendent Ferrara. He considered Ferrara a friend, and always referred to him by his nickname Il Gatto – a nickname given him by the journalist murdered on the orders of Salvatore Laprua.

'I agree. It would have been difficult for them to do something as sophisticated as that in the open air, especially at night.'

Anna Giulietti nodded.

'In order to prepare the explosive device they would have needed good artificial light. To attach the wires, obviously. And it would have had to be somewhere where they wouldn't be seen.'

'A garage?' Deputy Prosecutor Vinci asked.

'It's possible. Or else an abandoned warehouse.'

Prato and its surroundings were a predominantly commercial and industrial area, full of warehouses used by haulage firms and wholesale clothing companies.

The others nodded in agreement.

'So, Superintendent Rizzo and Major Alibrandi,' Anna Giulietti said, 'we have to search the whole area, starting with Prato, where the car was stolen, and then moving out to the area between Prato and Florence.'

'Right,' both men replied.

'That's just as far as the car is concerned. But the bombers must also have had an apartment to hide out in both before and after the attack. Which means they had accomplices. One at least.'

'And that could have been in Prato or Florence or anywhere,' one of the marshals said, grimly.

'I have full confidence in you, I know you won't let me down.'

That put them all in their place, they all thought, although no one said a word.

She turned to Fuschi. 'What can you tell us about the type of explosive?'

'So far we don't know much for certain.'

'But what do you know?'

'That it was a very powerful explosive, and was probably in the trunk or the back seat of the Fiat Uno. From the size of the crater, I'd say they must have used nearly a hundred pounds.'

'How was it detonated?'

'Probably by remote control, but it's still too early to be certain.'

'When will we know more?'

'We'll have to analyse the material that was found at the scene.'

'Yes, but when?' Anna Giulietti asked impatiently.

'The most comprehensive tests will have to be done in Rome because they require special apparatus which we don't have here in Florence. They'll have to use gas chromatography with a mass spectrometry developer—'

'All right, Dr Fuschi, you can explain that to me later,' she cut in. 'Your department and the Central Forensics Service will both report to me.'

'Of course, Signora Giulietti.'

'So, we'll have to wait for the results of the tests, but in the meantime, let's get back to operational matters. I think it's worthwhile questioning everyone living in the area, plus the owners of the damaged cars, and I want to do a blanket check of everyone staying in hotels and pensions around the Piazza del Cestello.' She gave a slight smile to the grim-faced marshal. 'We may strike it lucky.'

'We're already doing that,' Rizzo said.

'I'm glad to hear it, Superintendent Rizzo. But perhaps, to speed things up, you could share names and tasks with the Carabinieri.'

'Of course, Signora Giulietti. We'll divide up the area, if the major is happy with that.'

'Absolutely,' Alibrandi replied immediately.

'Then,' Anna Giulietti continued, 'we need to find out from the phone companies what mobiles were being used at that time on the Lungarno Soderini and the adjacent areas, and check them out.'

Rizzo would have liked to say that this would be a large and expensive operation, which, in the absence of any other points of reference, would almost certainly lead nowhere, but he restrained himself and kept silent.

They all nodded.

'Next,' she went on, 'I want a tap on all phones belonging to the family of Salvatore Laprua.'

Her words were like a bombshell, which was what she had been hoping. They all looked at her doubtfully, but no one spoke.

'Let's be absolutely clear about this,' she said. 'The investigation must adhere strictly to the Ferrara method. In other words, all options are open, and all theories should be examined in the light of the evidence before we decide to favour any particular one. And we have a lot to choose from: international terrorism, home-grown terrorism – Military Intelligence, Internal Security and Counter-Terrorism will be concentrating on those – the Mafia and God knows what else. But we do have reason to believe' – and here she made a gesture to include Rizzo – 'that the real target of the attack might, and I emphasise might, have been Chief Superintendent Ferrara. Isn't that right, Superintendent?'

Rizzo responded by recounting the events leading up to the

explosion, concluding with the fact that if Ferrara's Alfa Romeo had not stopped, it would have been the car hit by the bomb.

There followed another long silence, during which each man drew his own conclusions.

But their scepticism remained, and it was Major Alibrandi who took it upon himself to express it.

'It's a possibility, of course, but it could also have been an unfortunate coincidence. After all, the chief superintendent doesn't go by way of the Piazza del Cestello every morning. The bombers would have had to be very sure of his route, and how would they have known that – unless there was a mole in the *Squadra Mobile*?'

Rizzo stiffened. The very idea was absurd. He knew every man in his squad personally.

'On the other hand,' the major continued, 'we shouldn't forget that the bomb went off only a few yards from a military building. I'm sure you'll understand that I consider it my first priority to investigate the possibility that the army might have been the target. Don't forget that our participation in the operation in Afghanistan is a contentious issue.'

It was an irrefutable argument, and a point in the major's favour. That much was clear from the nods of agreement round the table.

'True,' Anna Giulietti was forced to agree. 'Given which, I'd like you to be the one to obtain the CCTV tapes from the Army Logistical Command and also from the Customs and Excise building on the Lungarno Soderini, if it hasn't already been done. But at the same time, I'd like you, Superintendent Rizzo, to establish who knew the chief superintendent's route. We can't escape the fact that the arrest of Laprua and the dismantling of his organisation, which was all down to Ferrara, happened very recently. The damage to the organisation—'

'Laprua's organisation,' Alibrandi had no hesitation in cutting in. 'Which was an independent initiative, like all Mafia operations on the mainland, where they feel much freer and don't have to play by Sicilian rules. But Laprua's family are in Sicily, and we know things are quiet in Sicily at the moment. No one there would launch a frontal attack on the State. It's a strategy that hasn't paid off in the past, and there's no way Caputo would allow it.'

Antonio or Antonino Caputo, known as Don Nino, who had been on the run for decades and was wanted by half the police forces in the world, was the acknowledged and established head of Cosa Nostra.

Anna Giulietti was clearly put out, because in her heart she knew that Alibrandi was right. Since Laprua's arrest, Sicily had been particularly closely monitored, but there had been nothing to indicate that the balance of power had shifted or that anyone had been planning reprisals.

'Rizzo?' she said, as if looking to him for support.

Rizzo would have liked to side with her, even though he did not understand why she was so insistent on favouring that particular angle. Could it be that she knew something he didn't? Frankly, the evidence to support her hypothesis was looking increasingly weak, especially as the idea of a mole in the *Squadra Mobile* was unimaginable. Ferrara himself, who was always careful to avoid basing an investigation on preconceived ideas, would not have approved, he thought.

'The major's right, Signora Giulietti.'

But the acting prosecutor's mind was made up. 'The Mafia, gentlemen, is a hydra with a thousand heads. Cut one off and two more spring up. It keeps going even when the bosses are in prison or on the run. Anyone who thought it had been defeated after the State reacted so firmly to the murders of Judges Falcone and Borsellino has had to think again. It's a terrible cancer which is spreading in ever more insidious ways over the whole of the country, and represents one of the greatest threats to our economy and democracy. We mustn't give an inch. I'm sticking with my request, and I take full responsibility for it.'

'We'll get the request to authorise the phone taps to you as soon as possible,' Rizzo assured her.

'When you do, I'll make sure it's granted immediately. Does anyone have anything else to say?'

Nobody asked to speak.

'In that case, the meeting is closed. Thank you, everyone, and good luck.'

11

When she saw him lying there, with that contraption clamped over his jaw preventing him from speaking, and his eyes open – 'The operation went very well,' the consultant had said – but staring into space, Petra's first thought was that the one thing that mattered was that he was alive. And then she thought – and it was the first time she had thought this with such conviction and such anger – that it was time she persuaded him to retire: he wasn't a young man any more, and he had given too much of his life to this dangerous profession and had got too little in return.

Ferrara had woken up in a confused state, probably as a result of the anaesthetic, remembering nothing of the incident and wondering why on earth he was in a strange room instead of in his own bed, and why he couldn't open his mouth, which felt annoyingly furred and numb. But Petra was there, which reassured him, and through a drip he was administered a mild sedative to allow him to sleep peacefully.

Petra prepared to face a long night. She would spend it going back and forth between her own room, where she made sure her husband was sleeping well, and intensive care, where Officer Franchi's family – his father, mother, sister and brother-in-law – were following his agony through the window of the waiting room. She watched with them, at a discreet distance and in silence – what could she possibly say that was suitable? – the luminous lines on the monitor beside the officer's bed, where he lay surrounded by tubes. From time to time he was shaken by a sudden convulsion that made the onlookers' hearts skip a beat, and everyone would look again at those lines and those white and green dots: the only thing anyone knew was that, as long as they moved and oscillated and formed graphs and diagrams, there was still hope.

Meanwhile, some one hundred and eighty miles away, in an office of the Ministry of Defence at Forte Braschi in Rome, the lights were still on.

Captain Somenti, just back from a stormy meeting with his chief, Nicola Spadaro, head of the Middle East division, had almost finished reading the reports which would stand him in good stead for his investigations into the attack in Florence.

He had been in Military Intelligence for more than a year now, and he still couldn't stand Spadaro. As far as he was concerned, the man was an idler, a playboy. He was almost never around, and in all these months had never entrusted Somenti with any important missions, only routine, insignificant ones. When the news had come in from Florence, given the urgency of the situation and the fact that Spadaro was not there, the director, General Mangiagalli, had gone over Spadaro's head and had ordered Somenti to leave for the Tuscan capital, which he knew well, to investigate the attack, on the assumption that this was a terrorist act with a Middle Eastern connection.

When Spadaro had got in that afternoon and heard what had happened, he had been beside himself. Unable to challenge his own superior, he had taken out his anger on Somenti.

'You shouldn't have accepted the job, simple as that!' he had screamed.

'I thought the general was in overall charge,' Somenti had retorted.

'You shouldn't think. Just report to me.'

'Yes, sir. Should I tell the general I've been ordered to stay in Rome?'

'Don't try to be funny with me! Do as instructed, but report to me personally. And report everything. Get support from the Florence bureau, but avoid passing on any information to them.'

Bloody malingerer! the captain had thought, and later he had vented his rage to Sergeant Giorgio Azzaro, a pot-bellied fifty-year-old with greying hair. 'How on earth did he ever get into Military Intelligence?'

'It was a political appointment, some time in the past. He's a civilian – and a bastard, I know. He had a brief period of glory from 1996 to 1998, when he was our liaison officer in Islamabad, during the civil war between the Taliban and the Northern Alliance. Since then, he's done so little that everyone's forgotten about him and he's simply stayed where he is. Now, with this new wave of terrorists from the Middle East, he's back in the eye of the storm, that's why he's itching to get involved.'

When the sergeant had gone, Somenti – a tall, handsome man of thirty-three, with dark hair, light eyes and regular features, son of a colonel in the Carabinieri who had died heroically in Sicily when Mafia violence was at its height – had tried to calm down by studying intelligence reports on the activities of Islamist groups in Italy, a particularly voluminous file since September 11. During his training, all the instructors had insisted on how essential it was to read all the available documents, and having an excellent memory he had always done well.

He had almost finished.

He had left for last a small green folder containing a report on one of the victims of the attack – someone else who had always done well. The label read: *Michele Ferrara, head of the* Squadra Mobile *of Florence. PRIVATE AND CONFIDENTIAL.*

It was a very detailed report, clearly drawn up by someone who knew Chief Superintendent Ferrara personally, not just by reputation like him. The document was unstinting in its praise for his brilliant career and his many successes, but also made a number of criticisms, which the captain highlighted in yellow to differentiate them from the phrases already highlighted in green, presumably by Spadaro – so he *did* work sometimes!

Written soon after the spectacular arrest of the Mafia boss Salvatore Laprua and the scandal that had shaken the Prosecutor's Department in Florence, the report observed:

> *Chief Superintendent Ferrara is a loyal,* sometimes too loyal [highlighted in yellow] *servant of the State, who does what he wants regardless of anyone else. Once he has chosen a path to follow, he sees it through to the end, whatever the consequences and/or the people involved. In so doing, he sometimes treads on unknown toes and* creates enemies in the most unexpected places [highlighted in green]. *A good example of this is the investigation into the so-called 'Monster of Florence', when he went beyond those directly responsible, whom he himself had identified and brought to justice, and pursued his investigation in powerful and high-up circles whose members were unlikely to let this go* without making him pay for it in some way [highlighted in green]. *Another example is the more recent investigation into Mafia activity and corruption in Tuscany,*

the ramifications of which may be manifold and not all immediately identifiable. I shall try to give some examples, all purely hypothetical, without making any claims to being exhaustive.

1. *The Mafia boss Salvatore Laprua, otherwise known as Zì Turi, arrested by Ferrara in August, headed an international drug trafficking organisation, a complex network extending from the cultivation of opium in* Taliban-controlled Afghanistan [highlighted in green], *much in our thoughts today, to organised crime in the United States, the destination of the load confiscated by Ferrara. And yet we know too little even now of the true extent of Mafia activities on an international scale to be able to say for certain what forces (national or international) may have been damaged by Ferrara's actions, thus provoking a* desire for revenge [highlighted in green].

2. *By isolating Laprua, Ferrara has broken the chain, thereby making it more difficult for other investigative bodies (especially the Anti-Mafia Squad and Internal Security, but also partly us) to have a complete picture of the Mafia's latest evolution, its expansion outside Sicily: a relatively recent phenomenon, largely unmonitored, and a possible cause of conflict within the Mafia itself. Seen from this angle, what was without doubt a successful police operation could be considered an obstacle to the course of justice, which may generate ill will and create animosity at various levels.*

   What appears obvious to the present writer is that Chief Superintendent Ferrara, although a dedicated and loyal police commander, is lacking in diplomatic and political skills [highlighted in yellow]. *He is interested only in pursuing his objectives, and is insensitive to the bigger picture of which his activities should merely be a part, and with which, precisely because of this insensitivity, they may also*

clash. This must be taken into account in any operation which requires his involvement.
M.

It was not difficult for Somenti to identify the anonymous writer. By a fortunate coincidence, when he got home, and while he was packing his bags, he watched a special TV programme on the events in Florence. Among the experts, who tended to see the attack as a warning from the Islamists before the imminent attack on Afghanistan, there was one who stood out from the rest: Angelo Duranti. He had been brought in to talk about Ferrara, whom he had known when he was commissioner of Florence.

It was Angelo Duranti – dubbed Mephisto by his subordinates for his sullen, prickly character – who had appointed Ferrara the head of the *Squadra Mobile* at the time of the Monster of Florence case and still respected him enormously, as became clear in the course of the broadcast. Although he did not descend into the somewhat polemical tone of the report Somenti had read, he talked about the chief superintendent in such a way as to make it obvious, at least to Somenti's trained ear, that the former commissioner, now retired, was working as an informant for Military Intelligence – not such a rare occurrence.

But his references to the Laprua case and the possible Mafia ramifications of the bombing did not go down well in the circumstances, and the presenter soon turned again to the military experts, who were more in tune with the changed times.

12

Former commissioner Duranti's words went down even less well – were indeed met with anger and derision – more than six hundred miles from Florence, in a modest house in the countryside between Palermo and Capaci.

'What the fuck is the guy saying? We didn't have anything to do with this mess.'

This judgement was pronounced by the Mafia boss Antonio Caputo, the oldest of the three men sitting around the little TV set in the kitchen. He was tall and well-built, but the years had clearly taken their toll. Unlike the other two, he was shabbily dressed. He had two day's growth of beard, his hair was white and shaggy, and his face lined. His eyes were bright and lively, even though they were streaked with red from all the wine he had drunk with his frugal meal of goat's cheese, dried tomatoes and olives.

'We don't have anything to do with Zì Turi any more either, since that day,' was the scornful comment of Antonio Molina, boss of the Caltanissetta district. 'Why are they trying to pin the blame on us? We don't give a fuck about that son of a bitch Ferrero or whatever his name is.'

'If we'd wanted to kill him, he wouldn't be in the hospital

right now, he'd be in the cemetery!' This from Salvatore Lume, known as Sasà, boss of the Palermo district, who could boast of 'hosting' the boss of bosses on his territory.

Antonio Caputo rose from his chair, walked a trifle unsteadily to the TV, an old set without a remote control, and switched it off.

'It wasn't us,' he said, pensively, 'but what if it was him?'

'Who?' Sasà asked.

'Zì Turi?' Molina said, incredulously.

'Why not?'

'Because he's inside, that's why. Which is just where he should be.'

'Jail's no hindrance to people like us, Totò.'

'Sure, you keep the same contacts, you keep your protection. But what protection can a man like that have, a man who wants to go it alone and refuses help, like some kind of golden eagle?'

Caputo's face seemed to relax, although he did not seem at all convinced. 'What about Laprua's sons?' he asked: he never referred to him as Zì Turi, which he found too familiar. Laprua was a traitor, someone who had left Sicily to do his own thing, someone who had rejected the hierarchy that ensured the Mafia's stability.

'They're all in Sicily. In their house, in Bellomonte di Mezzo. I saw them there myself, along with Pippo Catalfano, you can trust us on that.'

Caputo was not pleased to hear the name of the boss of the Castelvetrano district. Giuseppe Catalfano, known as Pippo, was the perfect embodiment of the new-style Mafia boss, as far from the old cloth-cap-and-rifle image as you could get: distinguished, refined, well-educated, he wore designer suits – rarely the same suit twice – and moved about in powerful, chauffeur-driven cars. He was one of the new breed that didn't greatly appeal to Caputo: they kept one eye – one slack eye – on their own territory, and the other on the limitless pastures of an increasingly globalised drugs trade. In his opinion, that was a fatal error: better to be king in your own patch, he always said, than a prince regent in someone else's empire.

More than once he had told himself that the Castelvetrano district was badly run, and that sooner or later he would have to bring it back firmly under his control with a new and more trustworthy boss, but he hadn't yet found the right person – or, primarily, the opportunity. Catalfano might be weak, but he wasn't an idiot; he was well protected politically and had never failed to proclaim his loyalty to his, Caputo's, authority.

'Pippo needs to know we have our eyes on him,' Caputo said in conclusion. 'He mustn't do anything we don't want.'

Molina and Sasà exchanged worried glances. They were both extremely loyal to Caputo, and from the beginning it had been their task to step in at the first sign of friction and prevent an uncontrollable feud from breaking out between Caputo and Catalfano. The last thing Sicily needed was a Mafia war: Caputo himself had said that.

'Anyway,' Molina suggested, changing the focus of the conversation, 'we need to inform Rome that we had nothing to do with this.'

'We could get one of your *pizzini* to the Basilisk, Don Nino,' Sasà proposed, referring to the cryptic messages on pieces of paper which the Mafia bosses sent each other and their contacts in the political establishment, to evade phone taps.

Caputo felt the strange spasm he experienced whenever that name, the Basilisk, was spoken, especially if it was someone else who had used it.

The Basilisk was Caputo's masterpiece, the Mafia's bridgehead at the heart of the State. He had practically brought him up from birth, like a son, almost stealing him from his mother's arms after his father's death. He had taught him the subtlest art of all: mediation. As a joke, he had given him the name of a deadly, treacherous creature – the Basilisk – and the name had stuck, the emblem of someone who was brilliant at forming advantageous alliances through persuasion, the ballot box, and, if need be, threats and blackmail.

His creation had proved equal to the task, and now the two of them worked hand in glove. Caputo had enough on the Basilisk to get him arrested, and the Basilisk knew all about Caputo's movements and his hiding places. Few men in the Mafia hierarchy even knew of the Basilisk's existence, and none of them had seen him. He was Caputo's. The consummate politician, the great mediator, who knows the strength and weaknesses of the parties involved, and bends them to his will when he has to.

Caputo stood up, walked slowly to the old green sideboard with the frosted glass panes, opened one of the drawers, and took out a school exercise book with squared pages. He tore off a page and started to fill it with numbers interspersed with letters, according to a rudimentary but effective code.

13

Pratica di Mare military airport, Rome.
Tuesday October 2, 9:15 a.m.

On the runway, a Falcon belonging to Military Intelligence was taxiing, waiting for the arrival of the two officers from headquarters at Forte Braschi. The pilot of the plane did not know their destination: for security reasons, as usual, he would be told it only at the last moment. That was fine with him: it meant he was not required to make a flight plan, although he would have liked to know if he would be back the same day, just so that he could arrange things.

His curiosity would be satisfied soon enough. He watched as a dark blue Lancia Lybra drove up to the plane and stopped almost at the foot of the ladder. Two men got out and came hurrying up the steps into the plane. Each of them was carrying a small case in one hand, and a bundle of newspapers in the other.

'Good morning, Captain!' said the younger of the two. 'I'm Captain Carlo Somenti, and this is my colleague, Sergeant Giorgio Azzaro.'

The sergeant shook the pilot's hand.

'Where are we going?' the pilot asked.

'Peretola airport, Florence,' Somenti replied.

'All right. Please take your seats.'

The door was immediately closed while the two passengers went and sat down in the first row of seats, but on opposite sides of the aisle so that each had a view through a window.

Before switching off his mobile, Somenti tried again to call the number he had been trying to contact for fifteen minutes, but this new attempt also proved fruitless. He went back to reading the newspapers, which he had interrupted on arrival at the airport.

'Have you seen *La Nazione*?' Azzaro asked, also busy with the papers.

'Not yet, but I'm curious to know what Farah has to say.'

'Read it. He's the only one who's a hundred per cent certain it was the work of Arab terrorists. The others are more cautious. They all mention September eleventh, of course, but they don't rule out other possibilities, especially as the head of the *Squadra Mobile* was involved. They're probably reflecting the uncertainty of the police and the Carabinieri, who surely don't know which way to turn. I don't envy them! But Farah has really got the bit between his teeth. Maybe he knows more than the others.'

Somenti hoped so, which was why he was trying to contact him.

He had met Farah when he was in charge of the Criminal Investigations Unit in Prato. He had been with the Carabinieri for ten years by then, during which time he had been moved from place to place, and Prato had been his last posting before he had joined Military Intelligence. Ahmed Farah had struck him as a bright, hard-working young man, well-known in the non-EU immigrant community, and very determined to be part of the Western world, having studied journalism in Florence, where he had lived since arriving from Cairo at the age of nine.

He loved Italy and respected its political and legal institutions, with which he had always been ready to cooperate. Right now, his help would have been particularly invaluable to Captain Somenti.

But what Somenti read was disturbing.

Ahmed Farah had seized on the terrible incident in Florence as an opportunity to launch a fierce attack on Islamic extremism, which he clearly saw as a major threat to the West, and which in his opinion was being spread by sleeper cells ready to strike. He mentioned the 'clash of civilisations' and accused the West of excessive tolerance, which in the light of the latest events came dangerously close to weakness. From this point of view, the attack in Florence was only a first step, a warning sign which the authorities would do well not to underestimate.

'If only half of what he writes is true, I hope they've already assigned him an armed escort. I doubt his co-religionists would let him get away with it!'

'What's to say he isn't right?' Sergeant Azzaro replied.

'Nothing at all, but that would mean he knows a lot more than we do. We haven't had any intelligence reports indicating that the situation has got to this point.'

'I wouldn't be surprised if he *did* know more than us. It wouldn't be the first time.'

Somenti did not reply, and they both fell into a pensive silence.

The insinuation had wounded the captain's pride. Just past his thirty-third birthday, and still with all the ambition of youth, he had seen Military Intelligence as an opportunity to advance his career. For the sake of it, he had even jeopardised his relationship with the woman he loved, Giulia, and the memory of that still rankled with him.

She was a physical education teacher in Prato, and was very beautiful. They had planned to marry, but when she learned that he had been called to Rome – to play at being a spy, of all things – she had given him an ultimatum: he could choose Military Intelligence and his damned career or he could stay in Tuscany with the Carabinieri and make sure their marriage worked.

It hadn't been easy.

And now here he was, increasingly depressed as he approached Florence, where there was a possibility he might see her, and with an older colleague casting aspersions on the efficiency of a Service he had idealised. Well, to counter those aspersions, he was even more determined to do well. This mission would be a test of his mettle.

He was still unsure how to handle the Florence bureau. His orders were to keep them in the dark about his findings. A strange request to say the least, unless for some reason the head of the Florence bureau wasn't considered trustworthy. He would certainly have liked to know what that reason was, perhaps he really ought to know, but Azzaro had no idea and he certainly couldn't ask Spadaro.

For the rest of the short flight, he tried to think of a way to avoid making the head of the Florence bureau suspicious. As the plane began its descent, an idea occurred to him: he would ask him if he could have his own base away from the bureau, perhaps a house in the country somewhere near the city. Officially, the reason was simple: to try and avoid attracting attention in Florence, where someone might well recognise him because of the time he had spent in Prato, which is almost a satellite town of the Tuscan capital. In reality, it would give him greater autonomy. Azzaro could act as liaison – which was what he had been asked to do anyway.

As Somenti started descending the steps from the plane, he switched on his mobile phone and, once he was connected to the network, saw that he had five messages. He listened to them. Three were from Spadaro, and he ignored them. The other two, which had come five minutes apart, were both from the same person and the content was almost the same both times: 'This is Ahmed Farah, just seen you've been trying to contact me, call me whenever you like, speak to you soon.'

Somenti dialled the number, which he already knew by heart. The answer was not long in coming – after the second ring, in fact.

'Ahmed!' he said, as soon as he recognised that unmistakable voice. 'Somenti here.'

'Hello. Nice to hear from you. What have you been up to?'

'I changed jobs. They transferred me to Rome.'

'A promotion, eh? Good for you.'

'Let's just say that I'm dealing with rather more confidential matters now, matters that may have a connection with what you've been writing lately.'

'I see. Do you want me to come to Rome?'

'No. I'm in Florence. I only just got off the plane.'

'Would you like to meet?'

'As soon as possible.'

'I won't have time today.'

'How about tomorrow?'

'As long as it's late. Shall we say an aperitif about seven?'

'Perfect! What about that bar in the square near your newspaper?'

'Too crowded, too many journalists.'

'Right. How about the Belvedere?'

'Fine. See you then.'

'See you tomorrow.'

Somenti rang off and left the airport, followed by Sergeant Azzaro. A driver from the Florence bureau was waiting for them outside.

14

In the corridors and offices of the *Squadra Mobile*, there was as much chaos as the day before. Most of the officers had been there all night, and even those few who had got away hadn't gone home but to Careggi Hospital, to look through the window at their colleague Franchi and the machines that were keeping him alive, and support his family with timid, awkward words of comfort.

As he entered his office, Rizzo noticed a young woman talking to Fanti in the waiting room. When Fanti saw him, he apologised to the woman and followed him in.

'Chief, the young lady is the owner of the Fiat 126 which, according to Forensics, was parked right next to the car with the bomb.'

'What did you find out?'

'She says she parked her car about ten o'clock the previous evening. At that time, there was an expensive-looking car on the right and a van on the left.'

'So the car with the bomb wasn't there yet?'

'No. It replaced the expensive-looking car.'

'Or this expensive car gave up its space to it. Did she say what make of car it was?'

'If only! She's one of those women who can't tell the difference, she says they're all more or less the same to her. She noticed it was a big car – what she actually said was, "One of those luxury models, like a company car", and she remembers it was black or dark blue.'

'Okay, take her to see Chief Inspector Violante, he can get a statement off her. But before you do that, there's something I'd like to ask you. Do you keep a diary of the chief's car journeys?'

'You mean a record of the mileage?'

'No, what I'm interested in is the routes he takes to go from home to work and vice versa.'

'There's no diary, chief.'

'But they change every day, don't they? Who knows what that day's route is?'

'Nobody. The driver knows he has to choose a different route every day, so he decides. Unless the chief superintendent decides on another route, but in that case he'll almost always tell him at the time.'

'I see. All right, you can go. Thanks.'

He collapsed into the armchair, feeling somewhat reassured. If the procedure was as Fanti had described, that completely ruled out the idea that there could have been a mole, and along with it the theory that Ferrara had been the target of the attack: to prepare something like that, the bombers would have had to be certain that the chief superintendent would go past the Piazza del Cestello that morning.

He lit a cigarette and glanced at the newspapers. All the front pages were devoted to the attack. He read through the reports. There were many theories, but only Ahmed Farah's long article in *La Nazione* unhesitatingly laid the blame at the door of Islamist terrorists. He may have been the only one to do so, but he wrote for the most widely read newspaper in the city. What was worse, though, was that, one way or another, they all ended by saying that the public did not feel safe or well protected.

There had been three claims of responsibility on the internet: two on Jihadist websites, neither of them regarded as 'official', and one from an unknown revolutionary army that evoked the spirit of the Red Brigades. All three were considered unreliable, but the Secret Services and the Communications Squad were looking into them anyway.

He folded the newspapers and put them aside.

He then skimmed through the reports from his staff and from the patrol cars that had been combing the territory, setting up road blocks at strategic points and searching for arms and ammunition.

Nothing significant had been found.

He decided to go upstairs and see Commissioner Lepri, to bring him up to date and receive any instructions he might have. Outside his office, he pressed the button on the wall, to the left of the door, but had to wait a couple of minutes before the green light came on.

'Ah, speak of the devil. We were just talking about you.'

Lepri was not alone.

'Good morning, Superintendent Rizzo,' Stefano Carracci said. The director of the Central Operational Service in Rome rose from the armchair in front of the commissioner's desk to shake Rizzo's hand. From the ironic expression in Carracci's eyes, Rizzo gathered that the commissioner was not in a very good mood, and that he had accepted this visit from Carracci with bad grace.

While they were exchanging greetings, Riccardo Lepri invited both to sit down. His voice was not a roar, but it was not a bleat either – it was more like a growl.

'I was just telling Director Carracci,' he said, in the same tone, 'that in Ferrara's absence you're standing in as head of the *Squadra Mobile* so you're the person he should get together with to evaluate the letter he's just brought me from his office, together with one from the head of the State Police. Here, read it.' He handed him a document addressed to the Central Operational Service in Rome.

It was a report from the *Squadra Mobile* in Palermo indicating the presence in Tuscany of a mobile phone believed to be in the possession of a dangerous Mafia fugitive.

The fact that Carracci had brought it in person, together with a letter from Armando Guaschelli, the head of the State Police, underlined the importance of this development, which must have been checked and counterchecked. Rizzo couldn't wait to find out the details.

'Does anyone know what on earth is going on?' the commissioner finally exploded. 'Mafia and terrorism, all together, here in Florence? Have you seen the papers? Do you think anyone who reads them is likely to be attracted to the city? Not to mention the Florentines themselves! They can't be feeling very secure, with all the flak the press are throwing in our direction! The *Squadra Mobile* need to get a move on, Superintendent. They need to do something. Put a stop to the journalists' innuendos, reassure public opinion. Florence isn't some kind of inferno! If we do have fugitives hiding out here, then let's let get rid of them immediately. Get together with Chief Superintendent Carracci and flush out this criminal.'

'Of course, Commissioner,' Rizzo replied.

'All right, get on with it, let's not waste time. And good luck!' The commissioner sounded calmer now, recovered from his outburst. 'Keep me informed. I have complete confidence in you, Superintendent Rizzo.'

15

Rizzo went back to his office with Carracci, and sent for Inspector Riccardo Venturi, who had the longest memory of anyone in the *Squadra Mobile* and was also a dab hand with computers, and Inspector Antonio Sergi, known as Serpico because of his resemblance to Al Pacino in the film.

The previous evening, Carracci told the three men, the *Squadra Mobile* of Palermo had sent him a letter indicating the presence on the mainland of a mobile phone in the possession of a Mafioso named Gino La Torre, who was affiliated to the Castelvetrano family. Wanted for murder and other crimes, he had been on the run for some years now, and his name was on the list of the thirty most wanted men in Italy. The head of the State Police had given specific instruction not to let up on the search, and the Sicilian police in particular were relentless in their pursuit of him.

La Torre's dark, square face, with its long, smooth black hair and several days' beard growth, was well known to Rizzo and his men: they saw it every day on a poster in the corridor of the *Squadra Mobile*.

'I immediately contacted the head of the *Squadra Mobile* in Palermo to ask for more details.'

Carracci paused for breath.

'It seems they've been tapping all the phones registered to La Torre's wife and family, and that Vodafone have instructions to help them track down the location of any phones called by these users. And here's where it gets interesting.'

He paused again, briefly.

'Yesterday they found out that a mobile registered in the name of La Torre's wife Lia contacted another mobile in the Prato area. The contact only lasted about thirty seconds.'

'Isn't it possible that it was the wife who was in Prato?' Serpico asked. 'And that could have been for reasons that have nothing to do with her husband.'

'No, it's not possible. The woman hasn't moved from Castelvetrano. We know that for certain because our colleagues have her under surveillance.'

'But if the phones are being tapped, we should know who spoke, shouldn't we?' Venturi asked.

'Unfortunately not. Whoever was being called didn't answer. After a few rings, the recorded message came on.'

'Whose number was it?' Rizzo asked.

Carracci paused again, took a sip of water, and put the glass back down on the table. 'The number is registered to a company called Matteo Parenti of Mazara del Vallo in the province of Trapani. First indications are that it's a fishing business.'

Like Laprua, Rizzo thought. It was as if what had just been thrown out the window had now come back in through the door. Laprua, too, had been in charge of a fishing company, which he had used as a cover for his drugs ring. The same thought must have crossed the minds of Sergi and Venturi – they were both looking at him – just as it must have crossed Carracci's mind earlier: the look on his face was that of a man who knows he has just dropped, if not a bomb, a least a big firecracker.

'So it's very likely that it was actually Gino La Torre calling. What time was the call?'

'That's the other interesting fact: at 12:32 on the morning of October 1, 2001, an odd time to be calling a fishing company.'

'Maybe even more interesting than you think,' Rizzo said, increasingly bewildered. 'The Fiat Uno used for the bombing was stolen in Prato on the night of September thirtieth to October first. Which suggests the Mafia may have been behind the attack, with Ferrara as the target. And to think I'd just ruled that theory out!' He went on to explain that such a theory implied the presence of a mole, something he considered quite impossible.

'Perhaps Ferrara wasn't the target,' Carracci observed. 'It's not always easy to figure out what the Mafia's intentions are. But it does look as if there's a connection between La Torre and the attack, so we have to look into it. For a start, we need to find out all we can about this Matteo Parenti company of Mazara del Vallo.'

'Absolutely. Inspector Venturi will get on to that as soon as we have authorisation from the Prosecutor's Department, right, Riccardo?'

'You can count on it, chief.'

The meeting was interrupted by the sudden arrival of Commissioner Lepri, who threw the door wide open without ceremony. He looked badly shaken, his face drawn and ashen, almost a ghost of his usual self. With his head down, he walked slowly to the table around which they were sitting and in a voice breaking with grief announced the death of Sebastiano Franchi.

16

At 8:10 a.m. on Wednesday October 3, a mile or two from Tavarnuzze, on a dirt track off Provincial Route 69, which descends from Impruneta down to the Via Cassia, a man sat at the wheel of a stationary black Mercedes S500, keeping his eye on the road.

He was waiting.

Any moment now, the Lancia Thema would pass on its way to Florence, as it did every morning.

On the empty passenger seat beside the driver of the Mercedes was the mobile phone, with the number to be called already programmed.

About half a mile away, behind a little concrete hut where road repairing material was kept, two young men in jeans, sweaters and boots were sitting on the ground chain-smoking. They only had to press a button. A simple enough thing to do, but they were nervous.

Next to them lay a jacket, and on it a mobile phone had been placed. They were waiting for the call.

It finally arrived.

They got to their feet, then bent their knees slightly to get a better view. Just two minutes later, one of them pressed the button.

The woman sitting alone in the back of the Lancia darted her head from side to side, looking in all directions. She had heard something. A kind of sharp crack, like a gunshot. But the driver didn't seem to have noticed a thing.

'Didn't you hear that?'

'What?'

'That shot.'

'Some boys in the fields with a popgun,' the driver replied. 'Or maybe a hunter.'

In the end, Anna Giulietti blamed it on her nerves: recent events had put her on edge. But it was not until she was on the busy Via Cassia that she felt a little calmer. She wondered if she ought to mention it to Rizzo.

She certainly would have mentioned it to Ferrara if he'd been around.

She was missing him, she thought, and that troubled her.

Although she refused to admit it, or even to think about it, she was well aware of the fact that, if Ferrara had been the target of the attack, there was a strong likelihood that she was next on the list.

Yes, she was definitely missing him.

17

'You're playing a dangerous game.'

Ahmed Farah shrugged. He was about thirty, with a sallow complexion, and a long, thin, almost ascetic face, framed by a thin, short beard, like a prophet. Beneath his hooked nose, his thin lips often curled in an amused smile with an almost imperceptible underlying bitterness. His eyes, too – lively, mobile and mostly happy – proved on closer examination to conceal depths of sadness and melancholy.

He was highly motivated, determined, intelligent and tireless. He had risen though the journalistic ranks and had made quite a name for himself. In the current climate, his knowledge of Arabic had proved highly advantageous, and he was making the most of it.

He had been explaining to the captain that there were no mosques in Florence, and that the faithful met in apartments, which made things harder to keep an eye on. Nothing at all was known about either of the two groups who had claimed responsibility. Whether the claims were true or false, he had remarked, they helped to stir people up, and he could sense the temperature rising in Florence.

'It's a dangerous world these days, don't you think?' he said in reply to Captain Somenti's observation.

'All the more reason not to go looking for danger,' Captain Somenti said.

They were sitting at a table outside the Belvedere bar, with the city at their feet. They were alone apart from a couple sitting some distance from them. The first lights had come on and were already shimmering on the Arno, which was tinged with red by a spectacular sunset.

'What about you?'

'It's my job. I chose the Secret Service, as I think you've guessed.'

'For me, it's more than a job. I come from that world, I know it well, I know there are things stirring there that can explode at any moment. These people are in a minority, but they're everywhere and they've been indoctrinated to seek martyrdom. They could become almost unstoppable. Maybe they already are! Not only could they jeopardise global stability, they could drag the whole Arab world, most of which wants nothing to do with them, into an insane, suicidal war. To protect that world, I have to do what I'm doing. But in addition to that, I'm half Western, and I love the West. As you can see, it's a position that forces me to play what you call a dangerous game, whether I want to or not.'

'Have you at least asked for an armed escort?'

'No, I'd prefer not to have one, it would restrict my movements. But I know that the Ministry of the Interior has taken it upon itself to request one for me. That's why, if we're going to work together, we have to hurry, before my hands are tied.'

Better to have your hands tied than your mouth silenced forever, the captain thought, even though he knew how potentially useful their relationship was.

'Work together in what way?'

'I have my sources in those circles, who inform me of any suspicious moves. I can even get names, but that's as far as I can go. Which doesn't get us anywhere.'

'Whereas I could check out the suspects, is that what you mean?'

'You people have the means. The terrorists use mobile phones a lot. If I can get hold of their numbers, you can put a tap on them, right?'

Somenti felt a shiver down his spine. 'It's dangerous, and it's not a game.'

'I know that,' Ahmed replied, raising his aperitif glass and smiling radiantly, the shadows put to flight by the glitter of his white teeth. 'Chin, chin!' It was as if he had won the lottery, and his joy was contagious.

Somenti clinked glasses with him. 'Cheers, Ahmed!'

It was almost 10:30 p.m. when a shadowy figure climbed down into the three-foot deep depression on the right-hand side of Provincial Route 69 as it descended from Impruneta. He bent over, picked something up, then set off in the opposite direction. He came to a brand new off-road vehicle, which was waiting with its engine running, and got in.

After less than half an hour, the vehicle drove into the garden of a small house, where a black Mercedes S500 was already parked. It stopped and the two occupants got out and entered the house. One of them was a short, dark-haired, dark-skinned man in his late twenties, with two gaps in his teeth where the incisors should have been, the other was just a little taller and had greying, almost white hair.

There were two men in the house, one of them young, the other a short, square man of about fifty.

'So, Jan, do you want to tell me what happened?' the man with the greying hair asked the younger man.

Jan was the only one with a light complexion. He was tall, slender and fair-haired, twenty-six years old, and could easily have come from a North European country.

He ignored the question and turned to the short, dark young man from the vehicle, who was carrying a bundle with both hands. With a movement of his chin, he indicated a small wooden table next to the wall. 'Put it down there,' he said.

He took off the wrapping to reveal three smaller bundles. Each of them was tied separately with adhesive tape. One by one, he examined them. His short, stocky companion watched over his shoulder, face tense.

After a few minutes, Jan said, 'Look,' and pointed to a kind of large sausage made of explosive gelatin.

'Why the hell did you put the detonator there?' his companion asked.

'I could have put it in any of them, but gelatin was the best.'

'Pity it didn't work!' the other man said, his nerves on edge.

'I wasn't to know that.'

'I remember the package containing it wasn't hermetically sealed,' said the young man who had brought in the bundle.

'No point arguing about it,' the man with the greying hair said. 'We have to get other detonators and more gelatin. Good stuff this time.' He turned to the young man without incisors. 'Go now and try to get back as soon as possible, within forty-eight hours at the latest. I don't think we have much time to play with. The longer we wait, the harder it'll be for us.'

18

The funeral service for the victims was held in Florence Cathedral two days later, in the presence of the city authorities and the head of the State Police, who had come from Rome with a representative of the Ministry of the Interior.

Also from Rome were selected marksmen from Special Forces, brought in to reinforce the impenetrable cordon that enclosed the square.

Petra Ferrara had left the hospital, and during the ceremony she stood beside Sebastiano Franchi's parents, sister and brother-in-law, close to the coffin, which was draped in the Italian flag. The grief-stricken old couple were finding it hard to stay on their feet. Before the service, an endless procession of important people and colleagues of the victim had passed before them, including a large number of young police officers stunned by the tragedy and capable of communicating their grief and anger only with their eyes – but, to the dead man's parents, those eyes said much more than the words of the authorities.

Coming out of the church, Guaschelli walked to the hearse between Franchi's mother and father, giving each an arm to lean on. Franchi's sister and brother-in-law followed them.

Petra found herself next to Rizzo and Anna Giulietti, who asked her how Ferrara's convalescence was progressing.

'He's had two more small operations, but he's slowly getting better. He's still under sedation, and very confused. Unfortunately, he can't talk, with that thing on his jaw. Whenever he's awake, he seems lost in thought, and quite restless. He's torturing himself. I get the impression he's trying hard to remember something.'

'Have you tried getting him to write things down?' Rizzo asked. He was desperate to establish contact with the chief superintendent, desperate to know why they had chosen that route and, above all, why the car had stopped so inexplicably.

'Yes, but he refused. He seemed quite irritated. That's why I think he's still confused. It's as if he's trying to emerge from a fog.'

'These things take time,' Anna Giulietti said, trying to reassure her, although she knew perfectly well that time was of the essence right now and that Ferrara's absence was a big problem. That wasn't to take anything away from Rizzo, who was doing a great job. But the very fact that Ferrara was involved in this business made him irreplaceable, and she was sure that his contribution, whenever it came, would provide a big boost to the investigation.

She just had to resign herself. And keep going.

'Please let us know as soon they allow visitors,' Rizzo said.

'You'll be the first, don't worry.'

'Could I be the second, Signora Ferrara?' came a voice from behind them.

They turned.

'I just wanted to say hello,' Ahmed Farah said.

Petra smiled, but did not reply.

'As an acquaintance, I assure you, not as a journalist. It's up to him to tell me when the time is right, I know that.'

She smiled again, and nodded slightly, but said nothing. She felt uncomfortable, not because of Farah, but because of the person with him: a tall, dark-haired young man with light-coloured eyes who kept looking at her in what seemed a slightly questioning way.

Rizzo also wondered who he was. He had never seen him before. But in a situation like this, you couldn't know everybody, he might well be a colleague of Farah's, a journalist from another city. He stopped thinking about who he might be, but his curiosity lingered: the man, it seemed to him, had been looking at Petra with unusual intensity.

Captain Somenti continued watching them as they walked away.

As far as the investigation was concerned, there had not been any major new developments, except for the interim findings on the composition and quantity of the explosive.

According to the forensics experts in Rome, it had been a cocktail of explosives, including dynamite, T4 and TNT, as well as others they would only identify after doing tests with more sophisticated apparatus. To judge by the size of the crater and the damage caused, the quantity could be estimated with a fair degree of reliability at between ninety and a hundred and ten pounds. As for the detonator, they had confirmed Fuschi's guess: a remote control had been used.

19

In the offices of the *Squadra Mobile* that Friday, October 5, people had been coming in and out all day, and were interviewed at a frenetic pace. Some had come to provide information, in the strictest confidence, others to complain about being summoned and having to waste their time. But despite all that activity no clear picture of the bombers had yet emerged. Nobody seemed to have seen anything suspicious, nobody had been able to supply any information that made it possible to build up a description, however vague. The bombers remained ghosts.

The phone companies – Tim, Vodafone, Wind and 3 – had already started to send the first records relating to the subscribers of the mobile phones being used in the area of the attack, and a tap had been put on all phones belonging to Salvatore Laprua's sons, who lived in Sicily, and his wife, who still lived in Viareggio.

A large operations team had been created, including members of the Central Operational Service, who had been drafted in from Rome. Within the team, they had subdivided the tasks, with everyone assigned to a particular aspect of the investigation.

Rizzo, just back from the funeral, was busy going through the day's correspondence when he heard a knock at the door.

'Come in!'

It was Inspector Riccardo Venturi.

'Sit down, Riccardo.'

'Thanks, chief.'

'What have you got for me?'

He had noticed that the inspector was carrying a file in his right hand which did not look as if it contained many papers.

'I discovered something I think may be of interest,' he said, with a touch of pride. 'Have a look and see what you think.'

'Okay.'

Venturi handed him the file.

Rizzo opened it.

The first thing he read was that in August that year, the presence of Gino La Torre had been reported at Forte dei Marmi, on the Versilia coast. The sighting had been contained in a report from the Florence centre of the Anti-Mafia Squad, who had been led to him thanks to a car rented by one of La Torre's supposed accessories at Pisa airport.

Salvatore Miano, born in Castelvetrano on January 15, 1953, was suspected of being an accessory of the fugitive La Torre, thirty-seven years old, also from Castelvetrano. In the course of investigating Miano, they had established that on Tuesday August 21 he had left at Punta Raisi airport in Palermo an Opel which he had rented in Pisa. It had been driven away from Pisa at 4:25 p.m. on August 7, having been hired from the Europcar agency by a man who had shown a licence registered to Salvatore Miano and had paid with an American Express card registered to the same name. By the time it had been returned in Palermo, it had done 973 miles. During the period it had been rented, it had incurred a number of parking tickets, including two on successive days, on the promenade of Forte dei Marmi, near the Jolanda bathing establishment.

The owner of the establishment and the lifeguard who worked there had both recognised the photos of Miano and La Torre without hesitation: they had been their clients during the peak period in August, in other words, the days of the August Bank Holiday.

Rizzo then read an extract from the statements made by the owner, a woman, as quoted in the report:

'They usually came mid-morning. They had rented a gazebo for the whole of August, paying in advance. There were four of them altogether. The men had two women with them, who weren't from around here because they didn't have a Tuscan accent. Like the two men, they spoke in dialect. It sounded Sicilian to me – Southern anyway. But after less than two weeks they left, even though, as I said, they had paid in advance for the whole month, and they didn't even phone to ask for a part-refund, as sometimes happens, though not often. I was surprised, but then it occurred to me that something serious must have happened and I didn't think any more about it.'

According to the witness, both women were about the same age – early thirties – and the same height – about five foot two. One was slim with bobbed chestnut hair, the other well-built, with long dark hair. They must have rented an apartment in the area, she thought: at least that was what she had gathered from a brief conversation she had had one day with one of the two women, the well-built one.

'And it couldn't have been too far,' she had added, 'because one morning, one of the couples arrived by bike and the other by car, an Opel, I think.'

The report ended by saying that, despite a thorough search of the area, it had not been possible to locate the apartment, nor had inquiries at the hotels and pensions along the Versilia coast yielded positive results.

'Now that is interesting!' Rizzo said when he had finished reading. 'Castelvetrano is in the Trapani area, like Bellomonte di Mezzo, which is where Laprua's from!'

'Precisely, chief.'

'Let's look into this.'

'It would be nice if we could find that apartment.'

'It sounds as if our colleagues have tried everything.'

'We could always try again.'

They were both thinking the same thing: at the very same time that the investigation had been taking place into the murder of the journalist Claudia Pizzi, an investigation that had led to the arrest of Zì Turi, the fugitive Mafioso Gino La Torre had been in the same area, apparently on holiday. The abrupt departure of La Torre and his three companions more or less coincided with the height of the *Squadra Mobile*'s activities: it was on Monday August 20 that the police operation had begun.

Too many coincidences in one go!

His curiosity increasingly aroused, Rizzo started looking through the papers again.

There was a copy of La Torre's personal file.

It gave details of his family – including his wife Lia, maiden name Cassese, who was thirty-two years old and also from Castelvetrano – the cars registered in his name and his wife's, his phones, the property he owned, his criminal record, his affiliation with the Castelvetrano Mafia, the names of his known and suspected associates.

Rizzo lingered over the record. There was a bit of everything. In the early days, burglary, armed robbery, grievous bodily harm. A large haulage company had been forced to hire him, a nice arrangement for the local Mafia, giving them inside information on valuable hauls, which were then regularly stolen. More recently, he was believed to have been involved in a number of Mafia-related murders – a sign that he had moved up within the organisation.

Gino La Torre was now believed to be a middle man for the suspected new district boss Giuseppe Catalfano, performing all kinds of duties including, when necessary, those of hitman – at least according to a Mafioso who had cooperated with the Sicilian judges, although his testimony was disputed.

'What about the phone records?' Rizzo asked. 'Where are you with those?'

'I'm having a look at them. Those which have arrived so far.'

'We need a report for the acting prosecutor, Riccardo.'

'Do you want me to do it?'

'No, you carry on with your work. Ascalchi can take care of it.'

He sent for Ascalchi, went over the new developments with him, and gave him Inspector Venturi's file.

20

Although there was not yet an actual Chinatown in Florence, many Chinese businesses, especially in clothing and leather goods – not all of them legal – had established themselves in the area between the outskirts of the city and the Campo Bisenzio and Campo Prato.

The area, which included a Chinese bank and even a small local TV channel, had, over a short space of time, become a kind of no-go area, where even the police often did not dare intervene. If a crime was committed, the Chinese preferred to deal with it themselves rather than turn to the authorities.

It was Saturday, around noon. Ahmed had chosen a tiny restaurant – really more of a takeaway, with a handful of tables – where they would be able to talk freely.

The room had bright green tiles of dubious cleanliness, and the whitewashed walls were slightly yellowed. Little bottles of Chinese beer, soy sauce and saké sat on a single shelf. The food was nondescript, identical to the food in thousands of similar places all over the world.

'Okay, what I can tell you for sure is that two men arrived in Florence two days before the bombing. The younger of the two is called Adjmal Yousazai, the older one, who's probably the leader, is Mullah Hamdullah. Apparently they've been looking for someone called Assad, who's here in Italy. They seem very keen to find him.'

'Are you sure they're Taliban?' Somenti asked, anxiously.

'No, but I'm sure they're Afghans and what I've told you is the rumour that's going round. They've also been seen with a Dutchman who's said to be an arms trafficker.'

'What's his name?'

'He calls himself Jans or Hans, I didn't quite catch it, but that's obviously not his real name.'

'Can you get close to the two Afghans?'

'Not me, but if they're trying to recruit people, I should be able to get to them indirectly. That's what I think they'll try. If the one thing they were here for was the bombing, you'd have thought they'd have already left, wouldn't you? But they've stayed, which means they probably want to use the attack for propaganda purposes.'

'If it was them,' Captain Somenti objected.

'Do you doubt it?' Ahmed smiled, and his white teeth gleamed.

'All the claims of responsibility turned out to be hoaxes,' Somenti said, remembering what he had read in the press. 'The newspapers are talking less and less about terrorism. They don't rule it out, but they don't exactly endorse it either.'

'Not all of them. You should read *La Nazione* more often. You're right, though, a lot of them are starting to be sceptical. Their main objection is that the Piazza del Cestello isn't a plausible target for international terrorists, with all the other things you can find in Florence.'

'But you haven't changed your mind?'

Ahmed Farah gave him an intense look. 'You just have to put two and two together.'

Somenti, not sure what he meant, raised a questioning eyebrow.

'The reason there haven't been any genuine claims is because the Piazza del Cestello wasn't the target. The bomb went off by mistake. One of the victims, the one closest to the explosion, was an illegal immigrant, an Arab, remember? Coincidence? Or maybe he was doing something with the car? Let's say he was supposed to move it a few hundred yards. Where is the Piazza del Cestello? Not far from the Pitti Palace and the Ponte Vecchio, not all that far from the Uffizi either. All rather more striking targets, don't you think?'

Captain Somenti shuddered. 'You mean they could try again? Is that why they've stayed instead of leaving immediately?'

'What do you think?'

'It wouldn't be so easy for them now. Security's been tightened.'

'Unless the threat level drops and the investigation shifts to other areas.'

'Which is what seems to be happening. At least officially.'

'And that makes it all the likelier that they'll try again, and sooner rather than later. Which means only one thing.'

'We don't have much time!' Somenti said.

In the afternoon, Rizzo was summoned to the commissioner's office.

He found him sitting behind his desk, head bent over a document he was holding in his hand. It was from the Prosecutor's Department, a request by Acting Prosecutor Giulietti for maximum cooperation from the police in pursuing the investigation into the bombing, an investigation which at the moment seemed to be ever more oriented towards the Mafia.

'These prosecutors!' Lepri burst out, grimacing and tossing the paper into a corner of his desk before the superintendent had even sat down. 'Female ones worst of all! It seems the only kind of crime that matters is Mafia-related, as if that was the only problem faced by the State. Have you read it?'

Rizzo was temporarily lost for words.

'Didn't you get a copy of this letter from Acting Prosecutor Giulietti?' Lepri picked it up and held it out. 'It's addressed to you, too.'

Rizzo read it. 'No, Commissioner, I haven't received it yet, but I have received detailed instructions to pursue investigations into a number of Mafiosi.'

Riccardo Lepri made no attempt to conceal his disgust, which obviously put Rizzo in an embarrassing situation. The commissioner advised him to do as the acting prosecutor requested, but not to use too many of his men, as his squad ought to be dealing with more important aspects of the case, then said, 'I've asked the head of the General Investigations Division to involve his counter-terrorism section in the car bomb investigation.'

Rizzo knew that the General Investigations Division were providing whatever information they could, as was standard practice, but he had not been expecting them to be fully involved in the investigation itself. Caught off guard, he did not know what to say in response. He sensed a lack of trust, and was about to defend the conduct of his squad when Lepri started speaking again.

'You know, Superintendent, the head of the General Investigations Division does have his informants, and, more importantly, he has the support of Military Intelligence, and I think he may have some good leads which could throw light on the bombing.'

That was all Lepri was prepared to say, but it was clear that he was viewing the case from the international terrorism angle.

'I'd be happy if the General Investigations Division could solve the case for us,' Rizzo replied.

'We'd all be happy, Superintendent. But I want you to cooperate fully, make everything we learn available to them; the results of the crime scene investigation and the forensics tests, the investigations into the stolen car, and so on.'

'Of course, Commissioner.'

'And I don't want any leaks, especially to the press. We don't want people becoming any more alarmed than they already are. I'm sure you understand that. Some newspapers would leap on the Mafia connection like manna from heaven.'

'I'll be as discreet as I can, Commissioner.'

'Good, Superintendent. I see we understand each other. Well, that's no surprise. As I've already said, I have every confidence in you.'

Sure you have, Rizzo thought, pretending to be pleased. A clash with the commissioner was the last thing he wanted, especially with Ferrara absent.

When he got back to his office, he received a call from Sergi.

'I have something for you, chief.'

'Go on.'

Rizzo collapsed, exhausted, in the armchair and lit a cigarette.

The inspector started by saying that Salvatore Miano's car had been confirmed as having been rented at Pisa airport and returned in Palermo.

'But we already knew that, Sergi,' Rizzo cut in, unable to hide his impatience.

'Chief, I was just going over the results of the checks we ran. I've also obtained a copy of the rental contract. But I haven't yet told you the most important thing.'

'And what's that?'

'Here goes. On August 7,2001, flight BM11233 arrived at Pisa airport from Palermo. It got in a little bit late, at 4:05 in the afternoon.'

'Have you checked the passenger list?'

'Of course. Miano's name was on it, and so was the name of another passenger, Luigi Torri, who checked in at the same time, travelled without baggage, just like Miano, and sat next to Miano on the plane.'

'Ah!' Rizzo said, finally hooked. 'Very good, Sergi. That means you have another name to check out in Forte dei Marmi: Torri.'

'That's right, chief.'

'Go ahead, then. And keep me informed. Thanks.'

He put down the receiver and took stock of what he had learned. Salvatore Miano had arrived in Pisa, where he had rented a car. He had probably been in the company of a man who had been flying on the same plane. In order to get his airline ticket, Gino La Torre, the fugitive, whose real Christian name was obviously Luigi, had provided a false surname but one that was very close to his real name. It was a subterfuge other criminals had used in the past when trying to hide their true identities. In case their papers were checked by the police, the closer their assumed names were to their real ones, the easier it was to justify it as a mistake made by whoever had issued the ticket.

It was definitely an interesting result, and a further incentive to persevere with that line of inquiry. Whatever Commissioner Lepri said.

It occurred to him to inform his colleagues in the *Squadra*

Mobile of Palermo and ask them to find out whatever they could about the purchase of those tickets and about the name Torri. But it was late, and he made a mental note to phone Palermo on Monday morning.

21

Sunday October 7 in Forte dei Marmi was so hot, it felt as if summer was not quite over.

That morning, Inspector Sergi sent his men off to check the companies that rented bicycles, giving every officer photos of Miano and La Torre. He himself decided to visit the Jolanda bathing establishment.

He had no difficulty finding the place. It was just a few hundred yards from the hotel where he had spent the night, on the long stretch of beach filled with bathing establishments, which were now almost deserted.

As he approached the entrance, he saw a slim but athletic and tanned young man who was working near the first row of huts. When he came level with him, he showed his badge.

'Inspector Antonio Sergi, Florence *Squadra Mobile*.'

The young man looked at him questioningly. 'I'm the lifeguard here. How can I help you, Inspector?'

'I'd like to talk to the owner, could you call her for me?'

'The signora isn't here yet, but if you like I can phone her.'

'Thanks.'

The young man went into the bar, which was right at the

beginning of a row of huts, and when he came back he said, 'She won't be long.'

'Thanks very much.'

Sergi was tempted to ask the lifeguard a few questions, but he decided it might be best to talk to the owner first.

Less than fifteen minutes later, a neat-looking woman of about forty appeared. She had short blonde hair, and was just as tanned as the lifeguard.

He showed her his badge.

'I'm Gina Forte. How can I help, Inspector?'

He explained the reason for his visit. 'I know you've already been interviewed about this.'

'Yes, some people came from Florence, from the Anti-Mafia Squad, but I think I told them everything I know.'

'I've read your statements, but I'd still like a few more details.'

'Certainly, Inspector, I have no problem with that,' she said cordially. 'If I can help in any way.'

In the meantime, the lifeguard had gone back to work.

'Why don't we sit down?' the woman said, indicating a table shaded by a canopy covered with climbing plants, and offering him a coffee.

The inspector refused politely and took a small black notepad and a pen from his jacket pocket. Then he showed her the photographs of the two men.

'That's them, Inspector, I haven't the slightest doubt about that.'

'Could you describe the two women who were with them?'

'They were both in their thirties. One was about five foot two, and she had bobbed chestnut hair and a long nose.'

She didn't mention the long nose before, the inspector thought as he took notes.

'The other woman was more or less the same age and same height, but she had dark hair down to her shoulders, and was quite well-built.'

'Is there anything else you remember?'

'I'm trying to think, Inspector, but I really think I told the other people everything. It's possible Leonardo may remember something – he has more contact than I do with the customers on the beach.'

'Could you ask him?'

'Leonardo, can you come here, please?' she called, signalling to the lifeguard to come over. He approached and sat down at the table.

'Leonardo, the inspector would like to know about those customers who paid for the whole month and then left without a word.'

'Oh, yes, the Sicilians.'

'That's right,' Sergi said.

'They were a weird lot,' the young man said. 'You know, usually the customers here talk to each other, make friends. But not these guys. They were always on their own, never talked much to anyone else. They hardly said a word to me when I went to put up the sunbeds just after they arrived.'

'Can you remember anything else apart from what you've already told me?'

The young man concentrated. 'No, I don't think so. That's all I know.'

'All right, thank you.'

He said goodbye to them and set off for the town centre, where he had arranged to meet up with his team at midday.

By lunchtime they were sitting in the hotel restaurant. There were few other customers there, and they had chosen a table in the furthest corner, where they were sure no one would hear them. Whenever the waiter approached they would stop talking and stare at their knives and forks.

'So, Pino, they didn't hire the bikes, but bought them,' the inspector resumed, addressing Officer Ricci, who, to satisfy his monumental physique, was already on his second helping of linguine with crayfish.

'That's right.'

Ricci had been telling him that he had had no luck with the companies hiring bicycles, but that he had then found a shop in the centre where the owner had recognised the man in one of the two photos as having been a customer. It was the photo of Salvatore Miano.

'He told me he sold him two bikes in August, a man's and a woman's.'

'How did he pay?'

'In cash. That particular shop doesn't accept credit cards or even cheques, unless they're from people the shopkeeper knows, especially local people.'

'So the buyer, Miano, wasn't known to him?' It was more a comment than a question.

'That's right.'

'Anything else?' he asked.

'This person, Miano, had a woman with him, and, after paying, they immediately rode off together on the bikes.'

'Did he describe the woman?'

'Yes, he says he remembers her well. His description fits one of the two women mentioned by the owner of the Jolanda, the slim one with bobbed hair.'

'Anything else?'

'That's all, but I think it's quite important.'

Indeed it was, because it showed that the Sicilians must have been living in Forte dei Marmi itself.

'Anything from the hotel records?'

'Nothing at all,' Officer Ciccio Messina replied.

He told Sergi he had been to both the police station and the Carbinieri station in Viareggio, which covered that area, but had not found the names Miano, Torri or La Torre in any of the records.

'In that case, we need to check out the agencies that let apartments,' Sergi said. 'When we've finished lunch, we'll divide up the areas and go through all the agencies with a fine-tooth comb.'

'But it's Sunday,' Ciccio Messina protested weakly.

'I know, but some may be open. This is a tourist spot, and it's a nice day today. We can at least try. We don't have anything else to do right now, do we?'

The waiter approached with a large tray of mixed grilled fish, which he laid in the centre of the table.

'Let's eat,' Sergi said. 'You've all done well.'

22

The young man without incisors had not managed to meet the forty-eight-hour deadline. Acquiring explosives and carrying them around isn't like doing the shopping at the supermarket and going home.

By the time he got back to the house that Sunday, Jan and the other two men were livid with rage. But the sight of the explosive and the two detonators – one of them a spare – helped to calm them.

In place of the gelatin, he had brought forty-five pounds of a white, granular compound that looked like washing powder.

Jan immediately put on a pair of gloves and got down to work.

He had to take great care in handling the material: even the slightest friction could blow them all to smithereens. This time he placed the detonator inside the white powder, then connected the wires to a box containing two twelve-volt batteries, which he fitted inside another, larger box containing a motor-cycle battery. The remote would send an impulse first to the box and then to the detonator. Finally he made a package with handles on both sides to make the bomb easier to carry.

'Let's take that iron chest, too,' the man with greying hair ordered.

The young men nodded.

When placed in the depression, the crate would make the explosion more powerful. They were trying to anticipate every eventuality. They could not afford another mistake: things were already on a knife-edge, and only the complete success of the operation might get them back in their boss's good books.

After a spaghetti dinner, they all took a few hours' rest. Then, when it was still dark, three of the men set off.

They positioned the device in the same depression as the previous time and covered it with grass which they had cut from the garden.

It was 5 a.m. on a new day, Monday October 8.

The two young men went and settled behind the concrete hut, while the driver drove round the area. It was just before eight that he parked on the dirt track off Provincial Route 69 near Tavarnuzze.

It had been a difficult night. The most difficult of that long week.

Michele Ferrara had had a restless sleep, and had woken several times bathed in sweat. Each time Petra, who was constantly beside him, stroked his face and tried to calm him. She had twice had to change his pyjamas, but it had never even entered her mind to ask anyone for help.

She had been reminded at one point, strangely enough, of a woman in labour, perhaps because every time her husband woke he seemed less confused – as if he were giving birth to his own memories, his own feelings, his own life, which had been asleep for too long.

And it was true, he was remembering. One piece at a time. The ball of fire, Sebastiano Franchi's stunned face, the pain, the August operation, the arrests, Anna Giulietti, Salvatore

Laprua, the phone call from Liuzza – he had to tell someone, he had to tell . . .

Just before eight in the morning, he woke again with a jolt, and signalled to Petra to give him a pen and notepad.

I NEED TO SEE RIZZO AND ANNA AT ONCE, he wrote.

Petra looked at the sentence, nodded reluctantly, stood up and slowly went to get her mobile phone. Deep inside her, she felt a new heaviness. It was her husband she had been waiting anxiously to see again, not the chief superintendent.

Rizzo's home phone had rung at 6:50 a.m.

'This is Venturi, chief.'

'A bit early, isn't it?'

'I've spent all night going over the records of all the mobile phones in the area of the Lungarno Soderini on the morning of the attack.'

'And?'

'The chief's number was there, too.'

'Of course it was there. We were all trying to contact him. I assume our numbers and his wife's were there, too.'

'Yes, but there's also another call I thought I had to tell you about, because it coincides with the time of the explosion.'

'Go on.'

'Right. At 7:46, the chief received a call, which lasted just over a minute in all. From another mobile, registered to Silverio Liuzza.'

'Laprua's lawyer?' Rizzo cried incredulously, feeling the first shot of adrenalin of the day. 'So it was Laprua's lawyer who made Ferrara stop his car?'

'That I don't know, but I'd say it's definitely the lawyer. There aren't many Silverios in this neck of the woods.'

'We need to inform Anna Giulietti, and we need to find

out what they said. It might be the lead we've been waiting for. I'm just getting dressed and I'll be right there.'

But Anna Giulietti did not get to the Prosecutor's Department that morning. Or ever again.

She was on her way to Florence from her mother's villa in Impruneta – she had moved in with her mother to help her convalesce after a second heart operation – and was listening to the radio. The driver had tuned to a national station, and they were rebroadcasting President Bush's address to the American people, first heard the previous day at one in the afternoon, Washington time:

'Good afternoon. On my orders, the United States military has begun strikes against al-Qaeda terrorist training camps and military installations of the Taliban regime in Afghanistan. These carefully targeted actions are designed to disrupt the use of Afghanistan as a terrorist base of operations and to attack the military capability of the Taliban regime . . .'

When the Lancia appeared on the final stretch of the descent down to Tavarnuzze, the man in the black Mercedes gave the signal. A few moments later, an almighty blast shook the air.

The short, square man watched with a fascinated grin as a column of smoke rose into the air and shards of metal were scattered over a radius of forty or fifty yards. He thought he also saw a few fragments of human flesh, although that might have been his imagination.

The Carabinieri from the Tavarnuzze station were on the spot within minutes. They found the remains of the car still smoking. The shattered bodies of Anna Giulietti and the driver had been catapulted a distance of a few yards, and the first thing the officers did was cover the most intact parts with white sheets.

23

Rizzo had not gone to the office, where Venturi was waiting for him. He was just about to step into the shower when he heard the phone ring again. He let his wife answer it and slid inside beneath the jet of water.

'It's for you, Francesco,' Eleonora shouted to him.

His body already covered in soap, he turned off the water. 'What, now? Jesus Christ!'

'It's the operator from Headquarters. He says he has to speak to you personally. I told him you were in the shower and that if he liked he could tell me.'

'What did he say?'

'He said the director of the prison, Signor Mazzorelli, wants to see you urgently. It's to do with a prisoner.'

'Is that all?'

'Yes, but he insisted it's urgent, otherwise he wouldn't have bothered you. He's still on the line, do you want to speak to him?'

'No. Ask him to give you Mazzorelli's number.'

As soon as he was out of the shower, he called Mazzorelli.

'The prisoner Salvatore Laprua was found dead in his cell this morning,' the director began.

'How did he die?' Rizzo asked.

'We don't know yet. I've sent for the doctor on duty in our infirmary, he should be able to tell us.'

There was a pause.

'Has the body been moved?'

'No, it's still in the cell. I've given instructions not to move it before the deputy prosecutor gets here.'

'I'd like to see it.'

'Of course. We're waiting for you.'

There was not much traffic leaving the city at that hour, and it did not take him long to get to the prison. He crossed the Ponte della Vittoria, over the fast-flowing waters of the Arno, turned on to the Viale Talenti and drove fast in the direction of Scandicci until he saw the great grey reinforced-concrete mass of Sollicciano prison. He turned right, stopped outside the gate, and identified himself.

The officer authorised him to drive into the inner court-yard. Here, he had to pass through the security checks. He handed over his identity card, his service pistol and his mobile phone, which were placed in a special box. It was a ritual that everyone had to go through, even police officers. Another officer, who was waiting for him, led him along identical bleak corridors, all with the same ivory-coloured walls.

Mazzorelli was sitting reading a newspaper behind the huge half-moon desk which took up most of one wall.

'Good morning, Superintendent. If you can call it that.'

'Good morning, Signor Mazzorelli. Tell me what happened.'

'Please sit down. One of our officers found him this morning. There was a change of shift at seven sharp, just as there is every morning, followed by the usual inspection of the cells to make sure all the prisoners are present and correct. Every guard goes from cell to cell in his own section, stops at every cell, opens the spyhole and looks inside. Everything was normal.

Except in cell number 10 on the wing reserved for the most dangerous criminals: political terrorists and Mafiosi. Here, the officer noticed something strange. The prisoner was lying on the bed, and showed no reaction when he opened the spyhole and jangled the keys through the iron bars. The officer waited a moment, then made even more noise. Still no movement. The officer had no alternative but to go in. He walked slowly and cautiously towards the bed, as he had been taught to do during his training course, and stopped a few inches—'

'Do you mind getting to the point?' Rizzo cut in, wearied by the director's obvious passion for detail.

'The prisoner was completely still,' the director continued undeterred, even accentuating the dramatic tone. 'He was wearing silk pyjamas. His legs were slightly bent, his hands crossed over his stomach, and his eyes were wide open, as if staring at a point on the ceiling. His face was ashen, just like a corpse. The officer touched him and found that he was cold. He ran out of the cell, locked the door, rushed to the nearest internal phone, and called the chief prison officer.'

'What's the officer's name?'

'Giuseppe Bongiorno.'

'Can we go?'

They stood up almost simultaneously.

After leaving the building where the offices were, they walked through a large iron door, crossed a courtyard and entered another building on the left. They walked along other corridors, went through more gates which were opened with different keys on either side, and finally reached Cell 10. The chief prison officer was waiting outside it, along with Officer Bongiorno and a doctor in a white coat holding a stethoscope in his latex-gloved hand.

Once the introductions had been made, Mazzorelli asked the doctor, 'So, what do you have to tell us?'

'There was nothing I could do. He's been dead for several hours.'

One at a time they entered the cell. It was just over two feet by three, with damp walls, a narrow bed, a small wash basin and a lavatory bowl. A small, poorly made, time-worn wooden table stood against a wall, with a few objects on it: a plastic envelope for cash, a few disposable paper cups, packets of crackers, sweets and chocolates and a partly emptied bottle of mineral water.

There was a neon light on the ceiling. No TV set, not even a radio: in that section, the regulations forbade them. On the wall facing then, near the top, was a small window which let in hardly any light. Through its dirt-encrusted panes, solid iron bars could be seen. The cell was a concrete cube, bare and anonymous. Like most prison cells, but worse, because this was a cell that housed one of the most dangerous prisoners. There were no posters, no photos of football teams or film actresses, no calendar of women in risqué poses taped to the wall.

Rizzo walked up to the bed to get a better look at the body. He noticed a small, dark, suspicious-looking stain close to the right corner of the mouth.

'How did he die?' he asked the doctor.

'There's no outward sign of violence. I'm guessing heart failure, but only a post mortem will be able to confirm that.'

'We're waiting for the Deputy Prosecutor,' the director said.

In the meantime, the air had become even damper and stickier.

They left the cell.

'We can wait in my office if you like,' Mazzorelli said. 'Would you like a coffee?'

'Excellent idea,' Rizzo replied.

24

Less than twenty minutes later, the deputy prosecutor on call arrived and swept into the office like a tornado. It was Erminia Cosenza, known as La Rossa because of her flaming red hair. She was dressed in a pinstriped jacket and skirt and had fine legs, but she was best known for her authoritarian tone and brusque manner. The director brought her up to date as they were on their way back to cell number 10.

'Who discovered the body?' Erminia Cosenza asked when they had reached their destination.

'Officer Giuseppe Bongiorno,' the director replied, indicating the young man in uniform with his right hand.

'That's right, I was the one who found him, just after the start of my shift.'

'When was the previous inspection done, and by whom?' the Deputy Prosecutor asked, once again addressing the director.

But it was the chief prison officer, a tall, fat man in his fifties with a neat moustache, who replied. 'I'll go and get the register.'

He walked off, and returned a few minutes later.

'Here we are. The previous inspections were done at five past midnight, just after the change of shift, and then again at three, but in neither case was anything unusual reported.'

'I see. Who carried them out?'

'Officer Filippo Giambra, who finished his shift at seven o'clock this morning.'

'In other words, Officer Bongiorno took over from Officer Giambra?'

'Exactly,' the chief prison officer replied, wondering all the while, *What the fuck is she getting at?*

'Good. Any external signs?'

'None,' the doctor replied, taking it that she was addressing him. 'Just a very small stain near the lips, perhaps blood. He seems to have died of heart failure.'

That 'seems' brought a grimace to the deputy prosecutor's face.

'Have you spoken to Officer Giambra?' she asked Mazzorelli, but again the chief prison officer answered.

'No, but I'll try to reach him at home.'

'Can't you call him on his mobile?'

'He doesn't have one.'

'Okay, get hold of him and tell him to come back here immediately.'

'Of course.'

The chief prison officer walked off again.

'Right. I'll arrange for a post mortem. I want it to be done today. Director, have the body taken to the Institute of Forensic Science.'

'Of course, Deputy Prosecutor. Can we move it now?'

'If all the proper checks have been done, yes.'

'The doctor made an external examination of the body.'

'Yes, so I've seen,' she said, as if holding back on her comments. 'Have photographs been taken?'

'No.'

'Any forensic examinations?'

'No,' Mazzorelli repeated, embarrassed.

'So I assume the cell hasn't even been searched.'

'No, it hasn't.'

'Right. Which means that before we move him, we have to send for Forensics. Superintendent Rizzo, I leave that to you. I want the examination to be as thorough as possible, and to take in the kitchens and any left-over food, all right?'

'I'll see to it at once,' he said, and walked to the phone at the end of the corridor.

As he did, the chief prison officer returned.

'Well?' Deputy Prosecutor Cosenza asked.

'No. Officer Giambra isn't home yet, but I asked his wife to get him to call me as soon as he arrives. It shouldn't be too long now.'

'All right, let me know right away.'

Erminia Cosenza ordered the director to let her have the officer's reports as soon as possible, and made ready to leave.

She was stopped by Rizzo, who looked badly shaken.

He had just been informed of the latest attack.

They both left almost at a run, leaving the prison officers bemused.

Nicola Spadaro did not read Captain Somenti's report on the suspected Taliban activity, with its alarming speculation on a possible new attack in the Tuscan capital, which he found on his desk that morning. Somenti had called him a few times from Florence, but the calls had been rather pointless, and the young man was getting on his nerves. Besides, he had other things on his mind.

The United States had launched their attack, signalling the start of the invasion of Afghanistan by the coalition troops, and all the secret services of the participating nations were on maximum alert.

There was now an added reason: three American citizens

had been kidnapped on September 28, and were being held hostage by the Taliban, accused of being CIA agents. It was possible they were being used as human shields, which had not dented President Bush's resolve but had led the CIA to ask the intelligence services of their allies for help.

According to the information that had come into his office, there was no doubt whatsoever that the men were indeed agents. A highly confidential report was circulating, detailing the idea that the CIA had bought the support of the Afghan warlords, to the tune of millions of dollars. The money, in hundred-dollar bills, was to have been brought into the country and distributed by CIA men.

The first group, composed of three agents, had probably arrived in Afghanistan on September 27, the leader of the group carrying three million dollars in a suitcase.

Nicola Spadaro's brain was working frantically.

25

Like many of his colleagues, Inspector Riccardo Venturi had refused to be overwhelmed by the inevitable feelings of grief and frustration which spread through the *Squadra Mobile* at the news of the latest attack and the tragic deaths of Acting Prosecutor Giulietti and her driver. Rather, he had reacted with a renewed, ferocious determination, and within a short time had finished examining the phone records of Gino La Torre's wife Lia, and the Matteo Parenti company of Mazara del Vallo, whose mobiles had been in contact in the Prato areas. He had looked at all the calls made from and received by these two phones, and had then examined separately the data on the registered holders of all the phones which had been in contact with them.

Lia La Torre's records had been straightforward enough, and within half an hour he had a fairly clear grasp of the situation. There were a relatively small number of calls, all of them to family members and relatives of the La Torres, at least judging from the names of the registered owners. During the period under consideration, Lia's mobile phone had been used outside Sicily on only two occasions. The first time had been from August 7 to 20, the second on October 1.

It was on this occasion that the call in the Prato area, which they already knew about, had been made.

The phone records of the Matteo Parenti company, on the other hand, showed that there had been many calls, and from the telephone areas involved it was clear that their mobile had been used many times outside Sicily, especially in the Viareggio and Prato areas.

The inspector then sorted through the numbers called from this mobile and established that, with few exceptions, from the day it had been activated, the one it had called most frequently – on an almost daily basis, in fact – was the land-line registered to a Cosimo Caruso, who lived in Mazara del Vallo. In addition, there had been several calls to phones registered to people with the same surname, presumably relations of Caruso.

At this point he got up from his desk, went and sat down at the computer and logged on to the Web Investigation System. This was a system which had only been up and running for a few months, replacing the previous one. It made it possible to consult the inter-force data bank and rapidly obtain information on criminal records, complaints lodged, police checks, hotel registrations, gun ownership, car ownership, business interests, competitive tenders, and so on.

First he clicked on the link to the Chambers of Commerce. Here, he discovered that the Matteo Parenti Company dealt in the 'processing, refrigeration and preservation of fish and related goods, the wholesale trading of fresh and frozen fish products, and the retail selling of their own products in the place of production', that the director had been the eponymous Matteo Parenti, born in Mazara del Vallo on February 20, 1955, but that he had now been replaced by his partner Cosimo Caruso, born in Mazara del Vallo on April 2, 1951, resident at the same address Venturi had seen on the phone log.

Through other links, he was able to establish that Matteo Parenti had no criminal record, had never been investigated by the police and had died on July 16 that year. Cosimo Caruso, on the other hand, had a number of previous convictions for financial offences: fraud and using bad cheques. Nothing especially serious, though. He had no weapons registered in his name, and on two occasions had been stopped at police road blocks in Palermo. The first time he was alone in the car, while the second time he had had a passenger with him, one Leonardo Parisi, a resident of Palermo, thirty-seven years old, with a criminal record for illegal possession of a weapon, fraud and gambling.

At last Venturi took his eyes off the screen, printed the results, and drafted a report.

Not only did they know for certain that a mobile registered to Lia La Torre (but in the possession of her husband Gino) and a mobile registered to the Matteo Parenti company had both been used in the hours immediately preceding the bombing in the Piazza del Cestello, they now also knew who had been using the second of these mobiles. A company phone it might be, but it now seemed a virtual certainty that the user had been the one remaining partner, Cosimo Caruso, as witness the frequent calls to his home phone and the calls to phones registered to people having the same surname.

When he went to see Rizzo with the report, the superintendent was not in his office. He left it with Fanti, asking him to put it where it would be seen, and went back to his research.

26

Around the same time, Inspector Sergi and his men were combing the estate agencies of Forte dei Marmi, which had been closed the previous day. It was almost lunchtime, and so far they had obtained the same answer over and over, like a litany: 'We don't have any Sicilian clients, and we've never seen these people.'

The next agency on his list was in a main street in the centre of town which ran down to the promenade near the landing stage. When he entered, a woman of about fifty with long brown hair was busy showing photos on her computer screen to a comfortable-looking middle-aged couple.

'One moment,' she said.

To kill time, he looked at the notices on the wall advertising houses and apartments for sale or rent. In some cases, prices were quoted, and they seemed exorbitant to him, even for an exclusive resort area like this one. In other cases, the word 'negotiable' was used, an indication that the prices were probably even more astronomical.

At last the two customers left and the woman rose from her chair. 'Can I help you?' she asked.

Without further ado, Sergi identified himself. 'We're trying to locate a particular place. We think it was close to an apartment being used during August by two Sicilian couples.'

He was lying in order not to reveal that he was specifically interested in the Sicilians.

'Our clientele is entirely from Northern Italy or abroad,' the woman said. 'A few Tuscans, too, but really very few.'

'It's possible, signora, that the couples only rented the apartment for two weeks. In August this year.'

'I'm sorry, I really don't think I can be of help to you,' the woman replied, gently but firmly.

'Thank you anyway.'

As he was about to leave she called him back.

'Yes?' he replied, promptly retracing his steps, although without holding out too much hope. He was used to disappointments.

'Now that I come to think of it, I do remember some Sicilians. But they didn't rent an apartment, they rented a villa through an old customer of ours. He told me he needed to put up some Sicilian friends of his for the whole of August. I remember that, because less than two weeks later he gave us back the keys, saying that his friends had had to go back to Sicily because of family problems, but didn't ask for any kind of refund.'

Is this it? Sergi wondered, with a glimmer of hope. 'Who is this old customer of yours?' he asked.

'He's from Milan, but he comes here every summer with his family.'

'Can you tell me his name?'

He had taken his notepad from his pocket, ready to take notes, but he sensed from the woman's expression that she might be having second thoughts, afraid she had said too much.

'Don't worry, signora. Our investigation has nothing to do

with who took the villa. As I said at the beginning, we're interested in a place which is near where these Sicilians were staying. I can't tell you more than that but there's nothing to worry about.'

'I understand, Inspector, but this agency has always distinguished itself for the fairness and discretion of its dealings with its customers. It's the oldest estate agency in Forte, you know. My parents ran it before me, and my father's father before them.'

'I repeat, there's nothing to worry about, signora, I'll make sure this person doesn't know. In the unlikely event that he were to ask me how I found out that he had rented the villa, I'd say it was from a confidential source which I wasn't at liberty to reveal.'

Reassured, the woman opened a book with a shiny black cover and leafed through it until she came to one of the last pages. 'His name is Antonio Vita and he lives at 46 Via Boccaccio, Milan. He's a fish merchant, quite big, I believe.'

BINGO! Sergi said to himself, euphorically.

Remaining as impassive as he could, he asked, 'Did you ever see these Sicilian friends of his?'

'No. It was Signor Vita who came here and signed the contract. And it was Signor Vita who gave us back the keys – before time, as I said.'

'Had Signor Vita ever rented any other houses on behalf of friends before?'

'No. This was the first time. Signor Vita has a very beautiful villa here in Forte – he bought it through us about ten years ago, when the prices were still relatively affordable.'

'And where is this villa he rented?'

'It's a two-storey villa not far from his own.'

Sergi would have liked to ask who the owner was, but he held back: he had probably already gone as far as he could.

The next day he would go to the Land Registry Office and find out the location of Antonio Vita's villa. In the meantime he would phone Rizzo from the hotel and bring him up to date.

27

The following day Fanti brought Rizzo Venturi's report, which did nothing to raise the Superintendent's morale, still shaken by the death of Anna Giulietti.

He also brought him an envelope containing the preliminary findings of the post mortem on the body of Salvatore Laprua, written by Dr Francesco Leone:

On October 8, 2001, I was requested by Deputy Prosecutor Erminia Cosenza to carry out a post mortem examination on the cadaver of Salvatore Laprua and to report my findings.

External examination of the body: the body is dressed in the following clothes: striped silk pyjamas, woollen vest, white cotton boxer shorts. He is male, 77 years old, 5 ft 9 in. tall, slight frame, with white hair, reasonably well nourished, muscular mass consistent with his constitution and sex. The following phenomena are noted: coldness and rigidity (possibly even too much!) in all areas, red (?) hypostases present in lower parts of the body. No signs of putrefaction. No abrasions or bruising on the face. Near the lips, which appear unusually dark, almost black, there is a small trickle of dried black blood . . .

Dissection of the cadaver: head/organs of the neck/ thorax/abdomen. In the course of the dissection, samples were taken from the organs and fixed in formalin, as were samples of viscera and bodily fluids for later toxicological testing.

Time of death: from an examination of the documents (in particular, the report of the doctor from the infirmary in Sollicciano) it would appear death took place approximately between the hours of 3 and 4 a.m. on October 8, 2001. This was confirmed by the abiotic phenomena subsequently observed, in particular the cooling of the cadaver, the rigidity and the hypostases . . .

Rizzo was well aware that after the life processes which produce heat cease, a corpse gradually loses temperature, which is dispersed over the surface of the body until it reaches the level of the external environment within eighteen to twenty-four hours. He also knew that an important factor in determining the hour of death was the nature of the hypostases, because their appearance changes with the passing of time.

He was struck, though, by the question mark after the mention of the red coloration and by the words 'possibly even too much' referring to the rigidity of the body. Both these things, together with the black lips, were strong indications that death had not been due to natural causes.

The pathologists' conclusion, however, was not very specific about this:

It is possible therefore to respond in the following terms to the queries raised by yourself:
- *death probably occurred at about 3–4 a.m. on October 8;*
- *death was due to cardiac arrest in the subject, who did not present any particular signs of myocardial interest;*

- *the unusual coloration of the hypostases, the blood and the urine do, however, suggest poisoning, which may have been a possible contributing cause, at least in our present state of knowledge;*
- *for the sake of completeness, and to supply more reliable answers, samples of parts of the organs and viscera were taken, therefore, for subsequent toxicological and histo-chemical tests designed to locate the possible presence of toxic substances. The results will be reported directly by the appropriate department.*

He felt a rush of anger.

If Laprua, too, had been murdered, then this case, with its unprecedented body count, was becoming a burden too heavy for his shoulders alone.

He really wished Ferrara was back.

28

It was almost midday on Wednesday October 10 when Inspector Sergi and Officer Pino Ricci parked their car in the open space outside the offices of the dispatch company. The gardener of the villa rented by Antonio Vita had indicated that this company was the one that had delivered to Sicily the two bicycles left by the tenants under a canopy in the garden.

'We're looking for the owner,' Inspector Sergi said to a young woman who was busy working behind a desk. 'We'd like to speak to him.'

'Who shall I say?'

'Police.'

The girl looked at him doubtfully. Sergi looked more like a film actor than a police officer.

'Look, here's my badge. I'm Inspector Antonio Sergi of the Florence *Squadra Mobile*.'

'One moment, I'll call him,' the girl said, rising from her chair in alarm.

She soon returned, followed by a short, fat, red-faced man of about sixty.

'I'm the owner, Anselmo Rossitto.'

Sergi told him that he was here about the bicycles his firm had been asked to dispatch to Sicily.

'How did you know about that?'

'The owner of the villa, Signor Luzi, told us.'

'I see.'

'All we'd like to know, Signor Rossitto, is where they were sent and who to.'

'Actually, I remember that job quite well, because after a few days the company who were delivering the bicycles for us phoned us to say there was nobody there and asked us if we had another forwarding address, even a phone number.'

'What happened then?'

'I told them the only address we had was the one we'd supplied. They never called again, so I assumed it had all been sorted out.'

'May I see the dispatch document?' As the man seemed hesitant, he added, 'We're not from Customs and Excise, Signor Rossitto. I'm not trying to find out if your documents are in order.'

The man put on an old pair of glasses with thick lenses, went to a metal filing cabinet, bent slightly, and started opening the drawers. Eventually, he pulled out a file.

Sergi read that the items had been dispatched on September 4, 2001 to Signor Salvatore Miano, 136 Via Giuseppe Garibaldi, Castelvetrano, and delivered on the seventeenth.

As soon as he left he phoned Rizzo, who complimented him on his excellent work.

As Rizzo put the phone down, Superintendent Ascalchi entered his office, holding a sheet of paper.

'What is it, Gianni?'

'The answer we've been waiting for.'

'Which one?'

'The one from American Express.'

'What do they say?'

'This is a list of payments on Salvatore Miano's credit card, and one of them is for two airline tickets on August seventh at Palermo airport. And guess what? I checked, and the tickets were issued in the names of Salvatore Miano, of course, and a certain Luigi Torri. You won't believe this, but it only took a phone call to find that out! Just like in that film—' He broke off immediately: everyone was always pulling his leg about his passion for the cinema.

'You certainly beat our Sicilian colleagues to it,' Rizzo said, and he meant it as a compliment. Not that he was trying to score points – he knew how busy they were in Palermo. And now they were going to be even busier! 'I need a detailed report from you as soon as possible, so that our colleagues can request an arrest warrant. There's no doubt now that Miano is aiding and abetting La Torre!'

When Ascalchi had gone out, Rizzo got Venturi on the phone.

'Keep tracking Miano's movements – the Prosecutor's Department in Sicily are going to want to know about them soon!'

He could not hide his satisfaction, although it was only a drop in the ocean, given the gloom that was now widespread throughout Police Headquarters.

But even with that gloom, the silence with which Venturi greeted his words seemed excessive.

'Well?'

'We've lost him.'

'What do you mean?'

Briefly, the inspector explained that, since they had started tapping Miano's mobile and his registered landlines on

October 6, as authorised by Acting Prosecutor Giulietti, they had heard practically nothing except on that first day. That Saturday, there had been a large number of calls from his mobile to his own home, then nothing more, apart from a single call on the morning of the eighth, from the Florence area, probably dialled in error because the contact had immediately been broken off at the other end and the call had not been repeated.

'Do you have the records?'

'Right here in front of me. I also have a summary of the conversation intercepted by our colleagues in September, after the Anti-Mafia Squad had alerted them.'

'Bring me everything.'

Venturi did better than that. Together with the records and the summary, he handed him the sheet of paper on which he had noted down the most interesting recent phone calls and their contents, as well as some of the unsuccessful calls:

On Saturday 23 September at 10:51 a.m. the mobile is operating in the Rome area, then at 1:40 p.m. his wife calls him and, after discussing personal matters, asks him if everything is all right. He says, 'Everything's fine', but he sounds irritated and cuts her off. At 9 p.m. his wife calls him again and he tells her he's just arrived and he'll call her later. She wants to know when he'll be coming home, and asks him, 'When are you going to eat cannoli here?' He replies evasively and tells her not to insist. He sounds a bit nervous. At 10:35 p.m. he phones his wife, and on this occasion the mobile is in the Florence area. He tells her he might be going to Prato and maybe he can go and say hello from 'you know who' to Vincenzo and Anna. In the following days there is no contact with the family, unless he used another mobile, but only short calls to other numbers which

*are still being checked out. On Saturday October 6, from
8.12 a.m. to 1 p.m. his wife calls him more than forty times,
but there is never any reply. Then at 1:10 a man answers
and tells her she has a wrong number, but the records show
that she in fact dialled correctly. At 4:10 p.m. his wife calls
again and this time talks to him and he says he's still busy
and doesn't know yet when he'll be back. On this occasion,
the mobile is in the Prato area. Then at 7:06 p.m. his wife
calls him again and asks 'Where are you, I mean, are you
all right?' and then immediately switches the conversation
to family matters. In the background men's voices can be
heard not far from the husband, talking in Sicilian dialect.*

*On Monday October 8, one last unanswered call. Since
then (it is now 11 p.m.), he has not used his mobile and his
wife has not tried to call him.*

'My God!' Rizzo exploded. 'We have to do something to
locate him, whatever happens!'

'But how, chief?' the inspector replied. 'We don't even
know what car he's using, let alone where he is right now. And
if he doesn't use his mobile, what can we do?'

Rizzo passed his hand through his hair, lit a cigarette, and
picked up the piece of paper again.

'I think all we can do for the moment is wait and hope he
uses his phone again. One thing you can do, though: ask our
Sicilian colleagues if Miano or his wife have any relatives,
even distant ones, named Vincenzo and Anna, living in
Tuscany.'

'All right, chief.'

But nothing was all right. Nothing at all.

29

'So, you've ended up a traitor?' Antonio Caputo, the boss of bosses, said finally, but without the contempt with which Mafiosi usually utter that hated word. Because this time it was different – the betrayal was an internal one. And it was playing into his hands, opening his eyes to a situation he had been guilty of underestimating.

When he had seen him that evening, Wednesday October 10, being brought across the fields by the look-outs who had intercepted him as he was approaching on foot – dark, squat, his smooth black hair longer than ever, his beard unkempt, his clothes without any trace of their original fine tailoring – he had barely recognised him. Then he had had him brought in, and Gino La Torre had told him everything.

About the attack on Ferrara, in which he had taken part, and about the attack on the acting prosecutor, from which he had dissociated himself when he had started to realise what the Lion was really up to.

'But who the fuck is he?' Caputo had asked.

'The Lion? Laprua's accomplice, the one who brought the drugs in from abroad and had the contacts with the Americans.'

If he was so important, how come he'd never heard of him? Caputo didn't like that at all.

'What kind of man is he?'

'I've never seen him. What I know I heard from Turi.' Meaning Laprua.

'Laprua never was good at choosing his friends. So, tell me all about it.'

'The orders came through Catalfano, who was one of Turi's men, like me. Like everyone in Castelvetrano. Turi was making us all rich. That's why when it came to killing the sons of bitches who screwed with him, I agreed.'

The confirmation that Catalfano was just Laprua's front-man, and that Laprua had continued to control the Castelvetrano district from the mainland, right under his nose, made the blood rush to Don Nino Caputo's head.

'He was making you all rich, eh? And what were you planning to do next? Kill me?'

'No, Don Nino, how can you say that?'

'I say it as I see it. And I'm starting to see clearly. Right now I don't give a fuck about the past! Laprua is dead, and now I have to think about the living. And I want to get that fucking Lion, I want to know what the fuck he wants and how far he's planning to go.'

'What he wants is to control the district in Zì Turi's place. I realised that when I saw he wasn't helping Turi. He let him rot in prison. He told us he was helping him, but he didn't give a damn. Quite the opposite. He might even have been the one who killed Turi. I know exactly what the Lion is up to. When Turi was arrested, he saw it as an opportunity to control everything directly. He holds the key to the drugs trade and Catalfano is under his thumb – he's only there because it suits him. Since Turi was arrested, Catalfano's stopped listening to me, and I used to be the one who gave orders – I mean Turi did, but I carried the orders. Catalfano used to lick my arse, but now I don't count! Now he only takes his orders from the Lion. When I realised that, I decided to put myself in your hands, Don Nino, because it just isn't right, you knew that all along, you knew it wouldn't work. Let me join you and you won't regret it.'

'You did the right thing,' the boss replied, and he lapsed into a pensive silence which La Torre respected. At last, he asked, 'What about the foot soldiers who were with you?'

'They're good boys, even the grandson. They don't really care if it's Zì Turi or us, as long as they know who's in charge. They swore loyalty to the head of the district, because he feeds them. That's why they follow his orders. But they're good boys.'

'No!' Caputo thundered. 'A good boy needs to know who's in charge! You have to bring them here. They need to realise what they've done.'

He was starting to grasp the enormity of the threat to his supremacy. The Lion's game was more subtle than even Gino thought: by exposing the workings of an important district outside Sicily – as long as it was only that one and he hadn't made inroads into others – and launching a frontal attack on the State as he had done, the man was already showing the world a new Mafia, one quite different from his.

'And find me the Lion,' he concluded. 'Now go and get some sleep, while I think.'

And think he did, long and hard.

It was late at night when he took the exercise book from a drawer in the sideboard and tore a strip off one of the pages.

The next day one of his men would set in motion the long process of getting a message to the Basilisk.

PART TWO

THE INVESTIGATION

Leonardo da Vinci included a basilisk in his bestiary,
citing its wicked habit of hiding up above
and staring at its victims
until they wither and die

1

In the end, even Commissioner Lepri had had to face facts. It wasn't just that the Carabinieri's Centre for Forensic Analysis in Parma had identified similar components in the explosive used in the attack on Acting Prosecutor Anna Giulietti to those used in the bombing in the Piazza del Cestello. It was also and more forcefully that, if the Piazza del Cestello was not a very credible target for Islamic terrorists, the acting prosecutor was even less credible. In fact, the idea was plainly absurd.

There was also the fact that Rizzo's investigation was increasingly leaning in one direction. Lepri hated having to admit the possibility – he refused to consider it anything more than that – that the Mafia were active on his territory. But he was unnerved by what had happened and had no desire to make a fool of himself again, as he had done when he had come down in favour of the terrorism hypothesis – along with most of the country, he told himself by way of consolation – so he had decided to adopt a neutral line which came dangerously close to indifference.

There were other possibilities, of course: home-grown terrorists, local gangsters, personal vendettas. But it was better to leave it all in the hands of the *Squadra Mobile*, let them sort out the mess, he already had enough on his plate dealing with the usual political and bureaucratic problems.

Of course, he would continue to support Rizzo. He quite liked the man – more than that hothead Ferrara, anyway – besides which, he couldn't be seen not to support him. But he would try and keep as much of a distance as possible until things became a little clearer.

When the Islamic bubble burst and even Rome had to admit the truth, Nicola Spadaro had the satisfaction of cutting short Captain Somenti's mission. Somenti, though, decided to take advantage of a few days' holiday he had owing to him and stay on in Florence. He may have suffered a professional disappointment, but one evening, quite by chance, he had run into Giulia again, as he was walking along the Via Tornabuoni. They had both been speechless at first, then had walked towards each other gingerly and had said a strained hello. But they had exchanged phone numbers.

He was beginning to feel that he was slowly regaining ground. He had had the impression that, deep down, she hadn't been sorry that they had met by chance like that: something in her eyes and in her slightly forced coldness had rekindled in him a hope he had thought was dead. Since then, they had seen each other twice more, and she had gradually thawed. She had gone so far as to tell him she was not seeing anyone at the moment.

Meanwhile, Sergeant Giorgio Azzaro returned to Rome, pleased with his trip. He had had nothing to do except for 'distracting' the head of the Florence bureau for a few minutes every day, which had left him plenty of time to get in some sightseeing at the State's expense.

The one person who was not pleased at all and refused to face facts was Ahmed Farah, who had continued to publish his diatribes – indeed, they had become even more virulent, if that was possible. He wasn't stupid, of course: he, too, had realised that Islamic extremists probably had nothing to with the bombing on October 1 – though there always had to be a margin of doubt where the Arabs were concerned. But that was a relatively minor detail. The threat to the West was still real enough, as was the presence of sleeper cells. And then there were those two recently arrived emissaries, Adjmal Yousazai and Mullah Hamdullah, around whom he was carefully tightening the net.

He knew now that the two men were continuing to make inroads into the Muslim community, especially among the young, some of whom seemed particularly attracted by their words – by their money, too, some said. From one of these young people, a relative of an acquaintance of his, he was hoping to eventually obtain their mobile phone numbers without arousing suspicion. But it was going to take time.

The most violent reaction to Anna Giulietti's death had been that of Michele Ferrara, who had torn off his neck brace and, without even informing Petra, and ignoring the consultant's protests, left the hospital early on the afternoon of Wednesday 10, wearing a pair of jeans and a black leather jacket he had wangled from one of his bodyguards. It wasn't just anger, it was a kind of anguish he had never imagined he would feel, a sudden sense of emptiness which, he realised, went beyond the loss of professional colleague or even a friend. The relationship that had been established between them had given rise to a feeling he found impossible to define.

He got in the first police car he found in the hospital car park, and did not even give the driver time to ask him if he wanted to be taken home.

'Headquarters, and make it quick!' he yelled, leaving the driver speechless.

2

'Fanti!'

The cry echoed along the corridor, and the secretary jumped in his chair as if his chief's voice had reached him from beyond the grave. And indeed, the man who threw open the door a few moments later seemed more like Ferrara's ghost than the real person: pale, thin, wild-eyed, dressed like a hooligan – or like a Narcotics officer, which came to the same thing – he seemed to be driven in a way Fanti had never seen him before, even at moments of high drama.

'Chief Superintendent, hello, welcome ba—' he stammered in confusion, leaping to his feet and knocking over a plastic coffee cup precariously perched on a heap of files.

'Get me Rizzo right away!'

'He's busy, chief. There's someone with him.'

'Who?'

'Laprua's lawyer, Signor—'

'Liuzza! Perfect! Just the man I want to see! I'll be right back, get me everything we have on the bombings. Even what we don't have, if possible.'

And just as quickly as he had materialised, he vanished.

Fanti tried to mop up the coffee stains spreading over the

cover of the visitors' book. He was sorry he hadn't had a chance to welcome his chief with the expression of joy he had been anticipating for days. He hadn't noticed that Ferrara hadn't even said hello when he came in: as far as he was concerned, although other chiefs might not always be right, Ferrara always was.

'Take it easy, don't let me interrupt you.'

There was too much smoke in his deputy's office, as usual. He had entered without knocking.

'Chief!' Rizzo cried, astonished to see him back so soon, dressed the way he was.

And so obviously in a foul mood.

The man sitting in front of him extinguished his cigarette in the overflowing ashtray and turned. He was short and plump, immaculately dressed, and with a rather affected manner.

'What an unexpected pleasure, Chief Superintendent! I thought you were still convalescing. How are you?'

'As well as I can be after losing first a loyal and innocent officer and then a colleague, a friend, a . . .'

Lover? Liuzza thought, such was the bitterness and contrition in the chief superintendent's voice. Not that it interested him in the slightest.

'I've only lost a client, and that's bad enough. I can't even begin to imagine what you're going through, but I do understand.'

'Is that why you're here? Because of what happened to Laprua?'

'I sent for Signor Liuzza to help us with our inquiries,' Rizzo said. 'He was only too willing to give us his assistance.'

'It's in my own interests for the truth to be brought to light, as you can imagine. I'm representing Signor Laprua's wife and children now, and naturally they want to know if there has been any misconduct or negligence on the part of the prison staff. I'm here to cooperate, of course, but it is my duty to inform you that, just as you expect something from me, I expect something from you, and that if this could also be used against—'

'Drop it, Liuzza!' Ferrara snapped. 'We know what our duty is and we've never held back from it, you should know that.'

Silverio Liuzza looked at him closely. 'I see how you're feeling. You've come out of hospital an angry man. Well, that's understandable. I suppose I would be, too. But be careful you don't lose your head. We all need you to have your wits about you.'

'Sit down, chief,' Rizzo said.

They were all three still in the same positions, the two men seated, Ferrara standing in the doorway.

He sat down next to the lawyer, showing that he had not taken his remarks amiss. Liuzza had not in fact been sarcastic, but sympathetic and understanding, as if he were sincerely suggesting that they put their heads together in a calm, rational way.

Rizzo looked on as the two men measured each other up, wondering if and when they would tackle the real subject he was anxious to talk to the lawyer about: the reason for that phone call at 7:46 on Monday October 1.

Instead, Ferrara said, 'It's all right, go on with your interview.'

'I was asking Signor Liuzza when he last saw his client.'

'The day of the bombing, about ten in the morning or just after. I went to see him to report back on something he'd asked me to do.'

'And what was that?' Rizzo asked.

Liuzza threw a glance at Ferrara, who did not reciprocate.

'I'm afraid I'm going to have to invoke lawyer–client confidentiality, at least for the moment.'

'Your client is dead, Signor Liuzza,' Rizzo insisted.

'Since the circumstances of his death are far from clear at the moment, I'm under no obligation to reveal to you any facts concerning him.'

'But you were about to reveal them to me?' Ferrara cut in.

Rizzo pricked up his ears.

Liuzza took the question as a signal to be more open. 'In a way. What I was supposed to report back to him about was our phone conversation. But of course that conversation never happened because of the bomb.'

'And what was it you were supposed to tell me over the phone?'

'That Salvatore Laprua wanted to see you, Chief Superintendent. He'd thought a lot about it, and had decided to cooperate with the police.'

Ferrara laughed at that, but it was a laugh that was more nervous than spontaneous. 'Come now, Signor Liuzza, you know as well as I do that bosses at that level never turn State's evidence. They can't, it's just not in their nature.'

'That's why I had to sweat blood trying to convince him that partially cooperating, although a major step, didn't make him a traitor, which of course he would have hated to be. It was obvious there was something that was eating away at him, and he could have been useful to you. It was only a matter of cutting a deal: he would have given you whatever information he felt comfortable giving you, without compromising his status as a man of honour, and in return you would have made his stay in prison less unpleasant and guaranteed the safety of his wife and sons, which was something that particularly concerned him at the time.'

'And what was this information?'

The lawyer looked from one to the other and shook his head. 'It must have been something extremely sensitive, because he wouldn't even tell me. And I'm not hiding behind lawyer–client confidentiality this time. It's the truth, I'm afraid. He would only talk to Ferrara, he said. Ferrara would know what to do with it, he'd decide whether to inform the prosecutor and give him the protection he wanted.'

'Then Ferrara gets blown up, and Acting Prosecutor Giulietti ditto. And he himself dies. I hope for your sake that really is the truth and you don't know anything else. I'm sure you're aware of the consequences if you were hiding anything.'

'I'm not hiding a thing. My conscience is clear, as a man even more than as a lawyer.'

'Let's go back to that last conversation,' Ferrara went on. 'You can talk about it now.'

Rizzo could see that his chief was taking over the interview, and he felt relieved. The shattered equilibrium of the *Squadra Mobile* of Florence was being restored.

'To be honest, there isn't much to say. I'd hoped to be able to present him with the result of our phone conversation, but you know as well as I do that it never happened. I told him about the bomb, and that you'd ended up in hospital, but I didn't know if you were dead or alive.'

'How did he react?'

'He became very withdrawn. He seemed weary. I think he knew something, Chief Superintendent. He was angry with someone – several people. He said they were fools. When I tried to find out what he meant, he changed the subject.'

'Is that the exact word he used?'

Rizzo, too, had found that strange, for some reason.

'He whispered it to himself, but I heard it distinctly. "Fools," he said.'

'I see. And was that all he said?'

'No. He said he didn't want me any more. According to him, there was nothing more to be done, there wasn't even any point in talking to the acting prosecutor as I had suggested. "It's over," he said, "This conversation is over, everything's over," I remember it very well.'

'Judging by what happened, I'd say he was right,' Ferrara concluded, angrily.

3

'Your wife has been looking for you,' Fanti announced, bringing them coffee in the small china cups used for special occasions. They drank it as Rizzo brought Ferrara up to date. It was excellent coffee, better than Ferrara could ever remember it being before: Fanti was becoming a real expert in combining different blends.

They had moved to Ferrara's office after Liuzza had gone, because Ferrara could not bear the smell of stale cigarettes. In his desk was a supply of Antico Toscano cigars: he hadn't had a cigar for ten days, and was really missing them. He lit one as he dialled his home number, but didn't enjoy it: he found it too strong, too acrid and bitter, as if he had never smoked one before. After only two puffs, he left it on the ashtray to burn itself out. He wished he could have done the same with the contents of the phone call, but his wife's anger at his premature return to work didn't seem like a mere passing storm.

Rizzo had been following the call. 'She's right,' he said, after Ferrara had put the phone down. 'But how come you didn't call her on your mobile?'

'I don't have one, it got broken in the attack . . . Fanti!' he called.

'Yes, chief.'

'Get me another mobile.'

'Straightaway, chief.'

'And don't you start, Francesco. I can't say this to her, but you know perfectly well how serious the situation is. Someone had no qualms about killing Anna and trying to kill me. They'll try again, and people like that don't make the same mistake twice.'

'Do you have anyone in mind?'

'The one thing that seems clear right now, from what you've told me, is that everything points to the district of Castelvetrano.'

'We'll ask our colleagues in Sicily to keep an eye on Catalfano in particular.'

'The man they suspect is the boss?' Ferrara sighed. 'There's no point. They've had him under surveillance for a while, but he's as cunning as a fox and very well connected. As soon as we go anywhere near him they'll accuse us of playing politics. Us! No, let's carry on doing what you've already laid out, you've done a great job. If we want to get to him, it'll have to be another way.'

'What I don't understand is how they found out you were going through the Piazza del Cestello.'

'I've been thinking about that, too, and I can't figure it out. The only person who knew was Franchi. He was the one who decided on the routes. Unless he confided in a colleague. I refuse to believe that one of our men could be playing a double game, but we'll have to keep our eyes open.'

'I'm already doing that.'

'But that's not the only thing that doesn't add up in this mess. If the Mafia's behind it, which seems to be the case, why has it gone back to using bombs? We all know Caputo was against them. Maybe he's changed his mind and it isn't only people from Castelvetrano or linked to Laprua who are running the show. Or is there a split within the Sicilian Cosa Nostra? Why target Anna and me, and why do it that way? Just to avenge Laprua?'

'Anna Giulietti actually thought he was the real brains, chief.'

'So did I, but that doesn't stand up after what Liuzza told us. Plus, we don't know why Zì Turi was killed, do we?'

'No.'

'A possible explanation could be that someone was afraid that the old man would reveal awkward secrets to us.'

'What Liuzza called "sensitive" information?'

'Precisely.'

'Which is why if we found out what that was, we'd already know who that someone was. If only it was that simple!'

'Someone – or several people . . .'

'"The fools"?' Rizzo asked.

'Ah – you noticed that, too?'

'What?'

'That it's jarring, like a tenor singing a wrong note.'

'Yes, I also thought it doesn't sound right, I don't know why. We aren't talking about schoolboys, though, are we?'

'It's because we're still Sicilians, that's why. And so was Zì Turi. I remember meeting him, I remember the way he spoke. No, a word like that just isn't him, a man like that would have said "dickheads", "sons of bitches", but "fools" – no, I don't think so.'

'So what did he mean?'

'I don't know, and we may never find out. Another secret he's carried with him to the grave.'

By the time Fanti came back with the new mobile, a huge box of pastries and bottles of sparkling wine, accompanied by all the men he could round up to celebrate the chief's return in style, Ferrara was gone.

He had left with Rizzo, leaving a note saying *We're with Alibrandi.* The files he had put on the desk were also missing, a sure sign that he wouldn't be back: he had obviously taken them with him so that he could look over them at home.

4

Major Alibrandi was pleased to see Ferrara up and about, and was proud to share with him the results of their examination of the CCTV footage from the Military Command and the barracks of the Customs and Excise Squad on the Lungarno Soderini. He had been just about to show it to an ex-colleague who had been transferred to Rome to work for the Ministry of Defence.

'This is a real honour,' Captain Somenti said, looking at Ferrara with open admiration. 'I've heard so much about you, but unfortunately never had a chance to meet you when I was in charge of the investigations team in Prato. We were very upset to hear about the attack.'

He did not specify who exactly he meant by 'we', but neither Ferrara nor Rizzo – who was trying to remember where he had seen him – felt the need to inquire. They had a pretty good idea, anyway.

'As I was telling my colleague,' Alibrandi resumed, 'there was a lot of pedestrian activity, as there is every morning. We managed to enlarge the image seven times, no more, and now we're trying to identify the people, but I don't think we'll get much. Three are foreigners, Arabs I'd say, and one is the man who got blown up with the car. The most interesting thing, though, is the night-time footage, even though it's of poor quality. Come, I'll show you.'

They moved to a large room filled with sophisticated equipment, where a number of young Carabinieri were hard at work.

'Pietro, this is Chief Superintendent Michele Ferrara, though you wouldn't guess it from his clothes,' Alibrandi said jokily, introducing them to a corporal sitting in front of a console and a large flat screen, 'and this is Superintendent Francesco Rizzo, deputy head of the *Squadra Mobile*. I think you already know Captain Somenti?'

The corporal broke into a big smile and leapt to his feet. 'Hello, Captain, good to have you back! Pleased to meet you, Chief Superintendent . . . Superintendent . . .'

'I'm only passing through, Pietro,' Somenti said to his ex-colleague, 'but I'm really glad to see you again.'

'Show them the footage of the cars from 2:46 onwards, starting with the camera from the Customs and Excise building,' instructed Alibrandi.

The corporal sat down again and tapped at the keyboard until a slightly blurred image appeared on the screen: the section of the Lungarno Soderini going from the front door of the barracks to the Piazza del Cestello and beyond.

The digital clock in the top right-hand corner of the screen was showing 02:26:28 when a white Fiat Uno appeared. As it neared the piazza car park, its left indicator came on, and it entered. The corporal then pressed a key on the computer and a shot of the opposite side of the square appeared on the screen, equally deserted, at 02:46. For a few minutes nothing happened, then at 02:58:16 the shape of a dark Mercedes S500 began to materialise. It was leaving the square and turning on to the Lungarno Soderini.

'That confirms what we thought,' Rizzo said.

'Precisely. The Fiat enters the square but doesn't leave, and the Mercedes doesn't enter – we had confirmation from the cameras on the police station in the Piazza del Tiratoio, which is the only other way into the square – but does leave. Between the two sequences, there's time to make the switch. Now we know for certain that the bomb was planted in the Piazza del Cestello a few minutes before three in the morning. There were two men in the Fiat Uno, that much we've been able to determine from enlarging the image.'

'And were you able to see the licence plate on the Mercedes?' Ferrara asked.

'No, Chief Superintendent, that would be too much to hope. It was too dark, the camera was too far away, and the tape had been used too often before. But at least we know the make and the model, and we know it's definitely a dark colour. We also know it has two quite visible scratches on the left side, long, irregular ones, as if someone had drawn a key along it out of spite.'

'I didn't notice that,' Somenti said.

'I'm not surprised, they're almost impossible to see at first. But look.' Alibrandi, who sounded quite pleased with himself, made a sign to the corporal, who gradually enlarged part of the image until the scratches were clearly visible, even though with each enlargement the already poor image suffered a progressive loss of definition.

Rizzo did not seem to share the major's pleasure. 'We already know they carried the device in a car. Where does this get us?'

'We cross-reference the data. We already have a number of suspects, don't we? Maybe one of them has a dark Mercedes S500.'

'But if they don't, we have to check their relatives, their friends, their workplaces. It'll take forever!'

'I know, but there's no harm in trying. I'm afraid that's all I have.'

'Thank you, Major,' Ferrara cut in. 'You've done well.'

'But the fact of it is, the death of the acting prosecutor seems to confirm that you were the target of the bombing in the Piazza del Cestello, Chief Superintendent.'

'Yes, it does. First me, then Anna Giulietti – and she's actually the reason we came. Any developments on that front?'

Alibrandi did not reply immediately, and Ferrara thought he detected a touch of embarrassment in the man.

'Apart from the fact that we're really shaken by what happened, I can tell you two things. The first is that Signora Giulietti expected something like this. She was quite nervous. She suspected that Laprua was out for revenge, and she thought it very likely that she was next on the list.'

'Did she tell you that?'

'No. She wrote it. She kept a personal diary, and her mother was kind enough to let us have it.'

'Can I see it?'

'It's with Forensics at the moment,' Alibrandi said, and it was clear that he was increasingly ill at ease. He was trying to gain time, but knew he couldn't keep his colleague in suspense for much longer.

'And what exactly did she write? Can you remember?'

'There's one entry in particular, from Wednesday October third. She writes that soon after leaving her mother's house for Florence that morning, just before she got to the Via Cassia she had the impression she heard something like a shot, which scared her. Then, seeing that the driver hadn't batted an eyelid and that nothing had actually happened, she let it go. But she'd clearly been rattled, because that evening she wrote about it in her diary, and admitted that she had been tempted to speak to Superintendent Rizzo, but that if you'd been there, Chief Superintendent, she'd certainly have told you.'

'She didn't say anything to me,' Rizzo said.

Ferrara felt a futile regret.

'But she did feel threatened, that much is certain,' the major said.

'She was the one who asked for security around you at the hospital to be tightened, chief.'

'Around me, but not around her!' Ferrara burst out, and his anger startled everyone.

Rizzo, too, was feeling guilty.

'I mentioned that there were two things I had to tell you,' the major continued, glad to change the subject. 'About a hundred yards from the depression where the explosive was, we found some cigarette ends, all recent. They were close to a concrete hut in a field at the side of the road. We hadn't seen them at first because they'd been covered over, but when we went over the area a second time we noticed the earth had been moved in one particular place and when we shifted the top layer we immediately found the cigarette ends.'

'Which probably means,' Rizzo said, 'that the remote control was activated by someone behind the hut, who'd started smoking while they were waiting.'

'And there were at least two of them,' Alibrandi said. 'There are two different brands of cigarette.'

'But the acting prosecutor was killed on the eighth,' Captain Somenti said. 'What's the connection with that noise she'd heard the previous week? Do you think they had already tried once, maybe with a rifle, and failed?'

'We can't rule that out,' Ferrara said, 'although it'll be hard to prove. Maybe there's no connection between the two things at all. Maybe Anna – I mean Acting Prosecutor Giulietti – was feeling particularly susceptible given all that was going on. But one thing's certain, Captain: in my experience, coincidences are always suspicious.'

'It shouldn't be that hard. Let's wait for the results of the tests. The cigarette ends have already been sent to Parma. We should soon know the blood type and hopefully the DNA of the people who were smoking them. They may also be able to tell if all the cigarettes were smoked at the same time, or if some were smoked on an earlier occasion than the others. I'll send them a specific request for that.'

'Good idea,' Ferrara said. 'And the DNA should be of enormous help in identifying the suspects. You're doing a great job, Major.' He sounded convinced but somehow distant, as if the compliment were a mere formality.

As they were all saying goodbye, Captain Somenti told Ferrara that he had to go back to Rome soon, but that, now that they'd finally had a chance to meet, he hoped they would be able to see each other again.

'Come and see me whenever you like,' Ferrara replied. He always felt an instinctive liking for young people who were intelligent and well-informed, which Somenti certainly seemed to be.

As Somenti walked away, Rizzo nudged Ferrara with his elbow. 'He's a friend of Ahmed Farah, chief,' he said. 'He was with him at the victims' funeral. He seemed particularly interested in your wife.'

5

'They're from Massimo,' Petra said as she handed him the two gifts from his oldest and most loyal friend: the latest novel by Jeffery Deaver, an American writer who often visited Italy and whom he had met at Massimo's bookshop in the Via Tornabuoni, and a CD of historic recordings by Maria Callas. 'He still doesn't know you left hospital early, before you were even allowed visitors!'

'Best not to tell him – I don't have time to see him now.'

'No, Michele, it's not right,' Petra said. 'It was bad of you to leave hospital, and very bad to go to work instead of coming home. You need rest, that's what the doctor said, and he wasn't joking. You can't just start working again like a madman. You should be thinking of me.'

He had never seen Petra so firm about what he chose to do in his job. It made him realise that their relationship wasn't going to be easy in the immediate future. He couldn't tell her she was the one he was thinking of, or that it wasn't work now, it was a matter of life and death.

'I'm fine,' he lied. 'Don't worry.'

'I don't believe you. You know, even Angelo Duranti called

you from his lovely retreat. You should follow his example and retire while there's still time!'

'Mephisto?' He was very fond of the retired former commissioner, and still saw him, although not very often.

'He phoned a few times. He was really nice. He's worried about you. You should call him.'

'I will, I promise. All I want right now is to have dinner and spend some time with you – and maybe Callas, too, if you're not jealous! Then a good night's sleep.'

Meanwhile, at Headquarters, having waited in vain for Ferrara to come back, Fanti had cleared the conference table in his chief's office of the huge tray with the words WELCOME BACK CHIEF spelt out in strawberry pastries and cream, chocolate and coffee puffs.

Knowing they would be stale by the next day, he gave them to the guards who were going to be on duty that night – at least they would have a sweeter time – as he was on his way out to catch his train home.

'These are from the chief,' he had lied, but deep down there was a bit of truth in it.

Late that night, Ferrara, unable to keep to his own plan, was still up.

When they had finished listening to the first act of *Rigoletto*, their favourite opera, and Petra had said she was ready for bed even though it was only just after ten, he had lingered in the living room. He had tried a cigar again – perhaps because he'd had a good meal he'd enjoyed it this time – and now he settled down to study the files which Fanti had left on his desk.

6

'Morning, chief,' Rizzo said. 'We have something for you.'

He and Venturi had been waiting for him outside his office.

'Early birds, eh? Something good?'

'I think so.'

'Come in.'

They followed him into the room and sat down in the visitors' armchairs.

'I'm all ears.'

'Chief,' Rizzo said, 'I think we may have identified Vincenzo and Anna.'

Ferrara looked at him, puzzled.

'The two names Salvatore Miano mentioned to his wife on Saturday September twenty-third, when he was in the Florence area. He said he might say hello to them from you know who.'

'I remember now,' Ferrara said, recalling the names from one of the reports he had read before going to sleep. 'And you checked and found out that neither Miano nor La Torre have relatives of those names in Tuscany, right?'

'That's right, chief, but now the boys have done a really through analysis of the phone records, and the results are amazing.'

Ferrara shot a knowing glance at Venturi, almost certainly the person who had really done the work.

'Go on.'

'Well,' the inspector said, 'we discovered that Cosimo Caruso's wife has a sister named Anna, who lives in Prato with her husband, Vincenzo, and a son.'

'As you probably read,' Rizzo hastened to add, 'the mobile in Gino La Torre's possession in Prato called a mobile registered to the Matteo Parenti company. From the intercepts, we know that this phone is almost exclusively used by Cosimo Caruso, the current director of the company.'

Ferrara nodded and took a few notes.

'By checking the records of all the phone calls made to and from the company's mobile and the Caruso family's landline, and then cross-checking, we now have a better idea why that call came from Prato.'

Rizzo paused and leafed through a few sheets he had in his hand until he found what he was looking for.

'Immediately after receiving the call from La Torre,' he resumed, 'Cosimo Caruso used his company mobile to call his own house. The call only lasted a few seconds – one of many calls from that mobile to the home phone. But less than five minutes later, there was a call from that home phone to a landline in Prato.'

'Ah-hah!' Ferrara exclaimed.

'And this landline turns out to be registered in the name of Vincenzo Lauria, who was born in Mazzara del Vallo but has been living in Prato for more than ten years. His wife's maiden name was Anna Cacioppo. She's the sister of Cosimo Caruso's wife Rita, maiden name Cacioppo.'

'Good work. Congratulations!'

'All down to the boys,' Venturi said modestly.

'And who is this Vincenzo Lauria?'

'I've checked the database. No criminal record, never been reported to the police. He works for a haulage firm in Prato.'

'And his wife?'

'Nothing at all on her.'

'I see. All right, make a few discreet inquiries and see what you can find out about this spotless family.'

'Right, chief.'

'Since that call from Caruso's house to the landline in Prato, have there been any others?' Ferrara asked.

'Not so far.'

'And before?'

'In the period of time we examined, from the first of July until today, just a few others, but few and far between.'

'Okay, Francesco, get to work and let me know.'

'Right, chief.'

'We also need to send these findings to the Prosecutor's Department and ask for authorisation to put a tap on the phone in the Lauria home – their mobiles, too, if they have them. And that's urgent, of course.'

'Of course.'

'You can go, but Inspector, I'd like you to stay.'

As soon as Rizzo had gone out, Ferrara turned to Venturi and asked, 'How come there's no user's name against this number?'

He was referring to the last number called by Salvatore Miano on Monday October 8.

'It must have been a wrong number. Nobody answered.'

'In which case it was the second time he dialled the same wrong number. Did you notice that?'

It was a detail that had struck him when he was looking through the phone records during the night. He had promised himself to talk to Venturi about it as soon as possible, and now the opportunity had presented itself. He hadn't wanted to do it with Rizzo there, because he thought it might be a serious oversight, and he preferred to deal with it himself. There had been a previous call to the same number, and on that occasion, too, the phone at the other end had rung a few times before being cut off. What had brought him up short – not that Venturi could have known this – had been the date and time: the morning of October 3, at about the time Anna Giulietti was supposed to have heard some kind of shot, if he remembered correctly what Major Alibrandi had told him. Not only that, but in both cases the phone being called, as was quite clear from the records, had been located in the Florence area, including La Certosa and therefore also Impruneta.

'No, chief, I didn't notice,' Venturi said, embarrassed. 'Can I see?'

'Here,' Ferrara said, showing him the previous page.

Venturi looked from one page to the other a couple of times and in the end had to admit that it really was the same number.

It had probably been a number stored in the memory of Miano's mobile phone and might not have any connection with the case, since on neither occasion had there been an actual conversation. But he couldn't say that: it was obvious his chief was expecting him to find a name for that number, and if that was what he wanted, that was what Venturi would have to do.

'I'll get right on to it, chief.'

7

Ferrara phoned Major Alibrandi and asked for a copy of Anna Giulietti's diary as soon as possible, explaining that he now had reasonable grounds for believing that it might contain elements useful to the *Squadra Mobile*'s investigations into the Mafia connection. Then it struck him that he ought to inform Erminia Cosenza, who was now acting prosecutor and had taken over the reins of the investigation. He decided to go in person to the Prosecutor's Department.

He left it to Fanti to phone ahead and announce his visit.

'Chief,' Fanti said, 'while you were with Inspector Venturi, that Egyptian journalist from *La Nazione* called, asking to speak to you.'

'If he calls again, tell him I had to go out but I'll be back as soon as I can.'

'Yes, chief, the usual thing.'

'I'll call him, don't worry!'

Soon afterwards, he found himself having to make his way through a crowd demonstrating in front of the Prefecture, holding up banners demanding accommodation for the homeless. They had blocked the street and were sitting on the ground, and the police and Carabinieri were trying to persuade them to move. Ferrara had got out of the car and had told the driver to wait for him outside the Prosecutor's Department, once he had managed to get through. He walked quickly, like a man who knows where he is going and does not want to be late. He took the Via Panzani and crossed the Piazza del Duomo, dodging a tide of Japanese and American tourists queuing to enter the Baptistry. Then he cut across the Piazza della Repubblica to the building housing the Prosecutors' Department, arriving only a few minutes later than he had planned when he set out.

Acting Prosecutor Cosenza was not surprised to see him up and about: news travelled fast in those circles and everyone knew by now that Ferrara was back in action. It wasn't in the papers yet, but it certainly would be by the next day. Ahmed Farah's phone call was proof of that.

'Do you really think it's a significant coincidence?' she asked him when he had finished.

'I don't know, Signora Cosenza, but it seems to me we're navigating without a compass, and when that's the case we latch on to anything we find, because you never know. What I do know is that Anna Giulietti was someone with her feet on the ground, she didn't fantasise, and she always had a sound instinct for an investigation. If she had a strange feeling that morning, we should find out all we can, don't you think?'

'Of course. I agree with you on almost everything.'

'Almost?'

She was looking at him with a slightly amused air, which made him nervous. 'If I were a man I wouldn't dare to pass judgement on what a woman fantasises about, it's an area where you men are a bit out of your depth, especially you, Chief Superintendent.' She changed tone. 'Be that as it may, don't spend too much time over it. If it doesn't lead any- where, just drop it. This case is complicated enough as it is.

We're navigating without a compass, yes, and the water's definitely rising!'

'Are there any new developments?' he asked coolly, irritated by what he preferred to dismiss as women sticking together.

'Unfortunately, yes. Look at this.' She handed him a small file. 'These are the results of the toxicological tests on Salvatore Laprua. As you can see, it's the worst possible development!'

'Murdered?'

'There are clear traces of poison. That's what the experts say.'

The poison, Ferrara read, was probably a derivative of curare and had been found in significant quantities, especially in the liver.

'Superintendent Rizzo suspected as much,' he said. 'I think you probably did, too.'

'Let's just say I didn't rule it out.'

'But from what I gather there weren't any medicines in the cell, let alone poison, and the prison officers and the forensics team who searched must have checked everything, every corner, and especially the food. If they had found something, or even had the inkling there was something, they surely would have reported it.'

'Obviously, someone administered that poison. I've already had the toxicologist and Dr Leone on the phone and they both told me Laprua must have swallowed it, there was no other way.'

'Did they tell you what the immediate effects are of that kind of poison?'

'It doesn't have any immediate effects. It obviously depends on the dose, but the person who takes it usually feels quite peaceful. Within a few hours he's dead.'

'Laprua was alone in his cell, no contact with anyone except the prison officers. How could anyone have got him to swallow poison?'

'I know it seems unlikely, but facts are clear and incontrovertible, as you can see from those results.'

In the pause that followed, each of them tried to think of a plausible hypothesis.

'All we can do,' Erminia Cosenza resumed, 'is go back to the beginning and start over. First of all, we need to interview the prison officers who did the night shift and the morning shift.'

'Have you had their reports?'

'Yes, but they don't say anything more than we were able to find out that first morning.'

'And the director's report?'

'Same thing. Nothing. We also have a report from the prison doctor, and another one from the chief prison officer with the names of the staff who dealt with Laprua and his visitors. In fact, Laprua only ever had one visitor, apart from his wife: his lawyer, Silverio Liuzza, whom we know well.'

'When did he last visit him?'

She took a sheet of paper from the file and gave it a quick glance. 'Monday October first, the day of the attack. The first attack, I mean.'

'Just his lawyer and his wife? Didn't his sons ever visit?'

'No.'

'Strange.'

'The whole thing's strange, Chief Superintendent. The only thing we can do is re-examine the case in the light of the results and do all we can to identify who brought in the poison and administered it to Laprua.'

'Why do you assume someone administered it to him? Couldn't he have given it to himself somehow?'

'Suicide, you mean?'

It was a hypothesis that had not even crossed her mind, as it had not crossed Rizzo's.

'It can't be ruled out,' Ferrara said.

'You met him. Did he seem the type?'

Frankly, no, Ferrara had to admit. Zì Turi was a Mafioso of the old school, tough, battle-hardened. There was one thing he remembered, though, and at that moment he would gladly have given half his severance pay, or even all of it, to have seen the expression on Laprua's face when he said to his lawyer, 'It's over.' Those two words had stuck in his mind, as if they bore some mysterious message, but the meaning of that message had also ended up in the grave.

Out loud, he said, 'I agree, it's not very likely.'

'But we won't rule it out. So let's take things one step at a time.'

'Okay.'

'First of all, we need to find out all we can about the two prison officers, Bongiorno and Giambra.'

Ferrara nodded.

'Let's tap their phones and make some discreet inquiries about them. In the case of Giambra, we'll have to check out Palermo, too. He's Sicilian and worked in the prison there.'

'Right.'

'We'll listen in for a few days, then interview them here in my office. They are our prime suspects, don't you agree?'

No, he didn't, but he said nothing. Maybe she was right, but a lot of things happen in prison that no one knows about. And besides, the two officers were too obvious as suspects. Why would they expose themselves like that, unless they had acted out of some kind of desperation?

'All right, Signora Cosenza, I'll get Rizzo on to it – he's already investigating the death.'

'Excellent choice, Chief Superintendent, I'm pleased.'

At that moment someone knocked at the door.

'Come in!' the acting prosecutor said.

'Good morning, Signora Cosenza. Oh, you're busy. Chief Superintendent Ferrara, how nice to see you! I've been looking forward to welcoming you back. I missed you, you know. Are you all right? Discharged you a bit early, didn't they?'

It was Francesco Leone, the pathologist.

'Only because I insisted.'

'Please sit down, Dr Leone.'

The pathologist, who was familiar with Ferrara's blind tenacity when he got an idea in his head, sympathised with his colleagues at the hospital. He sat down on the other chair in front of the desk.

'I've just been bringing the chief superintendent up to date.'

'I imagined so.'

'Here you are, Doctor,' she said, handing him a typewritten sheet of paper. 'I've drawn up a list of the questions I'd like you to answer as soon as you can. And this copy is for you, Chief Superintendent.'

All the expected questions were there:

Could the Chief Pathologist tell this Department: the exact nature of the toxic substance ingested; the means of administration; the quantity administered; the vehicle through which the poison was introduced into the organism; the way it was eliminated; when the poison was ingested and, in particular, if it was the principal cause of death or whether it could have been a crucial contributing factor?

'Fine,' Leone said.

'How much time do you need?'

'Thirty days, but I hope to get through it more quickly than that.'

'I'd be grateful if you could. All right, you can both go now.'

But as they were on their way out, the acting prosecutor suddenly called them back.

'What is it?' Ferrara asked.

'Just a moment.' She rose from her chair, walked up to them, and said in a low voice, 'We have to keep these results completely secret and only inform those directly involved in the investigation. I don't want any leaks to the press.'

'Don't worry, Signora Cosenza,' Ferrara said, and Leone nodded.

As he made his way back to Headquarters, Ferrara wondered if the acting prosecutor had been specifically alluding to Commissioner Lepri, who was not 'directly involved in the investigation'.

8

Meanwhile, Rizzo, Sergi, Venturi and Superintendent Ascalchi were taking stock of the disappearance of Salvatore Miano and the investigations in Forte dei Marmi.

'What about this Antonio Vita? Do we have anything on him?'

'Nothing specific,' Venturi said. 'Most of his phone calls are to business contacts. He is involved with horse racing and gambling, but there doesn't seem to be anything connected with our investigation.'

'All the same, he's the one who provided a hiding place for our friends. I think the time has come to search his home and interview him. He may know where Miano is, may even be sheltering him.'

'I volunteer!' Ascalchi piped up enthusiastically: as the good Roman that he was, he didn't feel much sympathy for the Milanese.

'Request a search warrant,' Rizzo said. 'I'll inform Ferrara.'

But before Rizzo could get to Ferrara, the chief superintendent was intercepted by Ahmed Farah in the corridor that led to his office.

'I found out you're back, Chief Superintendent, and I just came to say wel—'

'Drop it, Ahmed, I know perfectly well you've been stalking me. You owe me an explanation, so come with me, there's no time to lose.'

They went into the office and sat down facing each other. Ferrara lit a cigar.

The journalist put on one of his famous disarming smiles. 'It's not what you think, Chief Superintendent.'

'And what do I think?'

'I don't know, but I was only looking for you because I like you and I wanted to know how you were. I told your wife.'

'We'll talk about my wife later. Let's talk about the case instead. I think that probably interests you more than my health.'

'Maybe, but not for the same reason as you. I'm not on the news desk any more, I've been promoted. Right now, I'm investigating international terrorism, keeping an eye on my fellow Arabs here in Italy.'

'Is that why you're involved with the intelligence services?'

Ahmed was almost caught off guard, but reacted with good humour. 'Nothing escapes you, does it?'

'Which brings us back to my wife. You and Somenti were seen together at the victims' funeral. And he seemed very interested in Petra.'

'In you, Chief Superintendent, in you, not your wife. He was in Florence because of the bombing.'

'And now?'

'He's unemployed. Al-Qaeda seems to be out of the frame now, so Military Intelligence don't see any point in pursuing something that doesn't concern them.'

Ferrara noted a hint of sarcasm in Farah's words. 'You don't agree?'

'I've always been taught that, until the contrary has been proven, everything is possible. And so far it seems to me that nothing has been proven.'

'There's some strong evidence building up, believe me, and it doesn't point to Arab terrorists at all.'

Ahmed Farah stopped smiling, leaned forward, as if to underline what he was about to say, and said in a low voice, 'I do believe you, but I'm not satisfied. We're living in confusing times, fertile ground for U-turns and betrayals, backstabbing, alliances between enemies. We're on quicksand, and anything can turn out to be the opposite of what we thought it was. I know you've decided to concentrate on the Mafia, and it doesn't surprise me. In fact it wouldn't surprise me if in all this mess our paths finally converged. Don't forget that, at another time of confusion, when the allies landed in Sicily, they were only able to do so because they'd made a pact with the Mafia.'

'That's just a theory.'

'Come on, Chief Superintendent, it's history, and we're still paying the price.' The journalist had assumed the air of a man who knows that what he's saying is obvious, and as such it would be pointless for anyone to disagree with him. 'And now Florence is turning out to be a strange meeting place, a kind of modern Casablanca where all of a sudden Mafia bosses and Taliban leaders come together and bombs go off and people die in prison.'

'Hold on. You don't have any proof there's a connection between these things. Or do you?'

'No, you're right. Maybe there isn't any connection. Or just maybe there is. Don't forget, the Taliban have the poppies and the Mafia traffic in drugs.'

'But do you know who these Taliban leaders are?'

'I have my suspicions, and I've already passed them on to Captain Somenti.'

'Let Military Intelligence deal with it, then. This is a dangerous business, don't get any more involved than you need to.'

'Look who's talking.'

'Yes, but I mean it.'

'All right, then.' He smiled, showing his white teeth again. 'I'll be as careful as you are.'

'Don't joke about it, Ahmed.'

'I'm not joking. It's just that I'm afraid Somenti has taken his unemployment too seriously. He seems to have lost interest. I think he has other things on his mind.'

'I see. Well, if I get a chance, I'll try and speak to him, don't worry.'

'Thanks. But do it. Don't underestimate what I've told you.'

As soon as the journalist had gone, Ferrara asked Fanti to send for Rizzo, who had asked to see him.

'Inspector Venturi is also waiting to speak to you, chief.'

Ferrara looked at his watch. It was getting late and he still had to tell Rizzo about Acting Prosecutor Cosenza's instructions regarding the prison officers.

'I don't have time now, ask him if he can wait.'

'He says that's fine,' Fanti said after a few minutes. 'I'll call Superintendent Rizzo immediately.'

A few minutes later, his deputy was bringing him up to date on the latest developments and in particular on his initiative regarding Antonio Vita.

'Well done. Send Ascalchi, yes. He's a good officer, we can trust him.'

'I agree.'

'What I want you to do in the meantime is investigate the prison officers in Sollicciano. Acting Prosecutor Cosenza regards them as prime suspects in what has turned out to be another murder.'

'Laprua!' Rizzo exclaimed. But he did not seem surprised. 'I've been expecting it. I was hoping I was wrong, of course, hoping it was just me. You know how it is, this profession sometimes makes us too suspicious.'

'True, but it also sharpens the instinct, and yours wasn't wrong, unfortunately.'

9

'You're a real idiot,' a colleague of his had said when Captain
Somenti had told him that the reason he had left Giulia was to
make a career for himself in Intelligence. 'For a looker like
that, I'd have turned down the chance to be President.'

Now that she was here, sitting opposite him in this restaurant by the sea in Viareggio, her face illumined by the candle
on the table between them, those words came back to him like
a truth carved in Carrara marble. He was feeling slightly
befuddled: it was partly the cold Vermentino, partly his
inability to understand why life had to give us such impossible choices. He still loved Giulia as much as ever, and he still
loved his job as much as ever. Or wasn't that true any more?
Since he had seen her again, he had started to harbour some
doubts. Whenever they came, he would try to suppress them,
but the fact remained that his recent professional frustrations
had made him more uncertain than ever.

'I know what you're thinking,' she said. 'I've thought about
it a lot, too. But it won't work, believe me.'

'It's the only thing you say that I don't believe, Giulia. We
love each other, we've always loved each other. It's fate, how
can you not understand that?'

'You've always been a fatalist,' she said, with a kind of sad jokiness. 'I think we choose our own path, and I don't want to make a mistake. I've already made too many.'

'What do you mean?' he asked, barely raising his voice, afraid that she was referring to him.

She lowered her dark eyes and did not reply.

'Have there been others? Tell me!'

'You don't have the right, Carlo,' she replied, raising her head and looking him straight in the eyes.

'How can you say that? You know perfectly well I'm still in love with you!'

'Please calm down,' she said, lowering her voice and looking around in embarrassment.

But right now he didn't give a damn what other people might think.

'What should I do? Can you tell me that?'

'Okay, I'll tell you,' she replied in a determined tone, and she stood up and headed for the exit.

By the time he paid the bill and got out of the restaurant, she had already walked quite a distance along the beach.

When he finally caught up with her, his anger had abated a little. Giulia was silent. He walked beside her, wondering what his next move should be. The beach was dark, the air already cold and slightly damp. She shivered and pulled her shawl around her, and he had to force himself not to follow his instinct and embrace her.

As they walked, the backwash beat on the foreshore with a slow, regular rhythm, an eternal soundtrack to an infinity of love affairs that had burgeoned and died here, and the captain wondered, with a mixture of sadness and anger, how to categorise theirs: it had burgeoned, but had it already died?

'There was someone else,' she finally said.

The stab of jealousy was unbearable. It was even worse

hearing it said out loud than imagining it. He kept silent in order not to scream.

'But it's over,' Giulia added.

'What do you mean exactly?'

'I don't want to talk about it.'

When, much later, he parked his car outside Giulia's building, after an interminable journey along the autostrada in a silence broken only by the music of Pink Floyd coming through the speakers, he made a clumsy attempt to move closer and kiss her, but she quickly drew back.

'I'll call you,' he said as she got out of the car.

'If you like,' Giulia replied, in a sad, neutral tone that lingered with him as he drove along the last stretch of road to his temporary home in the Tuscan countryside near Florence.

10

The following day it was Rizzo's turn to go to the Prosecutor's Department, to be present at the interview with Anna and Vincenzo Lauria. As the tap on their phones – the landline and a mobile registered in the husband's name – had not yielded any significant results, Erminia Cosenza had decided to call both of them in.

A police officer had been despatched with the summons the previous evening to their detached house in an area filled with textile and wool factories.

The first to enter the acting prosecutor's office was the wife, Anna Lauria, maiden name Cacioppo. She was thirty-nine, short and well-built, with a dark complexion and shoulder-length chestnut hair. Her eyes, also chestnut, darted all over the office as soon as she stepped inside, as if she were searching for something or someone. She seemed lost.

'Please, signora, sit down,' Erminia Cosenza said, indicating a small armchair in front of the desk, to her right.

'Hello,' she replied, and her voice was slightly shaky, a fact which did not escape the acting prosecutor.

'Don't worry, signora, relax. This gentleman on my right is my colleague Deputy Prosecutor Vinci and this other gentleman is Superintendent Rizzo.' The woman timidly shook hands with both of them.

'You know, I'm not used to being summoned,' she said as soon as she had sat down. 'This is the first time.'

'I understand it may be rather daunting, finding yourself here, so let me tell you straightaway that you are being interviewed as a third party with knowledge of the facts.'

'What does that mean?'

'That you're not under investigation.'

'My God, that's all I need!' she cried, and covered her face in her hands.

'It's all right, signora,' Vinci intervened. 'I think you may have misunderstood. We're not accusing you of anything. We simply want to ask you a few questions and we need you to tell us the truth.'

The woman nodded and waited, calming down.

The first questions were about her family situation, her work, her husband's work, her acquaintances in Prato. She replied that she had been married about ten years and had an eight-year-old son, that she was a housewife, and that she did not know many people in Prato, only a few of her husband's workmates and their families.

'What work does your husband do?' Erminia Cosenza asked.

'He works for a haulage company in Prato. They deliver goods in Prato and the Florence region.'

Then she was asked more specific questions about her family origins, her relatives and possible interests in Sicily, and now the woman put up defences.

'Signora, we have absolutely nothing to do with our relatives down there in Sicily. Our life is here, in Tuscany. We only go down there once a year, in summer, during the school holidays, so that our boy can get a bit of sun.'

'Do you have a house by the sea?'

'Us? If only! We barely manage on my husband's salary! We make sacrifices all year so that we can rent a couple of rooms for the month of August.'

'Have any of your Sicilian relatives visited you recently?'

The reply was immediate and curt. 'Not recently, not ever.'

'Or any friends from Sicily?'

'No.'

Erminia Cosenza would have liked to ask if they had received any phone calls from Sicily lately, but she decided to leave that one until later: for the moment, she didn't want the woman to suspect that they were tapping her phone.

She did not insist, but instead asked first Vinci, then Rizzo if they had any questions. Both answered no, the interview was terminated, and Anna Lauria, after reading the transcript and signing with a trembling hand, said goodbye and left the room.

Immediately afterwards, her husband came in.

Vincenzo Lauria was forty years old, short, dark and thick-set, with a receding hairline and prematurely greying hair, generally rather coarse in appearance.

'Signor Lauria, do you have relatives in Tuscany?' Erminia Cosenza asked.

'No.'

'How about in Sicily?'

'My mother, brother and sister live in Sicily, in Mazara del Vallo.'

'Does your wife have any relatives there?'

'Yes.'

'How do you get on with them?'

'So-so. We don't see much of each other. The only time we see them is in the summer, when we go to the seaside.'

'Do you know Cosimo Caruso?'

'Of course, he's married to my wife's sister.'

'How do you get on with him?'

'So-so. The way you do with a brother-in-law.'

'When did you last see him?'

'I'm sorry, signora, but why are you asking me that? Has he done something wrong? We really don't have anything to do with him.'

'No, he hasn't done anything, we're just checking a few things.'

A pause, then: 'I saw him last summer in Mazara.'

'Has he ever visited you in Prato?'

'No, never.'

'Have you phoned him recently?'

'No.'

'What about your wife?'

'No.' The tone was firm and blunt.

'Does your brother-in-law have any children?'

'One son. His name is Sandro and he's at university.'

'What is he studying?'

'That I don't know. I only know he goes to university.'

Erminia Cosenza decided not to pursue the question of the brother-in-law for the moment and changed the subject. 'Do you have friends in Mazara del Vallo?'

'No. I only go there in summer. To be honest, I feel like a stranger there these days. I don't have any friends, I don't see anyone.'

'Did you know Matteo Parenti?'

'No. This is the first time I've heard that name.'

'Have you had any phone calls recently from your brother-in-law or anyone in your family?'

Vincenzo Lauria did not reply immediately. He lowered his eyes to his lap and gave the impression he was trying hard to remember. Then he replied, 'No. Definitely not, and I'm sure my wife and son didn't get any calls either, because they would have said. But I can ask my wife if you like – or have you already asked her?'

'No, we haven't asked her, but we will.'

Erminia Cosenza decided that her initial caution on the matter of phone calls no longer made sense. She asked Rizzo to go out in the corridor, where Anna Lauria was waiting for her husband, and ask her the same question. He could take down her answer on a report sheet.

Rizzo left the room.

Erminia Cosenza resumed the interview. 'Have you had any of your Sicilian relatives or friends staying in your house recently?'

'No, never. I already told you, I don't have any Sicilian friends, and no one from Sicily has ever been to my house.'

'Are you absolutely sure?'

'Yes. Why? Do you think they have?'

'Signor Lauria, I'm asking the questions, not you,' she retorted, in an authoritative tone.

'I'm sorry, I didn't mean to offend you.'

'It's all right. I just want you to know how things stand in this room.'

At that point, Rizzo came back, went up to the acting prosecutor and whispered in her ear that Anna Lauria had given the same negative answer as her husband.

'All right, Signor Lauria, if you have nothing else to add to what you've already said, we can terminate this interview.'

'I've told you all I know.'

Erminia Cosenza had the statement printed. Vincenzo Lauria read it over and it was then signed by all those present.

When Lauria had gone, she said, 'Superintendent, you saw how they reacted to my question about the phone calls. Let's not waste any time. We need to search the Laurias' house. It's obvious they're lying.'

11

On Sunday Ferrara decided to pay a visit he felt he could no longer postpone. Petra wanted to go with him and, as it meant a little trip to the seaside, he made no objection. A good lunch in a nice little restaurant might be just what they needed.

They took the A11 autostrada, which was quite congested that morning. During the journey Ferrara tried to imagine how the widow would react. But the woman had been as silent as a sphinx the only time he had seen her, and he hadn't been able to work her out.

When they reached Viareggio, he left Petra to look around the shops along the promenade and walked to the Laprua apartment.

The front door of the building was open. He climbed the stairs to the apartment and rang the bell.

The widow opened the door without asking who it was and then stood there pale-faced, dressed in black, giving Ferrara a withering look which went right through him.

'I'm sorry, Signora Laprua, I should have phoned,' he said, holding out his hand.

The woman shook it, then moved aside and let him in. She walked ahead of him to the same room he had been in when he had come to see Laprua in August. The room was just as clean and tidy as before. The thick curtains at the windows were drawn, and the only light in the room came from two table lamps.

'Come in,' she said in a thin voice, and indicated the armchairs.

Ferrara sat down on the edge of one of the armchairs, unable to relax. The woman did not sit down, but started pacing restlessly from one corner to the other with her arms folded over her chest.

'Why have you come?'

'I need to talk to you.'

'You should have saved yourself the trouble. Aren't all these deaths enough for you?'

'I'm very sorry.'

'It was you who put him in prison!' she replied with a grimace. 'You killed my husband!'

'I was nearly killed myself, and you know it.'

'I know you're alive, and my husband isn't. That's what I know!'

'Someone did kill him, that's highly likely. All the evidence points to it. I may bear some responsibility, but one thing I tell you: whoever killed him, I'm going to find that person.'

The widow's grimace became a sneer, which quite surprised him. It was an expression not so much of mistrust as of contempt.

'Forget it, it's nothing to do with you. He's dead, let him rest in peace!'

'I can't. At least tell me this: did he have any illnesses?'

'He was an old man, he suffered from the usual ailments. His heart was sometimes a little erratic, but nothing serious.'

'Was he taking any medication?'

'Occasionally a pill for his heart.'

'Did you visit him?

'Every Saturday.'

'How did he seem to you?'

'The same as always.'

'And last Saturday?'

'The same.'

'Any other visitors you know of?'

'No. Only his lawyer, and the father.'

'The priest?'

'The one from the prison. My husband was a believer.'

'I understand.'

'No, you don't understand a thing,' she said in a conclusive tone, making it clear the visit was over. But it seemed to Ferrara that she also meant something else: that she knew, but that he wouldn't get anything out of her.

When he rejoined Petra, he suggested they look for a restaurant, but she had had another idea. It was still early – why not pay a visit to his old friend Duranti, who had been so worried about him? It would only take half an hour from Viareggio, and it was such a nice day. Ferrara phoned him and received a joyful invitation to lunch.

The former commissioner had retired to a house in a place called Zanego, on the road that climbs the hill from Montemarcello to Lerici. He lived there alone, surrounded by his books, and by the plants he lovingly cultivated in the plot of land surrounding the house, from where he enjoyed an enviable view of Porto Venere and the islands.

Ferrara visited him from time to time, although much more rarely than he would have liked. They had become firm friends, and Ferrara loved to consult him on matters of law, as Duranti had acquired a vast knowledge over the years, made all the keener by his innate wisdom and by constant study. Petra, on the other hand, always came away from these visits with valuable gardening tips, which she then put to good use on the terrace of their apartment.

Duranti greeted them under a canopy in the garden, where he had built an outdoor kitchen. A pan was already steaming, waiting for the spaghetti to be added, and sauce was simmering in another, spreading an irresistible smell of seasonal mushrooms. The table had been elegantly set for lunch.

'You shouldn't have,' Petra protested.

'If I don't put out my best china on the rare occasions when I have visitors, what am I going to do with it?'

Petra took an apron from a hook on the wall, grabbed a wooden spoon, and went to check on the sauce.

'How I envy you this kitchen!'

'Don't even talk about it. If only you knew the trouble I'm having at the moment!'

'What kind of trouble?' Ferrara asked.

'I had an inspection from the local police, and it turns out the kitchen is against planning regulations. They were very decent, very polite, but someone has been spying and reported me, so naturally they have to do their duty.'

'The bastard!' Petra said, her German accent suddenly accentuated. 'What business was it of his? It's so beautiful! What bother is it to anyone? In my opinion, it enhances the area!'

Duranti made no comment on the informer. Perhaps he thought the way she did, but being an upholder of the law he would never admit it.

'I'm sorry, but being an expert on the law, shouldn't you have known?' Ferrara asked, genuinely surprised.

'I know about serious crimes. Who could ever have imagined that I would risk a fine for something as trivial as this? Someone like me!'

'It's ridiculous! What are you going to do?'

'Everything I possibly can, within the law. Anyway, the architect who refurbished the house for me before I built the kitchen is dealing with it, she's good and I'm sure she can sort it out. But I don't want to bore you with my problems. They don't amount to much compared with the problems of the world.'

Over lunch, Petra, much to Ferrara's surprise, asked about the architect.

'She has a practice in Sarzana. She was the one who suggested I buy this ruin and then refurbished it for me.'

'Are there any others like this round here?'

'Not many, but every now and again you can find something.'

'You're not planning to find a house here, are you?' Ferrara cut in.

'Why not? Isn't it a wonderful spot? You could rest and devote yourself to writing your memoirs. You certainly have plenty to write about, and it could be helpful to people planning to join the police force.'

Now that he saw where she was going with this, he decided to cut the conversation short. 'It's not time for that yet,' he said.

Duranti looked at her, and thought he caught a secret message in her eyes. He said nothing.

After lunch, the two men sat down on deckchairs to enjoy the warm autumn sun and contemplate the sea, while Petra went for a walk in the fields to look at the herbs and wild plants.

'Talking about problems,' Duranti said, 'I'm worried about you.'

'I know. This case is quite something. I can't get over poor Anna Giulietti!'

'It's obvious now that this was a Mafia operation, nothing

to do with terrorism. And you were the target, Michele. You should listen to your wife.'

'But Laprua wasn't involved,' Ferrara went on, ignoring the suggestion. 'After all, they killed him, too.'

'I know. I'm afraid you have to look higher.'

'The third level?' he asked, and at the same time wondered how Duranti knew that.

The former commissioner nodded.

It was a classification that experts in the Anti-Mafia Squad had coined to refer to Mafia crimes. First level crimes were committed to keep the Mafia going from day to day: extortion, drug trafficking and so on. Second level crimes comprised those committed in order to consolidate power, such as murdering members of rival families. The third and final level included all the crimes that did not fit into the old mechanisms, involving that area of the organisation in which the biggest bosses and their business associates dominated.

'And that's a quicksand,' Ferrara said, shuddering as he remembered Farah's words. He well knew how difficult it was to pursue an investigation whenever you came close to that third level, like the 'hidden powers' suspected of master-minding the wave of Mafia killings in 1993: he remembered how the investigation had inexplicably stalled and then come to a standstill once the perpetrators and their bosses inside Cosa Nostra had been identified. 'A quicksand where, accord-ing to a journalist friend of mine, there may even be collusion between the Mafia and the Taliban, and all kinds of double and triple crosses.'

Duranti shrugged. 'Who knows? I'm familiar with that friend of yours. Not personally, but I keep up with the news and always read *La Nazione*. Tell him to be careful.'

'I already have.'

'And you should retire, as I have, or stay in your own field, which is already deadly enough in itself. Don't get mixed up in things that aren't within your remit.'

'Understood.'

Petra's return brought them back to more pleasant topics, and they lingered until they saw the sun go down behind the hill of Porto Venere, turning the sky purple and leaving a trail on the sea, where the first lights of a ship at anchor glittered.

12

He found Inspector Venturi waiting for him in his office that Monday morning, anxious to repair an omission for which he could not forgive himself.

'I found it, chief.'

'Found what?'

'The registered owner of the phone that was called from Miano's mobile on the morning of October eighth, and before that on the third.'

'Who is it?'

'It turns out to be a Dutchman named Jan van Gorcum, born in Amsterdam, March nineteenth, 1975.'

'So you were right, Riccardo, it must have been a wrong number. Twice, though! I don't know . . .'

Venturi lowered his eyes in embarrassment, but immediately looked up again. 'Actually, chief, I hadn't finished.'

'Oh?'

'The thing is, this Dutchman lives in Sicily – in Agrigento, according to the address he gave the phone company when he signed the contract.'

'Well, well, what a coincidence! Keep checking. Send a fax to the *Squadra Mobile* in Agrigento asking for information on him.'

'Already done, chief.'

'Good work, Riccardo. Now get on the phone and make sure they received it. That way they know it's important, otherwise God knows how long they'll take to reply.'

Meanwhile, a team led by Gianni Ascalchi were at the residence of Antonio Vita in Milan. The search warrant had been issued by the Prosecutor's Department in record time, and now, not having found Salvatore Miano as they had hoped, they were sifting doggedly through a big harvest of documents. There were also a couple of thick diaries filled with notes and appointments, an address book full of names and telephone numbers, all from Sicily, and a number of very large sheets of lined paper covered in names, dates and figures.

Ascalchi's attention was especially drawn to a number of receipts and other papers, all relating to horses. The receipts were from races at various courses, including Montecatini and Palermo, while the documents recorded the purchase and sale of pedigree horses.

'Whose names are these, Signor Vita?' he asked, holding the large sheets in both hands.

Antonio Vita's face darkened. 'They're the names of horses,' he replied, in a thin voice.

Ascalchi looked at him and smiled. He didn't need to ask any other questions. These papers related to illegal bets and were usually destroyed after use. He would have a chance to go further into the matter during the interview, which looked like being juicy: it was well known that there were criminal elements, including the Mafia, involved in illegal gambling on horse races. At the end of the search, Ascalchi informed Vita that he was under arrest for gambling offences – just to leave him a souvenir of his presence in Milan.

But the interview, which took place the following day in a room in Milan Police Headquarters, proved disappointing. Antonio Vita's lawyer began by requesting, and obtaining, permission to have a conversation in private with his client – something the law allowed subject to the consent of a magistrate or, if a magistrate was not present, a police officer, who could only refuse it for a valid reason. After this the interview proper only lasted a few minutes, the time it took to go through the usual formalities (the presence of a defence counsel, the accused person's particulars, economic status, criminal record and previous convictions), because Vita declared unhesitatingly that he wished to avail himself of the right to remain silent. It was obviously a decision he had agreed on with his lawyer, dictated either by fear or by the fact that he was seriously implicated in the case. Either way, it could not help but cast further suspicion on him.

'In that case, Signor Vita,' Ascalchi said, 'I have to inform you that the investigation will go ahead anyway, and the legal procedure will take its course.'

The interview was terminated.

13

At almost exactly the same time, the interviews of the prison officers Giuseppe Bongiorno and Filippo Giambra were taking place in Florence. Their telephones had been tapped, but nothing useful had emerged, and Acting Prosecutor Cosenza had decided not to waste any more time.

According to the information about Giambra and his family that had come from Palermo, there was no evidence that he had any contact with anyone who either had, or was suspecting of having, a Mafia connection. His wife, it had been established, was not Sicilian: she was from Pistoia, as was her family.

By the time Ferrara and Rizzo arrived at the Prosecutor's Department, Officer Bongiorno had already been in the acting prosecutor's room for several minutes. They knocked and entered.

'Ah, good morning, you've come just in time, I was about to begin the interview.' It was obvious that Erminia Cosenza had had no intention of waiting for them. 'This is Officer Giuseppe Bongiorno. Officer Bongiorno, you've already met Superintendent Rizzo. His colleague is Chief Superintendent Ferrara, head of the *Squadra Mobile*.'

In civilian clothes, Giuseppe Bongiorno looked even younger than his thirty years. He was clearly nervous and uncomfortable, and sat with his hands crossed on his lap and his head bowed. An understandable state of mind, because this was the first time he had ever been interviewed by an examining magistrate. As he had already presented Director Mazzorelli with a detailed report, this summons to the Prosecutor's Department had to mean they considered him a suspect.

'Now, Officer Bongiorno,' the acting prosecutor began, 'can you tell me all about the last time you inspected Signor Laprua's cell?'

'But I told you all that the morning it happened.'

'Please tell us again, in detail. We have the good fortune to have the head of the *Squadra Mobile* with us now, and six ears are better than two.'

The officer passed his tongue over his lips, and once again went through everything he had done and seen during his shift, basically repeating what he had written in his report.

The interview was quite short and the officer left the acting prosecutor's office after barely half an hour. Erminia Cosenza had realised quite quickly that they were not going to get any more details from the officer, because he had probably said all there was to say. Besides, Officer Giambra was more of a suspect: the post mortem had confirmed that Laprua's death had occurred during his shift.

It was his turn now.

He was forty-two years old, and for more than twenty of those years he had worked in the prison service. First in Sicily, in Palermo, the city where he was born and grew up, and then in various prisons in Tuscany. He had arrived at Sollicciano two years earlier. His Sicilian origins and his time in Palermo had fed suspicion that he might be the culprit.

'You were the last person to see Salvatore Laprua alive,' the acting prosecutor began. 'Could you tell us when and how many times you saw him during your shift?'

'I've already written all that in my report,' the officer replied in a determined voice, almost as if to emphasise how pointless this interview was.

Ferrara and Rizzo exchanged glances: they both knew that a reply and a tone like that were not guaranteed to ingratiate him with Erminia Cosenza.

'I advise you to relax,' she said, calmly but firmly. 'I know perfectly well what you wrote; I have your report right here in front of me, can you see? But I want you to be more specific. I want you to tell these gentlemen and myself exactly what you did and saw.'

'How do you mean, more specific?' the officer asked, somewhat scared, glancing at Rizzo and Ferrara.

'We've already said that you were the last person to see Signor Laprua alive. Do you think it's strange that we want you to give us as many details as possible?'

It was clear that she was starting to lose patience.

'When I saw him, the prisoner Laprua was fine.'

'When exactly was that?'

'I saw him twice. It's in my report.'

'But at what time?' she insisted, deliberately ignoring the fact that this, too, was in the report.

'The first time was just after midnight. It was during my first inspection, after I came on duty.'

'And the second time?'

'Around three in the morning.'

'Are you sure?'

'Yes, I'm sure, it's in my . . .' he started to reply, and then suddenly seemed to deflate, as if exhausted by the tension and by having to repeat what he had already stated. 'I've always done my job, signora, I've always followed orders.'

'I don't doubt that, but you must understand that we need to look into things a bit more closely.'

'I understand, I understand. Tell me what you want to know – I don't know what else to say.'

'During your shift, did anyone come into your section – one of your colleagues for instance?'

'No, there was no reason for any of my colleagues to come into my section. Everyone has his own routine and you can't depart from it.'

'Are you absolutely sure?'

'Absolutely. The only person who was supposed to be in that section during that shift was me.'

'Did you leave for any reason, even for just a short time?'

'No. I was at my post the whole time. Why are you asking me all these questions? Didn't he die of natural causes? What have people coming into my section got to do with it?'

Instead of answering him, the magistrate chose to change tactics and tackle him head-on with a direct question.

'Why did you put in for a transfer from Palermo?'

Officer Giambra made a slight movement with his jaw, which did not prevent him from replying immediately, 'It was my decision. I did it of my own free will.'

'You weren't put under any pressure?'

'Absolutely not. You should know, signora, that my wife and her family are from Pistoia and she never wanted to live in Sicily. She didn't like it there, and neither did I.'

'Did you ever meet any of Signor Laprua's family or friends?'

'No, never.'

'Are you sure?'

'Very sure. Why, don't you believe me?'

'It's not that. It's just that you may have met someone and now you don't remember. How can you be so certain?'

'No, signora, if I say no, it's no. I can swear on the Virgin Mary.'

Erminia Cosenza turned to look at the two policemen.

'Signora, I've told you the truth,' Giambra said, more frightened than ever. 'If you don't believe me, I'm sorry, but I can't make something up just to keep you happy.'

'May I ask a question?' Ferrara said.

'Go ahead,' Eminia Cosenza said.

'Would you say Laprua was very religious?'

'Yes, very.'

'And did he often receive visits from the chaplain?'

Rizzo, who had already heard about Ferrara's visit to Laprua's widow, started to see what Ferrara was driving at.

'Yes.'

'Can you tell us how these visits take place?'

'The prisoners usually see Don Santo – that's his name – in his office, but he often comes to the cells, at any time, even at night.'

'Is there a register of these visits?'

'No, not really. The regulations give the priest free access to all sections of the prison, unaccompanied, at any hour of the day or night, especially in the evening when the prisoners tend to feel down.'

'All right, now think carefully. You told the acting prosecutor here that no one came into your section during your shift. Does that include the chaplain?'

Filippo Giambra hesitated.

The figure of the priest, so familiar in a prison and so free to move around, ends up becoming an almost invisible presence.

'No, I couldn't say for certain.'

'Thank you.'

'Any other questions?' Erminia Cosenza asked.

As no one responded, she declared the interview over. But

after Giambra had left the room, she turned to Ferrara in annoyance. 'Would you be so kind as to explain? What was all that about the priest?'

'Nothing really, just something that occurred to me on the spur of the moment,' Ferrara lied shamelessly, assuming his most angelic air. 'But it might be worth talking to him, don't you think?'

Erminia Cosenza was in a foul mood when she dismissed them. Not only had nothing concrete emerged from these interviews to implicate the prime suspect, now there was also the danger of a conflict with the ecclesiastical authorities, which was one of the things she most dreaded.

14

Avoiding your own commissioner isn't an easy matter if you're the head of the *Squadra Mobile*, especially when the only thing separating you is a flight of stairs.

So far, Ferrara had been spared a meeting thanks to the non-committal attitude Riccardo Lepri had chosen to adopt. But although he was keen to avoid Lepri in order to save himself the embarrassment of trying to keep him in the dark about developments in the Laprua case, as the acting prosecutor had requested, he realised he couldn't put it off indefinitely. Given that he had returned to work suddenly and unexpectedly, not even saying hello to the commissioner went far beyond mere discourtesy and might cause irreparable damage to a relationship which had never been exceptionally friendly.

He decided to call him.

'At last!' the commissioner replied, but his tone was unusually gentle. 'Before telling you off, let me say how pleased I am to know you're back in good health. You're well, I hope?'

'I owe you an apology. I know how worried you were and how kind you were to Petra, and I'm grateful to you for that. The reason I haven't shown my face is certainly not because I'm ungrateful, but the amount of work I've—'

'You don't have to apologise, Ferrara. I know how complicated the situation is, and I have every confidence in you. But
please, be careful. In every meaning of the word: don't overdo
it when you should be recovering, and don't take pointless
risks. There have already been too many martyrs of the State
in this tangled affair. Anna Giulietti's death has been a real
blow, believe me, and not only to me. There's a great deal of
anxiety in high places, and people are keeping a close watch
on what we're doing. So please, tread carefully!'

'Don't worry, Commissioner,' Ferrara replied, although he
would rather have done anything than tread carefully.

'And keep me informed.'

'Of course.'

When he had put down the receiver, he fished another
cigar from the leather case but, before he had time to light it,
Fanti materialised quietly in front of him and placed a bulky
envelope on his desk.

'From Major Alibrandi, chief. It says Personal and
Confidential.'

'Okay, thanks.'

'Should I open it?'

'No, thanks, you can go.'

He wasn't sure why the major was being so secretive. Anna
Giulietti's diary was a piece of evidence in a criminal investigation, not a personal and confidential matter.

Puzzled, he opened the envelope.

What he found inside hit him like a punch in the stomach
with its anachronistic and almost paradoxical humanity: it
was a hard-covered volume bound in beautiful green and
cream marbled paper, with a light-coloured leather spine
and a flap with a little lock to prevent access to the pages. A
personal journal, a jealous guardian of intimate secrets,
which made Ferrara think of a teenage girl's diary. It was not

something he would ever have associated with the image of Anna Giulietti, a self-confident, even cold woman, who once on a car journey had confessed to him her total devotion to work and her consequent sacrifice of a private life.

The cover bore the word DIARY and a label with a decorative border on which Anna had written in green ink in a beautiful English cursive script the date *June 2001* followed by a dash and an empty space to be filled in by the date when the diary was completed. Clearly, it was the latest in a series.

The lock had been opened and a yellow Post-it marked the page the major had mentioned – a page that apparently contained a reference to him.

October 3

Mother had some difficulty getting to sleep but eventually spent a peaceful night. She's better, thank God. BUT I CAN'T STAND IT ANY MORE!

I'M TIRED!

My back is broken and I feel swollen all over.

I kept her company and read her The Glass Menagerie *for the twentieth or thirtieth time. I wonder if her obsession with that play is a dig at me. She can be really wicked. And I'm stupid to be hurt by it! But it's pointless telling her over and over that I don't need a husband. What a bitch I am! She's old and weak . . .*

A husband, no, but a man?

A couple of days ago I looked at an old diary of mine, and reread the page for March 14, 1999. It was a Tuesday, we were on our way back from Certaldo, and Michele took me to have lunch at Latini's. I wrote that I could feel my heart beating like crazy and I was terribly self-conscious because one of my stockings had a very noticeable ladder. What a fool, I should be ashamed at my age! Is it possible I wrote that?

Yes, it's possible!

The truth is, I miss Michele, I miss him a lot! I hope he recovers soon, I need him beside me in this business, which is really starting to scare me. I'm so nervous that this morning, just after we left, and before we got to the Via Cassia, I heard a loud crack and immediately thought I'd been shot. My heart skipped a beat and my chest seemed to open up. Alessandro carried on driving as if nothing had happened, and when I asked him if he had heard anything he said it was probably hunters in the woods. I'M NOT CONVINCED. I'M NOT CONVINCED AT ALL. I hear hunters sometimes at dawn, or even earlier, but lately everything's been perfectly quiet. I didn't tell him that, though, in order not to scare him, too. I was still tense until we got to the Via Cassia. I thought of telling Rizzo, but then I didn't, I had too much to do and it went out of my mind. Maybe I'm blowing it up out of all proportion. After all, no one actually hit us!

But I would have told you, Michele, I'm sure of that. To feel protected? To make me feel important? To try and discover in a gesture, a look, a word, if you care about me, and if you do, how much?

Ferrara went home feeling very troubled, with the diary hidden in a brown envelope between some papers from the office, and as self-conscious as a husband hiding porn magazines from his wife. He had decided not to tell Petra, at least not until he himself had fully absorbed that revelation. Not to give her another reason to feel anxious, he told himself to justify his silence, but, never having hidden anything from her before, he felt embarrassed and was unusually taciturn all evening.

Petra had made tagliatelle with fresh, fragrant truffles, rabbit stewed in a tomato, wine and herb sauce, and a light, tasty strudel which she had adapted from a recipe of her mother's to make it more delicate. Neither the food nor the excellent Rosso di Montalcino helped, though, to lighten his mood. Petra put it down to problems at work, and she knew he never liked to involve her in such things. But this added to her conviction that his work was a prison sentence from which she had to help him escape as soon as possible.

Only after dinner, during which they exchanged such a limited number of words they could have written a haiku with them, did she feel justified in returning to a subject she was determined to pursue, gently but stubbornly.

'I was at the bookshop, Massimo says hello. I told him you're very busy but that you'll drop by as soon as possible. Did you know he's thinking of getting a manager in to run the shop and retiring?'

They were sitting in the armchairs, she with her coffee and he with a glass of grappa and the inevitable cigar.

'Can you imagine that? He could never do without his books!'

'More than he could before. He says books aren't what they used to be. Then he laughs and says neither are tomatoes, fruit, or fish. Or human beings, who are all barbarians now. Then he turns serious again and complains that everything's going to pot, it's time to let others get on with it. We've given all we can, he says, why don't we retire and enjoy what little time we have left to us? That's what he says, and it's also what I think.'

'I know,' he replied, but it was obvious that he was lost in thought and had stopped listening to what she was saying.

Petra sighed and went to bed to read one of the German

novels, not yet published in Italy, which she always stocked up on whenever they went to visit her parents.

Alone now, Ferrara took out the diary.

August 11

I went to see them in Marina di Pietrasanta. I like his wife, but why her? It's true, she's down to earth and probably gives him the solidity he needs. But when we're together it's as if she fades away, perhaps because he and I are united by interests that have nothing to do with her. BUT IS IT ONLY THAT? Every time I see him, even after a fight – or especially after a fight (like the one we had about Freemasonry, which I hope turns out to be a false lead because it could be very dangerous for him, and he's so reckless and indiscreet) – I feel that the understanding between us is so . . . intense? Oh God, I hate going all soppy!

He seems tense, he's lost a lot of weight lately. He's very worried about that friend of his, the bookseller, who he swears is innocent. How stubborn you are, Michele! Even when it comes to friendship. In that way you're the quintessence of the true Sicilian – not like the ones with their omertà and their exaggerated sense of honour but the ones with a deep feeling for friendship. A sacred feeling – and that's another thing I respect you for.

But that Massimo of yours is in real trouble and unfortunately I can't do anything to help him. I've promised, though, to unblock the request to see the victim's medical records, and I'll do it tomorrow, come what may.

He's a devil, that man: he looks at me with those hazel-green cat's eyes and gives me the impression he's

playing with me like a cat (it really suits him, that
nickname!) with a mouse . . . and the trouble is I like
playing the part of the mouse when he's the cat. If I can't
have anything else, I at least have that. A meagre
consolation! If only . . .

He closed the diary abruptly, then closed his eyes, too, and let his cigar die in the ashtray. He was angry and afraid at the same time.

Had he really been so blind as not to see what others were perfectly well aware of?

He suddenly recalled what Erminia Cosenza had said to him, with an amused look in her eyes: *If I were a man I wouldn't dare to pass judgement on what a woman fantasises about* – she had been talking specifically about Anna! – *it's an area where you men are a bit out of your depth,* especially you, Chief Superintendent! Or had he preferred not to see? And if that was so, had he taken advantage of it in some way? He wouldn't continue looking for the answer in that diary. Doing that felt like desecrating secrets which Anna had now carried with her to the grave. It was better that they stay there. The only way to know was to examine his own feelings. What had he felt for her? How sorry had he been when he had heard about her death?

He agonised for a long time, unable to come up with an answer. The further he dug, the dizzier he felt. A strange weakness took possession of him.

When at last he opened his eyes he realised that they were moist.

Petra had turned the light off in the bedroom. He thought of her with a mixture of tenderness and disquiet. She was the woman he loved, he was certain of that. What he wasn't completely certain of right now was whether you could love only one woman.

15

In an apartment in Prato, Captain Somenti was telling Giulia that he had to return to Rome. She responded, not – as he had briefly, stupidly hoped after she invited him to dinner – with the kind of compliant submission that would lead to a night of love and reconciliation, but by wishing him, in a slightly sarcastic and not very friendly tone, a brilliant career.

It was a suitable conclusion to a dinner that had been almost as silent as the Ferraras'. Throughout the meal, Somenti had been unable to get certain images out of his head: the ones he had found in the photograph album on the coffee table, which he had furtively leafed through while Giulia was in the kitchen getting ready and she had told him to 'make yourself at home'. As luck would have it, the pages he stumbled across showed the unmistakable beauty of the Valley of the Temples in Agrigento, mostly as background to her equally unmistakable beauty. Unfortunately, she was not alone in those photographs. With her, in poses which left no room for doubt, was a fair-haired young man, tall, cheerful and, he had to admit, decidedly handsome – almost certainly a bastard.

He tried to tell himself the affair was over. She had said so herself. But it was useless: the images haunted him for the rest of the evening, and he had to make an effort not to let his jealousy show, even though it was eating him up inside. When she wished him a brilliant career, he was certain she had lied to him, and it wasn't over at all, far from it. On his way out, he wondered if his career was really worth it after all.

'Salvatore Laprua's sons were killed last night. I just had a call from Trapani.'

Ferrara had just finished the coffee Fanti had made for him as he did every morning when Rizzo had come running into his office, breathless.

'Shit!' Ferrara said. 'How did it happen?'

'Apparently, three men armed with shotguns burst into the Laprua house in Bellomonte di Mezzo and opened fire on the people in the living room. They mowed down the boss's three sons and the wives of two of them. The third wife only escaped because she was upstairs at the time.'

'Is she the one who talked?'

'Yes, when she'd finished lashing out like a madwoman against everyone and everything. But hers is the only testimony they have about what happened. As usual, no one else saw a thing.'

Yes, as usual. Apart from the woman, who had been directly affected and only saved by chance, no one in Bellomote di Mezzo would talk. There would be a chill over the place for ages. The massacre would be long remembered, and so would the truth which almost everyone knew but would keep to themselves, on pain of death.

'So, farewell forever to the *pax mafiosa*. They were probably the same people who poisoned Zì Turi and almost certainly the same people who killed Anna Giulietti and planted the bomb in the Piazza del Cestello.'

'Of course. To avoid retaliation. You told me the widow knows, so it's likely she told her sons and they were getting ready to take revenge, don't you think?'

'Yes. A pity she'll never talk. Unless, now that they've killed her whole family . . . It may be worth another try, but not straightaway.'

Rizzo looked at his watch. 'I have to go, chief. I have an appointment with Don Santo.'

'Go, on then. In the meantime I'll try and find out more about this business, and I also want to talk to Alibrandi to see if there are any new developments on the Giulietti killing.'

But he did not get the chance to do either of these things: no sooner had Rizzo left the office than Fanti came in, looking agitated.

'What's up, Fanti?'

'This just arrived from Police Headquarters in Agrigento.' He handed him a fax, which he read immediately.

With reference to the request concerning Jan van Gorcum, born in Amsterdam March 10, 1975, we wish to inform you that the aforementioned was found dead this morning at dawn in the countryside near Canicatti. He had been strangled and his body had been put in a rubbish sack alongside another containing a second body, that of a young man identified as Marco Laprua, born in Bellomonte di Mezzo June 15, 1974, also killed by strangulation. Marco Laprua was the grandson of the well-known Mafia boss Salvatore Laprua, known as Zi Turi. On specific instructions from the local Prosecutor's Department, which has been informed of your interest in this individual, we ask you to supply a detailed explanation of the reasons for your request for information and in particular to inform us whether Jan

van Gorcum is implicated in one of your investigations
and if so in what capacity.

'Get me Venturi, Ascalchi and Sergi.'

'Right away, chief.'

When the three men arrived, Ferrara showed them the fax without any comment.

'What do we do?' Gianni Ascalchi asked.

'As far as the explanation requested by the Prosecutor's Department in Agrigento is concerned, I'll talk to Deputy Prosecutor Cosenza: that's a judicial matter and they can sort it out between themselves. But we need answers right now, we can't wait for the bureaucrats. I want one of you to take the first flight to Sicily and make direct contact with the head of the *Squadra Mobile* in Agrigento.'

Sergi and Ascalchi exchanged glances. Then Sergi asked Ascalchi, 'Do you want to go?'

'Sure, no problem. I've started to like being an accidental tourist, like William Hurt. I'll catch the first plane I can find.'

'Good,' Ferrara said approvingly. 'I'll phone Agrigento. By the way, there's been another development.'

They all looked at him.

'They also killed Laprua's sons.'

Silence fell like a stone curtain. The smile on Ascalchi's lips froze.

16

Scandicci had expanded so much that it was now less a municipality in its own right than a kind of satellite town of Florence. Apart from the prison, it also housed the church where Don Santo, the prison chaplain, was the parish priest.

Rizzo had preferred to meet him outside the prison.

He parked his Alfa Romeo 156 in front of the church, got out, walked round to the side street where the priest's lodgings were, and rang the doorbell. After a few moments, the door was opened by a short but quite well-built old woman with a lined face, dressed all in black. He took his badge from the inside pocket of his jacket and showed it to her.

'Good morning, signora,' he said. 'I'm Superintendent Rizzo.'

The woman looked at him with her dark little eyes. She seemed put out, but did not move and did not speak.

'I'm looking for Don Santo,' he went on. 'I'd like to talk to him. Don't worry, it's nothing serious.'

The woman's face did not relax. To her, prisoners and policemen both meant the same thing: trouble. And trouble was something Don Santo seemed to go looking for.

'I'll go and fetch him,' she said at last, reluctantly, in a voice that was strangely hoarse and shrill at the same time, and stepped aside to let him into a long, narrow corridor. At that moment, an elderly man appeared at the other end.

'What is it, Betta?' he asked.

He was tall, thin and distinguished-looking, with white hair and a dark complexion.

'This man is a police superintendent from Florence. He wants to talk to you.'

'Let him come in,' Don Santo said, coming towards him with his hand held out.

'I already have!' the housekeeper muttered shrilly, and walked away.

Rizzo had the impression that Don Santo was not surprised to see him. He followed him into the study, where he sat down on a wooden chair while the chaplain collapsed into a time-worn old leather armchair behind a small walnut desk on which stood a statuette of the Madonna and an old silver candlestick with three candles.

'So, Superintendent, to what do I owe the honour?'

'This'll only take a few minutes.'

'Oh, don't worry about that. It's not every day I get a visit from a senior police officer.'

Rizzo gave a slight smile. 'How long have you been the prison chaplain?' he asked.

'Practically forever, Superintendent.'

'Meaning what?'

'Let me explain. When they opened Sollicciano in 1981, the bishop asked me to be the official chaplain, but before that, ever since the fifties, I'd been the chaplain in the old prisons, Murate and Santa Teresa. But why did you ask me that?'

'I just wanted to know how much experience you have of prisoners.'

The old priest smiled.

'Basically I'm trying to understand how things work in prison,' Rizzo added.

'I'd have thought you knew that. But what it is this, just personal curiosity on your part?'

Rizzo had realised by now that the man was no innocent, and that he needed to be straight with him. 'No, I'm investigating the death of Salvatore Laprua.'

'I see, Superintendent,' Don Santo said, unperturbed.

'You knew him, I think?'

'Of course. I know all the prisoners.'

'When did you see him last?'

'On Sunday. The day before he was found dead.'

'Where?'

'In his cell.'

'Why was that? Didn't he go to mass?'

'Yes, but in the morning. I went to see him later, in the evening.'

'Why?'

'He'd seemed quite down in the morning, and wouldn't say why. So that evening, before I left, I went to his cell to say goodnight and see if I could give him any moral support.'

'And how did you find him?'

'The door was closed.'

The puzzled expression on the Superintendent's face did not escape the priest.

'Superintendent, according to the regulations the cell doors are supposed to stay closed at night, but the prisoners often ask to keep them open so they can talk to each other and get some air.'

'Obviously, he preferred to be alone.'

'I suppose so. Anyway, I was about to go when I thought I could hear a very, very faint moaning. So I opened the spyhole and looked in. He looked back at me and I had the impression he'd just been crying. He made a sign for me to come in.'

'Was he sick?'

'Physically? I doubt it. He was eating a chocolate. But he was depressed, even more depressed than he'd been in the morning.'

'Did he tell you why?'

'He told me that he missed his wife and sons, and that he felt as though he were in a cage and couldn't get used to it. He thought he was finished, and not even the word of the Lord could console him.'

'Did he ever talk to you about his past?'

'Listen, Superintendent, this is the way I handle things in prison: I never want to know anything about what the prisoners have done. Their past doesn't interest me at all, it really doesn't matter, it's dead and buried. And even when they want to talk to me about it, I say, "Look, I'm bored by all that, so don't tell me." It makes my job easier. How could I talk to a man if I knew he had killed other human beings or that he had raped women or, worse still, children? You see what I mean?'

Rizzo nodded.

'So, on principle, I prefer not to know anything. I even try to forget what I've learned from the press or in the secrecy of the confessional. I ask the Lord to help me forget it because it's my job to be a brother to everyone. You do understand?'

'Yes, I do, Don Santo. Was Salvatore Laprua very religious?'

'Very. He had a strong faith, at least from what he told me in the course of our brief conversations, and he seemed sincere. He certainly knew his Bible.'

'And in confession, did he ever reveal anything that might be of int—'

The priest stopped him with a gesture of the hand. 'I don't think I can tell you anything I may have learned, Superintendent. Not that I ever did learn anything. He never took communion, oddly enough. He said that he was no longer worthy, that the sins he had committed and those he would still commit made divine forgiveness impossible. I tried to convince him that none of us can know God's will, but he was adamant.'

Thinking of the crimes Laprua had on his conscience, Rizzo was more than ready to agree with him. But he didn't say that to the priest.

Instead, with a slightly frivolous smile, almost as if he wanted to lighten the tone the conversation had assumed, he said, 'Did you try any of those chocolates, too?' It was actually a question he had been wanting to ask for a while now, his curiosity aroused by the priest's mention of chocolates – this was, after all, a case of poisoning.

'No, he offered me a sweet instead.'

'Don't you like chocolate?'

The priest gave him an amused look. 'I see what you're getting at, but I'd rule out the possibility that he was poisoned with those chocolates. They were a gift from his wife. And besides, I assume you've tested the ones that were left in the box.'

The tests were in fact still in progress, but he could already predict the results. The frustration on Rizzo's face was obvious.

His chief, on the other hand, was at last receiving a positive piece of news. As usual, it was Inspector Venturi who had brought it in.

'After a long silence, Miano's mobile has been in use today. Just once: a call to his wife at home, from somewhere in the Palermo area.'

'What did they talk about?'

'He told her he was fine, but that he was going to be away a while longer, on business, and that she shouldn't worry about him, just take care of the kids.'

'Hmm, God knows what he really meant. It seems clear, though, that he wants to stay in hiding. How long is it since he last used his mobile?'

The inspector glanced at the sheets of paper he had in his hand. 'He phoned van Gorcum's mobile on the morning of the eighth. That makes nine days.'

'And at that time he was in the Florence area. What's he been up to since then? Anyway, the important thing is that we've found him again. Now try not to lose him and inform our colleagues in Palermo.'

'Right, chief.'

17

Ahmed Farah had become almost obsessively cautious, and had given Captain Somenti detailed instructions on how to meet him without being tailed. Somenti thought all this secrecy excessive. After all, they were only supposed to be saying goodbye. But when he saw him on his moped on the other side of the Ponte Vespucci, with his dark glasses and his helmet, pointing in the direction he wanted him to follow, he realised something must be up.

Farah was waiting for him at the next bridge. He made him get up on the saddle behind him, gave him a helmet, and set off again at high speed. After following a tortuous route, he slowed down and finally stopped in a square on the outskirts of the city dominated by a shopping centre. Only when they were inside the centre did he take off his glasses and helmet so that Somenti was able to see again his keen, intense eyes.

'You know something?' the captain said, playfully. 'You're a dangerous driver.'

'And you should know by now that danger is my business.'

'I can tell that from all the trouble you take to say goodbye to a friend.'

'Wrong. This isn't goodbye. We're still working together, aren't we?'

They sat down at a café table. Not far from them, a mother was cutting a slice of pizza into pieces while her little daughter watched her wide-eyed, her chin already dripping with oil, and an old couple were arguing without taking their eyes off their shopping trolley.

The surroundings were sufficiently noisy to protect them from prying ears.

'They're certain now it was the Mafia, Ahmed.'

'The bomb attacks, yes. But the war on terror isn't over, is it? In fact, it's only just begun. And things are hotting up, believe me.'

'Did you get the numbers?'

With a triumphant smile, Farah took a small piece of paper from his pocket and handed it to him. On it were the names Mullah Hamdullah and Adjmal Yousazai followed by the numbers of their mobile phones. The captain pocketed it.

'When are you going back to Rome?'

'I still have two days, plus the weekend. I have to be back on duty on Monday. I was thinking of leaving either Saturday or Sunday, but maybe I'll leave earlier, there's nothing more for me to do here.'

Ahmed assumed that the disappointment he clearly heard in Somenti's voice was due to the outcome of his mission, and his face lit up. 'Better still! That way you can get the phone tap set up immediately. The sooner it's done, the better. You'll see, with what emerges from this, they'll give you a medal. Forget about the Mafia, this is the real thing!'

Somenti smiled bitterly. He couldn't somehow feel the same excitement as Farah, even supposing it was all true and his promotion was all sewn up. He kept thinking about Giulia.

But he said, reassuringly. 'I'll do it straightaway,'

'Please, it's very important!' Ahmed said, briefly struck by doubts about Somenti's determination and fearing that his request would get lost in a mountain of red tape. 'You're the only person who can help me, so don't fail me now, not after everything I've done, all the risks I've taken and am still taking.'

'Don't worry, I'm not irresponsible,' the captain said. 'Or ungrateful,' he added at the last moment.

They separated at the exit. Somenti decided to take a taxi.

18

'First, you have to tell me the reason for your request. I'm in charge of the investigation, but the prosecutor's overseeing it and he wants to know.'

It was three in the afternoon on Thursday October 18. Vincenzo Raccuia, head of the *Squadra Mobile* of Agrigento, had kept Ascalchi waiting and then had received him with a kind of hostile wariness he had not been expecting, especially as Ferrara had phoned ahead to let him know he was coming.

'The prosecutor can get all the information he needs from Deputy Prosecutor Erminia Cosenza,' Ascalchi retorted, having no intention of being put in an inferior position.

'If you want to put it on that level, then let them talk. But I still don't understand why you're here. As if we didn't already have enough on our plates. This isn't the mainland here, this is border country! And if a Mafia war has broken out, as it seems to have done, then anything can happen. I think history has at least taught us that, don't you?'

Ascalchi cleared his throat and began again in a more conciliatory but far from submissive tone, 'I came here to work together with you, not to—'

Raccuia interrupted him before he could even finish the

sentence. 'I know you haven't come to pick a quarrel, and I don't want that either, but I do need an explanation before we can even think of working together.'

Raccuia's tone left Ascalchi no alternative. 'Of course,' he said. 'No problem.'

He told Raccuia about the telephone call to Salvatore Miano's mobile phone and the investigation into Miano in connection with the attack on Ferrara. As he spoke, Raccuia nodded from time to time and made notes on a sheet of A4 paper.

'So the attack on Ferrara had nothing to do with terrorism?' he said in astonishment when Ascalchi had finished.

'No, that's been ruled out.'

'And have you examined Jan van Gorcum's phone records?'

'Not yet, but we've requested them from the phone company and hope to have them as soon as possible.'

'Good. They could be useful to us, too, by helping us to reconstruct van Gorcum's last hours. Now we really can start talking about working together. In fact, we have to work together if that bastard had anything to do with trying to kill your Chief Superintendent!'

Encouraged, Ascalchi went on to tell him about the operation which had led to the arrest of Salvatore Laprua and the more recent investigation into his death in prison.

'Then it's the sons' turn and even the grandson,' Raccuia said, thinking aloud. 'But have you established a direct connection between these things and the killings of Marco Laprua and van Gorcum?'

Ascalchi had to admit that there was no proof as yet, only a tangle of theories. 'No.'

'So, as far as I can see, you're in the shit up there in Florence. You're even worse off than we are, and we're groping in the dark!'

'You've got it about right. Now do you see why I'm here? Maybe if we put our heads together, we can find a way through this mess.'

Raccuia nodded and briefly went over the facts of the deaths. The corpses of the two young men, both strangled with iron wire, had been found in two rubbish bags in the countryside near Canicattì. As for where they had got with their inquiries, it could be summed up in one word: nowhere.

'But what is this, do you think, a gang war?' Ascalchi asked.

'The M.O.s of the murders clearly point to the Mafia. Van Gorcum had no previous convictions, but Marco Laprua, although he also had no previous convictions, was Zì Turi's grandson. Although Zì Turi was living outside Sicily, he may still have been exercising influence. Or else causing trouble, in which case the killing of the sons and the grandson may be a clear signal that the district of Castelvetrano has finally repudiated Zì Turi's family and is now wide open for whoever was responsible for those deaths. That's possible, but there's one thing that doesn't quite fit.'

'What's that?'

'Whoever did it wanted the bodies to be found, which is unusual for a Mafia killing, and even left the victims' papers in plain sight.'

'How did you come to find the bodies?'

'Thanks to an anonymous phone call giving us very precise directions.'

There was a pause.

'And what about this van Gorcum?' Ascalchi asked. 'That's an odd name round here.'

Raccuia explained that Jan van Gorcum was the son of a ceramics merchant named Gioacchino Barberi, who in the past had been suspected of associating with the local Mafia.

'Then they dropped him, because he had a relationship

with a Dutch woman he didn't marry on account of the fact that she already had a husband in Holland.'

'Ah!'

'You know what they say. "Always fish in your own pond." These people really believe in that. They can't have been well pleased with Barberi's affair, or the fact that he had a son and gave him his mother's surname. Not the kind of thing you do in the Mafia.'

'I see.'

'We've questioned Barberi, but he wasn't any help. We immediately put a tap on his phone, but that hasn't told us anything yet either.'

'What next?'

'To be honest, we're at our wits' end. Now I think you can understand why the prosecutor was so keen for me to find out what exactly you wanted.'

'Yes, I can. Did van Gorcum live alone?'

'No, with his father.'

'And what did the father tell you about how his son spent his last days?'

'Nothing much. Only that he did all the things he usually did.'

'Such as?'

'Helping him at work.'

'Where?'

'Barberi has a ceramics shop in the Temple area, mostly selling to tourists.'

'Did you check that he was actually there?'

'We only have the father's statement to go on. There are no assistants and, as I said, the customers are tourists who are here today and gone tomorrow.'

'Will you go with me to see the prosecutor tomorrow morning?' Ascalchi asked.

'Of course. Do you want to speak to the commissioner, too?'

'I can do that later.'

Ascalchi did not particularly want to meet the police commissioner of Agrigento, well known in police circles for being a servile, bootlicking bureaucrat.

'All right,' Raccuia said, understanding the inspector's reluctance. 'In that case, let's meet tomorrow morning. We can see the prosecutor, and then I'll show you the place where the bodies were found.'

'Perfect. Till tomorrow, then.'

As soon as Ascalchi had left the building he phoned Ferrara to bring him up to date.

'Don't worry, Gianni. Erminia Cosenza has told me she'll call the prosecutor in Agrigento. In the meantime, would you do me a favour and send me a photo of the two victims as soon as possible?'

'I'll do it first thing tomorrow.'

'Thanks, Gianni, and if you need anything, just call.'

19

That night, with the moon obscured by heavy clouds, a black Mercedes S500 went off the road on the long stretch between Catellamare and Scopello, on the north-east coast of Sicily, and ended up in the sea.

The alarm was raised by a fisherman who, from his boat out at sea, saw the descending curve of the headlights in the darkness and heard the noise of the car smashing on the rocks before falling into the water. The rescue operation turned out to be long and difficult, because of the darkness and the strong winds, which sent the waves crashing violently against the rocks.

The carcass of the vehicle was finally hoisted by crane in the first light of dawn on to a Coast Guard trawler, which carried it to the port of Trapani. It was there that the police and the Carabinieri, with the help of the fire brigade, managed to extricate the bodies of two men from the wreckage.

Identification was not difficult, because they had their papers, still intact, in their pockets. They were Cosimo Caruso, from Mazara del Vallo, who had been in the driver's seat, and Salvatore Miano, from Castelvetrano.

The *Squadra Mobile* of Trapani immediately informed

General Headquarters, and Ascalchi learned the news from Raccuia as soon as they met that morning. Obviously it meant a change of plan, but Ascalchi was more than happy to tag along with Raccuia.

It was not until he was in the police car heading, with sirens blaring, for Palermo that he had time to call Ferrara. In recounting what had happened, he emphasised a gruesome detail: both men had their hands and feet tied, even Caruso, who had supposedly been at the wheel of the Mercedes.

Rizzo was with Ferrara, and heard him curse and then tell Ascalchi to send him as many photographs as possible of the Mercedes that had been fished out of the sea, especially of what remained of the left side. By the time Ferrara put the receiver down, he had a grim, worried look on his face.

'What happened?' Rizzo asked.

Ferrara told him, and then said, 'But I don't buy this gang war theory.'

'Why not?'

'First of all, because the victims are all from the Castelvetrano district. This doesn't sound like a war to redraw the map of the island and challenge Caputo's supremacy.'

'It could be an internal feud. For control of the district. Miano has been protecting La Torre while he's been on the run, and La Torre is Pippo Catalfano's man, so it's Catalfano they're striking at.'

'If he really is the boss.'

'Of course. But assuming he is, couldn't there be a connection between these murders and the death of Laprua and his sons? Maybe Zì Turi, having concentrated on Tuscany, didn't like the fact that he was becoming less powerful on his home territory. Especially as his sons were still there, and his grandson, who by all accounts was no angel.'

Ferrara looked closely at his deputy, impressed as always

by his clarity of vision. Then he suddenly stood up. 'Come with me!'

He moved so quickly that Rizzo had to make an effort to keep up with him as he raced along the corridor to the stairs.

'Where are we going?' he shouted, breathlessly.

'To see Laprua's widow! Everything revolves around Laprua!'

20

Rina Laprua greeted them as coldly as ever. Her pale face and red, watery eyes bore the marks of the blows that fate had lately been inflicting on her. But Ferrara also saw in those eyes a pride and a toughness that made him wonder for a moment if she might be the real boss of the Laprua family. He realised, once again, that he wouldn't get anything from her.

This awareness made him aggressive, and he had to make an effort to control himself.

'We haven't come only to give you our condolences, signora, even though we'd like you to accept them.'

The woman gave him a scornful look in response. 'What use are they? They won't give me back my husband and sons.'

'They offer comfort.'

'Only if they come from friends.'

'And we're your enemies, is that it?' Ferrara realised that he had raised his voice, but couldn't help it. 'Then let me tell you the other reason we're here. Last time you accused me of being responsible for your husband's death, and I've come back to pay you with the same coin, because you're the cause of your sons' deaths!'

'Don't say that!' the woman screamed. 'Out, get out!'

'No, we're not going until you've told us everything you know. It's because you've kept quiet that your sons have paid with their lives. Isn't that enough for you? Haven't there been too many deaths already?'

'Whatever I know is my business and my husband's. And God's. It has nothing to do with our sons, may they rest in peace. The Mafia killed them and I don't know anything about those things. I never knew anything, that was how Turi wanted it.'

'Then what *do* you know?'

Ferrara had lowered his voice, struck by her tone: the hatred had gone, replaced by genuine despair.

'Nothing,' she said in a whisper.

Rizzo, who was standing some distance from them, had noticed that drop in tension. He took advantage of it to point to a gold box full of chocolates identical to the one found in her husband's cell and asked in a sympathetic voice, 'Are these the same you took your husband?'

Rina Laprua stiffened again. 'What are you talking about? He never ate chocolates!'

'But the prison chaplain told me he did eat them, and that you took them to him.'

'He was wrong,' she said, categorically.

Ferrara made a sign to his deputy not to pursue it. 'If you want us to go, we'll go. We may never meet again, but I promise you one thing: we'll find your husband's killers, because we'll find the people responsible for the deaths of your sons.'

'You're wrong, Chief Superintendent. Find the people who killed my sons, because I want to spit in their faces. But no one killed my husband. No one!'

She said these words looking him straight in the eyes, as if entrusting him with a prayer and a secret confession. And Ferrara understood.

Later, as they were on their way back to Florence from Viareggio – Rizzo was driving because they had left in a hurry and had preferred to do without a driver – Ferrara complimented him.

'You never cease to surprise me, Francesco. You really do have amazing intuition. Petra may be right, I should retire and let you take over. The *Squadra Mobile* would be in good hands.'

'Are you making fun of me, chief?'

'I'd never allow myself to make fun of the man who has almost certainly just solved the Laprua case.'

'It's nice of you to say so, but I still don't understand.'

'Suicide. She said it herself. "No one killed my husband." No one killed him. He killed himself. With the chocolates, as you guessed. There must have been a poisoned one in case things got really bad, and he asked her to bring them to him in a nice gold box. She knew, and like a good Sicilian wife she obeyed. Zì Turi decided to take his life when he realised there was someone out there who was stronger than him, someone who'd even try to kill the head of the *Squadra Mobile* with a bomb in the centre of Florence. Remember what he said to his lawyer? "It's over." And there's something else, something you told me: he didn't offer the priest any chocolates, only sweets. He didn't want him to take the fatal one by mistake. He was keeping that for himself.'

'And he told the priest he didn't deserve to go to heaven,' Rizzo said, 'because of the sins he had committed, and the sins he would still commit. At the time, it didn't strike me, but now it all makes sense. Suicides can't go to heaven, and he was planning to kill himself that very night. But we don't have a shred of evidence, or else Erminia Cosenza could charge the widow, wrap up the investigation, and leave the two prison officers in peace.'

'As you say, there's not a shred of evidence. And we have plenty of other things to do than try searching for it. I think the widow's already paid a high enough price, don't you? The case of the officers will go cold by itself, don't worry.'

Rizzo left him outside his building. It was almost lunchtime and Ferrara, who ever since the day he had read Anna Giulietti's diary had felt the need to spend time with his wife, almost as if he owed her something, had assumed the unusual habit of going home for a light lunch every day.

Petra was waiting for him with a mozzarella, tomato and basil salad and a bottle of German beer, and the weather was mild enough to let them eat under the arbour on the terrace.

Even though Ferrara was still worried by the case, he seemed to have got over the bad mood he had been in at the beginning of the week. Trying to keep things as light as possible, he told her about his encounter with Laprua's widow: a small success – even if no one would ever know of it – which gave him grounds to be a bit more optimistic.

'I'm pleased,' Petra said. 'The sooner you solve this case, the better. And I hope it's the last one.'

'Come on, Petra, don't let's start that again. I'm still young, it's not time to retire yet.'

'I'm sorry to say this, Michele, but it isn't true that you're still young. Neither of us is young any more. And this is a country that needs young people. Think about it, and step aside.'

'I'll think about it.'

'So will I,' she said, knowing that she would be the only one to do so. It was a veiled threat, but Ferrara didn't know that.

Leaving home, he walked to the Prosecutor's Department, where he brought Erminia Cosenza up to date, and from there, still on foot, returned to Headquarters.

By now it was almost five, and he found Captain Somenti waiting for him. His first reaction was that this visit was a bit of a nuisance, but then he remembered that he had given the captain an open invitation, and that he was leaving soon. It would be extremely impolite to send him away, so he led him into his office and told Fanti that he did not want to be disturbed, unless there was a call from Sicily.

'I'm leaving, Chief Superintendent, but I really wanted to see you again before I went. I've always admired your work, and when I was on my way here I even hoped we'd be able to work together in some way. It would have been a great pleasure – more than a pleasure, an honour.'

'You don't seem happy to be going back to work,' Ferrara observed, studying him closely.

'Am I that transparent?' Somenti said, ironically. 'That's good for a spy!'

'Your friend Ahmed Farah noticed it, too. But he seems to be counting on your help. I hope you don't disappoint him, he's a good man.'

'Don't worry. I made a promise to him and I'll keep it. Anyway, it's my job.'

'Come on. Is it as bad as that?'

'I didn't think so, but yes, it is. It's as if these weeks in Florence have opened my eyes. It really meant a lot to me, being in Intelligence, you know? But it's not the way I thought it was going to be. I get the feeling people lose sight of why they're doing what they're doing. It's all political.'

'If that's the way you feel, I get the impression Major Alibrandi would gladly welcome you back into the Carabinieri.'

'Who knows? We'll see.'

At that moment Fanti came in.

'There haven't been any calls, chief, but these have been sent from Agrigento.' He placed a folder of eight-by-ten photographs on the desk.

They were the photographs of the Mercedes, taken on the dock at the port of Trapani. Ferrara spread them over the desk, searching for those that best showed the side of the car. The fall had crushed the bonnet and the roof, and dented the rest, but the shape of the vehicle was still quite recognisable. Bending over them for a closer look, he sifted through them, and a smile of satisfaction came to his face when he found two photographs on which two long, uneven scratches were still partly visible.

As if someone had drawn a key along it out of spite, Alibrandi had said.

'The major will be pleased!' he cried triumphantly.

But Somenti looked as if he had been turned to stone.

Ferrara realised that he was staring at the photos of Jan van Gorcum and Marco Laprua, which Ascalchi had included with the shots of the car, as Ferrara had requested. One of the men was blond, obviously the Dutchman, the other dark-haired and smiling widely at the camera, revealing the gaps where his incisors should have been.

'Do you know them?'

Somenti shook his head, his eyes still glued to the pictures. 'Who is that?' he asked at last.

'Jan van Gorcum, suspected of having taken part in the attacks here in Florence. He's from Agrigento, despite his name. At least he was. He's dead now, murdered together with this other one, who's the grandson of the Mafia boss Salvatore Laprua.'

Somenti closed his eyes and furrowed his brow.

He seemed to be in the grip of conflicting thoughts, but the expression which gradually appeared on his face was one of fear.

When he finally opened his eyes again and stood up, as pale as a ghost and clearly upset, he gave Ferrara an urgent, almost imploring look.

'I beg you, Chief Superintendent, come with me! There isn't a minute to lose!'

21

Giulia Roversi had only just got home and was about to take a shower when the doorbell rang.

She quickly put her tracksuit back on and went to open the door, thinking it was a friend. She was surprised to see Carlo, who she thought had already left, accompanied by a man of about fifty with quite long salt-and-pepper hair and rather feline hazel-green eyes.

'Carlo! What are you doing here?'

'Can we come in? This is Chief Superintendent Ferrara, head of the *Squadra Mobile* in Florence.'

'Yes, of course,' she said, puzzled and slightly scared. 'Has something happened?'

'No, don't worry. We just need to ask you a few questions. I'd have preferred not to bother you, Giulia, but this is quite important.'

'Please sit down.'

They sat down on armchairs around a coffee table. The photograph album still lay on it.

'Can I offer you anything? Coffee?'

'No, thank you,' Ferrara said. 'We don't have much time.'

'Fire away.'

'When did you first meet Jan van Gorcum?' he asked.

'I'm sorry?'

'We'd like to know when you first met Jan van Gorcum,' Ferrara repeated patiently.

Giulia looked at Somenti, bewildered. 'I don't understand. I don't know anyone of that name. What is this about?'

'Answer the questions please, Giulia,' the captain said.

'What is this? An interrogation?'

Somenti lowered his eyes and said nothing.

'That depends on you,' Ferrara said. 'On your answers. Are you sure you don't know him?'

'Of course I'm sure!' she burst out, indignation beginning to replace fear. 'What do you take me for? What are you thinking of?'

'I'm sorry, Giulia,' Somenti said. 'I shouldn't have looked in your photo album. I only did it to pass the time while you were in the kitchen. I wasn't trying to spy on you.'

'What are you talking about? Are you out of your mind? Spy on what? I don't have anything to hide.'

'May I?' Somenti said, picking up the album.

'Go ahead. I don't know what it is you want.'

'This,' he said, turning to the photos from Agrigento and pointing at the ones showing her embracing the fair-haired young man.

Indignation gave way to anger. How dare he? What was this all about? Jealousy? And the bastard had even brought a policeman with him! The whole thing struck her as ridiculous and unreal.

'That's my business! It has nothing to do with you, don't you understand?'

'Unfortunately, it's our business, too,' Ferrara cut in.

'Those are holiday photos. Why should the police be interested in Gianni and me?'

For a moment, Ferrara hesitated. Of course the young man did bear a very strong resemblance to the one on the photo sent by Ascalchi, but what if Somenti had got it wrong? The fear that he might be making a big mistake made him adopt a more conciliatory tone.

'Did you say his name's Gianni?'

'Yes. He's someone I met in Sicily. I was there on holiday, visiting my aunt.'

'Where exactly?'

'Agrigento. That's where my aunt lives.'

There was no doubt about it now. 'When did you meet him?'

'Last summer.'

'And his name is definitely Gianni?'

'Yes, of course.'

Ferrara and Somenti exchanged glances.

'Signorina,' Ferrara said, 'this man's name isn't Gianni, it's Jan van Gorcum.'

'That's not possible.'

'I'm afraid it is.'

A sudden silence fell. The young woman sat there dazed, her head bowed, her legs staring to move nervously.

'You mean he gave me a false name?' she said at last. 'But why? What has he done?'

'Just tell us how you met him and if you saw him again after that time in Sicily.'

'I'm sorry, none of this makes any sense. I'm not used to this kind of thing. I'm starting to feel scared.' Her voice had become choked. 'Carlo, help me!'

She burst into tears. They were real tears, not forced ones. She ran into the kitchen, and returned almost immediately, dabbing her eyes with a paper handkerchief.

'Calm down, there's nothing to be afraid of,' the captain

said, going to her and putting his arm round her shoulders. 'I'm here to help you. All you have to do is tell us what you know. Don't worry, the chief superintendent is a friend, you have nothing to fear.'

She put her head on his shoulder, the way she used to.

Ferrara was starting to believe her, but Somenti's confidence seemed excessive and premature.

'Tell us everything you know about him.'

Giulia Roversi freed herself from Somenti's embrace, a little embarrassed, and dried her tears. Then she began telling her story.

She told them that Gianni – she continued to call him that and Ferrara made no attempt to correct her – had been introduced to her by her aunt in a shop that sold ceramics, in the Valley of the Temples.

'Souvenirs of the place, drawings of Sicily, Sicilian carts, the Temples, lemons, you know the kind of thing.'

'Yes, I do. What happened then?'

The girl hesitated, embarrassed. Before continuing, she glanced at Somenti, who gave her a silent look of encouragement, even though he sensed that he wouldn't like what he was about to hear.

'One evening, Gianni and I went to a hotel,' she confessed, with her head bowed.

'Where?'

'In Cefalù, near Palermo. Gianni had invited me to visit the town, and then we stopped at a hotel by the sea.'

'What's it called?'

'I can't remember, but I must have a leaflet somewhere. I can look for it, if you like.'

'Later, perhaps, thank you.'

Anything that concerned van Gorcum might be of interest, and anyway it would be useful to check the girl's story.

'Did you spend the night there?'

She gave the captain another glance before again lowering her eyes. True, it was her business, not his, but she didn't like him to know.

'Yes. I phoned my aunt and told her it was late and I was staying overnight in Palermo.'

'I see. Go on.'

'The next day we went back to Agrigento. We continued seeing each other until I came back to Prato.'

'When exactly were you in Sicily?'

'In July, for two weeks.'

There was a pause, during which Ferrara considered his next question.

'Did you ever see Jan van Gorcum again after that, either here in Prato or in Florence?'

'Yes.'

'When?'

'Please, believe me, it's all over, we've broken up. I already told you, Carlo, didn't I? Why are you torturing me? What have I done?'

'You haven't done anything, Giulia. Unfortunately, Jan van Gorcum has.'

'Why? What has *he* done? Who is he?'

'All in good time. Don't be afraid. Please, just answer the questions.'

Giulia lowered her head again. She continued to squeeze the paper handkerchief in her right hand until it was a little ball.

'Yes, I saw him again, here in Prato. We saw each other for a while, up until a few weeks ago, when we quarrelled. Then I didn't see him again, or even talk to him on the phone. I didn't try to contact him, and he didn't try to contact me. To me, it was a clean break, I realised I was never really all that interested in him. It was just a summer fling. Women have them, too, you know, not just men. But he wasn't a bad guy. Why are you looking for him?'

'We *were* looking for him, but not any more. We found him, only he's dead. He was murdered, in Sicily.'

'Oh, my God, no!' she moaned, and started crying again. 'No, no, no.'

'He was involved with the Mafia, and was probably implicated in the Florence bombings. So anything you can tell us about him could be a great help to us, do you understand?'

Giulia looked at Carlo with scared, watery eyes. Then she turned to Ferrara.

'Chief Superintendent, Gianni – or Jan, or whatever – told me he was serious about me. I liked him but I wasn't in love with him. He turned up again in September, saying he wanted to be near me and had rented a house just outside Prato, where he was going to live while he studied at university in Pisa. At the time, I thought it was possible I might grow to love him, as sometimes happens when two people see a lot of each other and get to know each other better, so I agreed to see him again.'

'So he was registered at the university?' Ferrara said.

'He had been for a few months. He wanted to be an engineer instead of taking over his father's business in Agrigento.'

'I see. And did you ever go to the house he'd rented?'

'Yes, a few times, soon after Gianni moved in. I helped him to clean it up, and on one occasion – the last time, in fact – my sister-in-law came and gave us a hand.'

'Where is it?'

Giulia Roversi did not reply.

'Don't be afraid, you can tell me.'

'How can I not be afraid? You've just told me I was with a

dangerous Mafioso, someone involved in the bombings in Florence. And what if the people who were with him came after me?'

'But you didn't have anything to do with any of that,' Somenti said reassuringly.

'No, but I'm talking to you, I'm telling you everything. What about the people who know the kinds of things Gianni may have told me?'

Somenti had feared the same thing, which was why he had rushed here. And the fear had not gone.

'If it makes you feel any easier,' he said, 'why not come to Rome for a while?'

She did not say either yes or no, which he took to be a good sign.

'That might be a good idea,' Ferrara said. 'But first it's very important that you tell us where the house is.'

Giulia carefully weighed up the alternatives and finally decided to cooperate fully.

'It's a few miles north of here, in the country.'

'How did he find it?'

'From what he told me, through an estate agency that put an advertisement in a newspaper.'

'Could you tell me how to get there?'

'It isn't easy, I'd have to go with you, but I wouldn't like to be noticed.'

'Don't worry, we'll be as careful as we can. One last question. Why did you quarrel?'

'Because lately he hadn't wanted me to come to the house. I got the impression he had another woman.'

'I don't think he had another woman,' Ferrara said. 'But I do think he had something to hide.'

'I thought it was a woman, although he swore to me over and over that it wasn't. But I didn't believe him, so we quarrelled.

That was when I realised that I didn't really care all that much for him.'

'All right, shall we go?'

'Just let me get changed.'

She came back after a while, wearing a pair of jeans, a pink blouse and a blue sweater. In her hand, she had a leaflet, which she handed to Ferrara.

'The hotel in Cefalù,' she said, although it was obvious.

Threading their way through a labyrinth of streets, they left Prato and set off in a north-westerly direction along a provincial route lined by industrial plants and warehouses. After about four miles, they turned off it on to a side road which led to a less built-up area, and then on to another which after a while began to narrow and climb.

The Alfa Romeo 156 advanced slowly, following Giulia Roversi's directions. She had chosen to sit in the back while Captain Somenti occupied the seat next to Ferrara. She was leaning forward, with her head held low between the two front seats, as if trying to be as inconspicuous as possible. When they came to a fork in the road, Ferrara stopped the car.

A lopsided sign read *Welcome to Vernio*.

'We're nearly there,' she said. 'You have to carry straight on for another few minutes and then you'll see a dirt road on the right. That road climbs a bit and leads to the house.'

They set off again. At the same speed as before.

Ferrara easily identified the dirt road, drove up it, and after not much more than a hundred yards, they reached the house.

Giulia sat up. 'This is it!' she said, pointing. Not that there was any need. There were no other houses nearby, or at least none so close as to be confused with it. Unfortunately, that meant there would be little hope of getting anything useful out of the neighbours.

It was a white two-storey building from the 1950s, with a brown metal door and window frames. An iron gate and a little garden separated it from the road. It looked deserted.

Ferrara noted down the precise location so that they could find the house again, then did a three-point turn and set off back to Prato. By now, it was dark.

Driving back to Florence – alone, because Somenti had preferred to stay and take care of Giulia – he thought again about what he had not had time to say to Rizzo that morning, the other part of his reasoning about the supposed 'gang war'. Giulia Roversi's testimony reinforced the hypothesis that van Gorcum had been involved in the attacks, and it was very likely they would soon discover that Marco Laprua had been, too, as had Caruso, the 'driver' of the Mercedes S500, and Miano. They had all been thrown up as suspects in the course of the investigation, and they had all been silenced forever. Was it just a coincidence that they were also the only suspects on whom they had collected any substantial evidence?

What was certain was that their few leads had been practically wiped out. Someone had decided on a scorched earth policy.

Only one person was missing from the roll call: Gino La Torre, who had been on the run for a long time, and still seemed as elusive as ever.

22

Gino La Torre was looking in wonder at the huge blanket of concrete on the slope of the hill. It was like a shroud laid out to dry by the light of a dazzling moon, crisscrossed by lines that a famous artist whose name he could not remember had etched in it like wounds destined never to heal.

He was standing with Antonio Caputo on what remained of the last floor of a reinforced concrete skeleton amid the ominous ruins of the town of Gibellina, destroyed in the earthquake of 1968. The other men were scattered all around in strategic positions. They were all looking westwards along State Highway 119, waiting for the cars to arrive from Santa Ninfa.

When the first headlights appeared in the distance, a prolonged whistle echoed from hill to hill and the men got their weapons ready.

'Let's go down,' Caputo said, cautiously descending the staircase, which had remained miraculously intact. La Torre followed him, clutching his Beretta. Three of the foot soldiers were waiting on the ground floor. They surrounded Caputo, while La Torre took up position behind a pillar, protected by the darkness: he had no desire to be seen by the newcomers.

The two Mercedes parked side by side on the open space in front of the remains of the building, raising dust and rubble as they did so. Two bodyguards got out of one of the cars, and Pippo Catalfano stepped out of the other, with two more bodyguards.

'Good day to you, Don Nino,' Catalfano said as he walked in, followed at a distance by his men. He was trying to appear calm, to show that he had confidence in Caputo's benign intentions, even though he knew full well that he was totally in his hands: his bodyguards would be no match for Caputo's army.

'Good day, Pippo.'

'You know why I asked to see you,' Catalfano began without any preamble. 'You have to do something. I've lost seven men, seven of my best men. And Gino's disappeared, they may have killed him, too. You have to find out who's been doing this.'

While both groups of men stood without moving, some distance from each other, the two bosses had sat down together, using the stumps of pillars as makeshift seats.

'Why?'

'Because they were your men, too,' Catalfano replied, surprised by the question. 'Someone wants war, Don Nino, but we don't, any more than you do.'

'I know that. What I'm asking is: why me and not you? Aren't you capable of finding out who did this for yourself?'

Pippo was startled. This was not the kind of reply you'd expect from a boss of bosses, and it could only mean one thing: that he wanted to get rid of him. For the first time since he had arrived, he felt his confidence go, to be replaced by fear, a real, primal fear such as he had never known.

'No, no, you don't understand,' he stammered.

Caputo's eyes gleamed with an amused light in the half-darkness. 'Or do you need help from the Lion?'

The fear turned to panic.

'Don't joke, Don Nino, what's the Lion got to do with this?' Catalfano replied after a long pause, when he finally found the courage to speak.

'So you know who he is?'

'Of course! He belongs to Zì Turi, God rest his soul.'

'And now you want to take Turi's place, is that it?'

'Why should we want to do that?' he said, innocently and at the same time imploringly. 'That's all on the mainland, it's none of our business. Didn't you always support him yourself?'

'But the men who did those stupid things in Florence, that was you who told them to, wasn't it?'

It was like a blow to the stomach. Giuseppe Catalfano had no idea who could have given him away. But what he did know, what he knew now for sure, was who had killed those seven men, seven of his best men. Of all those who had taken part in the bombings, he had only managed to save two, sending Caruso's son Sandro to Germany and Leonardo Parisi to the United States. But they were fringe figures, not part of the inner circle.

He looked around, desperately, as if hoping for help from his bodyguards. But they were now fraternising with Caputo's men, who carried rifles and submachine guns.

'I wanted revenge for Zì Turi's arrest,' he said, trying to defend himself. 'His sons and grandson asked me. After all, he was one of us, even though he'd gone away. And as it was going to happen outside our territory, I didn't think—'

'That Antonio Caputo had to know?' His eyes were no longer laughing.

The silence that followed was even more like a shroud than Burri's concrete sheet.

Pippo Catalfano found himself mentally reciting a prayer as he awaited the verdict.

'You made a mistake. Antonio Caputo has to know every-thing. Always. Everything, do you understand?'

By Mafia law, a boss who makes a mistake pays with his life. Pippo knew that perfectly well.

'I'm ready,' he murmured, bowing his head as a mark of submission.

Caputo waited. 'You made a mistake, but I still need you,' he said at last. 'But be careful, you can't make another mis-take.'

'I won't make another mistake, Don Nino, I swear!' Pippo cried, almost in tears, and fell to his knees at Caputo's feet, heedless of the stones that dug into his flesh through the trousers, unable to believe such unexpected clemency.

'You must let the Lion know that we want to speak to him. As a friend.'

Even though it meant he would have to somehow get him to come to Sicily, the request seemed such a small thing that Catalfano almost burst out laughing.

When he finally got back to his car and the little procession set off again, Gino La Torre emerged from the shadows.

'You were too good to him.'

'The man's an idiot, that's all.'

'Finding the Lion was my job, I could have got him here.'

'You did well, the traitors won't betray again. But the Lion's another matter. The Basilisk says we should be careful, we need to sit down and talk. And he has to come here in peace, not in war. One of his men will bring him here. I don't know what the fucking advantage is of him coming here, but I trust the Basilisk.'

'Who *is* the Basilisk?'

He would have liked to tell him that it was none of his business, just as it was no one else's business in Sicily. It was his, Caputo's, business, and his alone. But he was tired, and he liked Gino La Torre a lot, the man had made the right choice, and had acted for him with speed and efficiency. That night, looking him in the eyes, he realised that he had finally found someone to take Catalfano's place. Catalfano's heir in waiting. And maybe his heir, too, when the time came: he could easily see him in charge of everyone.

'He protects us in Rome. I put him there. I've known him since he was born, even though his mother gave birth to him a long way away. Her husband was a cop. He died young, murdered, and I took care of the woman, gave her money, helped her to bring up her son. In a way, he was like my son, too. He didn't want for anything. School, university. I wanted him to be part of the State, to be at the top of the State. And he always took his holidays here, to learn the rules.'

'Why "Basilisk"?'

Don Nino shook his head irritably. 'Too many questions. What I've told you should be enough for you, until I decide otherwise.'

23

The next day, Saturday, the first thing Ferrara did was to give Inspector Venturi the task of tracing the name of the owner of the house rented by van Gorcum, and the second was to send the Prosecutor's Department an urgent request for a search warrant. Then he phoned Ascalchi. There were no developments in Agrigento – not that Ferrara expected any. He ordered Ascalchi to come back on Monday morning, which would at least give him a little time to enjoy the beauties of the place.

Just after ten, he had a phone call from Erminia Cosenza, asking him to join her for the interview with Antonio Vita, who was now also being investigated for aiding and abetting.

'He suddenly showed up this morning with his lawyer, who presented a deposition and declared that his client is ready to make a statement of his own free will.'

'Interesting,' Ferrara said.

The presentation of a deposition detailing the elements which, in his opinion, should clear him of the accusation was a privilege the law allowed an accused person. He also had the right to make a statement of his own free will, and the Prosecutor could do nothing but record the facts he presented in his defence without asking any questions.

'I've asked them to be here in an hour.'

'I'll be there.'

He left the office, feeling listless and strangely weighed down by routine.

He was already with Erminia Cosenza when Vita arrived.

'Please sit down,' she said. 'This gentleman is Chief Superintendent Ferrara, the head of the *Squadra Mobile*.' Then she called in her secretary, who would take down the statement on the computer.

'If you would start the tape recorder on your right, signora. Now write this.' She dictated: '"It is 11:15 a.m. on October 20, 2001, in the offices of the Public Prosecutor, in the Via Strozzi in Florence. I am Acting Prosecutor Erminia Cosenza, and I am here with Signor Antonio Vita, who is currently being investigated for the offence of aiding and abetting. In the presence of his attorney, Romolo Moroni of the Milan Bar, Signor Vita makes the following statement of his own free will." All right, Signor Vita, we're ready, please say what you have to say.'

'Signora, what I'd like to say is that I don't know the people named in the official notification, this Signor Miano and Signor La Torre. I've never seen them and I've never spoken to them on the telephone. All I did was do a favour for a friend from Palermo, a bookmaker at the Favorita racecourse, who asked me to help him find a small villa on the Versilia coast for some friends of his. As you discovered when you searched my home, I'm a lover of horses and racing, and I've made many acquaintances in racing circles over the years. I did what I could, just as a favour to him, and, through an estate agency in Forte dei Marmi, which sold me my own villa a few years ago, I found a small villa. My friend then asked me to pay the rent in advance, which I did, and to get the keys, which I was then to hand over to someone who would come and see me on his behalf. In August, a young man did in fact show up and I gave him the keys. This young man didn't tell me his name, only that he had been sent by my friend, whose name he told me.'

At this point he paused. Erminia Cosenza did not take her eyes off him for one second. She would have liked to ask him a whole lot of questions, especially the name of his friend, and show him the photographs of Miano and La Torre, but the nature of the procedure they were following prevented her from doing so. Meanwhile, Ferrara was wondering if the man had decided to make his statement after learning of Miano's death, knowing he could not contradict him. As for La Torre, being a fugitive made him an equally unlikely witness.

The expression in the acting prosecutor's eyes did not escape Antonio Vita, and when he started speaking again, he said, 'Signora, I can guess what you're thinking. "Why hasn't he told me his friend's name?" I know, it's a reasonable thing to think, but I'm in a difficult position. Racing circles are full of dubious characters, some of them almost certainly connected with organised crime, and I don't want to get in any trouble. I have a family and a business in Milan. I wouldn't like to have any problems.'

He paused again and looked at his lawyer, as if expecting him to make some sign that he agreed or disagreed with what he was saying. The lawyer did not move an inch, so Vita resumed his statement, with Erminia Cosenza still looking straight at him.

'All right, signora, I'll tell you the name. Otherwise, there wouldn't have been any point in my coming here and making this statement. My position wouldn't have changed in any way. I only hope I don't get in any trouble and I can continue to work in peace as I have all these years. The man's name is Leonardo Parisi, but they call him Leo. He's from Palermo.

He's about thirty-five, forty, and if it's of any help I can provide you with his phone number, which I have among my racing papers. I really don't have anything else to say. I just want to assure you that I've told you the truth, the whole truth, trusting in the law not to abandon me if I have any problems. And you know what kind of problems I'm referring to.'

Erminia Cosenza exchanged glances with Ferrara and then said to the secretary, 'Please write this, signora.'

She dictated: '"I, as Public Prosecutor, hereby declare that the statement has been taken down in summary form and has simultaneously been recorded. The tape was stopped at 12:15 at the end of the statement and has been put in the appropriate bag, which has been sealed and marked with the number 1 and will be attached to the present statement of which it constitutes an integral part. The written version of the statement, covering two pages, has been read, confirmed and signed, indicating, in relation to the person under investigation, that no methods have been employed to influence his free will, or to alter his ability to remember and weigh up the facts he had to expose." All right, Signor Vita, we'll check everything that needs to be checked and, if everything turns out to be true, you can rest assured that the State won't abandon you. If there's anything you need to talk about, phone Chief Superintendent Ferrara here.'

'Thank you, signora.'

'I'd really like to have that phone number,' Ferrara said. 'Here's my card.'

'Of course. Thank you.'

Erminia Cosenza rose from her armchair and shook hands with Vita and his lawyer. Ferrara did the same. Then the two men left.

'What do you think, Chief Superintendent?' she asked Ferrara when they were alone.

'Hard to say. He may have been telling the truth, but we won't know until we've checked it out. Maybe he really was only doing a favour for a friend.'

'At least we now have a new name to get the investigation going again. We were starting to run out of them.'

Ferrara nodded. He did not tell her that he had his doubts.

The investigation seemed to be under a curse, the suspects that mattered were disappearing before they could arrest them.

Curses like that meant only one thing: someone was pulling the strings.

24

On Sunday, Captain Somenti caught the 7:53 Eurostar to Rome.

Alone.

Once Giulia had overcome her initial fear, which did not take long, her attitude to him had hardened again. If anything, it had become even harder, as a reaction to her realisation that that tender moment when she had abandoned herself to his embrace had been the result of shock, and was out of all proportion to what she had really been feeling.

She had not even gone with him to the station that day.

It was Major Alibrandi who had gone instead.

On the ground floor were a living room, kitchen and bathroom. In a corner a spiral staircase led to the first floor: two bedrooms, another bathroom and a box room. At the back was a small garden, part of it laid out as a lawn, leaving space for two cars to park under a wooden lean-to and a niche for keeping firewood.

At exactly seven on the morning of Monday October 22, police officers from the *Squadra Mobile* and Carabinieri from

Prato entered the house, together with the owner, Alfonso Di Pietro, who had opened it for them.

'But I let the house,' had been Alfonso Di Pietro's immediate response when Inspector Sergi had got him out of bed in his apartment in the centre of Florence and asked him to come with him. 'I let it to an engineering student, a Dutchman.'

'Yes, we know, but we have reason to believe that your tenant isn't at home, and in any case we have to search the house and we need you to be present.'

He had shown him the search warrant.

The owner had given it a rapid glance. 'But why? What has he been up to? Oh God, I don't want to get into trouble! Look, I've never had anything to do with the police. The rental arrangement was above board, I can show you the contract.'

'Don't worry, trust us. All you have to do is come with us.'

Before starting to look through the rooms, Ferrara gave instructions to the forensics team, emphasising the importance of doing nothing to contaminate the environment as they went about their business.

'You'll need to photograph every object, every piece of furniture, everything. Obviously look for fingerprints, biological traces, anything at all. Use the Egis to find residues of explosive material. Look for anything else you consider might be of use.'

The Egis was a piece of equipment that made it possible to detect the presence of powerful nitro-organic explosive residue in rooms and on furniture, fittings, carpets, beds, even in dust.

Soon after nine, Inspector Sergi went up to Ferrara, holding a curious object in his latex-gloved hands, something like a home-made file. The handle was made from two 500-lire coins secured with adhesive tape; a knife blade cut to the shape and length of a file was held between them.

They were both wondering what it might be when they were joined by Officer Ricci.

'Look at this,' Sergi said. 'They found it in the inside pocket of a jacket in a wardrobe in one of the bedrooms.'

'I know what that is!' Ricci exclaimed, after a quick glance. 'Thieves use it for stealing cars, and also as a lucky charm.'

'Then he would have done better to take it with him,' Ferrara commented sharply, 'because it certainly hasn't brought him luck.'

'Pino, you take it away,' Sergi said, 'but put your gloves on first. Do all the tests you want, but I need to know what kind of car it can get into.'

'I'll do that first thing this afternoon, when the car show-rooms open again.'

'And start with the Fiats.'

'Right. With the Fiat Unos!'

'Great!'

Ricci put on his gloves, took the file and put it in a plastic bag.

When the search was over, Ferrara said, 'Good, now all that remains is to draw up a requisition statement.'

The statement listed all the objects taken away, indicating precisely where they had been found. Among other things, there were items of men's clothing in various sizes, glasses, plates, cushions on which the presence of hair had been noted, two combs with traces of hair follicles, four tooth-brushes, brown parcel tape, and some swabs taken from chair fabric, from the sofas and from a rug in one of the bedrooms.

Finally, after certifying that the whole house, including the garden and the niche with the firewood had been checked, and that no damage had been found to have been done to people or things during the course of the operation, he handed a copy of the statement to the owner. Alfonso Di Pietro signed it as a receipt, as required by law. He had not said a word the whole time, but now he asked, anxiously, 'Why take away all these things?'

'Because we haven't finished. We may have to come back after the results of the tests.'

'How long will they take?'

'I can't say, but we'll try to be as quick as we can, don't worry.'

25

At about the same time, not so far from there, Superintendent Rizzo was conducting a similar operation.

He presented himself at the door of the Laurias' house at 7:45 a.m., with an inspector, two forensics officers and two Carabinieri from Alibrandi's unit.

'Good morning, Signor Lauria,' he said when the man opened the door, in his work overalls. His wife was behind him, in the corridor.

'What do you want?' he asked in alarm.

'To search your house. We have a warrant from the Prosecutors' Department.'

The man was speechless for a moment, then turned to his wife and said, 'Anna, they say they want to search the house.'

'Let them in, don't keep them standing outside the door,' the woman replied, stepping forward. 'Come in, make yourself at home.'

Her husband moved aside and the men walked in.

'Here's the warrant, Signor Lauria,' Rizzo said.

Vincenzo Lauria took the document, read it through quickly and then passed it to his wife, who in turn read it, but more carefully.

'Before we start,' Rizzo said, 'we must inform you that you have the right to have someone you trust present during the search, even a lawyer, if you like, provided he can be easily reached and can get here in a short space of time. If not we can begin without.'

Vincenzo Lauria exchanged glances with his wife and then replied, 'We don't need anyone with us, and you can look at anything you want.'

Rather more distrustful than her husband, Anna asked, still holding the warrant, 'But are we being investigated for the things written here?'

'No, signora,' Rizzo said. 'The document refers to offences committed by persons unknown. You and your husband are third parties, and the law allows us to search your house.'

'I see. But we don't know the law, Superintendent, and we've never had a visit from the police in our lives. It's all right, but please don't turn everything upside down!'

'Don't worry, signora, we'll put everything back before we leave.'

The search began, and kept the men busy for about three hours, at the end of which a statement was drawn up, notifying the couple of the material being taken away because of its relevance to the investigation. This included:

From the living room on the ground floor: a swab taken from the fabric of a chair, suitably sealed in a bag; an address book with various names, addresses and telephone numbers;

From the bathroom: a comb, sky blue in colour, with traces of hair follicles, also sealed;

From the bedroom: samples of white pulverulent material present on the floor and inside the bed frame, sealed in bags;

From the garden: three samples of mould from various areas, sealed in containers;

*From the garage: a swab from the fabric of the seats of
the Fiat Punto owned by Vincenzo Lauria and a sample of
pulverulent material from the floor, sealed in separate bags.*

'Why are you taking all this stuff away?' Vincenzo Lauria
asked, when he was given the statement to sign.

'Because we consider it relevant to the investigations,'
Rizzo replied. 'It's in the statement.'

'I don't understand,' the man went on. 'I mean, I know
you're only doing your duty, but my family and I have nothing to do with all this weird stuff.'

Rizzo did not reply to this, simply said goodbye and left
the house with the others. On the orders of the acting prosecutor, all the bags were immediately taken by one of the officers
to Rome, where the contents would be examined using the
Egis system.

In the afternoon, Antonio Vita phoned Ferrara to give him
the telephone number of Leonardo Parisi – a name he found
vaguely familiar.

'Fanti!' he called, and the secretary was there in a flash, as
always.

'What is it, chief?'

'Does the name Parisi mean anything to you?'

'Leonardo?' Fanti asked, assuming a contrite air.

'That's right. Do you know him?'

'No, but he was a friend of poor Sebastiano's.'

'Franchi?' he said, incredulously, and a slight feeling of
dizziness came over him. 'No, forget it, it must have been
someone else, there are lots of people with that name.'

'You're right, chief, best to forget it, that's what I told
Sebastiano.'

'Why?'

'He wasn't exactly a trustworthy person, always hanging around at racecourses, always betting, you know what I mean?'

The dizziness got worse. 'Why, was Franchi a gambler?'

'He was trying to supplement his income. I think he did quite well. This Parisi must have given him some decent tips, if you ask me.'

'Did you ever see him?'

'No, but I heard his voice. One day when Sebastiano was in a hurry he asked me to do him a favour and call this Parisi to tell him he was running late. They were supposed to be going out together with some girls, he said. He was a Sicilian, I recognised the accent immediately.'

'When was this?'

'A few weeks ago, chief. In fact, just a few days before the bombing.'

The dizziness overwhelmed him.

'Could you call Rizzo for me, please?'

'Straightaway.'

Rizzo came in smiling cheerfully, thinking he would be asked to report on that morning's satisfactory operation. Instead, he found himself facing a grey, weary man, whose eyes and body seemed to be drooping under a heavy weight.

'Sit down.'

'What is it, chief?'

'Officer Franchi was friends with a criminal, the same man who asked Vita to find the villa in Forte dei Marmi for La Torre and Miano, the one who's into horse racing.'

'No!'

'I just found out from Fanti.'

'It must be a coincidence.'

Ferrara hoped and prayed that it was. He couldn't believe it was really Franchi, maybe because of a gambling debt, who had told the bombers the route they would be taking that day, thereby signing his own death warrant. But if he had, Ferrara preferred to think it was an involuntary lapse, perhaps something he'd said in all innocence to show off in front of those girls he'd been going to meet.

'But we'll have to interview him, anyway,' Rizzo went on, breaking into the chief's silence. 'What's his name?'

'Leonardo Parisi.'

'Leonardo Parisi? Do you mind if I call Venturi?'

'Go ahead.'

Rizzo picked up the phone and dialled an internal number.

'Venturi, haven't we come across a man named Leonardo Parisi?'

From the expression on his face as he listened to the answer, Ferrara could see that his deputy had been right. And when he put down the receiver, he confirmed it.

'Yes, it's him. He was stopped once at a police roadblock with Cosimo Caruso. Thirty-seven years old, from Palermo, previous convictions for possession of weapons, fraud and illegal gambling.'

Now Ferrara knew where he had seen the name before: he had read it in the reports he had studied soon after coming back to work. But why hadn't he remembered? Was he really getting old? Or was he starting to lose interest in an investigation he liked less and less the more it dragged on?

'Okay, ask Acting Prosecutor Cosenza to issue a summons, and interview him.'

He would let Rizzo conduct it. He preferred not to know.

26

Ferrara's mood did not improve in the days that followed, especially when it was learned that, after a fruitless search, their Sicilian colleagues had come to the conclusion that Leonardo Parisi was missing, most likely the victim of another Mafia killing. In fact, it had been getting steadily worse since the first concrete – and crucial – results had started to arrive.

The first was brought in by Officer Pino Ricci, who knocked at his door the following morning.

'Come in!'

'Good morning, chief.'

'What is it?'

'Chief, I did the rounds of the car showrooms, and the file opens all Fiat Unos but no other model of Fiat and no other make of car. And not only does it open the car door, it also starts the engine.'

'So anyone who had this tool could only have stolen Fiat Unos, is that right?'

'Exactly, chief.'

'Okay, Ricci, I need a report, detailing all the places you went, all the tests you did and the result. It's useful evidence.'

Is that all? Ricci wondered as he went out. With his wretched salary, a little bit of encouragement wouldn't have gone amiss. Ferrara didn't used to be such a bastard, he thought.

Rizzo must have thought something similar – though not, perhaps in the same words – when Ferrara informed him of Ricci's discovery some time later. But, instead of letting himself be influenced by his chief's air of fatalistic resignation, he decided to take the initiative, and the following day sent Sergi to Prato with specific instructions.

When Inspector Sergi arrived at Giulia Roversi's apartment, he found her with her sister-in-law, who was holding a baby in her arms. Without wasting any time, he showed first one, then the other, the album of photographs taken at the house rented by van Gorcum. Both recognised the furniture, Giulia Roversi with greater accuracy. The most important thing she recognised, though, was the jacket in which the tool had been found. She was categorical. 'That jacket was his.'

'You mean Jan van Gorcum's?'

'Yes.'

'Are you quite sure, signora?'

'Very sure. I have no doubt at all.'

'What about these other clothes?' he asked, showing her photographs of a suit, a winter jacket and a couple of men's shirts.

'Maybe the shirts, but I can't be sure. I'm certain, though, that I never saw him in that suit or this other jacket. I wouldn't want to make a mistake, but I don't think I ever saw them in the house.'

Her sister-in-law confirmed that she had never seen them either, which meant that Jan must have bought and worn these clothes after he had forbidden Giulia Roversi to visit the house. Or that they had belonged to other people, Sergi thought.

Satisfied with the results, as soon as he left he phoned Rizzo, who in the meantime had received a report from Dr Massa, the explosives expert at Forensics in Rome.

The analyses carried out with the Egis system had highlighted the presence of residues of powerful organic explosives (T4, TNT and gelatin) on the swabs removed from one of the bedrooms in van Gorcum's house, especially from the rug, as well as from the sofa in the living room. More traces had also been highlighted in the dust which had been removed from the floor in the entrance hall and the living room. 'These traces', the expert wrote, 'are indubitable evidence of secondary contamination by explosives.'

'Good work, Sergi,' Rizzo said. 'That means we need to go further, and check the ground around the house.'

'But chief,' Sergi objected, 'we already checked the ground and didn't find anything.'

'This time it has to be done with Ground Penetrating Radar. You'll have to go back tomorrow morning with the technicians and the apparatus.'

27

The telephone on the bedside table rang just before six on Wednesday morning. Ferrara answered it at the third ring. It was Dr Massa, from Forensics in Rome.

'I'm sorry for calling you so early,' he said, 'but I think it's urgent.'

'No need to apologise, I'm used to it,' he replied tonelessly, watching as his wife got out of bed. 'Go ahead.'

Massa told him that an examination of the pulverulent material from the floor of Vincenzo Lauria's garage and the swab taken from the driver's seat of the Fiat Punto revealed the presence of traces of explosive.

'What kind of explosive?' Ferrara asked.

'Definitely TNT and T4, once again. It's a secondary contamination.'

'I see. Thank you for letting me know, Massa.'

'Am I allowed to know what's wrong?' Petra asked him later, as they were having breakfast.

'Me?'

'Why, can you see anyone else here?'

Ferrara gave her a downcast look.

'If you want to know what I think, you've lost interest in

your profession, and I'm pleased. You answer the phone like an automaton, you do your work like a bureaucrat, and you come home every evening with your face dragging on the ground! Not even your doctor has told you to carry on with your police work. In fact he's ordered you to do the exact opposite and he's absolutely right. And don't tell me all you need is a bit of rest. This time I know what you need, and it's a nice house in the country, or by the sea like Duranti, a long way from Florence, from Headquarters and from the police, for all the years you have left.'

She might be right, Ferrara told himself later, in his office, as he was picking up the receiver to inform the Prosecutor's Department.

'That is good news, Chief Superintendent,' Erminia Cosenza said. 'At last! All right, let's not waste any time. Have Vincenzo Lauria picked up from home or work and brought to Head-quarters. This time he owes us an explanation. His wife, too. Make sure they're brought in different cars and wait in sepa-rate rooms. I don't want them getting together to agree on a story.'

'I'll get straight on to it.'

'And let me know when they're here. I want to interview them myself.'

Meanwhile Inspector Sergi was at van Gorcum's house, where he had gone before dawn to wait for the technicians who were bringing the Ground Penetrating Radar equipment. They were civil engineers: Forensics did not have that kind of machine, which was normally used for geological and archae-ological surveys. The inspector had had to turn to a centre for diagnostic engineering in Florence which carried out studies commissioned by the Ministry of Culture.

It was almost seven when the technicians got to the house,

and after eight by the time they placed the apparatus on the ground, ready to probe it according to a well-established procedure: along straight horizontal and vertical lines in order to leave no part untouched, even the remotest corner.

As the team moved the machine over the ground – it looked rather like a mower, but with tubes and wires sprouting from it – an engineer sat at a laptop on whose screen images of the subsoil with all its strata were projected in real time. It was an activity that required time and patience as well as technical expertise, the biggest responsibility being with the engineer at the computer, who had to read and interpret the data being transmitted to the computer by an antenna on the machine as it ran over the ground. All Sergi could do was wait and see if any anomalies were revealed.

As he waited, he peered at the computer screen. He hadn't the faintest idea what the lines on the screen meant, but he hoped he might be able to catch some positive comments from the engineer.

When he knew that the Laurias were on their way, Ferrara called the acting prosecutor.

'I'll be right there. Tell the Laurias I need to interview them again, but this time as persons under investigation, which means they'll need to have a lawyer present.'

'Right.'

'And then have the lawyer informed. If they don't appoint anyone, check and see who's on duty and have him advised.'

'Of course.'

The Ground Penetrating Radar was signalling something anomalous, and Sergi started bombarding the engineer with questions.

'You see that irregularity in the horizontal lines? That sug-gests the ground at that point isn't compact.'

'Ah, yes, I see.'

'And that may mean one of two things.' He paused to light a cigarette and take a drag. 'Either that someone dug a hole in that spot, which would have disturbed the original conforma-tion of the soil, or else that there was movement caused by growth in the roots of the nearby tree.'

'I see! How do we know which one?'

'To find that out, we have to take a sample, and then dig.'

'How far down?'

'About three feet.'

'When do we dig?' the inspector asked again, impatiently.

'When we've finished checking everything. For the moment, we'll put in a peg to indicate the exact spot, and when we're done we'll start digging, there and anywhere else the machine may have signalled in the meantime.'

'All right.'

'You know, Inspector, it may be useful to have someone come in with a Bobcat. You never know.'

Sergi looked at him, puzzled. 'What's a Bobcat?'

'It's a small excavator.'

'Okay, I'll get right on to it.'

It was the first time Sergi had moved away from the screen.

28

The interview with Vincenzo Lauria began at 9:49 a.m. Next to him was the lawyer Pino Castelli of the Florence Bar. Behind the desk, in Ferrara's place, was the acting prosecutor, with Ferrara and Rizzo on either side of her. Inspector Riccardo Venturi was at the computer to take down the statement and start the tape recorder.

Also present was Major Alibrandi – Erminia Cosenza had wanted him there.

After the usual formalities – name, marital status, profession, whether or not he had a criminal record – Vincenzo Lauria was asked to declare, 'I don't have a lawyer and I acknowledge that Signor Castelli of the Florence Bar has been appointed.'

Next, he was asked to choose an address to which all communications would be sent, and warned that he was obliged to inform the authorities if he moved from that address. In case of difficulty, all communications would be addressed to his defence counsel.

'I choose my house in Prato,' he replied.

'Signor Lauria,' Erminia Cosenza said, 'I hereby inform you that you have the right to remain silent but that, if you avail yourself of that right, the criminal procedure will still run its course.'

'I want to answer the questions, signora.'

'Good. Then I must notify you that are under investigation for illegal possession and transportation of explosive material. For the moment, I do not consider that I have to inform you of the sources for our evidence, as that may prejudice the investigation currently in progress.'

Lauria seemed thunderstruck, and looked at his lawyer as if searching desperately for help. Then he turned back to the acting prosecutor. 'What are you talking about? I've never had explosives, I don't even know how they're made. There must be some mistake.'

'No, there's no mistake,' she replied. 'Signor Lauria, I assume you are aware of the bomb attack which took place on October first in the Piazza del Cestello, here in Florence?'

'I saw it on TV and read about it the next day in *La Nazione*.'

'Where were you that morning?'

'You surely don't think I was the one who planted that bomb?'

'Please answer the question.'

'I was at work, same as every day.'

'We can check. Tell me, what kind of car do you have?'

'A Fiat Punto.'

'And how long have you had it?'

'About two years. Before that, I had another Fiat Punto.'

'Does anyone drive it besides you?'

'No. My wife doesn't have a licence and my son is only eight.'

'Have you ever lent it to anyone?'

'No, never.'

'What's your home phone number?'

'6728 4112.'

'Signor Lauria, have you had any calls lately from your relatives in Sicily on that number?'

'No, I told you that last time.'

'Has anyone phoned you from the family of your brother-in-law Cosimo Caruso?'

'No.'

'We know for a fact that at thirty-eight minutes past midnight on October 1, 2001, there was a call to your telephone number from a landline in the house of Cosimo Caruso in Mazara del Vallo.'

Vincenzo Lauria lowered his eyes, then raised them again and looked straight at his lawyer. 'I don't remember that call at all,' he replied at last. 'In fact, I never received it. I deny that my brother-in-law or anyone in his family talked to me.'

'You don't remember the call, or you never received it? The call is on your records, Signor Lauria. You're not telling me the truth, and that's a criminal offence.'

Vincenzo Lauria again lowered his eyes, and this time remained silent for quite a while.

'Could I talk to my client in private, signora?' the lawyer asked.

'Of course.'

'Thank you.'

'Inspector Venturi, please write: "It is 10:30, and the interview has been suspended to allow the defence counsel to talk with the accused, as requested by said defence counsel. The tape recorder has been switched off. The interview will resume in thirty minutes." Is thirty minutes all right for you, Signor Castelli?'

'Yes, thank you.'

Erminia Cosenza turned to Ferrara. 'Chief Superintendent, if you could make a room available for the conversation.'

'Of course. Inspector Venturi will see to that.'

Venturi led them into one of the waiting rooms, and took up position outside the door to stop anyone going in.

Ferrara, Rizzo, Erminia Cosenza and Major Alibrandi repaired to a nearby bar for a coffee and to talk over the case – although Ferrara, strangely, took no part in this discussion.

At 11:05 Vincenzo Lauria and the lawyer were again brought into Ferrara's office. They sat down on the same chairs as before.

'Signora, I—' Lauria began, but was immediately interrupted by the acting prosecutor.

'No, Signor Lauria, wait a moment, first we have to resume the interview.' She turned to Venturi, who was also sitting in the same place as before. 'Inspector, please write that it is now 11:07, the tape recorder has been switched on, and we are continuing with the interview.'

Venturi did as instructed.

'Now, Signor Lauria, you may speak. Tell us what you have to say, and when you have finished we may ask you some more questions.'

'The thing is, Signora, I've realised the situation isn't looking good for me and I don't want problems for my family because we don't have anything to do with . . .'

He broke off and looked at his lawyer.

'Just say it, Signor Lauria,' Erminia Cosenza said in a firm voice. 'Say what you have to say, and please look at me, not at Signor Castelli.'

'We don't have anything to do with my brother-in-law's family,' he finished. 'We've never really got on with them, because my brother-in-law is a "man of honour" and we didn't want to have anything to do with him and people like him, that's why we left Sicily.'

He paused, perhaps wondering if he had done the right

thing to say that, but it was done now and there was no turning back.

Erminia Cosenza broke the silence. 'So, Signor Lauria, you did receive that phone call?'

'Yes.'

'Go on.'

'My sister-in-law phoned and told us that her son Sandro was travelling by car with a friend of his, but they'd had a problem with the car near Florence. She asked us if we could put the two of them up for one night.'

'And what did you say?'

'It wasn't me, it was my wife who answered the phone. She said yes. I might have said no, but my wife just couldn't do it, after all it was her sister asking for a favour and her nephew who had the problem.'

'I understand. What happened then?'

'Well, about an hour later, maybe two, we heard the doorbell ring, and there was Sandro, with this other young guy, tall, foreign-looking, though he spoke perfect Italian. He introduced him and told us he was a friend from university.'

He paused again, and asked if he could have a glass of water.

After drinking it, he continued, 'My nephew asked us if he could put his car in our garage. He said they were going to try and repair it and they needed somewhere indoors and well-lit. I told him that was fine, there was enough room in the garage because my own car is quite small.'

'What make was their car?'

'A Fiat Uno.'

'What happened then?'

'Nothing. It was very late, so we went to bed. We told Sandro my wife would make up the sofa bed in the living room for them.'

'I see. And the following day?'

'The following day, Sandro and his friend were already gone by the time we got up. On the table in the living room we found a note from Sandro thanking us for our hospitality and saying they had managed to repair the car and had left because they really had to get going.'

'And did you ever see them again?'

'No. No, never had a phone call from them either. And Sandro's mother didn't even ring to thank us.'

'Do you still have the note they left?'

'I don't think so. I think my wife threw it away. You'll have to ask her. That's all, signora. Believe me.'

'Why didn't you tell us all this before?' Erminia Cosenza asked in a stern tone.

'Because we don't want anything do with those relatives of ours, they bring nothing but trouble.'

Erminia Cosenza tried going back over the story to get more details, but it was quite pointless: Lauria just kept repeating the same things. Then she showed him an album of photographs, including those of Jan van Gorcum and Marco Laprua, as well as those of other young men with almost the same physical characteristics.

Lauria looked at them and pointed to the photo of van Gorcum. 'That's him, that's the young man who was with Sandro. I'm sure of it. But I don't recognise any of the others.'

'That's fine for now,' Erminia Cosenza concluded.

The interview was terminated. The transcript and tape would be put in safe keeping for two months to avoid the contents becoming known to anyone else.

Next, Signora Lauria was brought in, with the same lawyer representing her. She fully confirmed everything her husband had told them and also identified Jan van Gorcum as the friend of her nephew who had been in their house. Both husband and wife were then detained at Headquarters, and the lawyer left.

Without further ado, Erminia Cosenza issued an arrest warrant for Sandro Caruso, and Ferrara faxed it to their colleagues in Sicily, although he was already pretty sure what the outcome would be.

29

Late that afternoon Ferrara received a phone call from Sergi.

'All done, chief. It's taken all day, but we finally have the explosive! It's a "sausage" and it was buried three feet down near a tree.'

'Good.'

'We're going to need a bomb disposal expert to remove it, chief.'

'Okay. Keep the place guarded, we don't want anyone going near it, and get everything photographed. In the meantime I'll find a bomb disposal expert and send him to you as soon as possible.'

'Chief, we also need some photo-electric cells, because it's going to be too dark soon to see anything.'

'I'll tell the fire brigade, don't worry.'

It was already dark by the time the bomb disposal expert removed the 'sausage'. It was made of gelatin, and a detonator was also found with the explosive.

Sergi phoned Ferrara at home and gave him the news.

Ferrara thanked him without any other comments.

Petra noticed that. 'Are you in a bad mood?' she asked.

'Tired,' he replied.

'Then go and have a shower,' she said with a wicked gleam in her eye. 'When you come out, I'll have a surprise for you.'

By the time he left the bathroom, the lights were off and there were candles on the beautifully laid dinner table. In the centre was a gleaming ice bucket, containing a bottle of Ca' del Bosco Reserve, a sparkling wine which, in his opinion, could bear comparison with the finest champagne. From the kitchen, where Petra was bustling about, there wafted a delicious smell of grilled fish.

'What are we celebrating?' he called out.

'My present,' she replied, coming out of the kitchen with a thin envelope in her hand. 'But first you have to open the bottle.'

As they drank a toast, Ferrara opened the envelope.

It contained five colour photographs. They showed, from various angles, a dilapidated stone building almost choked with brambles. On one of them, you could see the sea, and he immediately recognised the islands: Palmaria, Tino and Tinetto. An awful premonition made Ferrara's heart skip a beat.

'I met Duranti's architect, Cristina. She's very good. She's the one who found it. It's a real bargain!'

'No, Petra, wait. I don't want to dash your hopes, but now's not the time, I don't think we can afford—'

'You don't understand, darling,' Petra said, adopting her most innocent air. 'I've already signed the preliminary contract. It's ours. And it'll be beautiful, I already have the plans she drew up. Come on, let me show them to you.'

'What about the fish?' he objected feebly.

'Don't worry, I've turned off the oven.'

30

On Thursday October 22, Superintendent Francesco Rizzo
entered his chief's office, triumphantly waving a report.

'The results of the first DNA tests on the cigarette ends
have arrived, chief.'

'Ah,' Ferrara replied.

Ignoring the lukewarm welcome – he was getting used to it
by now – Rizzo continued, 'The experts have identified the
genotypes of two different men.'

'So now we have their genetic profile.'

'Precisely, and we know there were at least two individuals
lying in wait, and on two separate occasions, several days
apart, a week at the most.'

So Anna Giulietti hadn't been paranoid after all, there
really had been a previous attempt on her life. But why hadn't
she told Rizzo? If they had intervened in time and taken the
necessary precautions she might still be alive today, still with
them, with him. He suddenly recalled the sacrosanct words of
the murdered Sicilian judge Giovanni Falcone: 'People generally die because they are alone or because they have got
involved in something that is too big for them. They often die
because they don't have the necessary allies, because they lack

support. In Sicily the Mafia strikes only those servants of the State whom the State has not been able to protect.'

Not only in Sicily, not any more.

That thought increased his despondency, the memory of Anna his sadness.

'At least two?' he said.

'The experts don't rule out the possibility that there may have been others. Because the material they've had to work on was small and in a poor state of preservation, they haven't been able to run a full analysis of all the cigarette ends.'

'And we already know the names of those two men: Jan van Gorcum and Marco Laprua. Get the Agrigento people to send you some usable organic samples and pass them to the experts to see if the DNAs match, though it's pretty much a foregone conclusion.'

He sounded weary, as if he were going through the motions.

It was at that point that Rizzo decided that he couldn't take it any more. He summoned all his courage and openly challenged his chief, whose state of mind was in danger of lowering the morale of the whole squad.

'Are we allowed to know what's wrong, chief?' he burst out.

Ferrara gave him a look of annoyance. 'You sound just like my wife! Everyone keeps asking me what's wrong! To cheer me up, she's put me in debt for the next twenty years, so what bright ideas do you have?'

'I'm sorry, chief, but aren't we right? The men are at last starting to see their hard work bearing fruit, at last getting fantastic results, but they never get a single encouraging word from you, not even a "Good work, carry on, you're doing well."'

Ferrara had calmed down after his outburst. 'You're right, Francesco, forgive me. The men are doing a wonderful job, I must remember to thank them. But don't you get the feeling we're going round in circles? That we're watching the same film over and over again?'

'What do you mean?'

Ferrara made a vague gesture in the air. Then he looked around for a cigar, which he really needed at that moment. It helped him to think, and right now he was doing a lot of thinking.

'I don't know,' he said. 'It's just that we keep gathering evidence, important evidence, I grant you, about things we've already known for a while. We know by heart how it happened, we know who carried out the attacks, and we know who helped them, whether willingly or not doesn't really matter. It's all as clear as daylight, and yet we're still groping in the dark!'

As if determined to corroborate his chief's words and thoughts, the incomparable Fanti, with his miraculous sense of timing, took the liberty just then of interrupting them to inform them that they had just heard from Sicily that Sandro Caruso was now also missing.

'Or the victim of a Mafia killing,' Ferrara said gloomily.

Rizzo had to agree that once again Ferrara was right. He felt genuinely mortified, and did not know what to say.

Ferrara looked at him with a mixture of affection and anxiety, feeling he had gone too far. 'I'm sorry, Francesco, I don't want you to lose heart, too! The fact is, you're the best man I have, and if I can't tell you these things . . . It's depressing, I know, but the truth is, we're gathering evidence about people who are either dead or have just vanished into thin air. We're still stuck on the second level, that's the truth, and those on the third level are laughing at us!'

31

Late that afternoon, well past closing time, in the conference room of the Palermo branch of the Banca Popolare di Montepellegrino, a very special meeting was about to take place.

The first man to arrive, before the scheduled time, had been Pippo Catalfano, the organiser of the meeting. As usual, he was very well dressed. Some of his most reliable men, who had come with him, remained outside and at a distance, providing a discreet security cordon. As he waited for the others to arrive, Catalfano talked to the manager, who treated him with particular deference. Quite rightly, given that most of the shares in the bank, although in other names, were in fact held by Catalfano, and that it was Catalfano who had appointed him manager because he trusted him and appreciated his proven experience in the field of stock market operations.

Over the next thirty minutes, the other participants arrived in dribs and drabs.

The first was Salvatore Lume, known as Sasà, head of almost all the Palermo families, an impressive-looking man of about sixty, very tall – especially for a Sicilian – and always modestly dressed. He disapproved of drug trafficking, which was apparently to be the main topic of the meeting. With him was his eldest son, Giuseppe, destined to take over the reins when the moment was right. Giuseppe, too, was very tall.

Pippo Catalfano went up to them as soon as he saw them, embraced Sasà and thanked him for coming. Up until the last moment, there had been some doubt as to whether he or Molina would be there.

'Don Nino asked us,' Sasà explained, and Pippo knew then that there wouldn't be anyone missing.

The manager invited them to drink something, and walked with them to a corner of the room where a buffet had been laid out, including a tray of Sicilian cannoli and finger-sized 'cannolicchi', filled with very fresh goat's cheese ricotta, and dark chocolates decorated with candied orange peel.

Antonio Molina, district boss of Caltanisetta, and Luigi Rosati, head of the Catania families, arrived together. They had come from Catania in the same car. Rosati was relatively young, a high-flier who in a few years had established himself in the Catania Mafia, leaving behind him a long trail of blood and death. Tall and well-built, his hair still completely black, he was an imposing man. He dressed elegantly and with refinement and, like Catalfano, seemed more like a captain of industry than an old-style Mafioso with a cloth cap on his head and a rifle across his shoulders. He was perfectly happy about drug trafficking, which he ran in collusion with some families from the Calabrian Mafia who had been living for some years in Canada and Germany, where they laundered dirty money thorough apparently legitimate businesses. Both men approached the buffet and embraced Catalfano and Sasà.

Next came Don Pietro Uccelli, district boss of Enna, an old Mafiso with strong ties to his own territory, where not even a leaf moved without his say-so. He had just turned seventy and his ambition was to reach the end of his days at peace with all the other families, even though he did not agree with the spread of the drug market: sooner or later, he thought, it could well cause serious problems, even within his own patch. As soon as he saw him come in, Catalfano went up to him and embraced him, moved in part by his memories of the excellent relationship between the old man and his own father when he himself was still a boy.

'Thank you for being here, Don Pietro.'

'I only came because of your late father, Pippo,' he replied, in a friendly, almost affectionate tone.

'Have something to drink, Don Pietro,' Pippo said, taking him by the arm and walking with him to the buffet.

All the most important provinces were now present. The only one missing was the representative from Messina, not because he had not been invited but because he did not exist. Messina, although it had had its share of criminal incidents, was still considered a backward province, because of the lack of prominent Mafia personalities and the relative absence of Mafia activity. The Catania Mafia, though, were making inroads into the territory. The farsighted Rosati wanted Messina as one of his conquests, determined to have an organisation in place when the construction of the controversial bridge linking Calabria and Sicily finally got under way.

It was only now that Antonio Caputo made his entrance. He looked around the room and an expression of discontent came over his face. 'Isn't someone missing?'

The others looked at each other questioningly. Pippo Catalfano looked at his watch and went up to him. 'He's coming, he's coming.'

'Let's sit down, then.'

They all took their places in the comfortable leather armchairs around the solid walnut table, which had been polished until it shone.

Luigi Rosati, the youngest and most irreverent of those present, asked the question the others seemed reluctant to utter. 'Who are we waiting for?'

'The Lion,' Don Nino said.

Again, they all gave each other questioning looks.

'Zì Turi's associate. He wants to meet us and give us an explanation.'

At that moment the door opened and the manager, who had previously gone out and left them alone, now showed in a stranger and again made himself scarce.

Antonio Caputo gave a start. Pale and furious, he shot an angry glance at Pippo and cried, 'Who is this?'

He knew perfectly well who it was: if anyone knew the Basilisk, he did.

Catalfano swallowed and looked at both of them, silent and uncomprehending. 'The Lion, isn't it?'

'No,' the newcomer said. 'But it was the Lion who sent me.'

'You were always a fucking idiot and you still are,' Caputo spat bitterly at Catalfano.

'It isn't his fault, Don Nino,' the Basilisk said. 'I know you were expecting the Lion, but he couldn't make it. He asked me to bring you a message, and it struck me as an important one. You must forgive me, but he only told me today and I wasn't able to warn you, there was no way to get a message to you by the usual means.'

'Pippo, this wasn't what we agreed,' Caputo said, ignoring him, the blood beating in his temples.

'Be patient, Don Nino,' the unexpected guest insisted, gently. 'And please hear me out. This may be important for everyone, if not, I wouldn't be here. He'll come next time, you'll see.'

'There won't be a next time!'

'Calm down, Don Nino. You're right, but trust me.'

'I may be able to trust you, but no one slights Antonio Caputo! No one. So he couldn't come. Like hell he couldn't! He didn't *want* to come. What is it? Is he scared?'

The newcomer had approached the table, and now sat down between Molina and Rosati.

'They say Laprua gave him that nickname because he was very brave, but even a brave man may feel a little scared meeting the boss of bosses, so you may not be far wrong, Don Nino. You know who I am. A mediator, that's why you use me. And I know you. But even I feel a little afraid, to tell the truth.'

The others did not dare ask what their relationship was. There are contacts that everyone has the right to keep secret, especially a boss of bosses. If he had wanted to, he would have introduced him to the others. For now, it was enough for them that they had recognised each other, as long as Caputo trusted them it was fine.

'You know you have nothing to worry about, Basilisk,' Caputo said, and the revelation of the name spread like an electric shock. 'The Lion's another matter. He should have come and looked us all in the face, and he shouldn't have planted that fucking bomb in Florence. All the cops and judges in Sicily are up in arms. He got us in this mess, and you know that.'

'He says he had to do it. For all of you. The image and the international prestige of Cosa Nostra are at risk. That policeman confiscated two hundred and fifty kilos of prime quality heroin intended for the American market. The Americans are furious, they're threatening to turn to other markets and cut us all out.'

'Bullshit!' Don Nino cried. 'We don't give a fuck about international prestige, and we don't give a fuck about those fucking drugs!'

'One moment, Don Nino,' Luigi Rosati intervened calmly. 'Maybe, being outside of Sicily, the man sees things more clearly. The world is changing, we all know that. Why don't we talk about it?'

Caputo looked at the others, one by one.

No one took sides.

He sighed and again addressed the Basilisk. 'What does he want?'

'To go into business with you. He assures us he's reestablished contact with the Afghans, despite the difficulties of the war. He says he can replace the load that was confiscated and satisfy the needs of our American cousins. But he needs money. A lot of money. He's already made commitments, and the shipment is going to arrive soon.'

'How much?' Antonio Molina asked.

'Six hundred million dollars.'

They all looked at each other in silence. It was an enormous sum, even to these men who were used to handling fortunes. They would need to think about it carefully.

'With the prices the stuff is fetching in America now, you'll double your investment at least. Let's say a billion and a half, more or less. That's not being optimistic but realistic. A hundred and fifty per cent interest in ten days, two weeks at the most, as soon as the money is handed over. Less my commission of one per cent if you agree. And you divide the profits: eighty per cent to you, twenty per cent to him.'

Another silence, while they waited for Caputo's reaction. He had turned grim-faced and thoughtful. The offer was tempting, and when it comes to business even the strongest allies can waver.

After this long pause for thought, the boss of bosses made a sweeping gesture with both arms, meaning that he was leaving it up to each man present to choose.

It was a big risk for them: they were well aware that he was using it as an opportunity to test the loyalty of each family. And the Basilisk was his man, they all knew that now. What if it was a trap? But it could also be a huge opportunity, and open up new paths, such as the most ambitious of them were always searching for. The latent conflict within the Sicilian Mafia, the choice between isolation and globalisation, was about to explode. The consequences could be devastating, as the heavy silence that followed the boss's gesture demonstrated. They knew that the moment had come, and they each had to take responsibility for their own actions, as men of honour.

Don Sasà whispered something in his son's ear. Then he shrugged, sullenly, and addressed Caputo.

'Don Nino, you already know what I think. Drugs don't interest me. They require a commitment that's too much for me at my age. I want things to stay as they are, at least for the families I have the honour to represent.' He paused, took a sip of water, and concluded, 'That's what I want for the good of our families and all of Sicily.'

He placed particular emphasis on the word 'Sicily', perhaps to underline that life on the island would probably never be the same again if they agreed to this plan.

Caputo turned to Catalfano with a questioning look.

'I don't know if that's the right choice, Don Sasà,' Catalfano ventured somewhat hesitatantly. 'When you get down it, the Lion took a risk for us, and made commitments, and if now we turn our backs on him, think of the consequences.'

'What is that, a threat?' Don Sasà burst out.

'What are you talking about? I haven't decided anything yet, it isn't an easy choice. We've heard from someone who could be the future of Cosa Nostra, and we have to take him into account when we make this decision.'

'My friend, it's not just that I'm rejecting this proposal. You all know me well and you know I've always tried to find the best solution, even when I didn't completely agree. But this whole drugs thing will bring us trouble in the future. It will make us too many enemies, and all our activities could be put at risk. Salvatore Laprua always thought of himself, not of us. Let's not forget that. The Lion made those financial commitments without talking to us first. That's not how things are done among men of honour.'

'Let the others speak!' Don Nino ordered at this point.

The district heads of Catalanisetta and Enna said only that they associated themselves with the position expressed by Don Sasà. Don Pietro Uccelli regretted the conflict that had been created but said that he would not be able to accept the proposal.

Finally it was Luigi Rosati's turn. For a haul like that, he was perfectly ready to run the risk of this being a trap by Caputo: as it was, he didn't give a damn about Caputo anyway, and he addressed the Basilisk directly.

'Tell the Lion he can count on me and on the organisation I have the honour to represent, but I want my men in this operation. My earnings are at his disposal. I can contribute half the amount, and he would do me a great honour if one day he agreed to be my guest in Catania.'

Caputo absorbed the blow, and decided to choose the least painful solution for everyone, to at least try and prevent the partial victory obtained by the Lion, whose real strength he did not know, from having even more tragic consequences.

'Tell the Lion I'm expecting him, too, as he knows. And that we're not going to put a spoke in his wheels, as long as his activities do not interfere with ours and he doesn't put the peace we have in Sicily at risk.'

'I'll tell him.'

It fell to Catalfano, who was the host, to accompany the Basilisk back to the airport.

He chose to drive himself, because he didn't want anyone to eavesdrop, not even the most loyal of his foot soldiers.

Halfway there, he broke the silence which the passenger, absorbed in his own thoughts, had been observing.

'Are you worried?'

'Why would I be?'

'I don't know, I think the Lion was expecting a different result, don't you?'

'That's his problem, I just have to report back. I'm sorry about my commission, which will be reduced by half, but obviously I couldn't insist.'

'At least you'll make half, right?'

'That depends on him. He isn't really very generous. By the way, have you made your mind up yet?'

'Of course, but I want to tell him myself. What's the Lion like?'

'Brave,' the Basilisk replied, non-committally.

'Do you think he'll meet Don Nino in the end?'

The man did not reply immediately. He only did so when they were within sight of the airport.

'I don't know. But I have the feeling Don Nino's days are numbered anyway.'

The sharp, confident tone in which he said this almost made Catalfano hope it was true.

PART THREE

OBSTACLES

The basilisk is an image of the destructive power of evil.
Pliny called it 'the king of serpents'
who fear it for its poisonous breath

1

The smells hit Captain Somenti like a wave as soon as he set foot in the store. The main room had ochre walls with rich white stucco decorations and a vaulted ceiling, and the display cases were filled with flasks and bottles, some of them antique, of perfumes and ointments.

At the counter at the far end an assistant was serving a South American customer, but Somenti was not interested in buying. He quickly went through a door on the right and along a short corridor leading to the herb shop, where Ahmed was waiting for him, wearing a felt hat and dark glasses. It was he who had chosen the famous Santa Maria Novella pharmacy and perfume store in the Via della Scala for the meeting because it was mainly frequented by tourists.

The two men did not even greet each other. Somenti placed the paper bag containing the tapes on the floor by a door to the corridor and carried on walking to the far end of the room, where there were no staff at that moment, while the journalist headed in the opposite direction and picked up the bag on his way out.

Somenti returned to Rome by train the evening of the same day, Sunday October 28.

2

'*Schatzi*, darling, darling, wake up!'

It was Petra's voice calling him, Petra's hands shaking him gently to wake him. But he was finding it hard to return to reality and continued to toss and turn in bed. When at last he opened his eyes and found himself in his own bedroom, he touched his body and discovered it was soaked in sweat.

'Get up, Michele. Let's have breakfast. You've had a very restless night. You were talking in your sleep, but I couldn't understand what you were saying.'

'I don't remember a thing. I was talking?'

'That's right.'

'What was I saying?'

'I just told you, I couldn't understand any of it – just half sentences, garbled words, but your voice was strange, mournful.'

'Another nightmare.'

The clock said 7:03 on Monday October 29.

He got out of bed and went straight to the bathroom to take a shower.

He left home at the usual time and told the driver to take him to the Piazza del Cestello. Since those terrible suspicions had arisen about Franchi, a victim of his own naivety – he refused and would always refuse to think of it any other way – he had become even more cautious. Not only did he never take the same route twice, but he always chose the route himself every morning, on the spur of the moment.

He had never been back to the scene of the bombing, but now he decided he wanted to see it again, even though he knew that the road along that stretch of the Lungarno Soderini was still blocked off. The driver stopped the car, an Alfa Romeo 156, before they reached the restricted area, and remained beside it, watching, as Ferrara approached the square on foot. He stood looking at the spot in silence for a few minutes and for the first time became aware of the devastation the car bomb had caused. He remembered the terror of that moment, the worst he had ever experienced, and felt as though he had been miraculously healed, as though he were now living a second life.

Hard on the heels of this feeling was an unfamiliar sense of anger at the idea that he was in danger of wasting this new life. It wasn't possible, it wasn't acceptable, that someone was clipping the wings of the investigation in that way, eliminating the perpetrators one by one. What was particularly unacceptable was that he, Ferrara, should be forced to bend to that person's will, whoever he was. At all costs, he must find a way to fight back, he must find a new angle – he had been wracking his brains for days now.

With a rush of anger, he tossed away his cigar, unlit, and walked back to the car.

At that moment, his office mobile rang.

Ahmed Farah's name appeared on the display.

He decided to take the call, and, as the journalist insisted that he had some really sensational news, Ferrara asked him to come to his office.

*

'Not even I believed it when I said our paths would cross again one day, remember?' he said when they met.

'Get to the point, Ahmed.'

The journalist placed three cassette tapes and a bundle of typewritten sheets on the desk.

'I've spent all night listening to them, translating them and transcribing them. The recordings were made by Captain Somenti, tapping the two phone numbers I got for him. Mullah Hamdullah and Adjmal Yousazai, the two Taliban, remember?'

Yes, but what did this business of spies and Arab terrorists have to do with him? Were they planning a bomb attack in Florence? As if he didn't have enough on his hands with the Mafia bombs!

'So what are they up to?'

'More than you could ever imagine, Chief Superintendent,' Ahmed Farah said, lowering his voice and leaning forward, a smile of legitimate pride lighting up his face. 'They're stirring up the Arabs, and making contact with al-Qaeda affiliates in Italy, especially Tunisians. It's obvious they're planning to put together a solid network of terrorist cells here. Things that would drive the Secret Service wild, and not only the Secret Service.'

He paused for effect, which unnerved Ferrara. He admired Farah's enterprise, and almost envied Somenti and his organisation the acclaim they would get for this, but he really couldn't see what it had to do with him, except as a citizen. This wasn't about Florence or Tuscany any more, it was much bigger.

'And?'

Ahmed Farah's eyes and teeth glittered in unison. 'They're also in cahoots with your chosen enemies, Chief Superintendent, and in a big way. They're setting up a huge exchange: tons of the finest Afghan heroin in return for money or, better still, arms. That's why they were seeing that Dutchman, the arms dealer. They need arms to fight the Allies, or money to buy them.'

'Tons of heroin? Come on, Ahmed, that's completely unheard of!'

'A lot of things used to be unheard of, my dear Chief Superintendent. Like planes bringing down skyscrapers in New York.' Farah collapsed back in his armchair. 'It's all there, in that file. And brace yourself: the name of your dead rival Laprua crops up in the conversation, too.'

'Wait, don't go on. Fanti!' he called.

'Yes, chief?' his secretary said, appearing immediately.

'I want four photocopies of this file, for Rizzo, Ascalchi, Sergi and Venuti, and send for them immediately. And bring coffee for everyone, please, that good kind you make yourself.'

Fanti went back to his office feeling very pleased. It was the first time in far too long that he had had such a request, and it could only mean one thing, confirmed by his chief's tone of voice: he was his old self again, sometimes grouchy, sometimes stern, but also strong and confident.

Over coffee, Ferrara brought his men up to date and then asked Farah to continue from where he had left off.

'As I was saying, they even talked about Zì Turi. Part of this shipment is to replace what you confiscated from the organisation and allow them to honour their commitments to their American cousins, who in return guarantee to spread the drugs among the US forces in versions opportunistically modified to cause maximum damage. Not bad, eh?'

Ferrara and his men looked at each other, more astonished than ever.

'Have you already informed Somenti?'

'Not yet. I spent all night on this, Chief Superintendent, and I wanted you to be the first to know. And besides, Military

Intelligence are already translating the material, they have their own experts, they certainly don't need a poor hack like me! But you do.'

'So we didn't dismantle anything at all,' Ferrara said, looking at Rizzo and thinking how pointless his efforts and those of poor Anna Giulietti had been.

'That's why I was so keen to speak to you,' Farah said. 'Perhaps you can catch this man they call the Lion. Ever since they arrived, the two Afghans have been looking for someone called Assad. I thought it was the name of one of their Arab associates. But Assad *means* lion, and it turns out to be this man, the Lion, who's organising the whole thing.'

Ferrra looked at Rizzo. The realisation had hit them at the same time.

Silverio Liuzza had reported that Laprua had muttered the word 'fools' during their last conversation: 'cugghiuni' in Sicilian dialect. But he hadn't been saying that at all, he'd been saying ''U liuni' – Sicilian for 'the Lion'.

He picked up the file and leafed quickly through it. He looked disappointed. 'The mobile phone numbers aren't here.'

'No. Those are the actual recordings, the rest is with Military Intelligence. The only numbers I have are those of the two Taliban, the ones I gave the captain.'

'Give them to me, anyway. Or rather give them directly to Inspector Venturi, he's a wizard at interceptions.'

The inspector noted them down.

'Thanks, Ahmed,' Ferrara continued. 'You've been brilliant. Even more than you know. We'll take a good look at the transcript and I'll co-ordinate with Military Intelligence in Rome. You'll see, those two won't get away, we'll tap their phones here, too. And we'll get this damned Lion!'

'Please, whatever you find out, when the moment is right, *La Nazione* wants the exclusive!'

'Who else?'

'Okay, then, see you soon.'

'Can you leave us the tapes?'

'They're yours, I wasn't planning to take them with me. But I doubt that your Arabic translators, if you have any, could do any better than I did.'

Ferrara doubted it, too, but that was not why he had asked for them.

Once the journalist had gone, he asked Venturi to immediately get hold of an Arabic translator for the subsequent phone taps, then dismissed his men and threw himself avidly into reading the transcript, which was nineteen closely printed pages long. And into listening to the tapes, which he did over and over again, trying to fix in his mind the sound of the Lion's voice, to memorise its tones and cadences, and its quirks and defects if it had any.

It was a cultured, well-bred voice, without an accent, but not only had it been disguised in some way, it was also subtly altered, as always happens, by the use of another language. The man seemed to know Arabic quite well, falling back on his excellent English whenever he was unable to find a word or phrase. He only ever spoke to Mullah Hamdullah, clearly the head of the nascent terrorist network, whose English by contrast was somewhat broken.

3

ANTONIO CAPUTO, SOUGHT SINCE 1975, FINALLY
ARRESTED: that, or something similar, was the headline on
virtually all the front pages on the morning of October 30.

Boss of bosses captured in house near Capaci was the second
headline in La Nazione, which Ferrara was reading over
breakfast.

PALERMO. Hiding out in a modest peasant house a few
kilometres from Capaci, where Judge Falcone and his escort
lost their lives, the boss of bosses Antonio Caputo, known as
Antonino or Don Nino, has finally been brought to justice in
a brilliant police operation, after more than twenty-five years
on the run. Sought by the police since 1975, he was considered
the Italian Scarlet Pimpernel. He calmly admitted his real
identity to officers of the Central Operational Service and the
Squadra Mobile of Palermo when they entered his house
after neutralising the guards in the surrounding area without
a shot being fired. 'This arrest,' declared Salvo Almerita,
Police Commissioner of Palermo, 'is the result of a lengthy
and painstaking investigation by a special team comprising
officers of the Central Operational Service and the Squadra

Mobile, *who worked in absolute secrecy, using traditional police methods such as tailing suspects and tapping phones. Caputo was not betrayed by anyone, and we did not rely on informers.'*

Ferrara wondered why Salvo Amerita had added that detail. True, it was a tribute to the brave colleagues who had done something deemed impossible for many years and brought the hunt for Caputo to a brilliant conclusion. But it also seemed to be dictated by the need to protect someone – or did Ferrara only think that because his profession made him naturally suspicious?

Whatever the truth of the matter, what had happened was so big, it was likely to put everything else on the back burner for a few days, and that worried him. Everyone, from the Head of the State Police to the Anti-Mafia Squad, would be very busy, and that was likely to have a negative effect on his own investigation.

He had confirmation of this later when he got to Headquarters – where the arrest was the one topic of conversation – and tried to contact Military Intelligence in Rome. He found it practically impossible to speak to anyone in authority. They were all either busy or absent! He hoped they were busy hunting down the terrorists fingered by Ahmed, but he doubted it. Unfortunately.

And there was in fact another reason why Military Intelligence were so unavailable, connected to a news item that had appeared in the daily papers, although this one had been relegated to the inside pages by all the fuss being made about the arrest of Antonio Caputo.

Nicola Spadaro had found it in the *Corriere della Sera*.

WASHINGTON DENIES TALIBAN CLAIM
TO BE HOLDING AMERICANS
Tunnels in Eastern Afghanistan, possible
Bin Laden refuge, bombed
Mullahs' regime reins in Pakistani volunteers:
'Thank you, but we will need you later.'

FROM OUR CORRESPONDENT IN ISLAMABAD:
He says he does not know how many there are *[Three, of course, Spadaro thought]*, or where they are, or the circumstances in which they were captured, let alone when they will be released. All he will say is, 'Some Americans are under arrest.' More than one: that is the only thing that the Taliban ambassador in Islamabad, Abdul Salam Zaeef, is willing to say.

Together with his superior, General Arturo Mangiagalli, director of Military Intelligence, Spadaro had rushed to the Ministry of Defence for an emergency meeting.

Captain Somenti was unavailable for another reason: he was on the train, on his way to Florence to speak to Ahmed and, hopefully, also to see Major Alibrandi.

Perhaps Giulia, too.

4

The following day was even worse than Ferrara had feared, a real bureaucratic nightmare.

Captain Somenti was away on some kind of vague 'mission' and, although Ferrara left messages, he did not hear from him. Nor would Somenti's chief, Spadaro, answer his calls, and talking to his secretary was like talking to the wall. The Head of the State Police, Guaschelli, was preoccupied with the latest developments in the Caputo case. Caputo's threadbare wallet had been found to contain an old, yellowing photograph of a beautiful young girl. As he had obstinately refused to identify the girl, the photograph had been circulated among the police, but had not yielded any results. Some wanted to give it to the press, in the hope that it would jog someone's memory, but most, including Ferrara, did not see the point: the photograph was clearly very old and hardly mattered now. It could even have been a photo of Caputo's mother, may she rest in peace. The search continued, but discreetly.

After countless attempts, he finally managed to get hold of Guaschelli late that morning, only to be asked to send in a detailed report. 'As a matter of urgency!' Guaschelli said.

There was no point in Ferrara telling him that he had already had Fanti fax him the report, just as he had faxed copies to all the interested bodies, including the Carabinieri and the Prosecutor's Department.

When, on the afternoon of November 1, he went in person to Acting Prosecutor Cosenza to complain, he found he was the one being asked for a shoulder to cry on.

'I read it, Chief Superintendent, I read it. And I agree with you that it's first-class material, and that it would help our investigation enormously if we had the telephone number of this Lion. Military Intelligence must have it, because they did the phone taps. I've tried as best I could, but haven't got anywhere. Unfortunately, as you well know, I have no power over the Secret Service – they don't have to answer for their activities to any Prosecutor's Department. So I'm in the same position as you, neither more nor less. All I can do is carry on with what's left of the investigation, try and find Sandro Caruso and Leonardo Parisi, and hope that sooner or later Military Intelligence either condescend to return our calls, or get down to work on their own account and hand us the Lion on a silver platter. After all, what's on those tapes is their province. They have to do something, don't they?'

'Do you have any idea how long they could take to translate and transcribe the tapes, put the material in order and work out a plan of action?'

'I know, but what can we do? Patience is a virtue, they say, so we just have to be patient, Chief Superintendent.'

'All this patience makes us look weak, when we should be strong.'

'We're not weak. The State isn't weak. Don't forget the arrest of Caputo. That took hard work and – yes – patience. In the long run, the State wins, Chief Superintendent. We just have to wait.'

Ferrara nodded and took his leave.

Let's hope you're right, he thought as he went out, but there was something very strange about the fact that the true head of the Mafia, after sitting pretty for more than twenty-five years, should have been captured at precisely that moment. He didn't like to think that the Lion had had a hand in that arrest, too – although this Lion was certainly shaping up as the likeliest successor to Caputo, and seemed quite willing to provoke a war to get there.

No, he didn't like to think that.

But he did.

5

On Friday November 2, All Souls' Day, Chief Superintendent Ferrara decided not to go straight to Headquarters.

'The Porte Sante cemetery,' he ordered the driver. 'And stop on the way at the first decent florist's you find.'

The cemetery, adjoining the Romanesque church of San Miniato al Monte to the south of the city, on the other side of the Arno, now houses only prominent figures or those who have a family vault. Anna Giulietti, being of an old and noble family, had her last resting place there.

He found Anna's elderly mother already at the graveside, supported by a nurse. He greeted her, but, when she lifted the black veil from her face and he saw her eyes brimming with tears, he decided not to pursue the conversation. He placed his wreath on the grave and for a long time stood at a respectful distance from the old woman, in silence.

He remembered the beauty, in every sense, of his colleague, adviser, friend – and what else? He was still asking himself that question, and he still had not found an answer. He recalled her intelligence, her sense of duty, but also her unstinting loyalty, which sometimes led her to bend the rules just for him, even though respect for the rules was her life blood. They had fought and won many battles together, and she had fully deserved her recent appointment as acting prosecutor. How tragic that she had had so little time to enjoy it, and that she had paid such a high price for it!

He made a silent vow to her that he would not rest until he had avenged her.

Whatever it took.

When he realised that her mother was throwing him a discreet glance from time to time, he felt embarrassed, wondering if by any chance she had read her daughter's diary. But it wasn't embarrassment that made him take a step back to avoid her gaze.

It was to avoid her seeing his tears. For a man to cry might not be dignified, but for the head of the *Squadra Mobile* it would have been a scandal.

He put those tears down, not so much to grief, as to age.

More than six hundred miles away, Pippo Catalfano, district boss of Castelvetrano, was on his way to a very different kind of cemetery, although he did not know it yet. Nor did he know that he would have to make a stop along the way, a stop he had never imagined even in his worst nightmares.

His day had got off to a very good start.

Just before nine in the morning, his former lieutenant Gino La Torre, whom he had given up for dead, suddenly turned up at his house. He made a great fuss of him, treating him almost as the prodigal son. He had him tell of his many adventures escaping first from Ferrara's men, then from Caputo's, the latter a lot more lethal than the Sicilian police – he'd had no trouble evading them all these years! They both laughed over this, and then Catalfano told La Torre all about the epic meeting at the Banca Polpolare di Montepellegrino, how it had been mediated by the Basilisk, who was Caputo's man but impartial, because he was first and foremost a shrewd businessman, which was what a good mediator had to be. He had immediately understood which way the wind was blowing, and had told him that Caputo's days were numbered. Things were changing at last, even in Sicily – they would soon be sorted out, and then the two of them, under the guidance of the Lion and the Basilisk, would be in charge.

'There's a world to be won here in Sicily,' he had concluded, beaming. 'And you'll be with us at the top of the heap, Gino!'

Then he suggested that they should celebrate his return by going out and having a slap-up fish dinner, just like the good old days, and La Torre, who was down at heel, gratefully accepted. But first, he said, perhaps Pippo could go with him to his hideout to pick up his few things. It was a cave in the mountains, no more than eighteen miles to the north.

Pippo Catalfano calculated that he could easily get back in time. He gave instructions for his men – some thirty of them – to meet him at the restaurant, and set off his with his restored right arm in the direction Gino La Torre indicated.

A mile or two after the exit from the autostrada, as they were starting to climb up into the mountains along a secondary road, the driver tensed at the sight of a car in the rear-view mirror, following some distance behind. The next time he looked, he saw that it had moved closer, and that there were two cars now. The third time he looked, there were three.

He put his foot on the accelerator. 'We're being followed, boss.'

Catalfano turned, and saw with dismay that he was right. He heard La Torre's order in a firm voice, 'Let them follow you. And slow down, don't try to lose them.'

When he turned round again, pale-faced, he saw Gino

sitting there with a grim expression, a Colt in his right hand, pointed at him, and a Beretta in his left, held to the driver's head.

He said nothing, but started praying in silence.

'Okay, now take the left-hand road when we get to the fork.'

They travelled for a long time along almost deserted byroads, in a southerly direction, still followed by the three cars, now close behind, until they reached an area of open country near Agrigento, the sight of which made Catalfano shudder.

On La Torre's orders, the driver pulled up in front of a very high iron gate and sounded his horn. Immediately, the gate was opened. The car went through and all the way across a yard until it came to a brick building, where it stopped, as did the three cars behind it.

La Torre made Pippo Catalfano get out. Sasà emerged from the first of the other cars, Molina from the second, and Don Pietro Uccelli from the third, each of them followed by three armed men.

In total silence, they handcuffed Catalfano. With another pair of handcuffs, the driver was attached to the wheel of the car.

They went inside the house.

There were two rooms. One was very large and the other small and dark, with a toilet bowl barely visible in the light filtering in through a small window. In the larger room, amid crates of mineral water, jute sacks, ropes of various sizes and latex gloves like those used by surgeons, thirteen chairs had been placed in a circle, with a fourteenth chair in the middle.

'You, there,' Sasà ordered, nodding towards the chair in the middle.

Pippo Catalfano was forced to sit down and his feet were

tied. If he had still harboured some feeble hope, the sight of this place extinguished it completely. It was the warehouse, known only to a select few, nicknamed 'the chamber of death'. He had always considered it a medieval relic of the old Mafia he had hoped to replace.

'What do you want with me?' he said, desperation giving him the strength to protest. 'What have I ever done to you?'

'Never mind that,' La Torre said, enunciating his words clearly. 'You must tell us where the traitors are.'

'How am I supposed to do that? I don't know, I've never seen them. Only the Basilisk that one time in Palermo, and you all saw him.' He looked at each of them in turn, imploringly.

'But you talk to him,' La Torre insisted.

'Yes. I told you.'

'I know you did. But how do you talk to him? On the phone? Never in person?'

'I have no choice.'

'Give us the numbers, then,' La Torre said, with a sardonic grin. 'We'd be happy with that. We're good people, and we like you.'

'Of course, of course,' Catalfano said, and he quickly recited the numbers, which he knew by heart.

Then Don Pietro Uccelli said, 'Why did you betray us?'

'I haven't betrayed you, I—' he began, but immediately broke off because he knew it was pointless. Instead, he implored, 'Kill me with a single shot, don't strangle me. And don't dispose of my body. I'd like my children to be able to mourn over my grave.'

No one replied.

Pippo Catalfano closed his eyes.

The men looked at each other, waiting for a signal that no one any longer had the authority to give.

Then they all looked at Gino La Torre, investing him with the role for which Caputo, deep down, had already destined him.

It was up to him to kill the boss of the Castelvetrano district and take his place.

Gino walked up to him with a short rope in his hand, put it around his neck and started to squeeze, almost gently at first and then with increasing force.

Catalfano let out a guttural moan, his face became swollen and purple, and his eyes rolled up. His body was shaken by spasms as if he were being given a series of electric shocks. The spasms grew more intense, and then slowly diminished in strength until the body was completely still.

'Now if anyone wants to say goodbye they can,' La Torre said, moving aside. It was the customary invitation to the others to pull the fatal rope if they so wished.

In turn, each of those present did so.

They put the body in a trunk and one of the Mafiosi, the youngest of them, poured in the contents of an entire drum of acid. Within a couple of hours there was nothing left of the body. When it was pure liquid, they emptied it in the garden, where it formed a black patch which would disappear the first time it rained.

A second patch also marked the end of the unfortunate driver.

6

They had not yet put a tap on the Taliban's phones, and the *Squadra Mobile* was running on empty, which drove Ferrara mad. There was no lack of activity, but because of the inexplicable difficulties he continued to encounter, he did not feel that his efforts were focused on the main objective. Was it his fault? he kept asking himself. But he did not see what else he could have done, and the impasse was certainly not down to lack of trying. Apart from his professional pride and his need to protect himself, there was also – and this mattered more than all the rest – the promise he had made over the grave of Anna Giulietti.

To escape the sense of stagnation which he felt on the first floor of Headquarters, that Saturday he decided to go and see if the Carabinieri had any news for him.

Major Alibrandi greeted him with the usual courtesy, even though he was very busy.

The barracks was in a state of great excitement, but not for the reasons Ferrara would have liked. All the activity was connected with the Carabinieri's participation in the Afghanistan operation, and Ferrara saw officers from other parts of the army and even other countries.

The investigation into the Florence bombings seemed to have faded into the background, or even to have been forgotten entirely.

Major Alibrandi confirmed his suspicions. 'Now that all the main suspects have either died or disappeared, the case is practically closed as far as we're concerned. We've alerted all our stations to keep an eye open for Leonardo Parisi and Sandro Caruso, but there's nothing more we can do.'

'But did you see the report I sent you on the phone taps, with the information on this man, the Lion?'

'Yes, and I even talked to Acting Prosecutor Cosenza about it, but the ball's out of our court now. It's down to Military Intelligence, the Anti-Mafia Squad – and you, of course. Right now we have other fish to fry, believe me.'

It was pointless to insist.

Ferrara took his leave.

'Goodbye, Chief Superintendent. Oh, by the way, Captain Somenti asked me to give you his regards if I saw you. You remember him, don't you? I get the impression he really admires you.'

'Why?' Ferrara said, startled. 'Have you seen him recently?'

'Yes, of course, he's in Florence. Officially, it's to do with those phone taps you mentioned, and to see Ahmed Farah – who's now got an armed escort, by the way, courtesy of the Florence bureau of Military Intelligence. But actually, trust me, the reason he's here is much more personal. What do they say? *Cherchez la femme!*'

Of course: Giulia Roversi! How come he had never thought of that?

When he got back to the office, he tracked down her number and called her.

The captain was with her.

Taking advantage of the fine weather, they agreed to meet at the Caffè Rivoire in the Piazza della Signoria. Thanks to the long weekend, and the warm sun that bathed the statues and the facades of the old palaces with light, the square was swarming with the sounds and colours of cohorts of tourists. To Ferrara, it seemed like another world.

'Actually, I'm not here officially,' Somenti said. 'Farah asked to see me, and besides, I wanted to talk to Giulia again. I really can't get her out of my head. I think you've gathered that much, haven't you? And then the Florence bureau called me to say they'd had instructions to provide Farah with an escort – not before time, if you ask me. Not that he took it well, you know what he's like, but the orders come straight from the Ministry, so he'll just have to make the best of a bad job.'

'I agree with you. Ahmed is reckless, he needs protection. But to think, Captain, I spent so much time trying to get hold of you, and here you were, right here in Florence. If only I'd known!'

'I'm sorry, they didn't tell me. I'd have liked to come and see you, but I didn't want to bother you. Why were you trying to get hold of me?'

'Because of those phone intercepts. Have you read them?'

'No. When I left, the originals of the tapes had just gone to the appropriate department for deciphering and transcription. But Farah told me. It's truly astonishing, the number of terrorists who are taking root here. I immediately faxed my chief, and as soon as I get back I want to be one of the team that nabs them! We'll dismantle the network piece by piece, don't worry.'

'Good. But look, I'm not trying to interfere or grab the glory for my squad, only I'd like the Lion for myself, if possible. There are a few things I'd like to ask him.'

Captain Somenti smiled. 'Yes, Farah told me all about the Mafia's drugs for arms swap. I can understand your interest, especially after what happened. But he also told me you were already working on that angle.'

'I would be if I could have the support of your people,' Ferrara said. 'Do you have any idea why your chief won't return my calls?'

Somenti smiled, not in the least surprised. 'Who, Spadaro? He's a waste of space, Chief Superintendent. He's always out of the office, on some vague 'mission' or other. The only things he's interested in are women and his pension. We all know that.'

'So if I want help, you're the one to ask.'

'Anything I can do.'

'What I'd like is the Lion's number, if that's not asking too much.'

'Is that all? That's easy.'

'But I need it right away.'

'It'll have to be on Monday.' He smiled again. 'No point trying on a Saturday or a Sunday, even when there's a war on. You know what government departments are like. I'm going back to Rome tomorrow. I'll call you first thing Monday morning.'

'OK,' Ferrara said, resigned to the wait: he knew how these things worked.

Duranti had invited them again that Sunday.

It had been less an invitation than an appeal, and it would have been impossible to refuse. Besides, the weather was wonderful, and Ferrara had nothing else to do while waiting both for Somenti's phone call, and for the tap on the terrorists' phones to be authorised, so naturally he accepted. Petra, who felt quite at home now in Zanego, was delighted and had taken advantage of the occasion to make an appointment with the architect. She had taken care to buy two bottles of the best Brunello di Montalcino available on the market to take Duranti.

As it was a holiday weekend, the traffic was quite heavy. Along the winding exit that led from the mouth of the River Magra to Montemarcello, Ferrara, who was driving his elderly Mercedes, had to slow down several times behind cyclists out for a day trip, often riding side by side and taking up half a lane. And he was forced to a complete standstill when he reached the stretch of road looking out over the mouth of the Magra and the curve of the coast to beyond Viareggio, which was packed with cars that had stopped to let their passengers take photographs or simply admire the view. The air was so clear that you could see the distant outlines of Sardinia and even the island of Elba.

They reached Zanego just before midday.

Mephisto was on good form – in other words, in his usual foul mood. He greeted them with laments about the infirmities of old age as well as with a delicious chilled Vermentino by Lambruschi, a winemaker from the Luni area, which they drank beneath the notorious canopy.

For lunch he took them to Pescarino's, a pleasant restaurant so close by that they were able to get to it on foot along a path through the greenery, which in places became so narrow as to make it difficult for cars to get through – although that didn't stop drivers trying to find a way in just to save their lazy passengers having to walk a few steps.

They talked about various topics, one of them, inevitably, being the war in Afghanistan. Like everyone in the country, they had conflicting opinions about its usefulness.

Only when they had returned to the house and Petra had set off with the architect to inspect her purchase, which was not very far away, did Duranti tackle the real reason for his invitation.

'I'm still worried about you, Chief Superintendent.'

'I know, the case isn't over yet.' He went over the latest developments, including the tapes Ahmed had supplied.

Duranti did not seem particularly surprised – which did surprise Ferrara, although he said nothing.

'All of which takes you into that awkward territory I begged you to avoid, remember?'

'The third level – which seems to have become international.'

'Apparently, yes. You need to keep your distance, you and that journalist. And this is not just advice.'

The tone was more admonitory than anxious, which Ferrara thought strange.

'Don't worry,' he said, making light of it. 'I travel with an escort – apart from today, when I'm on holiday! And they've given him one, too.'

'I know,' Duranti said with a kind of smirk.

What did he know? That Ferrara had an escort, or that they had given one to Ahmed Farah? And why the smirk?

It suddenly crossed his mind that escorts might have a dual function: on the one hand, they protected your life, and on the other, they kept an eye on you, especially if they were supplied by Military Intelligence.

Alarm bells had started ringing and now sounded loud and clear in the perfect silence of the garden.

'Do you also know that Military Intelligence aren't returning my calls?' he asked.

Duranti looked at him for a long time, with sad, weary eyes.

Was he tempted to tell him something he wasn't supposed to know?

'I still have many friends in Rome,' he said, after a pause Ferrara had found interminable. 'I know a lot of things. Not all, but quite a lot. I also know that in some circles they're starting to look on you as something of a nuisance. You shouldn't meddle in things that are so much bigger than you, Michele. You don't have the skills for it – you're not exactly diplomatic. Let it go. Let other people deal with this Mafioso who's in league with the Taliban, other people who are more expert at a game you don't understand. Limit yourself to doing what you're paid for, and don't try to be a hero, a superman – the time for that has passed. The world is changing, other people hold the dice now. Listen to me, and stand aside.'

Ferrara could hardly believe his ears. The longer the old man spoke, the greater the anger and frustration he felt welling up inside him. This man, his teacher and his confidant, was telling him to step aside! Appealing to what he took to be common sense, he was dispensing advice that came dangerously close to being a veiled warning.

He still trusted and respected Duranti too much to believe that he was acting on orders from above. One of them was wrong, and he was not sure who. Not that it mattered: his reaction would not come from his rational mind.

When it came, it was from somewhere much deeper and more unfathomable. 'I can't,' he said. 'It's impossible.'

'Nothing's impossible,' Duranti said, already dispirited, knowing how stubborn, even obtuse, Ferrara could be.

Predictably, Ferrara gave him the most disarming look possible, a look of total conviction. 'I promised Anna.'

Duranti held his gaze, then lowered his eyes and shook his head, sadly.

8

The storm broke on Monday November 5, after a holiday weekend that had been relatively peaceful for most Italians, distracted only by the weather reports and sports news. And the person in the eye of the storm was none other than Armando Guaschelli, Head of the State Police, who was accused of having left an inexplicably long lapse of time between the capture of Caruso and the search of his hideout, which did not take place until five days later. It was argued that within that time the most compromising documents could have ended up in the hands of God knows who – a perfectly reasonable argument, since, as it turned out, no such documents were found.

Ferrara read the accounts in the newspapers with growing annoyance, feeling more alone than ever. With all this business, he was sure the report he had sent Guaschelli about the intercepts would now be ignored till the cows came home.

All he could do now was wait for Somenti's call.

Which never came.

Is that all? he had said when Ferrara had asked him for that number, but when he had said that, he had no idea what had been happening in the meantime at Military Intelligence.

That Monday, when Somenti had asked Sergeant Giorgio Azzaro to give him all the paperwork relating to the intercepts, the sergeant had looked at him as if he were an extraterrestrial recently arrived on earth or an American marine who had just landed in a hostile Middle Eastern country.

'You mean you don't know, Captain?'

'Know what?'

'Spadaro has grabbed hold of the file, and absolutely forbidden anyone else access until further orders from him or the minister.'

'Why?'

'State secrets apparently – so secret they're even forbidden to servants of the State whose business is secrets,' the sergeant replied with heavy irony. He sounded more disenchanted than ever.

'State secrets? They were obtained by a journalist! A journalist who knows everything! And if the press knows, then—'

'I wouldn't tell the chief that, if I were you.'

'But what are you saying? That we're doing nothing? With all the stuff that's in those intercepts?' It was only now that Somenti realised that the atmosphere in the office was the same as ever, with nothing to indicate that there was an emergency.

'Why, what *is* there?' Azzaro asked with a disarming smile, completely unfazed and without any real curiosity.

The captain turned his back on him and headed straight for Nicola Spadaro's office, hoping to find him there.

In fact he was, and, miraculously, he did not even make him wait too long.

As soon as Somenti entered, instead of greeting him,

Spadaro asked, clearly irritated, 'Are you sure the men we've provided as an escort for the journalist are good men who can be trusted, as I requested?'

'Yes, sir. I checked them myself one by one.'

'Then let's get down to business. You owe me an explanation.'

The captain had come in thinking exactly the opposite, but his superior's tone did not allow for objections.

'What about?'

'Don't act dumb, Captain. Those phone taps you set up weren't ordered by me. In fact, I wasn't even informed!' His tanned face was starting to turn red.

'Precisely because you weren't the one to order them. I did it on my own initiative at the request of—'

'Of a journalist! So now it's been decided that Military Intelligence is at the beck and call of the press, is that it? And who decided that – you?'

'It's not that. It's a long story, but when you get down to it what matters are the results, which are explosive and demand—'

'I decide that, damn it, not you!'

Captain Somenti felt his mind clouding over.

He was completely confused. Why was this usually bland and habitually absent bureaucrat being so zealous all of a sudden? Perhaps he had made a mistake, but Spadaro's reaction was out of all proportion, when you considered what he had discovered thanks to Ahmed. Indeed, it was completely absurd that a man who looked like a beach resort playboy should be wasting time reprimanding him while terrorist cells were spreading through the country like a cancer.

Gradually his confusion and bewilderment at Spadaro's verbal assault, and his naturally humble attitude towards his superiors, gave way to irritation.

'It's an established fact now, sir, that there are Taliban in Tuscany, in other words, in Italy, and that's due to me – if you don't mind me saying so – whether the means of obtaining the information was right or wrong!'

Nicola Spadaro sat back in his leather armchair with a slightly idiotic smirk and a suddenly pensive air. 'How do you know that?' he asked calmly, after a brief pause. 'When you left, the tapes had not yet been deciphered.'

'The journalist told me, the one we owe them to.'

'So you gave him copies, then?' There was genuine aston-ishment in his voice, as if the captain had just profaned the image of a saint or spat on the Italian flag. Then his tone became sarcastic again. 'This just gets better and better!'

'Of course I gave him copies, the material belonged to him – it was part of the work he's doing, which has been of such value to us—'

'Oh, so phone intercepts don't belong to the Service but to a foreign journalist. Congratulations! Since then, he's shown them to that pain in the arse, the head of the *Squadra Mobile* in Florence, who's been dogging my footsteps like a stalker. Now I understand why. Do you realise what you've done? Do you actually realise?' He was screaming now, his anger having not only returned but increased.

Yes, I do realise, Somenti thought, now completely calm and confident again.

'You've committed a very serious offence,' Spadaro, whose face had turned from red to purple, went on. 'It'd be a court martial offence if we were in Afghanistan, and there's nothing to say it won't be one here, too. Now go, get out of here, take some leave, and wait for the disciplinary procedure – and you won't get off lightly, do you understand?'

'Yes, sir!' Somenti replied, giving a military salute and clicking his heels. He left the room, slamming the door.

He would wait for the procedure, but in his own way.

As Azzaro looked on curiously, he walked to his desk, switched on his computer, and started writing a letter to the director.

Then he printed what he had written, read it over, went back to his desk and signed it.

Finally, very calmly, he gathered his things together and arranged them in two large cardboard boxes.

'Do me a favour, Sergeant,' he said, on his way out, buckling slightly under the weight. 'Make sure that letter gets to General Mangiagalli. Thanks.'

Azzaro waited until he had gone out before he stood up and walked to the other desk to pick up the letter. He read it, folded it, put it in a letter addressed to the head of Military Intelligence, and went to give it to his secretary.

Mentally, he saluted the captain, whom he envied.

9

'The Lion can't be touched, at least for now,' Nicola Spadaro said once again to Armando Guaschelli during a very confidential meeting held that afternoon in the presence of the Defence Minister and the Minister of the Interior.

The head of the State Police, who had already heard this assertion repeated *ad nauseam*, agreed. 'He can't be touched, okay, but for how long? His tip-off about Caputo worked out perfectly, you were right. But it's also true that the four days he's asked us for in return is having a boomerang effect, and I'm the one who's paying the consequences!'

'Don't worry about that,' the Minister of the Interior reassured him. 'We'll cover you. Let the papers scream – the next big story they get, they'll forget all about it. But what I'd like to know is why, now that we've got what we wanted, we still have to protect this Mafioso. We don't even know where he's hiding.'

'Because he can still be useful to us. *Very* useful. My office has discovered that he has, let's say, a business relationship with the Taliban. Which makes him a potentially valuable asset right now. And not just for us. Our colleagues in the CIA became very interested when I told them about him, because of their agents who are being held prisoner in Afghanistan. We've been looking together at the best way to use him. I can't say any more, except that, now that we have him in our power, it won't be difficult to persuade him to help us. It'll be an operation on a vast scale, which will not only lead to the freeing of the hostages, but may well inflict a decisive blow against the enemy.'

'I see,' the Minister of Defence said. 'So don't worry and do what you have to do, all right, Signor Guaschelli?'

'Absolutely!' said the head of the State Police, feeling that he had obtained what he most wanted.

As they were leaving the Ministry, Spadaro stopped Guaschelli on the steps.

'I need a favour.'

'Go on.'

'Get this man Ferrara off my back. He knows everything, and he's determined to pursue the Lion.'

'Don't worry, I'll deal with him.'

'Please do. The stakes in this game are enormous, and we wouldn't like anything to happen to him, would we?'

And with a jovial smile, he left Guaschelli on the steps and hurried towards the blue Mercedes that was waiting for him a short distance away.

The head of the State Police watched him go with a strange shudder. Even to someone like him, accustomed to rough and ready methods when necessary, these difficult times, in which it had become almost normal for one servant of the State to threaten another life, were starting to be a little bit uncomfortable.

It was not until a few days later that Somenti appeared in Ferrara's office.

In the uniform of a major in the Carabinieri.

314

The promotion had been automatic after his year's service in Military Intelligence, and his joining Alibrandi's unit had been a natural consequence of the many conversations the two men had had during the ex-captain's stays in Florence.

A possible disciplinary procedure was still hanging over his head, but he wasn't worried about that: he would appeal, if necessary. What mattered was how much better he felt. Not to mention Giulia's reaction, which more than made up for any future problems.

'It's been a liberation, Chief Superintendent, believe me. When I slammed that door shut, I felt lighter than I've ever felt in my life. It was as if a heavy weight had been lifted from my shoulders. That place is a nest of vipers. No, worse: of incompetents. Shrivelled-up old bureaucrats who can't tell the difference between an act of excusable indiscipline and a threat to national security. Those are the people whose hands we're in! I may have acted thoughtlessly, for God's sake, I don't deny it, but still, that's no way to treat someone who's conscientiously doing his duty. Even if I was wrong, and I don't think I was wrong – they'd realise that if only they took a closer look at what I gave them. That stuff's dynamite, and it could blow up in their faces.'

'When you reach my age, Major, you'll realise it doesn't always pay to be too impetuous. Resigning as soon as you get into difficulty isn't a good sign. But maybe that's not the whole truth, right? Let's say you grabbed the opportunity, and maybe you did the right thing, but forget all this talk about competence and principles.'

'I understand what you're saying. You'd have preferred me to stay, that way I would have got you that number. But it was quite impossible, believe me. I'd have stolen it if I could!'

'Don't worry, it's not your fault. It's obvious it wasn't meant to be.'

'What do you plan to do?'

'To tell the truth, I don't know. There are just too many obstacles, I don't think I can overcome them. Maybe I should also slam the door and go, I'd make my wife happy. What about you?'

'Major Alibrandi trusts me. If I can get him completely on my side, maybe we can go over the heads of the politicians and get the military top brass to do something.'

Ferrara shuddered at the thought of what this might mean for democracy. 'Good luck then, Major.'

'You, too, Chief Superintendent.'

What a world! Ferrara said to himself as he picked up the phone, intending to ask Fanti to tell his wife he would be home early. It mightn't yet be time to pack it all in, but it was certainly time to go home, as far as he was concerned.

But Fanti, quicker even than usual, was already standing there in front of him.

Only, instead of his usual industrious air, he looked pale and shaken.

The reason was the fax he handed him, anticipating a letter to follow.

It bore the heading of the Secretariat of the Head of the State Police, and was not the one he had been expecting for more than a week now.

To Chief Superintendent Michele Ferrara
Head of *Squadra Mobile*
Police Headquarters, Florence

A formal complaint has been made to this office
concerning the interference of the *Squadra Mobile* in the
activities of other bodies on matters within their area of
expertise, as evidenced by the report submitted by
yourself to this office on October 30 this year.

As such interference could cause incalculable damage
to the aforementioned bodies and to national security,
you are asked to suspend, with immediate effect and until
further notice, any and all activities having as their object
the suspected Mafioso known as the Lion, and any and
all activities in any way related to or ascribable to this
person.

The right is reserved to institute disciplinary
procedures, should it arise that you do not keep to the
present arrangement.

Armando Guaschelli
Head of State Police

Ferrara put the letter down, looked at Fanti, and smiled.
'Send for Rizzo, Ascalchi, Sergi and Venuti, and then come
back here.'

'Right away, chief, but—'

'Just do as I say, and don't worry.'

Once Fanti had gone, he calmly lit a cigar.

When his men were led in by Fanti, he showed them the
letter and said, 'Suspend the phone taps, Venturi. Francesco,
I'm leaving you in charge of the squad. You're in good hands,
boys, better than mine. I just want to ask one favour. Don't
say a word. Do as I tell you and leave this room without
speaking. Thanks for everything.'

Alone now, he took his badge from his pocket – the badge
he would have given his life for as a young man, the badge he
had almost lost his life for as a Chief Superintendent – and
tossed it angrily in the drawer next to the pistol he never carried with him these days, in defiance of the rules.

Then he went out.

His escort were about to follow him, but he said to the

leader, 'The service is cancelled. It's not needed any more. Tell the others and thank you.'

He dismissed the driver, too.

It was early, but the sky was overcast and it would be dark soon.

He set off on foot, without a specific destination.

From the window of his office on the first floor, Fanti saw him walk slowly away, his head bowed. When he had disappeared from view, Fanti returned to his desk, fished out a packet of paper handkerchiefs and blew his nose, even though he did not have a cold.

10

Ferrara walked home, but did not stop when he reached his building. Instead, he kept walking parallel to the river, completely unaware of the fake tourist who, as soon as he had turned on to the Lungarno degli Acciaioli, had trained a powerful pair of binoculars on him from behind the monument to Benevenuto Cellini in the middle of the Ponte Vecchio, and then had started following him at a distance, communicating his movements through the earpiece of a mobile phone.

Ferrara crossed the Ponte alle Grazie, not knowing where his steps were taking him, and started climbing towards the Belvedere. After a while, he cut off the main road and pushed higher still along streets and up steps swathed in greenery as the sky grew ever darker. When he was almost at the Porte Sante, he turned left until he reached the foot of the flight of steps that led up to the imposing church of San Miniato with its five majestic arcades on a facade of white and green marble. To his left, Florence lay below him, the lights already coming on.

He climbed the steps.

When he was in front of the church, he went through the arcade on the left which led to the cemetery, stopping before the gate at the shop run by the monks, where he bought a heather plant.

There was a sign saying that the cemetery closed at five o'clock in winter. Best to hurry up.

The thin, faded yellow lights from the chapels and the red flickers of the votive lamps imbued him with the sense of peace and security he was searching for. Everything else was already wrapped in gloom, and all he could see were the outlines of gravestone and crosses, but he did not need to see to find the way, his feet kept moving automatically.

He placed the plant at the foot of the grave.

He couldn't pray, but he could apologise. He didn't do it, because he knew that Anna would never accept his apologies. She would expect anything from him except surrender.

He stood there until a monk informed him they were about to close.

He left the cemetery like an automaton, descended the long flight of steps and went and sat down on one of the imposing parapets which formed the boundary of the gardens immediately beyond the road.

He looked at Florence, all lit up by now, as if for the last time. Everything had gone wrong, he was no longer in the mood to play this game.

As if to confirm this, he felt the cold contact of a gun barrel on the back of his neck and heard the click as the weapon was cocked.

PART FOUR

THE BASILISK

Basilisk, *adj.*, *humorous*, from Basilicata

1

Darkness, nausea, the smell of ether.

His body immobilised and aching.

Hospital? Accident? Explosion?

Sudden jolts, unwanted invitations to escape from the abyss of a deceptive sleepiness, to break the spell of this comfortable cocoon which was only just starting to reveal its malign nature. Horror, an inability to breathe, suffocation.

It wasn't Petra who was shaking him. And this was no nightmare.

He couldn't breathe.

He had to get out!

He tried to move his legs, trying not to be sucked in again, but his legs did not respond. His arms, too, were paralysed.

His mouth was covered with a gag and filled with a ball of gauze that still had the metallic taste of the anaesthetic. Tightly bound ropes kept him in a foetal position, an inert heap at the mercy of the unpredictable movements of whatever vehicle was transporting him.

That was the first thing that was clear to him when, after many attempts, he finally started to come to his senses: he was the passive cargo of a moving vehicle.

The smell of mildew, tyre rubber and motor oil convinced him that he was in the boot of a car.

After what seemed an interminable period of time, he felt the car slow down and finally stop.

He heard muffled voices.

Someone opened the boot, but he was not blinded by the sudden switch from darkness to light, nor did he feel the cool air on his face, because a thick black hood had been pulled over his head.

A good sign, Ferrara told himself. If his attackers didn't want him to see their faces, that might well mean they didn't intend to kill him.

'It's time to have a piss, Chief Superintendent,' a young, amused voice said.

'Why?' another voice said, laughing. 'This car's a toilet, why can't he piss in here?'

Both spoke in Sicilan dialect.

They untied him but did not take his hood off, and before making him get out of the boot they tied his hands again, in the front this time.

'Do whatever you have to do,' the man who had spoken second said, almost apologetically. They even helped him to get out and, when he felt dizzy and swayed, they supported him.

He suspected he was in a deserted lay-by on the autostrada, because he could distinctly hear the characteristic noise of cars and, more tellingly, lorries speeding by on the asphalt.

He thought of Petra. She would be worried, and had probably already called everyone to find out where he was. His men – he couldn't help still thinking of them as his – might well be scouring Florence by now, but what use was that?

He walked away to urinate at the edge of the grass strip feeling cautiously with his feet. He certainly needed it.

To fill up with petrol, they stopped with the radio at full volume. Again huddled in the boot and gagged, Ferrara could have kicked and moaned as much as he liked, no one would have heard a thing. And, as a further precaution, it must have been a self-service, because when he heard someone fiddling with the fuel cap he again heard the voice of one of the two Sicilians.

The next time they stopped it was for quite a while, and there were voices – not many, it must have been the dead of night, or already dawn – and noises typical of ports. When the car started again, moving in fits and starts, he guessed they were advancing noisily up a ramp, and he even thought he recognised the voice of one of the cabin boys on the ferry he took whenever he went to see his relatives in Sicily, but perhaps it was only an illusion.

Once they were off the ferry, they clocked up more miles, with one further stop for his bodily needs. It was hard to calculate the time, but it might have been another hour, or even two, before the car stopped again and the horn sounded.

He thought he heard the creaking of a heavy metal gate before the car started up again and then stopped.

They made him get out.

The men who had travelled with him were joined by others, and they pushed him across a patch of earth to a door, which they opened. One of them took him by the arm and pulled him inside.

They walked a short distance along what might have been a corridor. Then the man forced him to stop, fiddled with his hood for a few seconds, and at last took it off.

When his eyes had become accustomed to the sudden light, he almost fainted.

In the centre of a large room, amid crates of mineral water, jute sacks, ropes of various sizes and latex gloves like those used by surgeons, thirteen chairs had been placed in a circle with a fourteenth in the middle. The room smelled sour and stale. A smell of mildew and death.

The chair in the middle was facing away from him. As was the person sitting on it. A woman, with her hands tied behind the back of the chair and her feet secured to the legs, a gag knotted at the back of her neck.

He did not need to see her face. There was only one woman in his life still worth living for. Only one.

Facing Petra, sitting on one of the thirteen chairs surrounding her, was a man with a dark, square face, long, smooth hair and an unkempt beard, who no longer cared about being recognised. Ferrara immediately recalled his face from the poster in the corridors of the *Squadra Mobile*, in Florence, what seemed like a century ago. But he didn't have that dangerous Beretta in his hand then, pointing at Ferrara's wife. With a satisfied grin, he beckoned him to step forward.

2

'No reply from Ferrara's apartment, Superintendent. Just the answering machine.'

'It's obvious he doesn't want to talk to us, Fanti,' Superintendent Rizzo replied. 'What can we do? Let's take it easy.'

He was somewhat put out, perhaps not as much as the faithful Fanti, who would have at least appreciated a hello and found it impossible to take it easy.

Regretfully, they stopped trying.

'But I swear, Major, Spadaro is an incompetent!' Somenti protested.

'I understand what you're saying, but don't you think you might be a little biased? I mean, you do have a disciplinary procedure hanging over you, so any move you make could be interpreted as an attempt to defend yourself. The man's senior to you, he must know more than you do, and in his position he must be acting in the national interest. What valid arguments do you have against him? What do you know of the strategy of the higher echelons?'

'The only strategy they know is covering their backs. What

I know for a fact is that there are at least two Taliban in Italy, who are busy right now setting up a network which may become a powerful focus for terrorist activity, and I also know they're in league with the Mafia. Isn't that enough?'

Major Alibrandi thought this over for a moment. 'I don't know. It's not for us, for me, to decide, but the High Command. I'm sorry, Somenti, but there's really nothing else I can do.'

Somenti left his superior's office feeling disappointed all over again. He had really hoped that the Carabinieri would make up for Spadaro's stupidity, taking action without wasting any more precious time.

His hands were itching with inactivity.

'Really ingenious,' General Arturo Mangiagalli said, putting down the confidential letter signed by the head of the CIA, which constituted a kind of draft agreement, and looking with new eyes at Nicola Spadaro, who had just finished giving him a very brief summary of the plan.

He had obviously underestimated his subordinate. He thought of something he had often considered, which was that in peacetime people fell asleep, but it was during a war that you really saw the calibre of the best men – men like Spadaro.

'But what about this man the Lion, can we trust him?'

Spadaro looked quite inspired. 'Trust him? A Mafioso? No, chief, it's not a question of trust, it's a question of the clever management of people, as in all things. The man will be given a clear choice: he can finish his days in prison or perhaps killed by his own people, or he can live a long life, acclaimed as a hero, a man who helped to deliver a savage, if not fatal blow to international terrorism. Which would you choose?'

'But what if he tries to double-cross us? What if he keeps

the drugs for himself, and maybe the money, too, and just dis-
appears?'

'That's why the CIA want their men to be there when the
exchange happens, though still with us running the show. But
really, there's no danger, he won't do that. The truth, sir, is
that we have him by the balls. He went to Caputo's hiding
place hoping to find compromising documents, so that he
could blackmail whoever was protecting Caputo, but he
didn't find anything.' Spadaro gave a crafty smile. 'I made
sure of that personally.'

'So, according to you, he has no choice? But what kind of
man is he?'

Spadaro thought about this for a while before answering.
Then, as if having a sudden inspiration, he said, 'When you
see him, you won't believe it. Do you remember Spreafico?'

Spreafico had been the chief archivist, a gangling, lacklus-
tre individual, so humble and discreet that everyone made fun
of him behind his back for being so insubstantial.

'Well, he's exactly like him. A man who looks like millions
of other people, a man so anonymous, so innocuous, he might
as well be invisible. In the Lion's case, that's his real strength,
because behind that modest exterior lurks a very fine brain.
But don't worry, I have him in the palm of my hand. He'll do
whatever I tell him to do. It's my reputation that's on the line.'

And your career, the general thought. 'And he'll end up a
hero. Well, that's the way of the world. The difficult thing
now will be to convince the head of the General Staff,
Admiral Albertini. He won't like the idea of handing over an
arsenal to us, even if the CIA are guaranteeing to replace
them with newer weapons. And it won't be easy from a technical point of view, there are important people at various
levels who have to be convinced without being told the real
reason for the operation.'

'That's a *sine qua non*, I'm afraid. You know the Americans. Anyway that's his problem. After all he is in charge, isn't he? And if we can get the support of the Minister of Defence, he's bound to find a way.'

'I agree. Which means it's up to me. I'll organise the meeting.'

'Thank you, sir.'

'One more thing, Spadaro,' General Mangiagalli said, before dismissing him. 'This private report of yours about Captain Somenti – is it really necessary? After all, he is the son of a hero, a real one this time.'

And a relative of your wife's, Nicola Spadaro thought. Out loud, he said, 'But he may compromise the operation. He's got it into his head that the Lion has to be arrested and the Taliban network dismantled! Things are at a very delicate stage, they could go pear-shaped if anyone interferes now. Surely you realise that?'

'But couldn't you tell him about it and involve him in the operation?'

'An operation of this importance? In an office like ours? Absolute secrecy is the key to our success. All it needs is one mole, and the whole thing's ruined. It's bad enough that the head of the General Staff has to know, so can you imagine?'

'Have no fear, everything will be arranged at the highest levels, with the fewest possible people involved: Admiral Albertini, myself, you, and of course the minister. And everyone will be bound to secrecy. As for Somenti, he's young but he isn't stupid, I assure you. And he's loyal.'

'For me the important thing is that you know the reasons for his resignation,' Spadaro said, making the best of a bad job: he had always known that his superior would never listen to him about Somenti, and had thanked heaven when the captain had resigned. 'For the rest, do whatever you think fit, it's your prerogative and I trust you. Just make sure he doesn't do anything stupid.'

'Don't worry.'

After his subordinate had gone, General Mangiagalli waited a little while then picked up the phone and told his wife that she could reassure her sister: her son would be spared disciplinary proceedings.

Obviously Somenti would never know about that intervention from above. He would never have forgiven his mother if he had. He had entered the Carabinieri only after getting her to promise that she would never intercede on his behalf.

3

'Chief Superintendent Ferrara, what a pleasure to see you here,' Gino La Torre said, underlining the words with a theatrical gesture of welcome. 'It's a real honour to have you as my guest. But why have they gagged you? We need to talk.'

One of the two men ripped off the tape that had been gagging him, tearing a few pieces of skin from his thirst-parched lips at the same time. He spat out the ball of gauze which was already stained with the blood that immediately welled from the wounds on his lips.

His initial fear had been replaced by an immense anger. He tried to hold it back for Petra's sake – he could well imagine how terrified she must be, knowing that he was a captive too – but it rushed to his head, clouding his eyes, and the words tumbled from his mouth, hate-filled and uncontrollable.

'We have nothing to say to each other. You wanted me dead. Well, here I am. Kill me, but leave her out of this. If you're men and not dogs, let her go now that you have me!'

'Calm down, Chief Superintendent! That's not the way to talk when you're among friends. And we have to be friends, whether we like it or not. Come, sit down. And don't worry about your wife, she's our guest. And for us, the guest is sacred.'

'Shoot me, La Torre, shoot me now!'

Petra was crying, but he preferred not to look at her.

'No, no, Chief Superintendent Ferrara, you're scaring her, and I don't want her to think badly of me, or you! We went to a lot of trouble to bring you here. Why? To do you a favour, that's why. Sit down.'

This time, it was not an invitation, but an order.

'Yes, to do you a favour,' he went on. 'I want to give you two telephone numbers. I don't ask anything from you in return. Only that you do your duty. But of course, I shouldn't even need to ask that of Chief Superintendent Ferrara.'

Ferrara felt his head spinning. He swayed and finally collapsed on to a chair. 'What do you want of me?'

'I told you,' La Torre replied. He took a small piece of paper from his pocket and held it in front of Ferrara's eyes.

There were two names on it: the Lion, which startled him, and the Basilisk, which meant absolutely nothing. Next to each, a phone number with a prefix beginning with 4420.

'Those are London numbers,' Ferrara said, his interest aroused despite himself. He had no idea what kind of trap they were setting for him, but the Lion's phone number was dangerously tempting bait.

'But used here. Untraceable. They're clever, those two. They know that in London you can get pay-as-you-go telephones and SIM cards without even giving your name, you just use up the credit, and the phones are completely anonymous.'

'What of it?'

'Let's not play games, Chief Superintendent. You tap those phones and you track them down. We can't do anything. We've called them, tried to persuade them to come here, but they're clever, like I said. They only answer if they recognise the caller's name. If they don't, they let it ring or just switch off.'

'But why do you want us to get them?'

'We have our reasons. We want them in prison, you have to promise me that. If you kill them, better still. Especially the Basilisk.'

'But why? Who the hell is he? What has he done?'

'You surprise me, Chief Superintendent! With all the investigating you've done into the bombings, I can't believe you haven't come across him. A traitor, that's who he is. Someone who spat in the plate he was eating from. He used to be Caputo's man. Caputo carried him in the palm of his hand, like a son. Oh yes, just like a son. Then he betrayed Caputo to that son of a bitch the Lion. He was the only person who knew where Caputo was, because he went to see him, Caputo himself told me. He betrayed him. He betrayed him to the Lion, and the Lion was the man who tried to kill you.'

'So did you, if it comes to that. You were in the group that blew up my car and then the Prosecutor's, we know that.'

'What do you want, Chief Superintendent, a confession? With you tied up and me holding a gun? But I'll tell you the truth, because I'm a man of honour. You have to believe me when I say that I had nothing to do with the death of Prosecutor Giulietti. But your bomb, yes, I confess, I planted it. But I've repented, all right?'

Ferrara was starting to understand.

There really was a Mafia war. And these were Caputo's men, rivals to the faction loyal to the mysterious Lion. The head having been cut off, the organisation had reformed, as it always did with the Mafia, and in all probability it was the man facing him who was, or aspired to be, the new boss: Gino

La Torre, another illustrious fugitive who would slip back into the shadows forever if he, Ferrara, got rid of his rivals for him.

If Caputo had been betrayed, Ferrara told himself, that meant his capture wasn't just the result of a brilliant joint operation by the *Mobile* and the Central Operational Service, as the police commissioner of Palermo had declared.

Gino La Torre broke into his thoughts by ordering the hooded man who had remained in the doorway to untie Ferrara's hands.

Now they had established an understanding, there was no reason to fear any rash gestures.

But he and Petra were still being held at gunpoint, and Petra was still tied to the chair, despite his protests. They were making it quite clear to him that she was still their prisoner.

'There's a Panda waiting outside, which we rented with the credit card your wife was kind enough to let us have. We also used the card to book you on a flight from Palermo to Rome this evening. One of my men will go with you to Palermo, which by the way is nowhere near here. If you don't mind, we have to blindfold you again, we don't really want you to know where this place is. My man will get out along the way and you can continue on your own. You know what you have to do then.'

'What about Petra?'

'Your wife stays here. As our guest. And as I said, the guest is sacred. We're a hospitable people, as you well know. And a respectful people. We won't touch a hair on her head. Gino La Torre guarantees it. When the traitors are in prison or dead, we'll let her go. You have my word of honour. In prison or dead, Chief Superintendent. Both of them. Dead would be better.'

They blindfolded him, took him back outside, forced him

back into the stifling car boot, and set off, followed by the Panda.

They took his blindfold off on the outskirts of Piazza Armerina, not far from the Roman villa.

He knew the road, and it wasn't hard for him to orient himself. He reached Palermo airport with half an hour to spare.

He did not phone anyone. He was too afraid of what might happen to Petra. He was starting to have his doubts as to whether La Torre would keep his word. But the biggest question of all was: what could he do? The difficulties facing him were almost insurmountable. Acting Prosecutor Erminia Cosenza must know by now that he had been forbidden to investigate the Lion, and without her help it would be impossible to put a tap on the two phones. Even supposing he could get around that obstacle, there were all the technical aspects, the need to contact the phone companies, the unknown quantity of whether the two Mafiosi would actually use the phones.

What if they had other phones? The fact that they had answered calls from La Torre's men seemed to indicate that they were still using these, but for how long?

And finally there was this new figure, the Basilisk, this wild card pulled out at the last minute to shake up the game. His name had never cropped up in the course of their inquiries. On what grounds could he even investigate him, let alone arrest him?

How ironic this exchange La Torre was forcing on him really was! Of course, he wanted to get his hands on the Lion, almost as much as he wanted to save Petra: he couldn't forget the vow he had made over Anna Giulietti's grave. But if he succeeded – and however impossible that was, he had to believe he could do it – he would be helping the Mafia to regroup.

But that wasn't really a problem, because he didn't have a choice. The other problems were the ones he had to solve. He found a solution to the most immediate of them – the authorisation for the phone taps – when he was on the plane. Solutions to the others, he hoped, would follow.

4

'It's a simple plan, and the simplest plans are always the best. Practically no risk. Guaranteed results ranging from highly satisfactory to outstanding. A return of eighty to a hundred per cent on our investment, so to speak.'

As General Mangiagalli began presenting his case to Guido Albertini, head of the General Staff – a bald, flabby, thickset man pushing seventy, with the air of a servile and not especially bright bureaucrat – the minister nodded at almost every word.

The fact that the minister had gone to the trouble of coming to see him at the Palazzo Caprara, instead of summoning him to his office in the Palazzo Baracchini, had impressed Admiral Albertini, making him favourably disposed from the start to what the director of Military Intelligence had to tell him. That was one of the two things the minister had most wanted. The other was that this meeting should be absolutely confidential.

'Go on, I'm listening,' Albertini said, with rapt attention.

'The Taliban need arms, the Mafia need drugs. That's perfectly understandable, nothing abnormal or suspicious about it. Our intelligence services are second to none, if I may say so.'

Here he broke off for a moment to mention Somenti, praising his work – and naturally taking some of the credit himself – and giving the minister the opportunity to respond, which he did by saying, 'Really excellent.'

'In particular, Military Intelligence, which I have the honour to serve, has managed to secure the cooperation of an important Mafia boss, known as the Lion, who has already been extremely useful to us on another occasion. The fact that this cooperation is not entirely voluntary makes it all the more reliable. This man, this so-called Lion, has been in contact with envoys of the Taliban and has arranged an exchange. In return for a large quantity of drugs and the three CIA men being held hostage in Afghanistan, he will hand over – if, that is, you are gracious enough to grant my request – an equally large quantity of arms, some heavy but mostly light.'

Admiral Albertini was genuinely intrigued, all the more so as it seemed incredible to him that they were suggesting he supply arms to an enemy, with all the difficulties that entailed.

'Go on.'

'We contribute the arms, the Americans will supply the men and the technology. At a later date, they will replace all the arms with brand new ones. One of my subordinates, Nicola Spadaro, will be in charge of the operation. You will need to make a warehouse available to him, if possible not far from Livorno, stocked with ten thousand rifles, pistols and machine guns, and possibly also rocket launchers and ground-to-air missiles, although in much smaller quantities. The American technicians, all CIA men, will be taken to the warehouse by Spadaro. There they will render the heavy arms less effective and place bugs in the light arms. Thanks to these bugs, the US army, once they are on Afghan territory, will be able to monitor the movements of the Taliban troops. It's possible they could lead us straight to Bin Laden.'

The effect these words had on the admiral was predictable, and the general and the minister exchanged satisfied glances.

'You, admiral, apart from supplying the arms, will have to make sure that the port authority authorises the entrance into Livorno harbour of a Moroccan ship which will carry the load to its destination. It's all explained in this document.' He opened his elegant leather bag to take it out. 'It contains all the details of Operation Lion. All three of us will sign, if you agree to take part.'

Even if he had wanted to, the admiral would have hardly been able to refuse. The plan was fascinating, simple and brilliant, as Mangiagalli had stated at the outset, and, if the operation succeeded, it would enhance Italy's reputation, and his own, in the most historic way. In addition, the copy of the CIA's draft agreement, which was attached to the document, removed any lingering doubts he might have had – not that he had any.

He carefully read through the document, and then they all signed.

The document was stamped TOP SECRET, and it would be placed in the secret archive of the Ministry of Defence.

5

When Fanti entered the office that morning, dragging his feet wearily, he thought he could smell the strong odour of Toscano cigars, which had so often greeted him whenever Ferrara arrived before he did. This was turning into an obsession, he thought irritably, and he had to shake it off. After all, it wasn't the end of the world, one chief was as good as another, and they were chief and secretary, not husband and wife. But when he heard a cough, he took fright.

'Fanti! Is that you?'

It was the first time in all these years that, instead of just materialising in the chief's office, he cautiously edged his way in.

Ferrara was there, at his desk, with a half-smoked cigar in his mouth, grim-faced, drumming impatiently with his fingers on the wooden surface.

'About time, Fanti! Were you waiting for me to send a driver for you?'

He hadn't only come back to get his things, that much was clear at once. And for a moment Fanti did not know what he felt more: fear or relief. Ferrara was clearly in a foul mood, if not worse. He didn't think he had ever seen him like this.

'Bring me those other layabouts, Rizzo, Ascalchi, Sergi and Venturi. I want them here by nine on the dot, okay?'

It was now four minutes to nine.

Fanti was off like a shot. Within a very short time, all four men were in Ferrara's office. Ferrara did not explain where he had been, or why he had returned so unexpectedly. All he told them was that a very confidential and reliable source had given him two mobile phone numbers used by the Lion, which they were immediately going to tap. He did not mention the Basilisk. That would have made it even riskier. He was already getting them in trouble, there was no way he could ask them to go even further. He would be very surprised if either of the two men called anyone else. The only way the Lion's accomplice would be caught in the net would be through luck – if, for example, the Lion said something compromising.

'We already have one of these two numbers, chief,' Venture said when he saw them. 'And I can confirm that it's the Lion's. We intercepted a call from Hamdullah to that number yesterday afternoon. I've just been reading the transcript.'

Ferrara looked at Rizzo. 'So you continued tapping their phones? You ignored Guaschelli's instructions?'

'It's not like that, chief,' Rizzo replied, ill at ease. 'It's just that, you know how it is, these things take time, the machine starts automatically and records.'

These things take time, like everything else in Italy. For once he was glad. He didn't even mind that Rizzo was probably lying.

He turned to Venturi. 'And what did the transcript say?'

'The Arab was really pissed off. He said the drugs had arrived days ago, a large amount, and there was no way they could keep them. Only half the money had been paid into the Swiss account, and the ship from Morocco had already left port. The Lion tried to calm him down, he said he would definitely get the merchandise, it was only a matter of days now. The Arab gave him until Sunday. Any later, he said, and the whole thing was off.'

'Did you manage to track down the location of the phone being called?'

Venturi looked at Rizzo, embarrassed. Rizzo signalled to him to continue.

'Casal Palocco.'

'Where's that?'

'It's a residential area of Rome,' Ascalchi cut in. 'A very trendy neighbourhood, quite a distance from the centre, more towards the sea, near Ostia Antica. You remember Nanni Moretti's *Dear Diary*, the scene where he—?' Ascalchi broke off abruptly, after a scathing look from Ferrara.

'And are you tapping that phone? We have to get a precise location, so any calls he makes or receives will be valuable.'

His men's embarrassment increased. They had all been afraid they would be reprimanded for their transgression, but what Ferrara was asking was even worse.

'We can't, chief,' Rizzo said nervously.

'Who says so?' Ferrara asked in a weary, impatient, uncompromising tone.

'The acting prosecutor would never authorise it. Signora Cosenza knows there's been a veto on investigations into the Lion. Besides, it's an English number, she would have to put in a request to the police in Britain.'

'Only for outgoing calls. We're perfectly entitled to intercept calls received on Italian soil. And do you even have to tell Cosenza that the number is the Lion's?'

The men looked at him, more astonished than ever.

'You're still investigating the bombings, aren't you? There are two suspects missing, right?'

'Sandro Caruso and Leonardo Parisi?' Sergi asked.

'That's right. And we have two numbers, don't we? Would you know whose numbers they are if I hadn't told you? No. And she doesn't know either. Let's put in a request to the Prosecutor's Department, saying we've been told by an informant that the two men we're looking for are using those phones. We'll say that the phones are operating on Italian soil and we want authorisation to intercept the calls they receive urgently. We can also ask her to at least make a start on writing to the British police, so that we can access the outgoing calls as soon as possible.'

'But chief—' Rizzo said.

'We have no time to lose, boys, you heard what the transcript said. It's only a few days to Sunday. And I have to see this game through to the end. I was thinking I could give up, but I can't. I just can't, and that's it. If any of you don't feel up to it, I'll understand, and I'll carry on by myself. But I need to know. I'll leave you alone now, so that you can discuss it among yourselves. I'll be in the corridor. Come and get me when you've made up your minds.'

He left the room, but did not have to wait for long.

Two minutes later, the door to his office opened and Venturi came out and walked off in a great hurry without saying a word. From the doorway, Rizzo beckoned Ferrara back into the room.

'The inspector's gone straight to the intercept room, chief. Now, what do you want us to do?'

6

Three days later, Admiral Albertini dialled General Mangiagalli's number on his private line.

'Everything's ready for the operation we talked about,' he said, after a brief exchange of formalities. 'A courier is on his way to you with details of the warehouse and letters giving Nicola Spadaro and his men access and permission to take away what they need. The men there have already been informed.'

'Understood. I'll tell Spadaro. Thank you.'

'And good luck.'

'Thanks.'

In an ordinary investigation, three days are nothing, but when you're conducting it in order to rescue your wife from a murderer, three days can be unbearably long.

In those three days, there was only one very short call, on Thursday afternoon, to one of the phones they were tapping. It was to the Basilisk's phone, and came from a number registered to a company in Catania suspected of being a cover for the local boss, Luigi Rosati.

'On their way,' a Sicilian voice said.

'Understood,' the Basilisk replied – or perhaps it was the Lion.

The reason Ferrara was not sure was that this phone, too, was traced to the Casal Palocco area near Rome. The two men must be together, and it could well have been the Lion who answered: he had a clear memory of the Lion's voice and the way the speaker had said 'understood' did seem to correspond to it. But it was only one word, so he couldn't say for certain.

He dialled Ascalchi's number for the fourth time. 'Anything new?'

'Not yet, chief. We're doing the best we can.'

'Get a move on, time's running out!'

Ascalchi looked at Sergi and at the depressing spectacle of Casal Palocco, a ritzy neighbourhood that had grown too quickly, and was filled with villas, sports fields, apartment blocks and God only knew how many people. It was easy to tell them to get a move on when you were sitting comfortably in an armchair, but the reality on the ground wasn't the same as looking at a map on your desk.

'Yes, chief,' he replied, and rang off. 'You know, Serpico,' he said, turning to Sergi, 'I like the bastard as much as you do. But we're not getting anywhere here.'

Sergi shrugged. What could he say? Ever since Ferrara had come back and got them all involved in this mess, even he felt as if he didn't know him any more. He was starting to be unbearable, just as unbearable as having to tramp up and down this neighbourhood where the apartment blocks were called Island 14 or Island 29 South, the villas flaunted their wealth, and the streets were all named after Greek characters.

They turned off the Viale Gorgia di Lorentini into a side street and rang the entryphone beside the gate of the umpteenth villa, three storeys with a garden. After a few minutes, they rang again, several times. At last, an elderly voice replied, 'Who is it?'

'Police.'

'What do you want?'

'To talk to someone.'

'There's no one here.'

'Not even you?' Superintendent Ascalchi retorted.

'I'm coming,' the old man said, reluctantly.

He kept them waiting, and then did not even let them in.

'So what do you want?' he said again, through the bars of the gate.

'Have you seen anything unusual in the area lately?'

'What kind of thing?'

'A Sicilian who may have rented a house or be staying with someone,' Sergi said.

'What's he like?'

'We don't know.'

The old man looked at them in surprise and replied slyly, 'Then you'll never find him. People come and go all the time here. Apart from the older residents, it's all young professionals, air hostesses, stewards, and they bring home all kinds of people: weirdos, foreigners, tall, short, thin, Milanese, Sicilians.'

'All right, we get the idea. Thanks.'

'Get a description, or you'll wear your feet out,' the old man shouted after them as they walked away.

They continued on their route.

They were used to it by now.

'You know what I think?' Ascalchi said after a while.

'No.'

'That he's right. Let's drop this. We're just wasting our time here.'

'Ferrara will kill us.'

'For what?' the Roman said, ironically. 'Insubordination?'

7

On Sunday morning Ferrara heard the doorbell ring and went to open the door without taking any precautions. He hadn't bothered since his capture. If your enemy gives you his word and he's not stupid, there's nothing you can do.

'Good morning, Chief Superintendent,' Ahmed Farah said, entering the apartment.

'Hello, Ahmed, what can I do for you?'

'For me, nothing. It's you I'm thinking of. I wanted to warn you. Tomorrow I'm publishing the complete text of the intercepts, verbatim. With names and surnames.'

'Have you gone mad?'

'No. I'm just fed up.'

'I thought we had an understanding.'

'But you people didn't keep your side of the bargain. Don't you realise nothing's happened? Two weeks have gone by and everything's exactly the same as before, except that two weeks are more than enough time for a small army of Taliban to have prepared another attack. I've been thinking, and I've come to the conclusion that I was wrong to be so trusting. This is Italy, after all!'

Ferrara had peeked out of the window at the bank of the Arno outside his house.

Ahmed's escort was there: three men.

One of them was on the phone.

'I don't know if you did the right thing coming here,' he said, remembering Duranti's strange smirk: the men in your escort protect you, but they also keep an eye on you, especially if they're from Military Intelligence. 'I don't know if your guardian angels are pleased that you're visiting the head of the *Squadra Mobile*, who's a notorious pain in the arse, and who's supposed to have given up on these dealings of the Mafia and the Afghans.'

Farah bristled at these words, which seemed to him to confirm his suspicions. Everyone appeared to have given up, that much was clear now.

That hadn't been Ferrara's intention. He knew that Farah was right. All in all, faced with a hostile presence on their territory, the authorities had reacted in the most wrong-headed and confused way imaginable, resorting to the favourite sport of the Italians: punishing their subordinates for warning them that the shit was about to hit the fan.

But he couldn't say that. The one thing he had to do was stop Farah dropping his bombshell, because if he did the chances of getting to the Lion or the Basilisk were practically nil.

'Don't do it. You'd antagonise the very people who are protecting you. They're the ones who did the intercepts and they certainly won't want them made public, or they'd already have done it themselves. And if you go ahead with that scoop, they're going to make us look really bad. You're playing with fire, Ahmed.'

'I don't care, I'm used to it.'

Bastard! Ferrara thought. If he could, he would have arrested the arrogant hack on the spot. He would have done it if it wasn't for those three men waiting outside.

'They're going to kill you.'

'You can pray over my grave.'

'I don't know the Koran.'

'You can take lessons.'

'You publish that article and I swear I'll be teaching you a lesson!'

'I like you, Chief Superintendent,' Farah said, with a touch of pity in his voice. 'I came here thinking I was doing you a favour. But I've been wrong about that twice now.'

Ferrara let him go, then had to wait until he had calmed down before he could start to think rationally about what to do. He ruled out warning Military Intelligence except as a last resort, given their previous attitude and the poor reputation he enjoyed in Rome. He decided it would be much better to inform Major Alibrandi. The Carabinieri might be able to find an excuse to stop and detain Farah without making his escort too suspicious.

He spent the rest of the morning and the early part of the afternoon going over all the papers again, while he tried to trace Alibrandi. When he had finally got hold of him and told him everything, he decided there was no point staying at home and he might do better to drop into Headquarters, where he arrived just after three.

He went straight to the intercept room.

'Hello, chief,' Venturi greeted him, taking off his head-phones and getting to his feet.

'Hello, chief,' Ascalchi and Sergi echoed. There they were, sitting next to him.

'What are you two doing here?' Ferrara said angrily.

'We only just arrived. There was no point in us staying in Casal Palocco, chief, it was like looking for a needle in a—'

'I'm the one who gives the orders around here, Ascalchi! What the hell were you thinking of? If I tell you to do something, you do it!'

'Listen, chief—' Venturi said, trying to cut in.

'Like hell I will!'

'We got them.'

Ferrara reined in his anger. 'Who?'

'Mullah Hamdullah and this Assad, who answers the Lion's mobile. They've already spoken three times today, at 6:07 this morning, at 9:43 and then at 12:27. I only just got here myself, chief, and I was checking the automatic recordings to see if there was anything new. We've never had so many calls in such a short space of time. I think something big is happening.'

'Where's the translator?'

'Today's Sunday, chief, he's off.'

'For Christ's sake! Find me another one! I want him here right away, now, do you understand? By force if necessary!'

Yes, but who?

Ascalchi looked at Sergi as if it had finally been confirmed that his chief had gone mad.

Even Ferrara realised that he had gone too far. It also struck him that the only person they could call on at such short notice was Ahmed Farah. Which might not be such a bad idea: if he saw them still hard at work on the case, he might decide to give up his crazy plan.

He tried calling him, but his mobile seemed to have been switched off.

He frantically dialled Alibrandi's number and told him it was urgent they trace Ahmed Farah. After a few minutes, he called again.

'You *are* in a hurry, Chief Superintendent. I sent two men to get him at the newspaper. They'll tell the escort I have to interview him about a libel case we're investigating, I don't want them to think Major Somenti has anything to do with it. He's here with me, by the way.'

'Good, the two of you keep Farah there until I arrive. We could be at a crucial stage. And get rid of the escort, they mustn't see me come in.'

Before rushing into the courtyard to find a car, he ordered, 'Find Rizzo and wait here!'

8

The range of expressions on Ahmed Farah's face as he listened to the recordings covered all the possible gradations of concern, alarm and anxiety, which inevitably infected Ferrara and the two majors.

On the notepad in front of him, he took a few hurried notes in Arabic, followed by exclamation marks and question marks, pressing the pen into the paper with great force.

Whenever one of them, unable to stand the suspense, tried to urge him to say something, he would stop him with a commanding gesture of the hand.

Before the last recording had even finished, he asked for the tape recorder to be switched off and said, excitedly, 'The exchange is taking place tonight. It must be something big, they're using a lorry. The Taliban aren't just handing something over, they're taking something away with them. And I don't mean money.'

'What do you mean?'

'Merchandise for their cause. That's all they said.'

'Meaning arms?'

'Possibly. But a large quantity, to judge by the vehicles they're using!'

'What time tonight?'

'One in the morning, to be precise.'

They looked at their watches. It was 7:36 p.m. On a Sunday. No way of informing their superiors in time. They had to act on their own initiative.

'Where?' Major Alibrandi asked.

The journalist consulted his notes. 'In the yard of an abandoned villa about four miles after you come off the Florence–Pisa autostrada on to the Via Livornese, near Marina di Pisa. To be on the safe side, the Italian actually gave the co-ordinates: latitude 43°40′15″ and longitude 10°20′53″. No way of getting lost!'

'Muster the men and get them ready,' Alibrandi ordered Somenti. 'We need at least thirty men, fully armed. We have to secure the area on all sides.'

'Yes, sir,' the new major replied, his eyes gleaming with satisfaction.

'I'm going to round up mine as well,' Ferrara said, grabbing the phone to inform Rizzo.

'We've got hold of the translator,' his deputy said.

'Perfect. Tell Venturi to get in touch immediately if there are any further contacts.' Then, to Major Alibrandi as he was rushing to the exit, 'Let's meet on the autostrada, half a mile before the exit from the Pisa tollgate, to co-ordinate our positions.'

'Don't be late, Chief Superintendent. We won't wait beyond 10:15, otherwise we might not be able to take them by surprise.'

'We'll be there before you!'

'Can I come with you?' Ahmed Farah asked.

'Are you joking?' Major Alibrandi said. 'This is an extremely dangerous operation. Of course you can't come!' He could not have been more categorical.

The journalist did not insist. He raised his hands in surrender. He knew how to shake off his escort.

At 10:41 p.m. a reconnaissance patrol confirmed that the yard was still deserted. This small open space in the thick scrub that separated the road from the abandoned building, an old three-storey villa, was accessible from two gaps, one at the centre and one at the side. Other patrols, deployed at strategic points, radioed in that there were no suspicious movements on the approaches.

Ferrara and Alibrandi began placing their men in concealed positions. Some, led by Ascalchi and equipped with powerful self-generating floodlights, went inside the villa and straight up to the upper floors, where they took up their places. Others scattered through the surrounding fields. The vehicles were concealed on the side roads, ready to block any attempt at escape, near the junction of the Via Livornese and the slip road from the autostrada on one side, and up to a distance of five miles in the direction of Livorno on the other.

Ferrara, Rizzo, Alibrandi and Somenti co-ordinated the action from an unmarked car parked on a side road less than twenty yards from the villa.

The wait began.

Ahmed Farah had left his car in Marina di Pisa and begun the slow approach on foot. Having to elude both the police and the Carabinieri, he advanced extremely slowly and cautiously. Even if he arrived before they did, he calculated that he would not reach a useful vantage point until just before one, which was exactly when he needed to get there.

There was no moon, and visibility was poor. It was perfect for staying hidden, but he would have to get as close as possible if he didn't want to miss anything. It was going to be the scoop of his life.

At seven minutes to one, the Carabinieri – in an unmarked car keeping the fork in the road under surveillance – sighted a Volkswagen Golf, which passed their car, turned on to the Via Livornese, then on to the side road adjacent to the villa, entered the yard, and finally did a U-turn and drove back the way it had come.

'They're reconnoitring,' Ferrara said. 'They didn't notice a thing, they didn't even get out of the car. They must be feeling safe.'

The others agreed.

Three minutes later, another unmarked car, the one at the furthest point on the other side, radioed to the major that an army lorry had just passed, coming from the direction of Livorno.

'Damn!' exclaimed Alibrandi. 'Let's hope it turns off or goes past us soon! That's all we need, a fucking military vehicle to screw up the operation!'

Just then, another call came in on his two-way radio.

'White van, Florence number plates, approaching.'

'No! Shit, shit!'

They saw it immediately afterwards.

As it approached the villa, it put on its indicator. The military vehicle had disappeared. They prayed that it had turned off, but the men posted two miles away promptly informed them that it was still coming.

The van entered the yard and stopped.

From the opposite side, the headlights of the military lorry swept over the villa, then the indicators went on and the vehicle turned and entered the yard behind the van.

'What the fuck is going on?' Alibrandi said in a choked voice.

'You know something? I think we're about to see.'

Five men had got out of the van, heavily armed. Two of them walked to the military lorry, which had stopped a few yards away, and three went to open the back door of the van. From the lorry, a total of seven men got out, also armed but not in uniform. One of them went to meet the two men coming from the van, holding out his hand to them, while the others started to unload the contents of the lorry, imitating their counterparts at the back of the van, who had already taken out six wooden crates and were already bringing out others.

'Now!' Ferrara yelled into his transmitter.

Alibrandi, who had been watching the scene as if paralysed, collected himself and echoed the command.

Within a few minutes, all the cars had converged on the yard. Simultaneously, from the windows at the top of the villa, the floodlights were switched on and the voice of Ascalchi came through the megaphone, 'Stop! Police!' Through another megaphone, this one in the fields, a voice cried, 'No one move! Carabinieri!'

9

Blinded by the floodlights, the men in the yard froze. But only for a moment. Mullah Hamdullah, sure he had been betrayed, threw the Lion, who stood almost facing him, a look so full of scorn and hate that the Mafioso, stunned, uncomprehending and scared, could think only of making a run for it. And that was a mistake: he had barely had a chance to turn before a burst of submachine-gun fire from the Taliban brought him down.

That was the signal.

The other men ran to the shelter of the lorry, firing wildly, with returning fire raining down on them from all sides. It was an unequal struggle, which, given the numerical and logistical superiority of the police and the Carabinieri, did not last long.

When there were no more shots coming from the yard, Ferrara gave the order to cease fire.

They waited a few minutes. The smell of cordite hung in the air. The tense silence was broken suddenly by a weak moan coming form the army lorry.

At a command from Alibrandi, the Carabinieri started advancing in scattered formation, followed by Ferrara's men.

'Any casualties?' Alibrandi asked one of his marshals.

'Franceschini got a graze on his arm, Major, but it's not serious. Everyone else is fine.'

Ferrara's men, too, were unhurt, while of their adversaries only five seemed to have survived. There were two seriously wounded Arabs, and three other men who had taken shelter behind the military lorry, one lying on the ground in a pool of blood, another by his side, bending over him and sobbing, and a third on his feet with his hands up.

'There's another one here!' a sergeant suddenly cried, shining his torch under the vehicle on to a pair of eyes that were wide with terror. 'Out, come out, now!' he ordered, aiming his pistol at him.

'I surrender, I surrender,' the man, who was young like the others, protested in Sicilian dialect as he crawled towards the sergeant.

Meanwhile, Ferrara, Rizzo, Alibrandi and Somenti had reached the body of the man who had been shot by the Afghan. He was lying face down, his back riddled with bullet holes and soaked with blood. Alibrandi knelt beside him and looked at the others. Ferrara nodded: no point waiting for the ambulances or Forensics.

Carefully, the major turned over the body.

A pair of blue eyes stared out from the earth-caked face, and underneath the dirt, patches of tanned skin showed through.

Somenti turned pale.

'But that's … that's …' he stammered, 'that's Nicola Spadaro.'

For a moment – although it seemed interminable – there was a kind of panic among them. It was broken by Ferrara, who said, 'It can't be,' then yelled, 'Ascalchi! Bring me one of the prisoners!'

Ascalchi walked towards them with with the man who had taken shelter under the lorry.

'Who is this?' Ferrara asked, pointing to the body.

'That's the Lion. He was in charge.'

'Do you have General Mangiagalli's home phone number?' Alibrandi was asking Somenti when they were distracted by cries from a police officer who was inspecting the lorry.

'Come quickly! There's a whole arsenal in here!'

Ferrara was about to follow them when another officer came running towards him from beyond the yard.

'Chief Superintendent, come and see.'

Ferrara went towards him. There, behind a bramble bush, was another body. It wasn't the Basilisk, as he had hoped. It was Ahmed Farah.

'The bastard,' he thought, with a mixture of annoyance and affection. Farah might not have been the most likable of people, but he'd been smart and he'd been brave. He hadn't deserved to end up like this.

He ran back to the centre of the action, but instead of taking a look at the lorry, he went straight to the three scared young prisoners, all more or less unhurt, who were being led in handcuffs to the police cars by Rizzo.

'Which of you is the Basilisk?' he asked.

The men looked at each other, without understanding. Rizzo did not understand either, and looked at him. But he continued undaunted.

'The Basilisk, where is he?' he shouted. 'Is he dead?'

'Who's he?' the one nearest to him said.

Ferrara's fist hit him full in the face, breaking his nose. A second punch in the stomach made him bend double.

'Chief, what are you doing?' Rizzo yelled.

'There was another man with the Lion, where is he?' Ferrara yelled, ignoring both his deputy and the blood now flowing through the fingers the prisoner was holding over his wounded nose.

'He was alone,' the young man protested, plaintively.

Ferrara was about to hit him a third time, but Rizzo grabbed him by the shoulders and pulled him away. 'Take them away,' he ordered the other officers. 'Take them away!'

While they were waiting for the ambulances, the forensics team and Signora Cosenza, Rizzo took him to one side and tried to talk to him.

'What's got into you, chief?' This isn't like you. It's over – we've got them. You were right, you should be happy.'

'You don't understand, Francesco,' Ferrara said, cutting him off. 'Just drop it, okay?'

10

The helicopter landed at Pisa airport at 4:46.

Alibrandi and Somenti were there to greet General Mangiagalli. He looked pale, drawn, annoyed and at the same time scared.

'What have you done?' he said. 'Spadaro was on a mission authorised by the minister, a very sensitive and highly important mission.'

But he soon fell silent, tortured by doubts that had prevented him from involving the head of the General Staff until he had a clearer idea of what was going on.

During the car journey, he explained what the plan had been.

'But the men under his command weren't from the CIA,' Major Alibrandi objected. 'They were Sicilians. And they identified him as the Lion.'

When they reached the yard of the villa, Alibrandi asked the forensics team to take a good look at the weapons in the military lorry. There were no traces of bugs.

The newspapers greeted the news as the solution to the case of the Florence bombings, another brilliant operation by the head of the *Squadra Mobile* of Florence in association with Major Alibrandi of the Carabinieri. General Mangiagalli's resignation was passed off as an honourable retirement, and the head of the General Staff was given an award by the President of the Republic at a sumptuous ceremony in the Quirinale.

Ferrara refused all press and TV interviews. Nor did he agree to participate in any kind of celebration. But he did accept the congratulations of the head of the State Police and in return was given permission to participate, along with Rizzo, Ascalchi and a forensics team, in the search which Military Intelligence conducted in Spadaro's house two days later.

It was a four-storey villa covering three hundred and fifty square yards, with a large living room, five bedrooms, five bathrooms, a kitchen, a games room, two wide balconies, a garage, a cellar and a garden.

They started early in the morning. The first thing Ferrara did was to interview the domestic staff: a man who was both chauffeur and gardener, and his wife who was the cook and maid. He saw them alone, in the games room.

'Did he often have visitors?' he asked.

'Many women,' the woman replied.

'He was a real playboy,' her husband confirmed.

'But just recently, didn't he have another Sicilian staying with him?'

'What do you mean, "another" Sicilian?' the man said, almost offended. 'Signor Spadaro wasn't Sicilian.'

'Wasn't he?'

'No. He was from Palazzo San Gervasio, in the province of Potenza. Look.' He pointed to a photo on the wall: a black and white aerial view of a village on a peak in the mountains.

'Yes, I see. But wasn't there someone here he called the Basilisk?'

'No, there haven't been any men here in the last few weeks.'

'Are you always here?'

'Apart from Thursday afternoon and Sunday, which is our day off. Unless he wants me to drive him somewhere. But that almost never happens!'

Thursday afternoon, the day of the intercepted phone call!

'If there had been another man here during your absence,' he asked the woman, 'would you have noticed when you came back?'

'Oh yes, I think so. Men always make things dirty, they leave cigarette ends about and glasses and things like that.'

'All right, thank you, you can go.'

But it wasn't all right. It wasn't all right at all. Was it possible that they had been so clever as to wipe out all traces? It really seemed as if the Basilisk had never visited Spadaro, alias the Lion, at home.

He thought again of the puzzled expressions on the faces of the prisoners. He had reacted in a blind fury, preferring not to see that their ignorance was genuine – or perhaps he had seen it and hadn't been able to bear it. There was nothing to say that the Basilisk had to participate in the operation, but if he really was the Lion's accomplice or lieutenant, it was strange that he wasn't with him – either in his house or in the lorry. Was it possible that no one knew him, no one had ever seen him? A man who didn't leave a trace behind, no cigarette ends, no dirty glasses, nothing – a man who was perfectly invisible, as if he had never existed.

He left the room. In the corridor, he ran into some of the men from Military Intelligence, carrying a large cardboard box. Rizzo was with them.

'What's in there?' he asked him.

'You won't believe this, chief,' he replied, visibly excited. 'A whole pile of *pizzini*, in Caputo's secret code!'

They had to take away the PC, because no one could find

the password, and they also had to call a special team to crack the safe.

'Come and look at this, it's incredible,' Rizzo said, taking Ferrara by the arm.

Spadaro's study was a large, light-filled room, with big French windows on two sides, looking out on to a terrace with a view over the maritime pines in the garden. In the corner between the French windows was a large glass desk with a designer lamp on it. It was in a mess now because the men from Military Intelligence had turned it upside down, just as they had turned the cushions from the white sofas inside out and tossed them on the floor.

Rizzo pointed to the framed photographs on one wall, many of them dedicated to the stages of Spadaro's career, some showing him in Afghanistan, others in the company of military or political figures. But one in particular, the smallest of them, had particularly drawn his attention and now he showed it to his chief: a baby, presumably Spadaro himself, in the arms of a young woman standing beside a man in a police uniform.

Ferrara moved closer to it to get a better look, even more impressed than Rizzo had been.

The young woman bore a remarkable resemblance to the woman in the photograph found in Antonio Caputo's wallet. Too great a resemblance to be a coincidence.

'So his father was a police officer?' Ferrara said. He felt strangely agitated, and as he lingered over the truth of what he saw in front of him, a deeper truth struck him like a blinding light. 'Get Venturi to check it out immediately, Francesco.'

'I've already called him. He's working on it right now. He'll let us know as soon as he's found anything.'

'Good.'

11

In the afternoon the safe was finally opened.

Military Intelligence took possession of the most sensitive documents, putting them in envelopes which were immediately sealed. But Ferrara and his men were able to see the rest of the contents: the banknotes – lire, dollars and other currency, some of it from Arab countries – the passports in various names, the diplomas, the law degree, the certificate of enlistment, and the deeds to the house and to other property in Basilicata and Sicily.

'He was a pretty good forger, that's all I can say,' one of the Intelligence agents remarked. 'We found the equipment in the cellar. He even managed to forge a letter from the head of the CIA. Poor Mangiagalli can't get over it.'

Another agent came up to them holding a suitcase in his hand. 'And look at this. It's filled to the brim with American dollars.'

Nicola Spadaro, it transpired from Venturi's researches, had been the son of Benedetto Spadaro and Antonietta Nistico, both born in Palermo, where Benedetto had joined the police at the age of nineteen. Officer Spadaro had been transferred to Palazzo San Gervasio in January 1961, at his own request, after receiving threats from the Mafia. The move had not had the desired effect: his body had been found, just over a month after his son's birth, dumped in the countryside, bound in such a way that when he moved he had strangled himself.

The murder had never been solved.

When they stopped for the day, Ferrara withdrew into a stubborn silence.

In the car taking them back, beneath threatening clouds, to the centre of Rome, he thought again about the photo of the young woman with the baby in her arms. The agitation he had felt when he had first seen it had not left him. His fears for Petra were mixed with the nagging feeling that he had caught hold of the truth and still did not understand it.

He went over and over in his mind, like clips from a partly edited film, the moments that had brought him to the verge of the truth: the surprise on the face of the captured Mafioso, the word 'understood' uttered by the Basilisk or the Lion, the total absence of traces of the Basilisk in the Lion's house, the little photograph.

The driver, following Superintendent Ascalchi's instructions, dropped them in the Corso Vittorio, not far from the Piazza Venezia.

It was just after eight.

'Let me take you to dinner in a little place I know,' Ascalchi said, feeling duty bound, in his home city, to play the host.

'You go, I don't feel hungry,' Ferrara muttered. He had no desire to eat, let alone talk.

'No, chief, you can't go on like this. You've been reduced to a pitiful state, you've stopped talking, you're pale, you've lost weight. I'm sorry to bring this up, but hasn't your wife said anything?'

Petra.

For a moment he was almost tempted to come clean, but he held back in time. A roll of thunder distracted them.

They came out into the Campo de' Fiori as the first light drops of rain were falling. A few passers-by were taking shelter under those café awnings which were still up, others were running towards the Cinema Farnese.

The poster of the film drew his attention: the face of a man, red stripes, a light green background with other figures. And some words.

He suddenly started walking quickly towards the cinema, as if urged on by a hypnotic force, or as if it were the catalyst capable of answering all his remaining doubts. Rizzo and Ascalchi followed on, puzzled.

As they approached the poster, Ascalchi said, 'Ah. *I Basilischi* by Lina Wertmüller, with Santino Petruzzi and Stefano Satta Flores. Great film. Have you ever seen it? All about these young idlers who are always complaining about things but never do anything to change them. A wonderful picture of the Southern mentality in the sixties, set in a little village in Basilicata, Palazzo San Gervasio . . .'

He was still speaking, but Ferrara had come to an abrupt halt.

In his mind, images, thoughts, impressions, feelings, flashes of certainty, all fell into line with mathematical precision. The faces of the prisoners: they had never heard of him, *as if he had never existed.* The couple who worked for the Lion, had never heard of him, he had never come to the house, *as if he had never existed.* Two phone calls, one voice, he was certain of it now. Nicola Spadaro, Mafioso, spy, forger, inventor of names and identities, alias the Lion. The image of Spadaro's mother, kept in Caputo's wallet, Caputo who carried the Basilisk 'in the palm of his hand, like a son, oh yes, just like a son', as Gino La Torre had said.

He wasn't surprised when his private mobile rang at that moment. Nor was he surprised by the name that appeared on the display: *Petra*. The only woman who mattered to him, his one true love.

He had been owed that phone call for several days. He knew that now.

It wasn't his wife's voice he heard, and that didn't surprise him either.

'I'm sorry, Chief Superintendent. I didn't know. My friends have only just told me that the man in the newspaper, Spadaro, the Lion, was also the Basilisk. You killed two birds with one stone, eh?'

His answer was to yell, '*Where's my wife?*'

Rizzo and Ascalchi looked at each other in alarm.

'Calm down, Chief Superintendent. You kept your side of the bargain, and we are men of honour. Too many names for one bastard, eh? The bastard made your task easy. But it suits us fine. You can come and get her. We haven't harmed a hair on her head. You'll find her tomorrow at the Colleverde Park Hotel in Agrigento. We've put her in a suite. Like a queen. Don't worry, we're paying this time. She's our guest. I hope we never meet again, Chief Superintendent Ferrara.'

He hung up.

Ferrra lowered the mobile, waited for his two companions to rejoin him, and suddenly burst into a long, loud laugh; not hysteria, but a release.

Epilogue

'I want the best steak *fiorentina* in the world!' Duranti had said, descending suddenly on Florence and inviting Ferrara and Petra to dinner. Inevitably, they had ended up at Giovanni's in the Via del Moro, which had no equal as far as Ferrara was concerned.

'And to think I was the one who wrote a report on you for him!' Duranti cried after the *tagliolini* in hare sauce, changing the tone of the conversation, which up until then had been frivolous and light-hearted.

'So you work for Military Intelligence?' Ferrara asked, feigning surprise.

'Not any more. That son of a bitch Spadaro recruited me, can you imagine? Now I owe you a double apology.'

'You weren't to know.'

'But you, as usual, went your own way. What can I say? Congratulations. But don't push it. Strange case. Do you really think Spadaro was Caputo's son?'

'Who knows? Caputo's not saying. Maybe he doesn't know himself.'

'Come on! I wasn't to know, maybe he doesn't know . . . ! But you're right. There are too many things these days we can't know. The world used to be simpler: the good guys were on one side, the bad guys on the other, and you played the game. Things changed according to which side you were on, but once you'd chosen everything was very clear. Not any more.'

'Up to a point. The Mafia was a cancer, and still is.'

'And always will be, unfortunately. Right now you feel as if you've won a victory, just as you did when you arrested Laprua. But don't be under any illusions, you won another battle but you're losing the war. When you get to my age you'll realise that life is just like an investigation. Evil is always at an advantage, always a step ahead of you, perhaps because it always has a head start. When you think you've defeated it, it's already reorganising. Just like in the Laprua case. You and Anna Giulietti thought you'd weakened the organisation, and the organisation took its revenge. The old Mafia lent you a helping hand, all well and good, but that old Mafia is dying, God willing. There's less and less room in the world now for local potentates. It's the international potentates who are legitimising the underworld, linked to new men like Spadaro, who'll take their place, and men like you won't be able to do anything about it.'

Ferrara looked at Petra, who was following the conversation with a grave expression on her face. 'Does that mean it's time again for me to retire?' he asked.

'Think about it. You'll soon have a house to retire to, won't you?'

The chief superintendent looked at his wife and smiled. 'All right,' he said. 'I'll think about it.'

ACKNOWLEDGEMENTS

A heartfelt thank you to my wife Christa, for her gentleness and patience, and to my sister Rosa and to Davide for their valuable help with the Sicilian scenes.

I would also like to thank Doctor Stefano Grifoni for his suggestions on matters of forensic medicine.

And finally, a particular thank you to my literary agents and friends, Daniela and Luigi Bernabò, who offered me their wonderful house, where I finished the book, and to my friends Anna, Ruska and Roberto for being there for me.